SMALL TOWN HEARTS

SMALL TOWN HEARTS

lillie vale

Swoon READS
···································
NEW YORK

A Swoon Reads Book

An imprint of Feiwel and Friends and Macmillan Publishing Group, LLC

Our books may be purchased in bulk for promotional, educational, or business use.
Please contact your local bookseller or the Macmillan Corporate and
Premium Sales Department at (800) 221-7945 ext. 5442 or by email
at MacmillanSpecialMarkets@macmillan.com.

Library of Congress Cataloging-in-Publication Data is available.
ISBN 978-1-250-19235-6 (hardcover) / ISBN 978-1-250-19236-3 (ebook)

BOOK DESIGN BY KATIE KLIMOWICZ

First edition, 2019
1 3 5 7 9 10 8 6 4 2
swoonreads.com

To everyone who ever needed a second chance

one

An hour before closing time, a stranger walked into the Busy Bean.

Next to me, Lucy dumped coffee grounds in the compost bin. She bent over, flicking wet grounds off her fingers. "Hey, Babe, can you—"

"I've got it," I said, grabbing my notepad from the counter, already on my way. The guy was cute. If our new seasonal waitress had been out here, she would have tried to get to him first.

The boy hovered awkwardly near one of the corner tables. He was tall and lithe, with mussed brown hair that was on the side of gold, and a blue polo that brought out his eyes.

"Is anywhere fine?"

"Yeah," I said, gesturing to the available seating. "I can take your order here if you're ready or you can just come up later, if you need a few minutes."

Mystery Boy chose a table that came from a home and garden center, chipped stones in the mosaic face of a woman on the circular surface. The chair he sat on was wrought-iron and from a different patio set, the green seat plump and gleaming with the sheen of new leather.

He glanced at the chalk menu on the wall behind the counter. A smile bloomed over his face. "Nice art."

I followed his gaze. Lucy alternated between neat capitals and loopy lettering to advertise the regular items and the day's specials. Her daisy-chain border was in neon yellow, and some of the flowers had faces.

"Yeah, my friend's a regular Matisse," I joked.

The boy laughed, a rich, velvety sound, like the decadent filling inside a chocolate truffle.

I sensed eyes on the back of my neck, and I reached to rub the tingling patch of skin. I could practically *feel* Lucy's interest.

I pulled a blunt-tipped pencil and notepad from my apron pocket. "What can I get for you?"

Lucy's voice in my head went through a litany of the things I could give him. I squashed that voice. None of that was on our menu.

Since Elodie and I had broken up last year—since she'd broken my heart—I had gone on a handful of dates that never led anywhere beyond awkward "See ya arounds" and fended-off kisses at the end of the night. Most of them had been nice, cute and witty. Local boys who were salt of the earth, sunny girls who collected kisses like seashells. The first few dates, the butterflies had been flapping in full force, producing gale-force winds. I'd convinced myself I was crushing. I didn't want to *always* be Penny and Chad's third wheel. But when my dates' faces swooped close, eyes closing in anticipation . . . I couldn't go through with it.

It wasn't the act or intimacy of the kiss itself. I just had no interest in them. The other dates were middling at best, butterflies keeping quiet and still. Just nervousness, I'd figured. And then, one day, those butterflies were gone, too. It was just me left.

One corner of Mystery Boy's mouth crooked upward. I realized too late that he was looking at me with expectation. Jerked out of my reverie, I stared at him. "Sorry, I didn't catch that," I said, shooting him a sheepish smile.

"One of those days, huh?" he asked understandingly. After repeating his coffee order, he jerked his thumb over his shoulder to the glass-enclosed cake stand on the counter next to the register. "What kind of cake is that?"

"German chocolate. There's some delicious coconut-caramel frosting on it." Unable to resist, I added, "I made it myself."

He looked tempted for a second. "Just the coffee." His palm stretched across the large sketch pad he'd brought with him, the cover smudged with charcoal pencil.

I gave it a curious look, then smiled an easy grin. "Sure. You got it."

"Thanks," he said while opening the sketchbook. He poised his pencil over the blank page, already looking down.

At this angle, I could see half-moon smudges under each eye, like he hadn't been sleeping well. I didn't realize that my feet weren't moving until he glanced up, his golden eyebrows scrunched in surprise. Feeling heat creep into my cheeks, I turned and fled, retreating to the safety of the counter before I could do anything else to embarrass myself.

"Don't think I didn't notice you lingering over there with the *summer boy*, Babe Vogel," Lucy said. Her voice was low, but her smirk was at full volume.

"That? That was just good customer service." Cheeks still hot, I moved to the stainless-steel carafe, and in wordless unison, Lucy slid a white ceramic mug across the counter for me to fill.

"Uh-huh," she teased, fluttering her eyelashes at me. "Better get this over there. Along with some of that exemplary customer service."

I huffed, resisting the impulse to roll my eyes. "You know I've never gotten involved with a summer boy," I said, shimmying out of the way of the grimy dishcloth she swatted at me.

Despite what Lucy thought, I wasn't crushing on tall, blond, and gorgeous sitting in the corner table. Sure, he was aesthetic. And mysterious. And new to Oar's Rest, the sleepy little Maine seaside village that spilled over with tourists during the summer and turned into a ghost town the rest of the year.

Nestled on the coast, Oar's Rest attracted all kinds of people, but mostly the artistic kind. The kind of girls who tucked flowers into their hair and rode shiny new bicycles. The kind of boys who had paint and cigarette stains on their fingertips, battling for flesh. Writers who secreted themselves away from the real world and then slipped away from their rented houses and emerged in the fall with a bestseller.

Mystery Boy thanked me when I delivered his coffee, returning his attention to the sketchbook.

Lucy was waiting for me when I returned to the counter.

"Don't even say it," I warned.

"I wasn't going to say anything!" She threw up her hands. She let a beat pass. "Did you *see* his face? Go say something!"

I pursed my lips, eyeing him from across the room. "What? That's so weird. I'm not going to do that. He could have a girlfriend. And anyway, I hate when guys walk in and start to creep on me. It goes both ways. I'm not going to hit on him out of the blue."

"It's not that weird. Someone has to make the first move."

"Lucy," I said, lifting an eyebrow, "the cardinal rule of every beach town is that locals do not get involved with tourists. They always leave."

"I can't even remember the last time you went on a date," said Lucy. "And those girls and guys were *cute*."

I picked up a mug that didn't even need cleaning and began to rewash it just to have something to do. When I was nervous, I had the telltale habit of wringing the bottom of my shirt, and the last thing I wanted was for Lucy to know she'd hit a nerve.

She was right. I hadn't been serious about anyone in a few years because I'd been dating Elodie Hawkins on the sly. El had graduated a year ahead of me and gone off to art school in California. Going out of state wasn't enough—she seemed to want to get as far from Maine as she could without crossing an ocean.

A memory blurred into my mind's autofocus, sharpening until I could count the freckles spattered across El's nose and cheeks, her hair thrashing in the wind, the wisps of the cotton candy body spray she loved. If I closed my eyes, I could almost smell it. I could almost see the gray of the sky, the birds circling overhead. The sorrow in her eyes as she said she wasn't ready to tell people about us—about her.

"Excuse me."

I turned, facing Mystery Boy. "Hey, what else can I get for you?" I flicked my eyes toward the German chocolate cake.

His eyes followed mine and his grin widened. "Just wanted to settle my bill." He flopped down a five-dollar bill on the counter.

Counting out his change, I placed it into his open palm, intensely aware of my fingertips grazing his warm hand.

"Thanks." He turned to leave, then paused, seeming to wrestle with a decision. "I'll take you up on that cake some other time." With a final nod to me and Lucy, he headed for the door.

When he left, I let out a breath I hadn't realized I was holding. "Did that sound like he was planning on coming back, or like that's the last time we'll ever see him?" I wondered aloud. Though I'd been working at the Busy Bean for almost three years, this was the first time I'd hoped a tourist would be a repeat customer.

My curiosity wasn't lost on Lucy. "So you *are* interested in a summer boy." Lucy's voice held a grin. "And he's cute. Hint, hint."

"Maybe he's here for classes at the art center." I stared through the window at his retreating back, wondering where he was heading. "He had a sketchbook with him."

She shrugged. "Wouldn't surprise me. I think they're starting their summer program this week." She paused. "I heard Elodie Hawkins is coming back to be a mentor. Weren't you two friends?"

What? The wind was taken right out of my sails. El was coming back? She hadn't said anything. She could have texted, she could have emailed . . .

Elodie had left town, left me. I shouldn't care if she was coming back. I'd gotten over her. But there were some things I couldn't tuck away as easily. She was like a second beating heart inside me—tingling, magnifying, terrifying. This heart was carnivorous. It hoped and hurt at the same time. Hearing her name again filled me with a savage rush of life, something I couldn't hold back any more than I could keep the memory of *us* at bay.

Being the one left behind never got easier. After Mom, maybe I should have wised up. Nothing stayed the same forever, but when I remembered the soft, dazed look El wore right after I kissed her, I had thought that *this* could. *We* could. In possibly the biggest plot twist of my life, though, I'd discovered we couldn't. And just like that, everything I'd cherished for so long became a bitter enemy. Elodie left town, but the ghost of her was still here, haunting.

As I opened my mouth to ask Lucy where she'd heard about Elodie's return, I was interrupted by the storeroom door creaking open. Ariel, our new waitress, had volunteered to unpack some of our new inventory at the start of her shift, but instead of the sounds of moving coffee cans and creaking aluminum shelves, there had been silence all afternoon. I'd forgotten she was even there. It hadn't taken Lucy and me long to figure out that *organizing the inventory* was code for texting her friends in the privacy of the storeroom.

Ariel breezed out, already pulling her apron off her head. Her brown hair lifted with static. "So I've just about wrapped up in there—"

I blinked at the pile of boxes behind her before the door swung shut. "Really? It doesn't look like you've made any headway."

"—so I think I'm going to take off." She reached for the tip jar with an apologetic smile. "Mind if I bum a few bucks?"

Lucy made a strangled noise.

"No way," I said. "We divide the tips up at the *end* of the week. And there's still twenty minutes before we close."

Ariel's face turned red. "Right. Sorry." She withdrew her hand, cradling it against her chest. Her expression turned wounded. "It's just . . . something came up and I'd really appreciate it if—"

I wasn't in the mood to listen to one of her half-baked excuses. "Yeah, whatever." I frowned. "Go."

As she left, Lucy and I exchanged matching looks. Lucy sighed noisily. "How has she not been fired yet? She's the *worst*."

I took a peek into the storeroom. Nothing had been done, except some creative shuffling that might have fooled a manager who didn't know Ariel and her distinct lack of work ethic. With a sigh, I let the storeroom door close. "I'll talk to Tom when he comes in tomorrow."

"Good," Lucy said with vehemence. "I don't care if I have to work overtime. I'd rather make the extra cash than pull her weight for free."

She was absolutely right. I nodded in agreement.

We worked in silence to clear everything away before closing up. "See you tomorrow," I said as I locked Busy's door.

"See ya!" Lucy called over her shoulder as she jogged toward her boyfriend, waiting on the beach for her with his dogs. He took off his cap and waved it at me.

As the warm sunlight outside enveloped me, I almost—*almost*—forgot the cold dread that had gone through me when I heard of Elodie's return. My eyes sought out my lighthouse, small and distant above me. The place where we'd met most often, the one place in town no one would see us. And so, of course, it was the place where El felt the most comfortable. It was the only place she could be herself. The only place we could be a *we*.

What would I say to her if she really was coming back? Would she even want to see me? Did I even want to see her?

A boat coming back to shore blew its horn, a sharp, trumpeting sound that rattled me out of my thoughts. I felt like a girl overboard.

But it turned out there was no mayday call for returning ex-girlfriends.

♥ ♥ ♥

It was at the most beautiful moment of firefly twilight, when the sun had dipped just beyond the water, that I reached my best friend Penny Wang's houseboat. It was far enough from the beach that we were away from everyone's prying eyes, so Penny probably didn't think twice before waving me onto the deck with a bottle of beer in one hand and her phone in the other.

"Hey," I said, flip-flops thwacking against the pier.

"You took your sweet time getting here," she said in response, tipping the bottle to her lips. She sat cross-legged on the deck, phone balanced on one thigh. "I was just about to text you."

I joined her, sinking down and letting my back rest against the wall. "Everyone we know is out on the beach. Hard not to stop when everyone wanted to talk. Isn't it weird how all the people we didn't talk to in high school are suddenly acting like they're going to miss us?"

Penny snorted. "Graduation messed with their brains." She twirled her finger in circles next to her ear. "They're living in some parallel universe where we give a shit."

"Maybe in some universe we do," I said, laughing.

She typed something furiously on her phone before turning it facedown on her thigh. "All the me's in all the universes hate them unequivocally."

I didn't even have to think about it. "Then all the me's do, too."

"That's why you're my best friend," she said, bumping her arm against mine.

We stared out across the water, letting the silence last. I hoped she felt just as warm and squishy inside as I did. "So you won't believe this," I said.

"Hmm?"

"Elodie's coming back home." I let the bombshell drop, satisfied to see the surprise on Penny's face.

She leaned closer toward me, clutching the neck of the bottle tight. "Really? She told you that?"

"Hell no. You know she didn't want to keep in touch." She'd snipped me out of her life so easily. Even a year later, the bitterness and hurt rankled.

Penny's lips twisted into a scowl. "Ugh. Are you going to try talking with her again?"

I shook my head. "That ship has sailed."

"Good," she said. "I'd have kicked your ass if you got back with her after what she put you through."

"That's why you're my best friend."

"I mean, it was fine if she just wanted to break up," said Penny. "But she didn't have to be such a bitch about it. Cutting you out of her life like that was super shitty. She didn't have the balls to date you while she was here, but she managed to break your heart with no problem." She made an aggravated sound of disgust.

"I'm over it," I said. "But thanks for the ex bashing."

Penny smirked. "Any time." She held the beer out with her right hand. "To summer. And graduation. And to never talking to any of those fuckwads again."

I grinned and took a sip before handing it back to her. "And lying out on the beach and eating tacos and ice cream every day."

This was what I loved about summer, the free pass to be totally lazy and do things only if we wanted to do them. And nobody could say boo about it. It was like the rest of the year was an impostor some-how, and summer was the only time that everything moved back into place.

"God, yes. The tacos. Now I'm craving some bulgogi," said Penny. "I want pickled cucumbers so bad. And sriracha mayo."

The Korean steak tacos were her favorite, while I preferred the fish. Jeju BBQ was the only place in town that served street-style Asian tacos, and everything on their menu was pure rapture.

"Let's go get some." I bumped her shoulder. "Tacos are always a good idea."

"I wish. We have something to do first, though."

"If it's more important than tacos, it must be serious."

"Not kidding, B." She paused. "Hey, so this is kind of awkward, but I was wondering if you could you do me a favor?"

I scrunched my forehead. Penny didn't often ask for favors, at least not so obviously. So whatever this was, it had to be A Big Deal. "Sure. What's up?"

"Would you go talk to Chad for me and, um, tell him I don't want to see him?"

"What? Why?"

She didn't meet my eyes. "Because I broke up with him."

I rolled my eyes. "Yeah, sure," I said, swiping the bottle of beer out of her hands. Penny's houseboat swayed beneath us, gently bob-bing with the tide. "Ha ha."

"I'm not kidding. I told Chad we were through yesterday, but I didn't really handle it that great. He wants to come over, and I just know that if I see him so soon, I'm going to feel crappy and then—"

Penny let her hair spill out of its bun and wound the elastic around her wrist. She waited for me to take a swallow before snagging the bottle back. "Please, Babe?"

Our shoulders brushed as I turned to look at her in disbelief. "What? You dumped him yesterday?"

She pursed her lips.

"You . . . you didn't tell me." I was in the deep end. I was always the first one she went to when it came to Chad, when it came to anyone. Loss took hold in my stomach, filling my limbs with cold. "Why—why did you break up?"

"I didn't know that I was going to," said Penny. "It kind of happened out of nowhere. I wasn't planning it."

"So you broke up with him . . . just because?" They had been together for years. Since we were fourteen. Was this a joke? Was there something I wasn't getting? A minute ago, everything had been okay.

She looked back at me, stare for stare. There wasn't a hint of a joke in her eyes. I'd always thought her brown was much more beautiful than my blue—warm and friendly and all-encompassing. She didn't look that way now. Still, I waited for her face to break into a smile, for her to cry *Gotcha!* and tease me about how I'd fallen for it.

I felt sick, my stomach thrashing. Queasy, I looked away. I had this writhing *thing* inside me, something terrified and angry and wholly new. Something that Penny had birthed. Something that, worst of all, wanted to go along with what she wanted just so I could stop feeling this way. This sick, petrified way that told me that everything had just changed.

I wanted to heave. I wanted to scream. This was our summer—

Chad's and Penny's and mine. The very last summer we'd have before college.

From where we sat, cross-legged on her deck, I could see the wooden slats of the pier where we'd used chalk to draw a yin-yang sun and moon. The fiery sunburst orange and the calm blue melded together to form one shape that represented wholeness and harmony.

That was us, Penny and me.

"It just all feels so same-y," said Penny. Her voice sounded like it was coming from very far away. "Like we've been the same people our entire lives and nothing's changed. College is my chance—his chance, too—to start again."

I didn't like the way she said that. Like she'd been paused for the last few years. It hadn't been that way for me. These were the best years of our lives. How could she not see that?

She stretched her legs out and let her head loll back. Her voice softened. "Babe, I just . . . I think this is what's best for me."

I wouldn't argue with her. And anyway, it was done. It was already over. My opinion seemed unnecessary now.

"Could you just run some interference and make sure he doesn't drop by?" asked Penny. The edge of desperation in her voice didn't sound right, not on her.

I startled out of my fog. It was one thing to accept her decision; it was another to actually involve myself in the fallout. "How do you expect me to do that?"

"He texted me. Said he's going to come over." She dropped her eyes to her lap. "I didn't really give him a reason yesterday. Could you . . . could you do, like, a Breakup 2.0?"

This was too much, even for her. I gaped. "No way. He's your boyfriend. I'm not going to just—it's not my place, Penny. Oh my God. It needs to come from you. Properly, this time."

Her lips scrunched. "Just tell him I haven't changed my mind."

Crazy to think that if I hadn't started school a year late, we wouldn't have ended up in the same grade. The three of us had been friends since elementary school. Didn't she care that he was my friend, too? I wanted to scrunch in on myself, ball myself up like a wad of paper. I didn't have a lot of constants in my life, but Chad and Penny? I thought I could count on them always being there, all of us always being together. The three of us were a team. Without our friendship, I would have fallen apart the past year. Between my ex-girlfriend leaving for college and my mom spending less and less time at home, I'd clung to my friends like the lifelines they were.

She must have read the conflict on my face, because she sighed and handed back the bottle. "I don't think I can face him, B. It's just . . . it's Chad. It's not easy."

I laughed. "And it is for me?"

"We're starting college in September. People are supposed to break up before they go to college."

My arms flushed hot. *We* weren't starting college—they were. Penny had the habit of saying it like I'd be right there on their first day, but I wouldn't be.

"That's because most people go to different colleges," I said. "You two are staying right here in Oar's Rest. You don't *need* to break up."

"What if I just want to?" asked Penny. "What if I want to start fresh with someone new? What if *I* want to be different? Don't I have that right?"

14

The cold hand of dread felt its way down my spine as Penny's words echoed over and over in my head. With a little *snip snip*, could I be cut out of her life just as easily? When she talked about starting over, it was hard not to feel like she was shedding our friendship like a snake that had outgrown its skin.

Penny put the bottle to her mouth and took a deep swallow, buying me the time to collect my racing thoughts. Her silence made me feel paper-thin. It was just summer, but she was already thinking about fall. About being someone else in fall, someone who wasn't recognizable as my best friend or Chad's girlfriend. In that moment, she reminded me so much of one of the paper dolls we'd played with as children. Her mom had bought a book of them for us, sweet-faced dolls punched out of pages, who could be altered with just a change of outfit into someone new.

In the distance I heard the dull thuds of stroller wheels bumping over the pier. A seagull's caw as it swooped over the water and landed with nimble grace on a support beam. The sound of water cresting at the bow of a boat slicing through the stillness.

Penny touched the cold bottle to my knee. "So? Will you? Please?"

I couldn't say yes to her. There was no way. I ignored the *thing* in my stomach. Chad was our friend. Having this incredibly awkward discussion with him on her behalf would feel too much like us versus him. It was fine if Penny wanted to start college single, but I didn't want to choose sides.

It wasn't like when we were kids. It had been easy to be the mediator then, to fix whatever had cracked before it actually broke. When you had two best friends, it was just something you had to do if you didn't want to be torn between them. I didn't want to feel the pressure of having to choose. We'd never really had this conversation, but I couldn't help but feel a little betrayed anyway. I had never wanted to pick one of my best friends over the other. And yet here I was.

"Chicks over dicks," said Penny.

In this situation, it wasn't him who was the dick.

I rubbed the side of my nose, resenting her easy assumption that I was on her side. It wasn't that I wasn't, exactly, but I wasn't her henchwoman, either. It felt dirty and grubby to do her work for her. Not looking at her, I mumbled, "Right. Yeah. I know." I felt like it was expected of me.

A memory floated from the deepest recesses of my mind, softly blurred at the edges. When we were little kids, Chad had been chubby. He wasn't one of the boys who had made fun of Penny's lunches, but he'd joined in the laughter. So when he'd started hanging around us more often, making it clear he wanted to be our friend, Penny made him do all kinds of stupid things to earn our forgiveness.

It was her favorite game to make him ring someone's doorbell and run away as fast as he could, only we were always faster, so we were already giggling behind a hedge while he was huffing and puffing his way down the driveway. He was the one who got in trouble, not us. A decade later and it still made my mouth taste sour.

But she was my first real friend. The first friend who had chosen me back, not someone who was forced to play with me because our moms set up a playdate. The way we'd treated Chad was mean, and even back then, I'd known it was wrong, but Penny had the kind of charisma that made us want to pass her test of friendship.

Penny was like that. If someone said something to her, it wasn't just hers to deal with. It was mine and Chad's, too. And Penny was always willing to show up for a fight and have our backs. It made me proud that she unfailingly thought of us as a team, but for the first time, I didn't want it to be us against the world. Not if the world was Chad.

"Babe," snapped Penny, impatient now. She frowned at me.

She wanted me to tell her I'd do it. She was waiting for me to do what she wanted. The hard edge in her voice couldn't be softened even by the glow of alcohol.

Would I be the next to go if I failed her now? My vision swam. All I wanted was for things to go on like they always had. There was safety in things staying the same. A year from now, five years from now, all I wanted was for us to be the same, doing things together, being the people we'd always been. I didn't want to be the kind of friends who drifted apart after high school, the kind who could live in the same town and still be strangers. I didn't want to think about fall and college and uncertainties. I wanted what *was* certain. I wanted what was right now. Was that so wrong? Was it so unreasonable?

"Babe," said Penny. "I really need you. Please, will you talk to him for me?" She reached out to twine her fingers between mine. She squeezed. I understood. She needed me to be her strength.

The *thing* in my stomach was roaring at me. I squeezed my eyes shut. My friends were my everything. They meant more to me than any of my exes ever had. The only way this summer would be saved was if I saved it. I knew my role well. I could be the captain and get us through these rough waves.

"All right," I said. My shoulders hunched, defeated. "If you really want me to."

The tension lifted with her smile. "Oh my God, thank you, thank you, thank you! I just know if I do it, it'll turn into this whole big thing. Chad and I need a better reason to stay together than habit." She rolled her eyes. "We're not Rory and Logan."

She loved *Gilmore Girls*. I wasn't such a fan, but I watched it for her. "If you *were* Rory, though, then I'm Jess," I said. "Because I'm always there for you." It was hard not to say it with a little resentment, but she didn't appear to notice.

"You are," said Penny, pale skin shimmering in the hazy glow of twilight. Her smile was luminous as she leaned forward to lay her head on my shoulder. "You're the best, B."

The guilt that churned in an angry whorl dissipated when she pressed her cool lips to my curve of my shoulder. We stayed like that for a minute, or maybe it was more than that. The beer lay between us, forgotten, and the outside waves and chatter dulled to nothing.

The stillness was broken only when Penny's phone beeped. She tore herself away to look at the screen. "It's Chad," she said, holding the phone up as proof. "He just left his house." She typed something back, face inscrutable. "Feels too weird to have him back in my house after yesterday. I told him to wait on the beach. You can meet him there."

"The beach?" Guilt stabbed at me again. "Penny, I don't know—"

"It's not a big deal." She placed her phone on the deck and leaned against the wall. She cast a sidelong glance at me, lips pursed. "You said you'd do it."

It needled that she felt she had to give me a reminder. I'd played the go-between to smooth over many of their little tiffs, but this was a big deal. It wasn't like when they argued about how to spend Friday night or when Chad caught Penny returning someone's flirtations at her parties. Those times had been different. "But—"

"Go!" she said, her voice sharp with urgency. "He's going to just come over if you take too long to show."

"But I don't know what to say to—"

Penny shoved at my shoulder. "You promised."

She took a deep, shuddering breath. "Babe, I just don't want to see him right now. I don't want to feel bad about doing what I need to do. If I don't do this now, then . . . everything will always be the same. We'll always be the same. I can see it all stretching in front of me. College, engagement, marriage, children, just . . . all of it! I can't deal with love like this. Not right now. We just graduated. I want to be *free*. I want to feel like I'm growing up, like I'm doing real things. I don't feel like that when I'm with—" She paused. "With him."

But I'd heard that little crack in her voice. She hadn't been about to say *with him*. She'd meant to say *with you two*. Both me and Chad. Tingles shot up my spine. If this was my test, I would make sure to pass. I would do what she wanted.

The *thing* in my stomach calmed. I was doing what it wanted, too. I stood up. "Okay, okay!" I flashed my palms at her. "I'm going."

As I scrambled onto the pier, I almost lost my balance. Dotting the boards in front of her boat like a welcome mat were her yacht and sailboat doodles. Chad always encouraged her to pursue art—even when we were little kids, he'd been the first to buy her arts and crafts.

My breath caught as I looked down. Something uncomfortable stole across my heart. My foot had severed the yin-yang chalk drawing.

two

I intercepted Chad at the other end of the pier. He looked up from his phone, vague surprise crossing his face. "Where's Penny?" His blue eyes darted over my shoulder like he expected her to materialize out of thin air.

"Can we—" I looked around, faltering. There was nowhere for us to go that would be private. Even if Penny didn't care, and I was sure that deep down she did, I wouldn't break the news to him in front of other people. Especially since some of our high school dude bros were lounging nearby.

I found an abandoned stretch of sand that was more pebble than beach and pointed to it. Chad slowed his loping strides until we were side by side. From the frequent sidelong glances he threw me, I could tell he was itching to ask what all the secrecy was about.

Chad shuffled his feet in the sand. "What's going on?"

"I can't just want to talk to my best friend?" Part of me thought that if I delayed the conversation, it would be easier.

He snorted. "Come on. When's the last time you and I"—he gestured between us—"actually talked?"

As I opened my mouth to respond, he beat me to it.

"And I mean just us. Me and you. About real stuff, things that matter." He fixed me with a pointed stare.

He had me there. Conflicting emotions built up inside me until my chest felt tight and stretched. Penny knew that this was a big ask. But she'd asked it anyway. That was Penny all over, but this wasn't me. I wasn't okay with this. I wished to God I hadn't agreed, but now I was here and Chad was here, and there was no escape route. Penny was probably on her second beer by now, waiting for my text to tell her I had it all handled. Before, her faith in me would have been a comfort. Now it was a noose.

"Kinda worrying me here, Babe," said Chad. He kicked at the sand, and when I still couldn't unstick my mouth, he kicked some right onto the tops of my feet.

I shook the sand out of my flip-flops. "I heard about what happened yesterday."

His mouth opened and closed. He took a step closer, lowering his voice. "She told you?"

Now it was my turn to fidget. I slipped my foot from my flip-flop and dragged my big toe through the sand, creating a line between us.

"Damn," said Chad. "It feels weirdly more real if she's actually telling people."

I bristled. I wasn't *people*. Immediately, my irritation rerouted. It wasn't him I was upset with. What was I doing here? This wasn't my place. I had no right to break his heart, and now that I thought about it, really thought about it . . . Penny didn't, either.

What was her excuse? She wanted to be single? She didn't want to be one of those girls who went to college with a boyfriend and had to miss out on meeting new people?

None of that was a good enough reason to dump someone who loved you.

21

"Babe, seriously. What's up?" Chad took a step closer and settled his hands on my upper arms, as if he was trying to steady me.

The last time he was this close—the last time we'd talked about *real stuff*—he had said something neither of us had been ready for.

One of his buddies shouted at him from the beach and Chad half turned, waving him off. When he looked back at me, concern pooling in his eyes, I felt something inside me give.

This was Chad, my best friend. The guy who taste-tested all my cookies and cakes, even the ones that didn't turn out great. The guy who showed me how to build my first sandcastle when we were kids, and then chased the older kids away when they tried to demolish it. The guy who taught me how to change a tire and drive a stick, even though I told him these life skills would be totally wasted on a girl who didn't need to own a car. I couldn't draw this hideousness out. Not for his sake, or for mine.

"Penny doesn't want you to come around tonight," I whispered. "She wanted me to tell you that she isn't going to change her mind."

My words hung between us, suspended and fragile, like the smallest puff of breath could blow them away. It took a second for it to register on his face, and when it did, I wasn't prepared.

His cheek twitched as his expression morphed into disbelief, then hurt, then anger. He didn't need to speak for me to know everything he didn't say. I felt it, too. Cheated, somehow. The sadness was there, too, but more than that it was the feeling of being used.

Chad didn't move away, but he dropped his arms. They hung limp at his sides.

"Hey. C'mon. Talk to me." I caught his hands, even though they were like unyielding marble. "Don't shut me out."

"Did she tell you why?" His voice was hoarse. "Because she didn't really give me a reason."

"I . . . no."

"Really?" He shot me a confused look.

I shook my head. "I didn't even know until a few minutes ago."

"Oh."

"She . . . she may have said something about wanting a fresh start. Um, because of starting college in the fall. I think she just wants to feel new again. Like she's someone else."

"She could always change her mind. You know how she gets," he said. "Just blowing off steam. Because I didn't want to have dinner with her grandparents after graduation." He waved his hand, crumpled face now looking a bit less hopeless.

He made it sound like it was easier if Penny had decided to end things on a whim. Maybe because it meant she could decide to *un*-end things on a whim, too.

"It isn't like those times." I drew my lips under my teeth, letting my jaw apply blunt pressure, blunt pain. "She was for real. I think she meant it. No, no, she did mean it."

Some of the hope dwindled from his face. I hated that I was the one who had caused it.

He took a deep breath, tilting his face to the side. "Wait, so what does 'feeling new' mean, anyway? Be someone else?" Seeming to skip from denial straight to anger, his voice turned sharp. "Or be *with* someone else?"

The distinction was just one word, but it was so much more than that. The air was sucked out of me. Oh, God. I hadn't thought of that. It hadn't even occurred to me that she could want to be with someone else—someone who wasn't Chad.

"I bet it's fucking Vince," he said. "He's always hanging around her. Maybe it's already started between the two of them." He slid his eyes to me, nostrils flared. "You'd tell me if it was like that, wouldn't you?"

"Of course I would. If I thought she'd messed around behind your back, do you think I would be doing this for her? You know me a hell of a lot better than that," I fired back. "She doesn't want to be with you anymore. I'm sorry. She asked me to tell you so she didn't have to. I have no idea if it has anything to do with Vince or any other guy." I hesitated before saying, "And it had nothing to do with your not going out to eat after graduation."

It didn't. I would have known if it had, because Penny had just rolled her eyes when Chad said he was going to get baked with the guys instead. At Penny's insistence, I'd gone in his place.

"I should still talk to her," said Chad, looking more unmoored than I'd ever seen him. "Maybe we can still figure this out."

"You shouldn't," I said, jumping in front of him when he started to turn around. "It'd just make things worse. More awkward."

His eyes searched mine, raw and hesitant. "She really doesn't want me there, does she?"

It would be another dagger in his back if I confirmed it. I settled for saying nothing, but even that said it all.

My silence drew a brittle laugh from him. "Yeah. Okay. Great." He threw his hands in the air. "Thanks for the message."

"I didn't want to," I said, voice small. "You're both my best friends. It was awkward for me, too, you know."

"For you? It doesn't even affect you." He paused. "Shit, I'm sorry. I wasn't thinking. You're part of this, too. I didn't mean it like—"

I wrapped my arms around myself. "No, you did. It's fine. I was being—I didn't think before I spoke. I know you're hurting worse than me."

Chad's face was bathed in shadow. The sun had already dipped beyond view, the golden dusk giving way to dusty lavender. His face tilted in the direction of Penny's houseboat, looking more faraway than I'd ever seen him.

I wasn't so sure my being here was helpful. She should have been the one to break things off, properly. I'd thought maybe she was right at first, that I'd be able to do it gently and without drama, but now . . .

My stomach lurched. Penny was a coward.

Whether it was me or her, it didn't matter who did the hurting. It hurt Chad either way.

Self-loathing burned through me. I'd been flattered Penny thought that I had a way with Chad, that I was better with him than she was. But what about this was better? I could see it the way he saw it. Humiliation, to be told by a friend rather than his girlfriend. Shock, that it came out of nowhere. Hurt, that a relationship of four years didn't even merit a face-to-face conversation.

I couldn't stand the silence anymore. "God, this is so fucked up, isn't it?" I said. "Do you want to—I mean, if you wanted, we could go for a drive along the highway. Or head back to my place. If you want to just get away for a little while . . ." I trailed off, blinking. "Why are you looking at me like that?"

Chad smiled. It was tinged with sadness, but it was still there. "You're always thinking of me," he said, fondness coming through in the way his smile reached his eyes, crinkling the outer corners. "You're a great friend, you know?"

Before I could answer, he took a step closer. And then he was everywhere, invading my space with his strong arms and broad chest. With his face buried in the crook of my neck and my blonde hair tangled between us, I hugged him back.

The heaviness that had settled in a leaden pit in my stomach didn't disappear, but lessened somehow. I was cocooned by the scent of warm sunshine on his skin and spicy aftershave, and his hug felt like forgiveness.

He was the first to pull back. His arms tightened around me, all hard muscle and bare skin. His fingertips electrified. The moment was charged, and I knew we were on the precipice of something.

"Babe," he began to say.

I tensed, pressing my lips together. The softness in his voice, the tenderness in his eyes . . .

"Maybe . . . maybe we could give you and me a go," he continued.

There was something so comforting about being in the arms of someone you loved, but this—no, this was wrong. We couldn't have this conversation. Penny trusted us, trusted me.

Chad fell silent.

It was a warm summer night, but my body flashed cold. I knew what he wanted to say. He'd said it before, once, when we were drunk and Penny had fallen asleep. In the hazy dreaminess of dawn, while the gentle sways of Penny's houseboat lulled us into sleepiness, he'd whispered, "I love you, Babe."

We'd never spoken about it. In the light of day, I hadn't wanted to bring it up, hadn't wanted to know in what way he meant it. Later, it was easier to just assume he loved me as a friend—of course that was how he meant it, and I felt the same. But it always hung between us as the last real thing we'd shared.

"It could have been you," he said, breaking the silence.

His voice sounded too loud and too *everywhere*. Our hips were still touching, so with one soft push on his chest, I put space between us again. "What are you talking about?"

"You and Penny," said Chad. He ducked his head as if embarrassed. "I liked you both. It was just that she asked me out first."

Something inside me sparked. It was half anger, half interest. I stifled the latter to focus on the former. He had liked us both? As if the outcome didn't matter, as if Penny didn't matter. What an asshole.

"Wow," I scoffed. "That's pretty shitty. We're not interchangeable."

"That's not how I meant it!" Chad looked up, eyes flaring with emotion. "You're both my best friends. I love you both."

Years ago, I'd been at Penny's house for a sleepover when she'd dared me to call him and ask him out. I'd been too chicken, so she'd grabbed the phone from me and raced to the bathroom. I'd gone screeching after her, freaked out that she would say something dumb and embarrass me. She'd locked the door behind her, cackling, turning it off just long enough to very sweetly ask for Chad when his mom picked up the phone.

I had no idea how long I'd waited outside the door, uncertainty and excitement giving me that prickly having-to-pee feeling. Would he say yes? Or would he think it was super weird that I didn't have the guts to ask him out myself? When it finally opened, Penny was the one who had the date with Chad, not me. She hadn't realized how much I'd wanted him back then, not even when I shoved my way into her bathroom and slammed the door. I stayed there for half an hour, pretending I was sick, even when Mrs. Wang came to ask if I was okay.

I didn't want a reason to feel more upset right now. Hearing that it could have so easily been me wasn't the soothing balm that Chad had intended. It was dumping the whole salt shaker into an open wound.

The space between my eyes was beginning to hurt. "I should go."

"Babe, wait."

"You're her boyfriend," I said heatedly, but he cut me off.

"Ex-boyfriend." Chad exhaled. "Remember?"

I glared. Considering what had just happened, I wasn't likely to forget.

He lifted his hand tentatively, stopping centimeters away from my face. When I didn't move, he brushed his knuckles across my cheekbone. The featherlight tenderness seemed out of place somehow. Everything about this seemed out of place. "I wish," said Chad, "that it had been you. Maybe things would be different now."

There had been a time that I wished it had been me, too. Once, long ago.

But Penny had never let me feel, not for one instant, like I was the third wheel. Every step of their relationship, I'd been there. Every up and every down. She asked me to go birthday shopping with her, let me pick out a shirt for Chad that matched his eyes. She deferred to my judgment when I told her to give him some space. She asked me to spend the night, all three of us curled up in her bed, after an exhausting night of partying.

I knew what I owed her for wanting me as much as she wanted him. I also knew she would view the words Chad was saying—and the old, decrepit emotions he was stirring—as disloyalty.

"There hasn't been anyone for you since Elodie left," he murmured. "And now I don't have anyone, either."

His implication was clear. But was he really saying what I thought he was? Or was he just looking for some comfort in a what-could-have-been?

Flustered, I tried to find the right words. "It doesn't work like that. Just because we're both single doesn't mean that—" I broke off, dropping my eyes to the sand.

"We make sense. We could just try it. See how we feel after." Chad took a step closer. And then another one. "Maybe it'll be magic."

My head hurt, but it had nothing on the excruciating sensation that was sporadically clenching and unclenching my heart. Was he as afraid to be alone as I was? We were back on the precipice, but this time, I didn't want to pull away.

I wanted to fall.

So when Chad bridged the distance between us and tipped his head down to mine, I let myself fall over the edge. As his lips settled on mine and his hands squeezed my hips, I kissed him back not for myself, but for the girl I used to be.

For the part of myself, no matter how small, that still fluttered when he said he wished it had been me and him for the last four years.

I wasn't falling for him, I knew that. My feelings for Chad were very much in the past tense, faded into nostalgia. I was just falling for the moment. The what-could-have-been. The what-almost-was.

But this wasn't just a fall. This was a ruination.

three

When I woke up the next morning, it took a second for everything to sink in. And when it did, queasiness quickly followed. I stumbled to the bathroom, desperate to brush the bad taste out of my mouth. Last night's whiplash was still fresh in my mind. The way everything had gone so wrong, so fast. Perfect summer with my best friends? Ha! Whatever we were now, whatever this was . . . it was the antithesis of perfect. But a little trick I'd learned after Elodie left was that baking would get my mind off things. I was usually an early riser, but today I woke even before the sun came up and made my way, bleary-eyed, to the kitchen. It was time to cookie.

Within minutes, my narrow galley kitchen was in disarray. Flour, sugar, and eggs lined the counter in bowls, and by the time the oven had preheated, my arm was sore from mixing. A few drops of vanilla and a handful of dark chocolate chunks later, I had my cookie batter ready. I laid out two dozen cookies on my baking trays, sprinkled them with sea salt and crushed pistachio, and then into the oven they went.

There was no time to rest, though. I still had the doughnuts to make. Using the same ingredients, I browned butter in a saucepan before mixing it with everything else, then poured the cake doughnut batter into molds. I popped them into the oven right as the cookies came out.

While I worked, I focused just on the task right in front of me. The tacky feel of the dough in my hands, the ache in my shoulder as I whisked. The aroma of warm sugar escaping when the oven opened, the crunch of the sweet and salty pistachio cookies when I bit into them.

It was only when the doughnuts came out that my flurry of activity came to a stop, and the world came rushing back. Penny. Chad. My perfect summer hanging in the balance of what could potentially turn into A Great Big Thing.

I sighed, leaning against my now-spotless counters. It had been such a mistake returning Chad's kiss last night. It wasn't a bad kiss, exactly, but it wasn't a good one, either. If he'd been waiting for some magical moment full of fireworks and electricity, this wasn't it. I thought of myself as a pretty good kisser, but the total lack of *anything* on his face had given it all away—this wasn't the outcome he'd been expecting. Nostalgia wasn't all that it was cracked up to be. The kiss hadn't meant anything to either of us.

Our friendship would change when both of my best friends started college. Even though Oar's Rest Tech was right in town, I couldn't count on things staying the same. Maybe they'd make new friends. Maybe I'd be the one to drift away like a lost kite, no one to chase after me. I squeezed my eyes shut against the image. There were a thousand things that could happen. Maybe Chad would finally buckle down and start taking school seriously. Maybe Penny would make new girlfriends, people in her marine technology program who would share her interests. What was holding the three of us together, after all? High school? Memories? Blurry nights of booze?

Chad was right. We hadn't talked about anything real in a long time. These days it was all houseboat parties and lying around on the beach. Penny reveled in her role as party hostess—for her, fun usually involved a bottle or three. Chad and his friend John were fixing up a car together. And then there was me. Stuck in limbo. Penny had clearly changed, but I hadn't. I was still the same Babe. I didn't want things to change. And if they did, I didn't want it to be now. Not when we still had the summer for ourselves. I'd worry about everything else when it happened.

Half an hour later, Penny swung by my lighthouse home with a four-pack of ginger beer tucked into the basket of her bubblegum-pink bike. "Hey!" she called out.

Using the wooden stepladder, I made my way down to the ground-floor kitchen to open the door. The third floor was the bathroom and laundry room, separated by a wall; the second floor was a cozily cramped living room with all my furniture pointed at a bookshelf instead of a television. I could still remember the look on my friends' faces when they asked for my nonexistent Wi-Fi password. I preferred books to TV—any shows I sat through were usually just to bond with my mom. When I was younger, it was *Sex and the City* reruns. Now it was anything with glamorous, high-powered middle-aged women, and she watched them with her roommate, Abby. If I wanted to watch anything, I made do with the data on my phone and the public library's hot spot.

From my fourth-floor bedroom, I'd seen Penny coming. I swung the door open before she even had to knock. "Hey," I said breathlessly, running a hand through my hair like I had been in a rush to answer the door and not because I'd been standing behind it for a minute freaking out.

Her eyes zeroed in on the tote slung over my shoulder. "Where are you off to?" she asked, forehead scrunching.

"Work." I had a long shift today at the Busy Bean.

Honestly, I was glad to have the excuse not to linger and chat. With my kiss with Chad still branded on my memory—and my lips— it was impossible not to feel the scorch of guilt. Yes, they were broken up, but I doubted she would see it that way. It wouldn't matter that I didn't want to be with Chad, or take something that was hers, but it still felt like a betrayal. And I knew that.

I pulled the door shut behind me and pretended not to see Penny's face fall.

She touched the neck of one of the ginger-beer bottles. "I was thinking we could hang out. I just wanted to say thanks for handling . . ." Her hand fluttered between us. "You know, everything with Chad."

"Yeah, no, absolutely."

"You said he took it okay?" Penny paused, worrying her lower lip between her teeth. "He's cool still being friends?"

After he kissed me, the only thing I was concerned with was pretending it hadn't happened. We hadn't talked about what the breakup would mean for him and Penny. We'd parted ways, both flustered and reeling from the mistake, and I'd beat a retreat back to my lighthouse. But under her scrutiny, I could only give a tense, jerky nod. What else could I do?

In the twinkling twilight, it had been so easy to let the world fade away. I could still see the recklessness in his eyes, feel the warm breeze against my neck. The chatter on the beach and the crashing of the waves. I could remember what it felt like to be a kid again and to want Chad to want me the way he wanted Penny. But

I'd known, even before we kissed, that I wasn't that girl anymore. That was what no one told you about the road not taken. You can't go back to the start of something that was never yours to begin with. Sometimes you just had to deal with taking the wrong exit ramp.

Penny exhaled. "Well, thanks. It was pretty cool of you to help me out."

I remembered the bite in her voice as she'd hustled me off her houseboat. My chest tightened. She was mistaken if she thought I'd had a choice in the matter. I didn't want her to be fucking *grateful* now.

"Yeah," I said, bringing my hand to my forehead to shade against the brilliant glare of the morning sun. "No problem." I grabbed my bike from where it leaned against the candy-cane-striped lighthouse wall.

"We can bike down together?" Penny offered. Without waiting, she got back on her bike and used her heel to push back the kickstand.

The descent from my clifftop lighthouse wasn't steep, but the road was narrow and winding. The breeze carried traces of azaleas and roses, tickling my nostrils and kissing my cheeks.

As my thighs pumped, I tried not to look at her, tried not to give her any opening to continue the conversation about Chad. I just wanted to wipe last night from my mind. The embarrassment, the awkwardness, the kiss. A fresh shiver went down my spine and I pedaled harder, faster.

We reached the town center of Oar's Rest, forced to slow for pedestrians and cars. The ride down never got me out of breath, so I knew the tightness in my chest had everything to do with Penny's proximity and the secret that hovered between us.

Hang in there, just hang in there, I said to myself over and over like a mantra. In just a few short moments, I would be able to duck inside the shop and Penny would be on her way. Just hang in there.

As I waved to one of my regulars, a young mother pushing a stroller into the Busy Bean, Penny drew up alongside me. My muscles stiffened.

She came to a stop, angling her wheels so I couldn't go past her. "Hey, speedy, you didn't tell me it was a race!" she said with a laugh.

I smiled stiffly and swung my leg over the bike, getting off. "Guess you win."

Tom, the owner, was bent in front of the windows with a watering can. As he straightened from the window boxes, he raised his dark-brown hand, then called out cheerfully, "Morning, girls!"

"Morning, Tom." I wheeled my bike by the handlebars, sidestepping Penny.

"Hey," said Penny with a bright smile, undeterred. She swiped her glossy black hair over her shoulder. "Coffee smells wicked good."

It was hard not feeling a little intruded upon when she let her bike lean against mine on the rack in front of the shop. "You're coming in?" I asked.

She nodded. "Think I'll get something to go."

She followed me in, smiling and waving at the familiar faces of Oar's Rest. While she was waylaid by a table of young high school girls, I shimmied myself behind the counter, where Lucy was making coffees to go.

It was only once I donned my familiar green apron and breathed in the strong, aromatic blend of our house favorite that my unease faded. It was as if my apron was a suit of armor, strong enough to protect me from whatever came my way.

The Busy Bean, affectionately known to the locals as Busy's, was an eclectic cluster of kitsch and old-world charm. Nothing matched— not the mugs or the furniture. The tables and chairs were solid European workmanship, odds and ends that Tom had picked up at antique malls and liquidation sales, with the odd bit of patio furniture thrown in. I loved the jumbled look of the place, "tasteful eclectic," as Tom called it.

Now that I was here, it was easy to think of Busy's as my castle and the separating counter as my moat. It divided me and Penny, made me feel a little less emotionally and physically attached. Not quite a drawbridge, but it'd work in a pinch.

"Slow morning," I said, surveying the room.

Busy's earned its name during the summer months when the tourists descended en masse on our coastal Maine town. In the days leading up to tourist season, however, work consisted of chatting with the locals who came in with their books and portable chess sets, half-heartedly wiping down spotless counters, and offloading the day's baked goods before they got dry and stale.

"Mhm." Lucy pressed domed plastic lids on the to-go cups. "Everyone's down at the beach. Surprised you didn't see them."

Truth be told, I'd been a little distracted by Penny's presence, otherwise I was sure I would have been more observant. Hands behind my back, I tightened the apron strings. "Why? What's going on?"

"Sign-ups for the sandcastle competition start today!" Lucy chirped, sticking in the bright red straws. "You signing up?"

My neck prickled. The sandcastle competition was an annual tradition that came around every August, and competition was fierce. In the weeks leading up to the event, our town would spill over with tourists, and there wouldn't be a lot of space on the beach to practice.

In the kids' division, teams could have as many members as they wanted, since it was all about the fun of participation. When we were younger, Chad, Penny, and I had dominated the competition, but once we hit sixteen, we were in the adult group. It also meant everyone taking part was in it to win it, and there were some pretty savage pseudo-professional sandcastles erected on our beach. And because it was more competitive, teams were restricted to just two people. Since Chad and Penny were dating . . . well, it hadn't been a surprise who the odd woman out had been.

"Signing up for what?" asked Penny. She sidled up to the counter and leaned forward on her elbows.

I made eyes at Lucy, but she answered Penny anyway.

"The sandcastle competition," said Lucy. She shot Penny a grin. "Think you and Chad have what it takes to beat me and Lorcan?"

Penny's smile dwindled. It was no secret that she and Chad always came in second to Lucy and her boyfriend. Chad always stressed, coming up with convoluted plans to maximize the number of towers and fortify the walls against collapse. Penny hated getting sand everywhere, but she loved the limelight of being a winner's girlfriend.

"Hey, sorry. Too early in the day for trash talk?" Lucy made eye contact with the table of girls and waved them over to collect their drinks.

As the door banged shut behind them, Penny said, "I'm not competing this year."

Lucy's eyes flicked to me. "Are you?"

"Yeah," I said, shrugging. "There's usually someone left over who doesn't have a partner." Between my skill and my dud partner, we usually scored third place.

Lucy's face lit up.

I knew what she was going to say before she said it, and in that microsecond, the guilt was gasoline in my stomach.

"Babe, you and Chad should team up!" Lucy said excitedly. "Oh my God, now *that* would be a real competition."

She'd lit the match.

Penny blinked. "What? Oh, I didn't even—" She turned to me, forehead creased. "Do you . . . I mean, you could if you wanted."

It sounded like an offer, but was it a test? The idea of actually standing a chance to win first place was tempting, and I knew that together, Chad and I could pull it off. He'd been the one to teach me how to build sandcastles competitively. He'd taught me everything I knew. What angle to hold the tools that would get the best results. The creative vision to create something beautiful. The patience to erect that vision into reality.

I could still remember being thirteen and letting him take my hand, feeling the sprinkle of sand against my palm. Every grain of sand had a story, Chad had said. A history of the earth that stretched behind us so far that it was only the tiniest of pinpricks against the horizon. Chad didn't take a lot of stuff seriously, but building sand-castles was his religion.

I wanted to say yes. I wanted to be on the A team. I wanted to *win*. And yet . . . was Penny hoping I'd say no?

I searched her face for any sign of fakeness but came up empty.

Did I owe it to Penny to brush off Lucy's suggestion? To pretend like this didn't feel like my chance to come in from the cold? Like I didn't know that Chad and I could take home first if only we had the chance?

He'd been right when he said we used to be able to talk, just us. We'd been able to hang out and text each other without freaking out about whether we should include Penny. But when they'd started to date, it had changed everything.

It wasn't just me and him, or me and Penny. It became the three of us together, no secret too secret. Everything was laid bare between us. Nothing was secret, but we couldn't be open with each other anymore, either. Chad was right. When had any one of us *really* talked?

It was only group texts from then on, and hanging out became a trio activity. We'd made a few Golden Trio jokes—Penny insisted she was Harry, even though we all knew she was a total Slytherin— and at first, I hadn't seen it. That Penny couldn't, or wouldn't, trust us on our own.

The stare I exchanged with Penny had turned into a stalemate. I couldn't say anything, not if I didn't know what the right answer was. I was keenly aware of the dull, throbbing beats of my heart.

The silence had lingered too long. Enough for Lucy's friendly smile to waver into something awkward and uncertain. I wondered if she even knew what a minefield her innocent suggestion had been.

"Sure," I said at long last. I was testing the waters, so I made sure not to look away, not even to blink. "I mean, if you're sure you're not going to do it. The competition. With Chad."

"Uh, I don't think so." Penny's face betrayed nothing. "So, Luce, I'll just take my usual to go."

The couple sitting at one of the tables by the door scraped back their chairs. While Lucy began preparing Penny's drink, I headed to clean up the mess. Some coffee had spilled onto the table, milky liquid pooled in the dents and gouges of the wood. I took my sweet time clearing up. After carrying the used cups and plates back to the dishwasher, I swept away muffin crumbs and sopped up the coffee. By the time I was done, Penny had already gone. A glance out the window told me she was biking away. My heart twinged—this morning could definitely have gone better.

I wrung out the rag in the sink. Coffee dribbled down the drain in a steady brown stream.

"Is everything okay with you two?" asked Lucy. "It's just . . . I kind of feel like I stuck my foot in it back there. About you and Chad?"

I squeezed the rag even harder. "Nah, everything's good."

"You sure?" she pressed.

It wasn't my place to tell Lucy that my friends had broken up, and that I'd been way more involved in the process than I wanted to be. I shifted my feet, leaving the rag draped over the sink. "It's fine, we're fine, it's all fine," I said through a smile, although the words were more for myself than for her.

We're fine, we're fine, we're fine became my new mantra, although the repetition did zero to convince me. Partly because I already had the feeling deep in my gut that we weren't.

"Oh, shit. Babe." Lucy glanced at the wall clock. Both hands had aligned at the twelve. "Don't you have to go check in the dude who's renting your mom's house?"

"I almost forgot about that. I can't believe it's noon already." It felt like just a few minutes since Penny had left. "I better get moving."

"Fingers crossed he's cute!"

"Are cute boys all you think about?"

She rolled her eyes. "It's the *only* thing worth thinking about."

I rushed for the door. "Back soon!"

"You better. I'm not crazy about handling the lunch rush by myself!" Lucy called after me.

I made my way along the boardwalk toward my mom's house. My old house looked out on the beach, painted the color of lacy green fronds. The door was burgundy, and in front of it stood a boy. When he turned around, my eyes widened.

"You!"

It was the boy from Busy's, the one I had dubbed Mystery Boy yesterday. His eyes lit up with recognition, and the wood creaked as he stepped off the porch.

"Me," he agreed, using his thumb to point over his shoulder. "I wasn't expecting the cute waitress to follow me home." A faint smile played on his lips.

I breezed past the word *cute* with an awkward laugh. "I didn't follow you. This is my house. Well, my mom's house. I'm here to check you in."

Now it was his turn to laugh. "I guess that makes you my landlady."

"I guess that makes *you* Levi Keller."

He nodded and pulled a folded square from his back pocket, smoothing it out against his thigh before handing it to me.

My eyes skimmed the email confirmation. "Looks like everything's in order." I glanced at him. "You should have given me a call yesterday. I would have let you in early."

The corner of his mouth quirked up. "It wasn't a big deal." He tilted his head to the car parked at the curb. "I didn't want to bother anyone. I didn't really think ahead when I decided to drive here early," he said with a rueful smile.

I swallowed. Maybe if he'd given me that call, I wouldn't have gone to Penny's place. Rationally, I knew I couldn't blame Levi, but the unwelcome thought had taken hold: Everything that had happened last night could have been avoided.

"Anyway, my car was comfortable enough for one night." Even his eyes seemed to smile at me.

I moved past him to slide the key into the lock. From here, I could smell the clean detergent that clung to his clothing. My stomach fluttered. It was just the sweet smell of laundry. Why was I so hyperaware of it? I twisted the doorknob. Hard. "Come on in."

I didn't know much about him. All Mom had told me was that our renter was in Oar's Rest on an eight-week grant sponsored by the local artist colony and the historical society. Since the house was empty after I'd moved into the lighthouse, Mom decided to rent it out for some extra cash. Levi would be the first one to stay there.

Wait. I knew his name from somewhere. I rifled through my memories, hunting him down. The answer pressed gently against my mind, and I grasped at it, pulling tight. Cotton candy perfume and a laugh like a fairy tale. The bouncy, natural curls falling across her brown shoulders as she leaned forward, snatching the macaron from my hand.

One day I'll be in Paris for an art show and I'll eat these every day.
If Ladurée's are better than mine, you'd better not tell me, El.
C'est impossible! Your macaron is magnifique!

I remembered her feigning a look of total horror that any macaron could be better than mine, even if they came from the most famous pâtisserie in Paris. At the time, I'd glided past her Paris-for-one future, even though it was pretty much the most glaring writing on the wall I could have asked for.

I was trying to be cool and unaffected, but inside, my heart hammered in relentless beats. How had I missed this? Levi Keller. It had been a name I'd heard on and off when I'd been with Elodie, but it had faded from my mind in the last year we'd been apart. I sneaked a covert look at Levi. Was it him?

I could remember El lounging on my couch, scrolling through his Instagram feed on so many of our secret dates that it felt like she was in a relationship with the wrong person. The last time she'd done it, I'd dragged my head up from her lap and asked her to come back to me, please. She'd kissed me, quick and sweet, said "Just a sec," and gone back to her phone. It was only when I got up that she snagged my wrist and let her phone slide into the gap between the cushions. *I'm right here, Babe. I'm not going anywhere. C'mon, don't be mad.* And I couldn't be. Not at her, and not for long. At least back then.

Levi took a delicate sniff, then crinkled his nose like he was about to sneeze.

The house smelled like pine, thanks to the trio of overpowering scented candles on the mantelpiece. Memories accompanied the nostalgic fragrance: me, Chad, and Penny doubled over in laughter on the couch, watching C-list slasher flicks; Mom coming home late from her hostess job in Bar Harbor, but never too late to still spend time with me before bed. Our couch was imprinted with the memories of many midnight hot chocolates, Mom's favorite drink, and her firm insistence that neither of us would go to bed until my homework was done.

The entry was small, and Levi and I bumped shoulders. A frisson of electricity went through my arm. I glanced at him from the corner of my eye, but he hadn't seemed to notice.

A leather couch and two armchairs pointed toward the TV stand, and a laminated list of emergency numbers was underneath the remote. Painted driftwood from last summer's art exhibition hung on the walls, and there were probably more oversize shells on our shelves than actual books. Mom really loved playing up the seaside cottage aesthetic.

"Wow, this is great. I like the look in here," he said, glancing at the gigantic seashells and glossy photography books on the kitschy Americana center table.

I gave him a walk-through, explaining which knobs to fiddle with on our ancient washing machine, and pointing out the closest grocery store from the second-floor hallway window. He seemed especially impressed with the view of the beach from the master bedroom.

"So," I said once we were back downstairs, "there's milk and eggs in the fridge, bread on the counter, and some menus on the dining table if you want to eat out. There's also stuff for coffee and tea in the cupboards, and you can just help yourself to anything else you find in here."

"Thank you," said Levi, ducking his head into the kitchen for a quick glance. "That's really nice. I wasn't expecting a welcome package."

There was no reason for me to linger, and yet my feet were stuck to the floor. I searched my mind for something—anything—to say that would keep the conversation going, but what came out was: "So, art, huh?"

Oh my God, did I just—

Levi's lips twitched like he was fighting back a grin. "Art," he replied gravely.

"Cool." I swallowed, feeling my cheeks warm. "So, uh, my phone number is on the contact list next to the TV. If you have any questions, feel free to call. I hope you have a pleasant stay."

"I'm sure I will." His blue eyes held mine.

Realizing I hadn't told him my name yet, I added, "I'm B—"

He cut me off. "Wait, I'm good at this. Bella!"

"Uh, no." My left eyebrow scrunched.

"Becca? Becky?"

Taken aback, I stared.

"Bonnie?"

"Are you just going through all the *B*s?" I asked.

"Hold on, I'll get it in a minute." He eyed me for a long, inscrutable moment.

"You're not going to get it," I said with confidence.

He shot me a cheeky grin. "Hey, I'm on a winning streak right now. I'm really good at this."

"Could have fooled me," I muttered, but not so loud that he'd hear.

Levi kept his eyes on my face, brow furrowed deep like he was calculating the odds.

I folded my arms across my chest. He wasn't going to get it.

"Barbara," he said slowly, deliberately.

What?!

Okay, now that was pretty weird. I thought for sure I'd have him guessing for at least another ten names. Barbara wasn't really modern, and I always got a double take when I introduced myself by my full name.

He saw the twitch of my lips and his own smile bloomed. "Ha, guessed it," he crowed.

"Lucky guess," I said, folding my arms across my chest. I fought off my smile, trying not to be charmed by his silly grin—a losing battle.

Levi's eyes crinkled. "Oh, ye of little faith."

I hadn't gone by Barbara since first grade, when the teacher told the class to let her know if we went by a nickname. But he just looked so proud of himself that I let him have his win. It was oddly endearing, and anyway, it wasn't like we'd be seeing each other enough for the antiquated name to bug me, anyway.

"I'm tempted to put you to the test in guessing other things," I said.

"Go for it."

"Not scared I'll disprove your ESP?" I teased.

"Nah."

I was tempted to poke a little hole in his confidence. But then I remembered Lucy was waiting for me back at Busy's. With reluctance, I cleared my throat. "Sadly, gotta head back to work."

"Maybe I'll see you around?" he asked.

"Maybe," I acknowledged with a dip of my head, unable to bite back my smile. "You know where I'll be. And you have my number, so, um, just call me or drop by Busy's if you need anything, all right?"

"Aye, aye." One side of Levi's mouth lifted in a crooked grin. "See you soon."

♥ ♥ ♥

I'd made it back from the house just in time to catch the tail end of Busy's lunch rush, and in between plating up sandwiches, soups, and salads, I gave Lucy the entire play-by-play.

"Are you serious?" Lucy's squeal was deafening. "He's the one renting your mom's house?"

The regulars didn't look up. We were all used to her frequent high-pitched noises.

I laughed, swabbing the counter with renewed vigor. "Yeah, I know. I was . . ." I trailed off, unable to put it into words. "Surprised," I said after a long pause. "Crazy coincidence, right?"

"This is *perfect*," said Lucy. "You don't have an excuse anymore. He's staying in town for the next eight weeks. You could totally ask him out." Her eyes shone. "He's gorgeous, B. This is meet-cute material, I swear."

"Meet-cute? You've been watching too many rom-coms."

She tilted her head. "And you haven't been with anyone in ages . . ."

I'd been with Elodie, but no one except Chad and Penny knew that. I shook my head. "Just because I'm single doesn't mean I'm lonely. I have my friends."

"Sure," said Lucy, "but having a partner is different from having a friend. You can't just hold your friend's hand whenever you want to, or kiss them good morning, or . . . you know?"

She had a point, but the idea of getting to know someone new wasn't as easy as she made it sound.

I grabbed her hand. "See? I'm holding your hand right now."

"Okay, okay!" She pulled her hand free and laughed. "But you get my point."

"I can't hit on my renter," I pointed out, forcing a grin, though I felt far from amused. "'Owner's daughter hits on guests' is not what I want to see on TripAdvisor, thank you very much."

"Why'd ya have to make it sound so sleazy?" Lucy complained over the gurgles and glugs of the dishwasher.

"We don't even know if he's single," I reminded her. "Or if he's interested in dating anyone. Besides, he's just here for the summer." I chose not to share with her that he'd called me "cute." Lucy would read too much into it.

She rolled her eyes. "Details, details."

"Not everyone's as lucky as you and Lorcan," I said. "You two make it look easy. It's been, what, two years?"

"Yeah." Lucy gave me a curious look. "Hasn't Penny been with Chad for way longer, though?"

"Oh, right. Yeah. She has." I gave the rim of the mug a furious swipe, wishing I could scrub the words out of Lucy's mouth in as easy a gesture. My sun-bleached hair escaped the crook of my ear and fell into my face.

On reflex, my hand shot up to push my hair behind my ear. The movement drew my eye to the gold butterfly ring on my middle finger, a birthday present from Chad.

Chad. I still had no idea what to say to him. How to even talk to him after what we did. The one thing I knew was that it would be way easier than talking to Penny.

"Babe?" Lucy touched my shoulder. "I know I'm not Penny, but you can talk to me. You've looked kinda edgy all morning. Don't just say you're fine." She looked at me sternly. "Not unless you mean it."

Well, Lucy would find out eventually. "Chad and Penny broke up," I said. "That's why she's not competing with him in the sandcastle competition."

Lucy's eyes widened before she squeezed them tight in a wince. "Oh, shit. I knew I said something to make things weird, but I didn't know—"

"It wasn't you," I said. "It was already weird. She totally put me in the middle."

"What do you mean?"

"She didn't exactly break up with him right. So I had to take care of it."

There was a long, drawn-out silence. Lucy watched me wash the same mug over and over in what was, I knew, an aimless endeavor.

"You're kidding," she said. "She actually asked you to do that?"

"She needed me," I said, because it felt disloyal to say anything else. Even if I wanted to. And then, because I needed to tell someone, and I definitely wasn't ready to tell Penny yet, I said, "He kissed me."

Lucy lowered her voice. "*What?* He just decided to up and kiss you? That fast?"

I waited for her to tell me I was a terrible friend, that I had to come clean, that I was in the wrong—but she didn't. Her eyes welled with sympathy. Sympathy for me. Surprise and relief surged through me. Lucy was on my side.

She sighed and reached over to turn the tap off, forcing me to stop rubbing at the mug. "You'll wash the paint right off," she said with a forced, cheerful smile. She held her hand out and I passed her the mug, which she dried off with a drying rag and replaced with the others.

I snagged the black elastic on my wrist and looped my hair through. "Can we not talk about this right now?"

"Sorry." Lucy exhaled. "I can't believe that she—wait, can I just say this one thing before we drop it?" I nodded. "I can't believe she had you do that! They've been together forever! She owed him more than—and him! What is up with him? Didn't he care that he'd just been dumped? He just . . . he kissed you? Just like that?"

My hands tangled in a snarl of blonde hair as I wound my hair into a sloppy bun. She'd just voiced so much of what I was thinking, and her outrage felt like a warm, safe blanket wrapping around my shoulders. I shot Lucy a smile. "*Thank you.*"

She made a disgruntled sound in the back of her throat, like a cat working out a hairball.

"Trust me," I said. "Anything that you're thinking has already gone through my mind. Multiplied by a thousand. Raised to the power of freaking out."

My perfect summer was in jeopardy, and no boy, no matter how cute he was, would be able to save it. Only I could do that. With some serious CPR, although this time I'd stay as far away from mouth-to-mouth as possible.

I waved at a few customers on their way out the door, savoring the salty breeze that swept in along with our boss, Tom. He lifted his hand to tip an invisible hat, and his gruff voice called out, "Not too late for a sandwich, is it?"

"Coming right up!" I promised, already slicing into a round of blue cheese. I pulled away a creamy, marbled wedge and set it aside. "Hey, Lucy, can you—"

She was already on it. "Done, and done!" she pronounced, showing me two slices of rustic, thick-cut bread grilling in the pan, surrounded by a light, buttery froth.

We worked in unison, Lucy slathering apricot jam over one slice while I put blue cheese on the other, spreading it evenly with a butter knife. Then, while I began putting ingredients away, she stuffed arugula leaves between the slices and put the sandwich in the panini press.

"How's the day been, ladies?" Tom asked, leaning against the counter. He raked his eyes over our clean workspace.

I had to answer before Lucy did. Quickly, I jumped in. "Pretty good. Had a few new people come in for lunch," I said, trying to ignore the flutter in my stomach as I vividly remembered yesterday's blue-eyed customer.

The butterflies beat their wings in steady, insistent *flap flap flaps*.

"Looks like tourist season is going to hit us any day," said Tom.

"I'm already seeing more out-of-state license plates," added Lucy.

Tom grunted, scratching at his wiry black stubble. "Right on schedule. I always love to see 'em come, and I love to see 'em go."

We didn't need reminding. Tourists were all anyone in Oar's Rest could think about in the days leading up to T-Day.

The sandwich sizzled inside the panini press, fragrant sweetness spiraling upward when I lifted the lid to take a look. Using a spatula, I slid the perfectly golden sandwich to a plate. "Dig in."

Tom grinned around a mouthful of his first bite. Lucy and I exchanged a smile—we both knew how much Tom loved a savory grilled cheese with just the right amount of ooze.

"Everything come in okay?" He chewed, swallowed. "Ariel around?"

I thought of the new inventory still boxed and taped in the storeroom. Lucy's eyes were on me as I cleared my throat and said, "Um, well . . . she took off earlier for her lunch break."

Tom frowned. "Again?" At my nod, he sighed. "I'm sorry. Hiring her was a mistake. She seemed so earnest." He rested his cheek against his palm, the worry lines at the corners of his eyes deepening.

"Everyone's like that at the interview," I offered, compelled to wipe the dejection from his face. "I mean, even we"—I gestured at Lucy—"wanted to impress you."

"The difference is that you girls have *continued* to impress me ever since you walked into the interview." A fond smile stole across his face. "Do you think she should get another chance to impress us?"

"No," said Lucy.

I gave a half-hearted shrug. I'd never fired anyone before.

"Well, let me know. No sense throwing more good money after bad if that girl isn't earning her wages." Tom pushed his plate toward us. "Lunch was great."

As Tom ambled to his usual table in the back, waiting for his buddy Ralph to come in for their daily chess game, I let out a heavy sigh.

Lucy sucked in her cheeks. "Y'know, there's such a thing as being too nice a manager." She paused. "I hope you aren't going to give her another chance. She doesn't deserve the free pass."

For a brief second, the wild thought raced through my mind that if I earned myself some karma points, maybe the universe would reward me with some goodwill and make things less weird with Penny. Ugh, but that wasn't how good deeds worked, was it? You had to do things selflessly.

"Babe." Lucy poked my arm.

"Maybe you're right," I said reluctantly. "But if it was me, I'd really hope someone would give me that second chance." I wasn't just talking about work.

Lucy shook her head. "You can't always count on having a second chance. Sometimes you just get the one roll of the dice. Bam. You're done. Do not pass *Go*. Do not collect two hundred dollars."

She was right. She was absolutely right. Just as I was about to tell her so, I was cut off by the soft chime of the door opening, the bell knocking against wood. I opened my mouth with an automatic greeting, faltering when I saw who came in. The surprise was sucked out of me and replaced with something infinitely more complicated.

"Hey, Babe." Penny shoved her hands into the pockets of her overalls with an easy smile. The purple lace of her crop top peeked through the gaping armholes. "Can I get an iced coffee to go?"

I tuned out the background chatter as I made her drink, guilt tightening around my chest like a too-tight shirt. We went through the usual motions of *Hey, what's up?* and *Just a busy day, you?* but every time I looked at her, all I could see was her and Chad. Me and Chad.

Penny rubbed at a dark, sooty mark on her cheekbone. Looking at me from under hooded lids, she seemed to be waiting for me to say something.

I snapped the lid in place and slid the drink to her. "So how was work today?"

Penny had enrolled in a two-year marine technology program at Oar's Rest Tech so she could be a boat mechanic. She'd managed to get herself an apprenticeship over the summer for some on-the-job training. Since we were kids, she'd loved boats, whether they were on the open water or docked at the marina. For her eighteenth birthday, her parents had given her a houseboat of her own, but she'd only started living there after graduation.

"Great!" she said, her dark eyes lighting up. "Next week Rolly's going to teach me how to scuba underwater to pressure wash the underside of a boat."

"To get the algae off?"

"Yeah." Her shrug held a hint of nonchalance. "He's making me earn my stripes by teaching me how to scrape a boat on land first."

I winced in sympathy. The scum line on the hull, not to mention the other stains from rust and deposits, was notoriously difficult to remove. "That'll take forever."

"He says I've got to use some elbow grease to learn respect for the vessel." She rolled her eyes, but she was still smiling. "Put in the time and do it right."

For a moment, things were normal again. But her words plucked at me—had I already earned my stripes with Penny, or did I still have a way to go? We'd been friends for years. Surely we were at the point where I could tell her about that moment of madness on the beach. That I didn't want to be with Chad, but that if she was okay with it— and *only* if she was okay with it—I'd love to win first with him this year in the sandcastle competition.

My stomach twisted. If I told her Chad and I had kissed, everything I wanted this summer to be would go up in flames.

"I'm having a party on my boat this weekend," said Penny. "It'll be fun to get a little crazy before the tourists get here." Looking embarrassed, she ducked her head and clutched her plastic cup. "And I'm going to be pretty busy at the art center this summer. I, um, took Chad's suggestion about enrolling in a couple of classes. So it'd be cool to spend some time now while we still have it?" She looked like she wanted to say more.

I sucked in my lip. "Yeah, definitely. I'll try."

It shouldn't have been so weird, and a big part of that was my fault. But without the third person in our trio, my relationship with Penny felt like it didn't fit. Or maybe it was me who didn't fit.

Penny seemed to take my answer for what it was. She shifted on her feet, nodding. "Did you and Chad get all signed up for the sandcastle competition?"

I tried to dissect her words. Even though I hunted for an undercurrent, there wasn't one. Carefully, I said, "Not yet. I'll do it after work."

"Cool." She lifted the cup. "See ya!"

After she left, for one quick, hard stab of a moment, I wished everything could go back to the way things used to be. Before we graduated. Before Penny asked me to handle the fallout with Chad for her. Before Chad kissed me. Before I let him.

Life wasn't meant to be preserved in amber, though. Already, the soft-focus memory of being seventeen was blurry around the edges. It was like clinging to a cloud. At seventeen, life had been perfect. Invincible. I had my friends, my girlfriend, my mom. Then poof, all gone. How had things gotten so complicated? Was it like this for everyone? How did you hold on to your life when it was changing so fast?

four

Days passed, Thursday sneaking up on me in the blink of an eye. It was the summer of everything and nothing. Sleepy starts and sleepy ends.

No one was in a hurry to do anything because we all knew these were the last few days of summer when the town belonged to us, the people who had been here all along.

But soon, the mornings began with the peppering of hammer falls all over the town as local businesses started getting ready for the tourists. HELP WANTED signs went up, gift shop windows filled with new displays, and flowers bloomed in the streets.

Even Busy's did our part with newly painted trims and soaped and shined windows overlooking boxes of geraniums and lavender. A faint smell of paint lingered, so we'd put our fans on to clear the air.

"Must be almost tourist season!" Lucy remarked cheerfully as she pulled the ice-cold French press out of the fridge. Her bubbly vivaciousness couldn't be dampened, not even by the oppressive blanket of humidity that threatened to send my soft waves billowing into Hermione Granger circa *Sorcerer's Stone* hair.

"Must be," I agreed, watching her give the press a swish.

Busy's was the local watering hole for everyone in need of an afternoon coffee break, and iced coffee seemed to be the order of the day. Already, Busy's had emptied two of the enormous French presses and now we were on the last one.

Lucy and I were used to working in unison, so as she began to pour the chilled coffee over the ice cubes in the tall glasses, I set to work grinding more beans. The process for the perfect iced coffee was easier than people thought, but the time that went into it required a lot of planning ahead, and that was reflected in the price. We were still priced a lot cheaper than the nearest Starbucks, though, and our coffee tasted light-years better.

First, grind the coffee beans. Darker the better. Brazilian was my personal favorite. You couldn't grind the beans too fine, or else you'd end up with a grainy mess in your coffee. Too coarse and you'd waste the beans' flavor. I carefully poured filtered water into a clean French press along with the coffee grounds.

We had to let it sit for fifteen hours, minimum, in the fridge before taking it out. Tomorrow, when we had our first iced coffee order, we'd push down the plunger and serve the aromatic, chilly drink over ice.

Working together every day, in a small amount of space, had perfected our movements until we were always in sync.

"'Scuse me," said Lucy as she edged around me, her arm snaking for the fridge door. "Need the milk."

I waited until she withdrew the half gallon of milk before squeezing the press between pitchers of fruit juice. By the time I closed the fridge, someone was already waiting for me.

My smile turned from welcoming to flustered, and everything inside me tingled and sparked. I was attracted to him, there was no denying that.

"Hey," said Lucy, not sounding surprised.

"Hi, Lucy," said Levi. He shot her a lazy grin and shoved his hands into his pockets. In red gingham shorts and a white cotton shirt, he looked every inch a beach boy.

Levi's smile dimpled when our eyes met. "Hey there."

"Black coffee, coming up," I said, hand already on the coffeepot handle. It was his standing order and one that I'd gotten familiar with the past few days.

Instead of seating himself, he waited by the counter, watching me fill the cup in a steady stream. "Can I ask you a favor?"

"Sure."

"Do you think you could"—he pulled a map out of his pocket and laid it on the counter—"gimme some pointers on the prettiest places to paint in Oar's Rest?"

In the top right corner of the map were the words *Oar's Rest Tourist Office*. It was folded in fourths, with the tourist office circled in red on the map and squiggly arrows pointing in various directions up the roads. One of the arrows led up to the lighthouse.

He ran his hand through his hair. "I haven't had much of a chance to explore. I've been at the art center."

"Oh yeah? How's that been?"

"Unbelievable," he enthused at once. "Everyone is so talented. It's amazing to be around that kind of energy."

I pointed a highlighter-yellow fingernail against the tiny depiction of the lighthouse. "This would be the best place."

He looked down with interest. "Cool. Thanks." But he didn't leave. It was like he wanted to say something more, but didn't know how.

Conflict warred inside me. I liked Levi, but I had also wanted this summer to be all about me and my friends. How did a summer boy factor into that equation? Then again, my dream of the perfect summer already seemed like it was sinking. I hated change, but maybe just this one time, a teeny tiny one would be okay?

I wanted to keep the conversation going, hopefully in a more articulate way than I had last time. "It's sort of a twisty road, so it's better without a car," I said. "I don't work tomorrow, but Lucy needs me to cover for her a couple hours in the morning. I'm totally free after the breakfast crowd. If you want, I could take you up there."

Levi nodded. "I'd love that. Thanks." He hands folded around the cup. "I'll meet you here?"

"It's a date." My mouth clamped shut. Had I really just said that?

He didn't appear to notice. Relieved he hadn't seemed amused, or worse, weirded out, I pretended to be busy rearranging the spoons. When I looked up again, he was at his usual table, already sketching, totally oblivious.

Whew.

By the end of the day, only two slices of cake remained in the glass dome. I packed them up for Tom and his friend Ralph, waving off their money when they both reached into their pockets.

In twenty minutes, Busy's would close for the night, but Levi showed no signs of leaving. He was still scrunched over his sketchbook, feverishly sweeping his hand across the page.

Tom glanced over his shoulder, catching the direction of my gaze. He tucked the portable chess set under his arm. "That the kid who's staying in your house?"

Insistently, Ralph smoothed out a crumpled five-dollar bill on the counter. "Talented," he commented. "And hardworking. I was on the selection committee."

I firmly pushed the money back to him with a smile. "No way."

Both men were like grandfathers to me. Whether it was showing up to horrible plays in elementary school—out-clapping every other parent there, even when I forgot my lines—or helping me move into the lighthouse, they were there.

Tom's encouragement of my baking, even researching the law to make sure I could sell my confections in his coffee shop, presented itself in mixing bowls, imported spices, and pastry books at Christmas. And Ralph's deft fingers had painted a mural on the ceiling of my lighthouse, a blue-and-white sky, and sunflowers in the kitchen, birds on the banister of the stairs.

When it came to these two, my treats were on the house. No ifs, ands, or buts about it. After a few more futile protests, they ambled out, arguing good-naturedly about their chess game.

Lucy had already taken off, and there was nothing left to do. Except kick Levi out.

Okay, I wasn't going to do that. I glanced at my cell phone. He still had a good ten minutes.

I could always find *something* to look busy, even if it meant refilling all the sugar cellars again, though I had already done it yesterday. Together, Lucy and I had managed to catch up on all of Ariel's work, so I couldn't even hide out in the storeroom to kill time.

I idled at the counter, scrolling through my phone. Chad's face popped up on Instagram, captioned *No place like home* with the sailboat and beach umbrella emojis.

I exhaled, then swiped up so fast that his face went spinning into the ether.

Next I checked my bank account, happy to see that my savings account had grown since last month. Tom was still a long way from retirement, but when he was ready, I hoped to have enough to take over Busy's for him. While he'd already dropped hints to me that it would be staying in the Busy's family, I still wanted to make him a fair—no, *generous*—offer.

When I grew bored, I studied Levi. Surreptitiously, of course, so he wouldn't notice. From under lowered lashes, pretending to still look at my phone, I lost myself in the quiet grace of his hand moving across the paper. His eyes were intent on his work, nose scrunched up as he bent closer to the page. His arm moved more feverishly, sending the pencil in short scratches.

My phone chimed. Penny's name popped up on my screen.

Levi jerked his head up, frowning at the interruption. His face cleared after a second and he got up. "You waiting on me?" He loped toward me, coffee cup in his hand. He'd been nursing the same one for hours, until Lucy had insisted on a free refill.

"A little bit," I admitted. "Don't wanna push you out the door, though."

He laughed. "No worries. I'm the only one here, and I'd feel bad if I made you stay just for me."

"Thanks," I said, taking the cup he held out. "You didn't have to bring me the—"

"I was heading here anyway." His cheeks were pink. "Figured I'd save you the trouble."

He settled his bill, insisting on paying for the refill.

"It was free." I rifled in my apron to find the key to the antiquated cash register. When the cash drawer sprang open with an obliging twist of the brass key, I tucked his five inside, counted out three dollars in change, and then closed the drawer. The little metallic click resonated in the silence.

His smile grew flustered. "Seriously, I can't accept—" He put one dollar back in his wallet, but left the others on the counter.

I raised a challenging eyebrow at Levi. "I'm all locked up for the night."

He eyed me, then dropped both ones in the tip jar.

My lip twitched. "Well played." I acknowledged the move with a half bow.

He was fighting a grin, too. "Thank you."

A few quick punches and pulls and the electric appliances were turned off, odds and ends were put away, and the leftover coffee grounds were dumped into the old aluminum canister that the beans had come in.

Levi watched with interest as I thwacked the last of the grounds into the can. "We sell it for garden and compost piles," I explained.

"Is there a lot of money in that?"

I heaved the heavy canister under the counter and turned my back to Levi as I scrubbed the filter clean and replaced it in the coffee machine. "Not really, but the owner of this place—that's Tom, he was in here earlier—I asked him whether I could start this initiative as a way to keep our grounds out of the landfills, and he loved the idea. He said if I could find a way to make money out of it, it was all mine."

I shrugged, straightening up and working a kink out of my

spine. "But it's not about the money." I pulled the apron over my head and hung it on a round peg next to the sink, half-draped over Lucy's.

"I wish more people cared about the environment. I think what you're doing is really great."

I rounded the side of the counter and headed for the door. About to push it open, I was surprised when Levi reached it faster and held it open. "Thanks," I muttered, hoping he didn't see my cheeks flame. It was a little embarrassing how flattered I was at his admiration.

A blast of warm air hit me and I inhaled the sweet, sweet scent of sand and sea. It was more intoxicating than any bottled fragrance— even the clean scent that was clinging to Levi. I glanced at him. His head was tipped up and his eyes were closed. A tiny smile played on his lips, like he was enjoying the same thing I was. I knew I'd remember that smile a lot longer than just tonight.

Levi's eyes opened and he caught me staring. "Sorry. I just—I really love that smell. It never gets old. Do you . . . do you smell it that way, too? Or are you used to it?"

"Every time still feels like the first," I said with a smile.

Before the door closed, I snagged my arm behind Levi and turned off the lights. While he waited, I pulled the door shut, locked up, and slid the key down the front pocket of my shorts.

"Have a good night," he said as I reached for my bike.

It was propped against the peeling green paint of the Busy Bean's wall, sans chain and lock. In Oar's Rest, neighbors looked out for neighbors.

"You too." I wanted to say more, and from the way he was looking at me, he might have wanted to say more, too.

"So, um, I meant to ask . . ." Levi visibly reddened.

I cocked my head. "Yeah?"

"I overheard some of the people at Busy's calling you 'Babe' over the last few days." He scratched his neck, then made a face. "Doesn't it bother you?"

"Uh . . . no?"

"Not even when the old guys say it?"

It took me a moment to get it. My lips twitched as I tried not to smile. "Why would it?" I asked innocently. A beat. I had to let him out of his misery. "Babe is short for Barbara," I explained.

The relief in his exhale was palpable. "You had me going for a minute. It was driving me crazy, because I wanted to ask you but I wasn't sure how it would sound," said Levi. He shot me a sheepish grin. "Um, so I'll . . . I'll see you tomorrow, then? If we're still on."

"Yeah, of course." Another beat. My stomach fizzed pleasantly. "Do you have a bike?"

"No." His eyes twinkled. "City boy, remember?"

"Won't be a problem." I knew where I could get one. "Meet me here at ten o'clock tomorrow."

"I'll be here," he said.

As I pedaled away, I resisted the urge to look around. It was a strange sensation to like someone else. Not physically, although there was that, too. But just the rapport and chemistry that came with finding someone who fit you. Someone who never seemed like a stranger, even though that's what they were. I'd been part of a trio for so long that it was rough figuring out how to make it work with someone new, where it was just us two. El had been the first.

It startled me how very much I wanted Levi to be the second.

five

The next day, I borrowed a bicycle from the local bike rental for Levi. I left it next to mine in front of Busy's. I'd never been eager to leave work before, but today I was counting down the minutes.

My excitement didn't go unnoticed by Lucy, who threw me curious glances as I peeled the apron over my head. "Thanks for covering for me this morning," she said, mouth working into a funny smile. She touched her jaw and winced.

"Still sore?" I asked.

She nodded. "Eating all your delicious food has contributed to way too many cavities."

"Hey, you're not blaming me for that." I lobbed my apron at her.

"It's a compliment!" She caught my apron and hung it up. "Anyway, I don't want to hold you up." She grinned. "Enjoy your date!"

I gave her a look.

"Day," she said. "I totally meant to say 'Enjoy your day.'"

I laughed and headed for the door. "See ya later."

Once outside, I shaded my eyes against the sun. The street was quiet, only the low buzz of voices from the beach breaking the stillness of the late morning. The door of a shop opened, bell jangling, and I instinctively turned.

My breath caught.

Elodie.

Her curly brown hair was pushed over one shoulder. The sight of her bare neck shot prickles down my spine, electrifying toward the backs of my knees. She was saying something to her mother and swinging a shopping bag from her wrist.

I exhaled through my nose. The last time we'd spoken, we'd been at my lighthouse. The air had whipped our cheeks pink, sent our hair flying into tangles. She'd been crying, or I'd been crying, and all I could taste was salt as she'd kissed me goodbye for the last time. She wanted a clean break, a chance to leave and be someone new. She didn't want midnight texts or silly Snapchats or longing confessions of how much I wanted her back. I would have gone with her, if only she'd asked. I would have been her secret for as long as she wanted, if only she hadn't buried me along with the rest of her old life.

California had been good to her. Elodie was a natural golden-brown, but now she was glowing bronze from the sun, and more freckled. Unlike my skin, hers wouldn't turn pale in the winter.

Mrs. Hawkins touched her ballerina bun like she was checking that it was still there. Satisfied that it was, she dropped her hand from her sleek platinum hair. Her heels, preposterously high, drew her to Elodie's height, but even her summer tan couldn't compare to her daughter's tawny radiance.

Elodie and her mother were coming closer. Closer. I willed her to look at me. She had to see me standing there.

Elodie began to turn toward me, and my mouth lifted into a welcoming smile, but then—

She touched her mom's arm and pointed toward a shop on the other side of the street. She was still too far away for me to make out what she was saying, but her mom nodded, and in one excruciatingly quick moment, their direction changed. They were moving away from me.

Horror rose in my stomach, my throat swimming with all the things I wished I could say to her: *Why? Why? Why?*

I tried to console myself by thinking she hadn't seen me, but I couldn't shake the sense that she had. That she'd seen me waiting for her, and had deliberately gone the other direction.

When she was on the other side of the country, she existed in vague ex-girlfriend terms. It had been easy to push the hurt away. But this Elodie was back in my town, memories given life. Flesh and blood.

And she'd just treated me like a total stranger. All the hurt came rushing back, tenfold.

I wanted to crumple in on myself, but I didn't have long to be deflated. A silhouette approached from the beach, blackened with shadow. The features sharpened into focus as he got closer, and my heart felt a little less bruised when I saw him raise a hand in a wave.

Levi wore khaki shorts and a periwinkle formfitting shirt with a tiny green alligator over the left breast. The Ray-Bans tucked into his shirt flashed metallic blue. He had a canvas backpack with him, the straps digging into his shoulders.

I cleared my throat and gestured to the cherry-red bike next to mine. "Hop on."

"Thanks. Where'd you find the bike?"

"Borrowed it from a friend who owns a bike shop."

Levi gripped the handlebars and swung one leg over the seat. "Ready when you are, Cap'n."

And then we were off.

♥ ♥ ♥

We passed the florist on our way up. She couldn't wave back to me because of an armful of flowers, but over the profusion of pink and purple hyacinths, I saw her broad grin.

"You know everyone in Oar's Rest, don't you?" Levi called.

I grinned into the wind.

The heart of the town ran parallel to the beach, the grime from the sand and sea staining the bottoms of the houses black and gray, a gradient against the pastels. When you biked higher, the houses were less weather-beaten, and could afford to be painted white. We passed wisteria-draped hotels and restaurants set into the cliff wall. A few of the owners waved to me as they turned the CLOSED sign on the door to OPEN.

"There's chowder today, Babe!" called out Mrs. Mackenzie as she flapped red-and-white-checked tablecloths over her outdoor seating. "I'll set some aside for you."

I slowed down just enough to answer her. "Thank you! I'll come by after the tour!"

"What tour?" Levi asked over the sound of pedaling and wind rushing past our ears.

You'll see, summer boy.

Craggy rocks and cliff-bound lanes navigated us to the top of the hill. We had to pause every so often to haul our bikes onto the sidewalk whenever a car rumbled past.

"Tired yet?" I called over my shoulder to Levi.

"No way!" he responded. Then, after a long pause, "But we're almost there, right?"

I grinned, though he couldn't see me. "Yes!"

The houses broke away on either side until the only thing in front of us was a grassy slope up to the lighthouse. We had to pedal harder and faster until we reached the top, where the land flattened and we could slow down.

"That was," Levi said, his voice sounding strained, "exhausting."

I hummed, braking until I came to a slow and gentle stop. Levi glided next to me, his black-and-white sneakers landing in the close-cropped grass.

"This is gorgeous." He used the toe of his shoe to nudge the kickstand down.

We stood next to each other, shoulder to shoulder, looking at the town below. We'd traveled in a C shape to come up the hill to the lighthouse. From behind, houses dotted the landscape, and below was the colorful town, each sherbet-colored building winking up at us.

Levi started to unzip his backpack. "Can I set up anywhere?"

"Anywhere," I confirmed.

I watched him set to work, pulling a complicated wooden contraption out of the bag and straightening it so it resembled a tripod, three legs settling into the ground. He placed a thin square of canvas against the easel, adjusting it until it was smack in the middle. The easel wasn't pointed at the sea, but at the town below.

"Is it okay that we're here?" he asked, sticking a paintbrush in his mouth while he rooted through his backpack. He came up with a watercolor palette box, a small tub of water, and a sketchbook.

"I should hope so," I said, smiling. "I live here."

"You live—" He pulled the paintbrush out of his mouth and looked up at the candy-cane-striped lighthouse. "*Whoa.*"

"Yep." I shaded my hand against my face to block the bright sun. "Want something to drink? Juice, water, soda?"

"Water's fine," he said. He was still gaping at the lighthouse in wonder.

I wheeled my bike to the lighthouse wall, unlocking the door and pushing it open with my elbow. Inside, my home was dark. The only natural light came from the windows in my top-floor bedroom, but I was pretty used to the darkness, so I didn't need to flip on the lights.

The fridge was stocked with fruits and vegetables. I pushed aside a bunch of kale to grab a bottle of water for him and a homemade cranberry-lemon seltzer for me. The drink was of my own devising, one of the many cold beverages I liked to tinker around with in summer in hopes of finding the next yummy concoction to serve at Busy's.

The cranberry-lemon was a winner, but I had a feeling it would taste better as a syrup poured over ice shavings. I'd need a taste test and Tom's go-ahead before moving ahead with it, though.

On my way out, I squinted, immediately kicking myself for not grabbing a pair of shades while I was inside. One hand was shading my face, the other holding the bottles between my three middle fingers.

"Want my sunglasses?" Levi asked. "Thanks," he said as he accepted the bottle, overlapping my simultaneous "No, thanks."

We smiled at each other, both acknowledging the awkwardness of the moment, before Levi tore his gaze away to take a sip. My eyes trailed from his chin to his neck, and I swallowed hard. Before I could be caught staring, I sat cross-legged in the grass and turned toward the Oar's Rest overlook. Sitting next to me, he began to sketch.

If I'd met Levi a few days before, maybe things with Chad wouldn't have gone down the way they did. Maybe I'd be introducing him to my friends, bringing him around Penny's houseboat for one of her weekend parties. The four of us would be sipping Moxie on the beach, waiting for our smoky, buttery shrimp to come off the barbecue. We'd laugh, tell stupid jokes, get to know each other— some of us for the first time, some of us finding each other all over again. Talking, really talking. The way we used to.

A fly grazed my arm before continuing on its journey. I watched it for as long as I could before I went almost cross-eyed. I wondered where it came from, where it would end up. Was it born here, in this place I'd called home my entire life? Or, like Levi, was it just a traveler passing through? Who knew where it would end up. Who knew if it would ever be back here.

People were good at leaving. My mom, Elodie. They weren't as good at coming back. Getting attached to Levi would only lead to my own heartbreak. With my mom, with my friends . . . I had roots. History. Years of shared experiences that tethered us together. If it was so easy for them to cut the strings, what chance did I have with someone new? Someone who had a past of his own, one that didn't include me.

Uncertainty ballooned in my gut, sickly and stale like day-old fries. Getting involved with a summer boy was dangerous. Because Levi Keller wasn't mine to keep. I had to remind myself of that.

This was supposed to be the summer of *us*. Of me and Chad and Penny. My palm brushed the grass, the blades tickling. I couldn't get my friends back on track if I was distracted, not even if the distraction in question was inches away from me, sun skimming his cheekbones until he glowed. Even if he was looking at me with soft eyes, like he wanted to understand me, get to know me . . .

"You're quiet," Levi said. "Penny for your thoughts?"

I startled. My fingers closed around the grass, bunching it up tight in my grip. Hearing my best friend's name sent a frisson of electricity down my back. "Just thinking how peaceful it is up here," I said.

"Your parents don't mind?"

"Don't mind what?"

He gestured to the lighthouse, our strong and silent sentinel. "You living here by yourself. Don't get me wrong"—he grinned— "it's beautiful, but also . . . there's something a little solitary about it."

I acknowledged his words with a nod. "Some people do find it a little creepy. In the winter when the nights get darker, when the fog gets so dense you can't see a foot in front of you . . ." I shook my head. "Don't laugh, okay?"

"I would never," Levi promised.

"I like the romance of lighthouses. The mystery." I shot him a look to make sure he was not, in fact, laughing at me. "After almost being shipwrecked, Benjamin Franklin wrote a letter to his wife and said he was more likely to build a lighthouse than a church. Because the strength of a lighthouse *is* from its being alone. From being a beacon of light in the darkness, a finger showing you which way is home."

He was silent for so long that I began to regret my honesty. Had I made it weird? The lighthouse wasn't just that *thing* looking over the town, not to me. It was history and romance and heartbreak and everything in between. It was my life. In every window I'd pressed my nose against while waiting for Elodie to show up. In every groan and creak the lighthouse made in winter, letting me know I wasn't alone. In every memory that settled in between cracks and corners and crevices.

Not everyone understood what it meant to love something that much. So they tried to make you feel a little embarrassed, downplayed your passion and made it sound silly or nerdy or weird. People had been like that in high school; dismissive and snickering about my interest in baking, about Penny's interest in boats. So many of our friends were more like Chad, content to smoke and drink and lounge on the beach. Only Chad wasn't like the rest of them, so that was why it worked. That was why the three of us worked. Or, at least, that's how we used to work.

Just when I was sure Levi wasn't going to say anything, he cleared his throat. "I really like that," he said. "Maybe it guided me here, too."

I lowered my voice cartoonishly. "Were you lost in the dark?" I meant to tease him, but his face grew serious, and I realized that maybe my words had hit home. I darted my eyes away.

"I was, actually," he said. "A couple of years ago, I started posting photos of my art online. Just for exposure. And because I wanted anybody, even if they were strangers, to notice me. I couldn't share it with my friends. It wasn't what they'd consider cool art. Landscapes, flowers, portraits? Yeah, no." He laughed. "They were so bored whenever we had a class trip to a museum. They'd have laughed if I'd shown them—" He broke off. "Sometimes it's easier to be the real you when you're with strangers. You know?"

I chanced eye contact with him. I did know.

"I got noticed, I guess is the way you'd put it. People began talking about me. People actually *in* the art scene, professionals. Things sort of took off from there. My parents got involved, decided I should have an agent." Levi shrugged. "I love creating art, but I want to go to college. I want to figure out if there's something else I love, too."

"I sense a 'but' coming," I said.

He dropped his eyes, stared at the outline of the lighthouse he'd drawn. The sketchbook lay in the grass between us, but he made no move to reclaim it. "Dad thinks college would be a waste of money. He never went, and he figures that I don't need to, either. Not if I already found what I'm good at. And Mom . . . she doesn't really listen to me anymore. This agent she found, some sleazy dude who only cares about making money, told her I should limit my output of paintings so I look more exclusive. That's . . . that's not the kind of artist I want to be, or the kind of art I want to create. It should be for everyone. It *is* for everyone."

There was a kind of nakedness in his eyes as he spoke. Heat furled in my stomach. It was easy to talk to people, to talk a lot but not actually say anything, and fool yourself into thinking that was enough. But with Levi, I was talking about real things. Things that mattered. I'd forgotten how much I missed being able to talk like this with someone. The last person had been—

Elodie's face wisped into my mind, and I savagely blew it away. Like a gust of breath on a dandelion, I banished her. I didn't want to think about her in this moment.

"Then you should," I said impulsively. "Share your art. Share it with the world. Do it your way."

He smiled, crooked and sweet. "You think?"

Without thinking about it, in a touch as casual as any I'd shared with Chad and Penny, I lightly touched his knee. "I do."

His eyes practically twinkled at me. "Thank you." He made a

move as if to grab his sketchbook from the grass, but instead, he covered my hand with his.

My heart strummed deliciously. There was no denying it. I was attracted to him. There'd been chances over the years to get involved with summer boys and girls, but I'd never once been tempted. I thought about Chad and his fear of being alone, his wanting to replace Penny with me just so his world didn't go out of orbit. Was I like that, too? Was I trying to use Levi to replace what I had lost? Though his hand was warm against mine, I felt a chill at the idea of Levi as a stopgap.

Navigating back to safer waters, I pulled my hand free and handed him his sketchbook. As I looked back at the lighthouse, I said, "And, um, you asked if my parents minded."

He nodded.

"It's just me and my mom. I don't have a—well, I mean, I do have a dad, somewhere. I just don't know him."

He stayed silent. Gratitude thrummed through me. He never rushed to fill the silence. He waited, he listened. He let me come at my own pace.

"We never talked about him much. It never mattered to me, though. I didn't need him. All I could get out of Mom was that he was a summer boy, too."

He picked up on that last word. "Too?"

"Like you."

The breeze lifted his hair, teasing the golden waves until they fluttered back down to his forehead. He swiped them aside.

"She works on a cruise ship," I continued. "I think she was thrilled when I turned eighteen, so she could go off without the guilt. She

75

gave me some money, and I put it toward getting this place at the end of my junior year. I always loved the lighthouse, and when the opportunity came up to rent it . . . it was a no-brainer. I've only been here a year, but I already can't imagine being anywhere else. There's a saying about this town. Kids learn it in school every Founders' Day."

"What is it?" he asked.

"That Oar's Rest is a place to rest your oars. It's home," I said simply.

He was quiet for a long moment. Then, "I'm jealous," he said, so adamantly that I was taken aback.

My laugh was startled. "What?"

"You're living in your literal dream house. Do you have any idea how rare that is?" Levi couldn't look away from the lighthouse, face glowing from more than just the sun. "My mom's always talking about getting out of the city, moving to upstate New York and building a house. I remember this one weekend as a kid where she convinced my dad to drive up there and look at houses. But we never actually did it."

I could hear the regret in his voice. "Maybe she still will."

He shook his head. "Nah. For most people, I think that's the point. The dream stays a dream."

Considering that, I tipped my bottle toward him. "Then here's to the dream."

"And to the dreamer," he said, returning my toast.

We fell into companionable silence, watching the gulls soar over the water and a long row of cars get backed up on Main Street. White crests of cerulean-blue waves crashed, the wind carrying muted squeals of delight from a young family on the beach.

The pier was missing planks in a few places, and orange safety cones cordoned off the area. Even from this distance, I could make out two men in yellow hard hats and blue overalls walking along the pier, one swinging a toolbox while his partner carried new slats of wood over his shoulder.

They wrenched the old and broken wood out and replaced it with the new boards, hammering them into place and testing the weight. The scrapped wood would go toward building the model boat on the beach that the whole town would help to construct, only to set it on fire at the end of summer. Another old founders' tradition, this one would reclaim Oar's Rest at the end of tourist season.

The minutes passed with the warm breeze on my cheek and the soft scratches of his pencil rasping against the canvas. All I could see of the preliminary sketch were boxy outlines of houses. He used feather-light strokes, the pencil faint against the white of the canvas, and made even fainter by the glare of the sun. His right arm moved all over the canvas while his left intermittently raised the water bottle to his lips.

I almost hated to break the serene moment, but a question had popped into my mind. "Out of all the places in the world, why Oar's Rest?" I asked.

The pencil touched the tip of his nose. "Would you believe me if I said I just closed my eyes and shoved a pushpin into a map?"

"No." I paused. "Is that what you did?"

He smiled. "Yeah. My dad had this huge map in the den where he put little pins on all the places he wanted to visit. He got so mad at me when I was little and pulled some out. I just got so . . . I hated that stupid map. And when my parents kept insisting college wasn't the right place for me right now—for my career—I hated it even more.

So I grabbed some of Dad's red pushpins and the first one landed on Oar's Rest. I loved the name. It sounded unreal, and when I looked the town up online and saw the artist residency program, something just clicked."

"Did you tell your parents you were coming here?"

He shook his head. "I left a note. Told them I needed to clear my head. If Dad looks close, maybe he'll notice the extra pushpin where it's not supposed to be." There was an undercurrent of bitterness to his voice.

I didn't know what, if anything, I should say. I lay down on the grass, hair fanning out under me. I started to let my iPhone's most-played song list begin to play, only to frown and switch to a different song.

After I did that about three times, Levi said, "You're one of those, aren't you?" He turned around, the paint box in his hands. Inside were at least fifty small wells of watercolors, all of them well-used, because I could see white plastic peeping out from the nucleus of each one.

"One of who?"

"Those people who love all the songs on their iTunes until it's on shuffle and then they can't stand them."

"I'm the freaking president of that club," I replied, laughing. I turned off the music, gazing up at him. Sunlight settled in the hollow of his throat, in the curve of his ear. The cutest freckles were starting to form on his nose.

"Do I have—" Levi immediately glanced down to check his shirt for paint spatter.

"No." My cheeks burned.

"So you were just checking me out?" he asked, sounding not at all weirded out by it.

Without a beat, I said, "No, I was ogling your art."

His lips twitched. He didn't believe me.

Unease strummed along my spine. The connection I'd made with him couldn't go beyond friendship. He was a *summer* boy. I wasn't made for temporary and fleeting—I wasn't good at it.

"Honest," I said, pretty sure I was fooling no one. Cringing inside, I was relieved he didn't press me on it before he began painting. Every so often he would pause to clean his brush in the tub of water he'd brought with him, and the swishing sound threatened to lull me into a doze. Soon, the bottom corner of the canvas was speckled with the colors of Oar's Rest.

While his back was to me, I raised my phone and took a photo of him. It felt silly, but I didn't overthink why I wanted to immortalize the moment. Maybe I just wanted something to hold on to when the inevitable happened and he left, too. Or maybe—

No, I wasn't going there.

He swung around just as I dropped the phone in my lap. "Thanks for bringing me here."

"You're welcome," I murmured, scooping my hair away from my neck. The sun was making me hot, the inside of my hair getting wet from sweat. I propped my arm under my cheek and curled up, watching him work. There was something hypnotic in his movements, the way his back moved as he scattered color over the canvas. Something I committed to memory, just in case. My eyes closed just for a second.

Here's to the dream. And to the dreamer.

♥ ♥ ♥

The next thing I knew, Levi was gently shaking my shoulder.

"*Whaa?*" I groaned.

"Babe," he whispered insistently, "there's a huge group of people coming up the hill. I think they're heading here."

Levi's face flickered in my vision for a few minutes, golden and tanned against the backdrop of the sun. Then his features focused—a narrow nose and disheveled hair sticking straight up from the wind.

"Oh, right on time." I sat up, stifling a yawn. "I've got to get started. Are you okay here on your own?"

"My own?" Levi's brow furrowed. "The people—"

"Are tourists," I finished. "They're here for a tour of the lighthouse."

Every summer I did lighthouse tours, Friday to Sunday. "You can watch," I told him. "But it's not that exciting, so if you wanted to just sit around looking artistic, that's cool, too."

"You mean be your prop?"

I could tell he got a kick out of it by the way he tucked his paint-flecked brush behind his ear.

"Exactly." I launched myself upright, teetering for a second, but his hand shot out to steady me. "Thanks."

A few minutes later, the sweaty, red-faced tourists had reached the top of the hill and I was waiting for them with a cooler of water, juice, and soft drinks. The cooler's lid was open, and on the inside was a giant yellow Post-it, the price written in thick black Sharpie.

"Welcome to the Oar's Rest Lighthouse!" I said. "There are ice-cold drinks available in the cooler! Just two bucks each."

Levi quirked an eyebrow. "Isn't that kind of expensive?" he asked in a low voice as I passed by.

"Supply and demand," I whispered.

The tour lasted about thirty minutes. I walked them around the lighthouse, told them a little bit about the history of the fishing town of Oar's Rest, peppered with humorous anecdotes about local life. The kids were especially interested in the ghostly legends and seafaring superstitions that I'd grown up hearing, and the adults couldn't keep their chuckles at bay, either.

After a quick walk-through of the grounds, I brought everyone to the lighthouse keeper's quarters, the home next to mine where originally, the keeper and his family would have lived. It was a tight squeeze, but we all got inside in the end.

The electrical wiring had been shot to pieces, the real estate agent had told me when I'd moved in, and the wiring was from the last century. There was woodworm in the ceiling, and before the historical society had gotten their hands on it, vagrants had set up camp inside, so it smelled a little like urine and rotten food. The disrepair of the three rooms of the keeper's quarters couldn't be solved with TLC— it needed something a lot stronger.

And so the historical society had outsourced the cleanup to a cleaning crew, and they'd come in and scoured the place clean. After that, the quarters and the lighthouse had changed hands a few times. Some rich guy had bought it with the intent of settling in Oar's Rest, only to discover that small-town living didn't agree with him. His asking price was sky-high, which meant no one was willing to buy it. He filed for bankruptcy a year later.

The historical society had scooped up the remodeled buildings again, hoping to maintain the place as a cultural monument of the town. They leased it out for a rock-bottom rent with the addendum that the new renter, me, had to provide tours during tourist season.

Inside, the quarters had been renovated into a museum. Glass cabinets housed relics and mementos of the past, like photographs taken by the families who had lived here and foghorns and thick, ancient knots of rope. Placards provided colorful visuals of maritime history, and one wall was reserved solely for a timeline of famous ships that had come in and out of harbor. Old pictorial maps were available to browse through, and everyone was enamored with the sparkling Fresnel lenses and Coast Guard medals.

To wrap up the tour, I recommended a few places for them to get lunch and locally made ice cream. The kids immediately began clamoring to leave, the youngest ones tugging on their parents' hands and shorts.

I closed the cooler lid, watching as the tourists picked their way down the hill, hands outstretched to keep them balanced. I grinned at Levi. "Bet you're glad you had a bike. Did you see their faces by the time they made it up here? Lobster red."

He laughed, and I finally noticed how far he'd come on the painting. "That's beautiful," I said, taking a step closer, our shoulders grazing. "You got the colors just right."

He'd managed to get the soft hues of the houses and the crocodile green of the grass. The upper left of the canvas had a curve overlooking the houses below. I looked closely at it until I figured it out.

"The lighthouse!" I turned to him. "It's beautiful. I bet a lot of people would want this."

He studied my face. "It's not for sale."

The ease of our friendship made it so easy to forget that he was a summer boy. Made it easy to let my heart get involved. Hearts were fickle things, always willing to beat for the exact wrong person. First Elodie, who couldn't *be* with me the way I wanted us to be together. Now Levi, someone who would be as fleeting as this summer itself. I had to harden my heart. I had to remember that Levi wasn't mine to keep.

"Right," I said faintly. "You probably need it for your residency. There's usually a big summer show at the end of the program."

His eyes looked more gray than blue. For a second, it looked like he wanted to say something. Levi's lips parted, and the intensity of his face made me yearn for a thousand different things that I hadn't even known I wanted until now.

I waited, but then the moment was gone.

"Want to grab lunch?" he asked. "I'd love to try real New England clam chowder."

Relieved by the change of subject, I couldn't help but tease him. "Is this you trying to get out of eating at my place? I promise I won't charge you two bucks for a drink."

He didn't seem to notice. "Let's go," he said, laughing as he put his stuff back in his backpack. "Would you mind if I left the canvas here?" After a pause, he added, "I mean, assuming that you'll let me come back to finish it."

"Sure," I said quickly.

It would give him a reason to come back.

And even though I hadn't worked out what—if anything—I hoped to get out of being friends with Levi Keller, I wanted him to come back, too.

six

The next day, I met Lucy on the beach before work. Around us, some early birds had already started prepping for the sandcastle competition. Lucy bounced her well-loved, graying volleyball on her thighs. "Hey, you entering the Clamshell Queen pageant?"

That was a bit of a loaded question. Penny's mom had played fairy godmother when Penny and I had entered two years ago. She'd helped us design our gowns and taught me to use her sewing machine to stitch it all together, making sure my stitches were straight and neat. Penny had won the pageant that year, and no one had cheered louder than me.

The next year was a different story. That was the year I'd won, and the crushing look of hurt on Penny's face had broken my heart. I'd taken the tiara off my own head and placed it on hers, announcing to the entire crowd and all the judges that we were best friends and we'd win—and lose—together.

A couple of weeks ago, Mrs. Wang had told me to come by so she could take my measurements, but I hadn't gone over. I had to talk to Penny first. I couldn't let what happened with Chad hang over our friendship. I already had a plan in place—I'd make up a batch of Penny's favorite oatmeal raisin cookies and bring them over to her houseboat. Then I'd broach the topic and explain what had happened that day on the beach when Chad had kissed me. I'd tell her that it meant nothing. I was definitely not into Chad, and despite the kiss, I didn't think that he wanted to be with me. It was foolishness, that was all.

"I don't know if I'm entering this year," I said. "Kind of depends on what happens with Penny."

"You can do it with me. My mom's super stoked I actually agreed to do it this year and wants to take me dress shopping in Bar Harbor." Lucy shot me a grin before bumping the volleyball off her knee. The ball soared through the air in a gentle arc.

"We've done it together the last two years," I pointed out, sending it back to her. "And it's cheaper with Mrs. Wang. I don't have the money for an expensive dress."

Lucy returned it with a powerful spike, sending me in a fumbled dive. Despite her petite stature, she was a powerhouse of energy.

Two feet short of the ball, I landed on the soft sand. "I thought we were playing for fun," I said, brushing the sand off my knees.

I didn't buy her innocent look for a moment as she said, "We are."

Our second game had the same result, a flurry of short, explosive motions culminating in me biting the sand—again.

"I wish it hadn't taken us so long to get around to doing, you know, stuff like this," said Lucy, bouncing the ball over to me.

"What do you mean?" This time, I managed to return it.

"Just . . . sometimes it felt like just because you had Penny and Chad, that sort of stood in the way of our getting closer?"

"We've hung out before." But I couldn't really put my finger on when.

Lucy laughed. "Nah, we haven't. Not like this." She sent the ball back to me.

I scampered after it, wincing as it hit my wrist bone in a sloppy return. It was a knee-jerk reaction to protest, but she was right. People who had hit their friend quotient tended not to look outside the equation.

Lucy snatched the ball out of midair and tucked it under her arm. "I hope things get back to normal for you, obviously, but it's nice to see you without your posse." She made a face. "Makes the rest of us lowly peasants feel like we have a shot at getting to know you."

"Oh my *God*, Lucy." White-hot embarrassment streaked over me. "You're not a lowly peas—I love you, okay? You're the best."

She studied me for a long moment. "Can I say something?" She bit her lip. "Something that you potentially won't like."

"Go for it."

"I didn't have a lot of girl friends in high school. Or, um, a lot of friends in general? It always felt like once people had their tribe, they didn't have a lot of time for new friends. I never really got it, you know? Why people felt like x number of friends was all they had space for."

I knew where this was going.

"And we've hung out before, obviously, but we've been spending more time together . . . lately. Which is really nice," she rushed to say. "But it just made me think about high school again."

She thought I was only hanging out with her because I didn't have anyone else. Shame burned hot in my face.

Lucy must have read some of what I was feeling. "I don't want you to feel bad, Babe! Just know that I'm here." She opened her mouth, about to say more, but then her eyes darted away.

I followed her gaze. Lorcan was talking with some of the fisher-men, and from the concentrated furrow of his brow, I figured he was haggling prices for the morning's catch.

"Hey," I said. "Remember when you were younger and you threw sand at him? You screamed that you were going to marry him when you grew up."

Lucy laughed, then made a face. "He was only a *year* older than me. But he was thirteen, a teenager. It seemed so old back then."

I cackled, remembering how mortified and amused he'd been. Though he'd been in my grade, he was never really part of my circle. With a twinge, I realized that what Lucy claimed was truer than she knew—I'd never really talked to Lorcan much because I thought Chad and Penny were all I would ever need.

Elodie's face winked into my mind, swiftly replaced by Chad's and Penny's. Even as I focused on them, traced their features to my memory, they began to get hazy. Lost to me. In the blink of an eye, they were blotted out, replaced by a golden-haired boy and his blue eyes.

As if she could read my mind, Lucy asked, "Did you put any moves on Levi yesterday? I'm telling you, Babe, he is so into you."

I quirked an eyebrow. "Based on?"

Levi seemed to enjoy my company, and had laughed and joked with me yesterday, but maybe that was just his personality. I didn't want to read more into it than that. Especially since I'd been on the awkward receiving end of guys who had misread my own friendli-ness for romantic interest.

"Um, the fact you took him to your totally romantic lighthouse?

And went out for lunch after?" Lucy put her hands on her hips and leveled a no-nonsense look at me. "C'mon, that's at least second base."

I flushed. "What are you, ten? Levi and I are just friends."

"There's no such thing," she said.

I raised an eyebrow. "Friends don't exist?"

"Oh, friends exist. But the way you two eye-sex each other every day at Busy's goes way beyond friendship."

"We don't—"

"Trust me. You do."

Now my face was hot for a totally different reason. Deflecting, I said, "I remember not so long ago you were too tongue-tied to even go up and talk to a boy. If Lorcan hadn't worked up the courage to talk to you, you'd both still be mooning over each other."

"I couldn't trust myself to keep my cool around him! You know what a serious case of foot in mouth I have," said Lucy. "Doctors have told me it's inoperable. I'm cursed with it for life. Side effects include incredible awkwardness and loss of coherency."

"Loser," I said lightly.

"Well?" Lucy demanded, impatient for details.

Pretending not to know what she was asking, I gave her an innocent, wide-eyed look. "Well what?"

"Did anything happen between the two of you?"

"He just came to paint! Not everything is about sex."

"Yeah," said Lucy, grinning, "but some things should be."

I glanced toward Busy's, where Tom was just making his way outside with his watering can. Like clockwork, we could count on him to be out there every day at eight a.m. "Shit, we've gotta go. Ariel already texted to say she was sick"—"Ha! Sick!" groused Lucy—"so it's just us this morning. Race you back!"

Hours later, my lower back felt stiff and sore from being on my feet all day. I felt like a Sim with a low energy bar. Stifling a yawn, I turned just as the door opened and a customer came in. What little energy I had left in me ebbed away entirely.

Elodie Hawkins, in the flesh.

With her statuesque height and high cheekbones, she'd always looked ready for the runway when we were in high school. She was the girl voted Most Likely to Succeed, and no one ever forgot it.

"Guess who's back for the summer!" she said through a laugh, throwing her arms out. As if it was so easy to breeze back into town— back into my life.

I seethed to see two tables erupt into cheers and *How's college, E?* Some of the kids who had graduated in her year had occupied the table closest to her, and they quickly scooted chairs to make room for the prodigal El.

"Told you she was coming back," Lucy murmured over the drone of the dishwasher. "Hey, she'll probably run into Levi at the art center." She nudged me.

I gave a half-hearted shrug, unease pooling in my stomach. Elodie still hadn't looked at me. The humiliation of her avoidance yesterday was fresh in my mind, and the hair on my arms prickled. She looked even prettier today. Up close, I could almost count the constellations of her freckles. I remembered thinking once that no matter how blustery the day, seeing her made me feel like I was warmed by summer rays. Now I just felt cold.

"Oh my gosh, Babe, is that you?" Elodie made a show of looking around the room. It was only the slight downturn of her full lips that hinted at her emotions.

I wouldn't call her El. "Hi, Elodie," I said, trying to smile as she approached, although I was pretty sure it was laced with Splenda sweetness.

She wrapped her arms around herself, like she was warding off the chill she'd brought into the coffee shop. She glanced over her shoulder at the table that was waiting for her, then back to me, like she wanted to say something more. "How have you been?"

I kept my voice as clipped as I could as I responded, "Fine."

Lucy's eyes volleyed between us. "So how's school? You were in California, right?" she asked, breaking the tension.

"Yes!" Elodie's whole face seemed brighter. "CalArts is amazing!" she said. With an embarrassed smile, she added, "That's what we call it there."

Lucy caught my eye, and I knew she was fighting back a laugh. "Whoa. Cool," she said.

"California Institute of the Arts," said Elodie.

I kept my face blank, even though she seemed intent on holding eye contact. I knew the name of her school, abbreviated and full, and didn't need a reminder of the place that had lured her away from Maine.

Elodie waved a hand at my cakes in the glass display case, still smiling. "We had some amazing food near campus, but I found myself missing these so much."

Missing *these*. Not missing me. Not missing us.

"Glad you missed something about home," I said tartly. "Back for anyone in particular?" I wanted to take the words back the moment they were out there. It sounded like I was fishing, like I wanted her to tell me she was back for me. I knew she wasn't. Oar's Rest was her home; her family was here. It made total sense that she was back for the summer.

But it was too late. Elodie's mouth tightened and her eyes flashed. She leaned over the counter and lowered her voice enough to say, "Would it matter to you if I was?"

Stung, I pulled back. She was trying to goad me. And I'd practically invited her to do it. I wouldn't pretend that I was fine. She'd *ignored* me. She didn't have to acknowledge our relationship, but she didn't have to actively avoid me, either. I'd been without her for a year. I'd learned how to move on, even though it hadn't come naturally. When my mom started taking longer and longer work trips, I had accepted it. But with Elodie, there had been too much confused anger and grief to make acceptance come easy. Each step was a milestone, each day was a little easier. I'd known, of course, that our relationship was over, but my heart hadn't been ready to face it until now. We were *done*. It crossed my mind in that second that we made better strangers than we ever did friends.

I put the mask back on. Wearing my heart on my sleeve had only brought me pain. Though it galled me to wait on her, I forced myself to say, "Can I get you something to eat or drink?" It would have been on the house before.

"Can you do any of the drinks without sugar?" Elodie asked, tapping her French-manicured nails against the counter. "I'm trying to cut back." I saw the glitter of the rings she wore, contrasted against the color of her skin. She never used to wear this much jewelry— maybe it was a California thing.

"Yeah, of course," said Lucy.

"Okay, I'll have a small caramel hazelnut. No whipped cream, no sugar, and easy on the creamer."

"Hey, Elodie, c'mere!" John called out, scraping his chair against the floor so he could mime a lewd grasping motion. His father owned the hardware store, and John had gone into business with him last year so Martin & Son could finally live up to its name. "Babe," he said, grinning at me, "quit hogging her!"

Oh, he was welcome to her.

"Coming!" Elodie trilled right back, spinning around to give him a dazzling smile. But while Lucy prepared her drink, she stayed at the counter.

I could feel the tension strumming between us, and was incredibly grateful when Lucy defused some of it by saying, "I love your rings."

Lucy's words broke the silence, and Elodie let a genuine smile pass over her face. She twisted her left hand to give Lucy a better look. Her glossed lips curled into a foxy smile. "Thanks. It's kind of silly, but I like to reward myself with a little something after I finish a piece." She tapped the ring on her middle finger, a thin silver band with a turquoise teardrop center. "This was from last month, to celebrate the end of the semester."

The door of the coffee shop opened and a couple came in with two young children. "I'll get this," Lucy said quickly. She skedaddled with a wave to Elodie, leaving me with the rest of her transaction.

I held Elodie's drink out, but she made no move to leave. She cradled the coffee cup against her chest and bit her bottom lip, looking chagrined. Ignoring the beckoning whines and calls of her friends, she leaned against the counter.

She swirled her straw. "So what have you been—"

"Can I get you anything else?" I asked, determined to play it cool. I wouldn't have an emotional response to her. Not again.

"Are you seeing anyone?"

Why the hell was that her business? I sucked in my cheeks. It wasn't fair. Elodie wasn't allowed to just swan back into my life and expect me to answer her questions. Maybe last year I would have. But I wasn't that girl anymore. And Elodie, too embarrassed to even say hi to me in front of her mom, was *exactly* the same girl.

The seconds inched by. Elodie pursed her lips. "Babe."

That one word threatened to undo my glued-together pieces. I forced myself to keep civil, even as my insides thrashed and nausea rose in my throat.

"Is this about . . ." She passed a hand over her face.

When I didn't say anything, Elodie sighed and looked down. "I'm sorry. I . . . I know you saw me yesterday. I just—I couldn't. I was with my mom."

Even though I'd promised myself I wouldn't do this, I found myself saying, "You could have just said hi."

Her cheeks pinked. "I know. Believe me, I felt like such a coward turning away from you, but . . . you know the deal with my parents. They just wouldn't—I mean, for God's sake, my mom's as Waspy as you can get. She's so judgmental about stuff like this. And just telling her wouldn't be enough—she'd want to talk it to death." Elodie exhaled in frustration before sweeping a surreptitious glance around us. "Sometimes I think she thinks sexuality is a trend. If I'm not ready to put labels on anything, I'm definitely not ready to defend myself to her. Or to anyone."

"It was just hi, that's it. She wouldn't have read anything into it. One word wouldn't have given you away." I didn't want to hear her excuses. "It's not like I would have said or done anything to out you," I whispered.

But I could see from the look in her eye that even that would have been too much to ask for.

I paused. "Did you think I would?"

She didn't answer me directly. "Maybe I did it for myself, too," she said. Her eyes slid away from me, but I'd already seen the sheen of wetness. She didn't blink, and I knew why. "I told you before I left that I just wanted a clean break, that I didn't want to hang on to . . . to anything from here. And I meant it. But that doesn't mean I didn't spend the last year regretting it."

Meanness burned inside me. "You feeling sorry doesn't change anything."

"No, no. Of course not." She seemed startled. "I . . . I should join my friends." She lifted her cup, still unblinking. "Um, I'll see you around, I guess."

"I guess," I echoed, watching her drift back to her table. The tips of her dark brown hair skimmed the waist of her high-rise shorts, swaying as she walked. She might have gotten her dark curls and light

94

brown skin from her dad, but the extent to which she cared about other people's opinions was all from her mom.

"Thank God I missed all that," whispered Lucy as she joined me behind the counter. She dumped a tray in the sink and turned on the faucet. "You could cut the tension with a knife. '*CalArts, that's what we in California call it.*' Jeez, how pretentious." Lucy punctuated the sentence with an eye roll. "And what was all that clandestine whispering going on between you two? Why did she say—were you two, like, *together* together?"

"It was nothing. Just some stupid drama from last year that we never really resolved." It wasn't my secret to tell, anyway. I hoped Elodie could feel the holes my eyes were boring in the back of her head. "Trust me, Lucy. I couldn't care less about her. The sooner she goes back to California, the better."

"Hey, sweetie, what's going on?" was the first thing Mom said when she answered her cell phone. Then, fainter, "Abby, it's my daughter. No, no, don't pause it." Mom's breath came across the phone line, along with the distinct sound of a closing door.

"Did I interrupt your movie?" I asked, punching buttons on the microwave to reheat last night's dinner, four-cheese macaroni with truffle oil.

"No big deal, sweetheart. Abby's just nursing a bit of a broken heart, and you know Katherine Heigl movies always cheer her up."

"What happened?"

"Her fiancé doesn't want to settle a date for the wedding." Mom dropped her voice. "The wedding might be off."

I vaguely remembered meeting Abby's fiancé. Nondescript sort of dude with serious commitment issues. Something that Mom had agreed with, and Abby had willfully ignored. "I would say I'm sorry to hear it, but I think she's probably dodged a bullet."

Mom's sigh sounded heavier over the phone. "Sometimes a roommate just has to listen instead of saying 'I told you so.'"

When I turned eighteen, Mom decided to move to Bar Harbor. She and her friend Abby worked on cruises from May to October, and in the winter months, Mom made jewelry for the Etsy shop she ran. By the summer, she would have hundreds of pieces ready for the charmed tourists in Bar Harbor and Oar's Rest, too.

When Mom was a little girl, her mother had taken her beachcombing and had shown her how to make jewelry with their finds. Sand dollar earrings, cowrie shell necklaces, sea glass pendants, and silver spoon bracelets. The first spoon they found, probably washed up on the beach from someone's summer house, Gran taught Mom to bend into a cuff bracelet. She wore it to this day, claiming it was an antique and would probably be the only thing of value in my inheritance.

"So, um, I guess you'll be sticking around Bar Harbor for Abby, then?" I asked, shooting a wish into the universe that she would be coming home soon. I wanted my mom, but I didn't know how to ask for her.

"I should be able to stop by sometime next week before my ship leaves."

It wasn't the answer I was looking for.

"Maybe you and I can even go shelling, if you're free," Mom added, as though it was *my* schedule that made it hard for us to get together.

The microwave beeped and I swung open the door. The aromatic fragrance of steamed cheese and earthy truffle wafted out. I poked a fork into the center of the macaroni before carrying it out to my small dining table.

"Yeah, Mom. Sounds good." My words felt about as empty as her promise.

She didn't want to end the conversation, intent on grilling me for details about our tenant, but I told her my dinner was getting cold and I'd FaceTime her later. By the time I hung up, my macaroni was lukewarm.

After doing the dishes, guilt reared its ugly head when I realized I'd made a vague commitment to go to Penny's party. Even though I wasn't sure I wanted to go, I felt like I should. I took my cookies with me as a peace offering for when I came clean about what had happened with Chad.

I decided to walk down to town instead of biking. I needed to work up the courage to talk to Penny, which would have been a lot easier to summon if I knew what I planned to say. In Oar's Rest, friendships lasted forever. Tom and Ralph had been friends since they were three, and I'd always hoped for that same kind of bond with Chad and Penny. I wanted a lifetime of watching fireworks from the houseboat, eating sweet strawberry granitas on the boardwalk, measuring my life in cups of coffee and summer freckles.

But graduation had changed everything. I'd been content to stay at Busy's, and had ignored the college financial aid forms the guidance office sent home. Looking back, I don't know what I'd expected to happen. That all three of us would stay immortalized at seventeen, preserved like mosquitoes in amber, teenage Lost Boys who never grew up, maybe.

I'd never expected everyone's path to take them in a different direction—away from me.

The walk to town took a little over twenty minutes. A curve of the road overlooked the beach, with just enough room for two cars to pull up. One car was empty, guidebooks and a clipped bag of potato chips in the back seat. In the second car, a young couple was kissing in the front seat.

These tourists were the first harbingers of summer. In a few days, Oar's Rest would be theirs.

"Hey!"

The door of the grocery store closed behind Levi. In his hands were two shopping bags, a baguette and some leafy greens poking out the top.

"Hey," I called out.

He jogged across the street to meet me. "I had a really good time yesterday." He put the bags on the ground. "I was about to cook dinner tonight. Would you like to join me?"

Hesitation danced on the tip of my tongue. I should say no. Just as the houseboat would always hold the memories of sleepovers and Fourth of July fireworks and too much beer, the places I shared with Levi wouldn't belong to me anymore. That was the risk of summer boys. They always outgrew summer.

But here was Levi, looking at me like he wanted me to say yes. And I wanted to, even if it meant breaking my own rule. I wanted to know who I could be when it was just me—when I wasn't a package deal, a buy-one-get-one Chad and Penny. I wanted to know who *he* was.

"I already ate," I said. "But I could watch you eat?" Realizing that sounded weird, I added, "I mean, I could keep you company."

We shared an awkward smile over my little stumble. Well, I'm sure mine was awkward. He just seemed happy.

Belatedly, I realized I'd just overwritten my plans for Penny's party. If I wanted to get the three of us back together—my perfect summer back, too—then I couldn't get sidetracked by whatever this thing was between me and Levi. Even if I wanted to. I hated to dim his smile, but at the end of summer, he would leave. My friends would still be here. They, not him, needed to be my priority.

I hefted the weight of the cookie platter in my hands. "Actually, I may have said yes too soon," I had to admit, face scrunched with ruefulness.

Levi's face fell, but recovered quickly.

"It's just . . . I told a friend I'd go to her party tonight. But you could—you should come." I pointed to the docks. "It's the houseboat with all the lights."

He lifted his bags. "But what about—"

"We can drop them off first."

"Is it okay that I just show up with you?"

"Absolutely," I said.

And the flush of heat that crept over my skin had everything to do with the temperature, and nothing at all to do with the adorable boy standing in front of me.

Nope, nothing at all.

♥ ♥ ♥

It was warm and I could feel the beginnings of perspiration on the back of my neck. The sun was streaked with the colors of clementine skin and blood oranges. The first stars were almost visible.

Even from the beach, I could hear the raucous laughs and music coming from Penny's houseboat. It wasn't a modern monstrosity of plastic and glass, something out of a millionaire's playbook. It was rustic wood, painted electric blue, with yellow trim and smudged windowpanes overlooking scrawny flower-box petunias.

I could see people milling about on deck, drinks in their hands. Everyone glowed with the sun. The pier stretched ahead of me, boats moored on either side. Wrist-thick rope coiled around sturdy wooden poles, anchoring the boat to the dock.

Everyone saw us coming. Against the warm gold of the sun and the sand and everything in between, Levi's white tee and my white sundress stood out like beacons. Several shouts of *Babe!* heralded our entrance.

Lucy, dressed in a navy-blue crop top and skirt, waved from Lorcan's crab shack. She used a napkin to swipe at her forehead. People were sprawled on the sand, waiting for their meals. Summer nights were busy ones for a one-man operation, and Lucy helped him out whenever she could.

The sizzle of fire-grilled lobster and shrimp married with the tang of salt water carried over with the balmy breeze. My mouth watered. Grilled seafood was my favorite smell in the world—freshly ground coffee beans came a close second.

"I love this view," said Levi, pointing to the colorful shacks and cottages dotting the beach. "These are all the original fishermen's cottages, aren't they?"

He'd been reading some of the pamphlets I'd left in the house for him. My heart blew up. I liked him even more.

He closed his eyes, letting the last rays of sun warm his face, lips curved into a beatific smile. His face radiated the same kind of wonder and appreciation that I felt every day in this town.

"The town is pretty strict about maintaining the authenticity," I agreed. "There's lots of regulations about renovations and paint colors and stuff."

I pointed to Lorcan's restaurant, La Mer. "Eaten there yet? It's the best fresh-caught crab you've ever had in your life."

"Never eaten it. Too many, uh, arms and legs."

I laughed, relishing the revolted expression on his face. "You eat drumsticks, right? Chicken wings? Exactly where do you think those come from?"

"The freezer section," Levi said, shooting me a grin.

We were close enough to the houseboat for people on board to turn and wave at me energetically. I raised my hand in return, spotting Penny's glossy black head as she wove through the crowd like an eel.

"Babe!" Her shriek carried across the air. Her skinny arms went around me in a bone-crushing hug. "You're here!" She released me from her hold long enough to stare deep into my eyes and go in for a peck on my lips, her signature greeting. Her pupils were dilated, eyeliner smudges at the outer corners of her lids and Twiggy-esque clumps of mascara on her lower lash line.

Her eyes landed on Levi with surprise, then slid to me in question.

"This is Levi," I said. "He's renting my mom's house for the summer." I gestured to my friend. "Levi Keller, Penny Wang."

"Whoa, small world." Levi ran a hand through his hair. He gave her a smile. "Hi, again. Sorry for crashing like this. Cool party."

I looked between them. "Sorry . . . you've met?"

"He's going to be my mentor at the art center," said Penny. "We just got the email today about our matchup. I had no idea you'd be so—" She laughed. "Young."

Levi's smile grew. "Yeah, the word *mentor* makes me think of an old dude with glasses."

"And probably a dweeby sweater," said Penny.

Ice broken, I relaxed. For a moment, I had thought Penny wouldn't like my bringing Levi along. I wasn't in the habit of just showing up with people.

"Hey, I baked these for you." I handed her the plate of cookies.

Her face brightened. "Thanks!" Before I could stop her, she turned to one of the guys and said, "Hey, Vince, could you just put these out on the counter for everyone?"

I opened my mouth, but it was too late. He'd already taken the plate from Penny with a wolfish gleam in his eyes. A second later, he'd stuffed one in his mouth.

Those cookies were for *her*. They were her favorite. I hadn't wanted them to be put out as a party snack. But I knew they'd all be gobbled up by the end of the night.

As Vince ambled to the kitchen, Penny sized Levi up. "You want some weed?"

Levi started.

"The drinks are back there," said Penny, pointing behind her. "Coke, wine, beer, you can pick your poison." She shot him a teasing grin. "Tap water if you're not into having fun."

My eyebrow twitched. There were more ways to have fun than getting blackout drunk.

"Uh, okay. Can I get you ladies anything?" Levi gave me a faint smile.

I began to move toward him. "That's okay, I'll go with y—"

Penny grabbed my arm. "Wine, please. Right to the top."

He looked at me.

With my friend's arm manacled around mine, there was nothing I could do except shrug. "Beer, please."

"I'll be back," said Levi.

Penny waited until he was out of earshot, edging between grinding bodies, a pucker etching deeply into his brow. Then, "Babe, what's going on?" Her voice dropped. "You're with a *summer* boy?" She made a soft, strangled noise.

I shifted uncomfortably. "These people are mostly your friends, not mine. Without Chad here . . . I just didn't want to be hanging around by myself while you did whatever you were doing. I didn't want it to be weird."

"For you?" Her face scrunched.

"Well, yeah." I shifted my weight, looking at the polished wood below my feet.

"I don't get why."

Because you wrecked my perfect summer when you broke up with Chad! I wanted to shout. *Because he kissed me, and even though it would never have gone any further, I still feel like I'm betraying you! Because I don't know how to talk to you about all these changes—about any of this!*

My stomach surged and crashed like waves against a rock. It had nothing do with the cloying smell of weed or the swaying of the boat.

I closed my eyes. Before it all changed, things hadn't been simple, but there was a consistency to life. Chad. Penny. Me. Hysteria bubbled up. What had I been thinking, getting attached to Levi? What good was attraction when everything else was falling apart?

I stared out across the water. The sun was low in the sky, almost within reach of the grasping mortals below. It reflected red and yellow on the water, rippling like molten gold. The salt air and the heat made for a heady combination, more intoxicating than any perfume.

In the elongated silence that followed, Penny repeated, "I don't get why." This time, it was said with a hardened edge.

"Don't you?" I whispered.

Penny's face softened. "Did something happen?" She touched my shoulder. "Whose ass am I kicking?"

In one sentence, she reminded me what a good friend she could be. But before I could say a word, Levi was back.

Penny pressed her lips to the glass immediately. When she pulled away, her pale lips were stained merlot.

"Thanks," I said, accepting the ice-cold beer. I wrapped my fingers around the neck, knowing that I felt too sick to take even a sip.

"No problem." Levi's fingers toyed with the bottom of his shirt, eyes carefully looking everywhere but at me.

Did he catch any of that? I watched his expression, unable to gauge what, if anything, he'd overheard.

Coming here was a mistake. Even with Levi acting as my buffer, my life raft, I felt out of place. Like maybe it wasn't my world that was different, but me.

The realization scraped across me, steel wool against tender innards. The awkward silence was broken by the off-kilter twangs of a guitar and someone's tinny voice attempting a rendition of Johnny Cash's "Swing Low, Sweet Chariot."

"Oh, and Chad *is* here, by the way," said Penny, cutting the awkwardness with an airy hostess voice. "Hey, cool to meet you, Levi." Someone dancing jostled her arm, and her wine sloshed.

It felt like the world was braking. Not slow and gentle, but screeching to a stop, burning rubber. My nose tingled and I sucked in a shaky breath. "Wait!" I must have heard her wrong, because there was no way he would be here, not after—

Penny met my gaze. Her eyebrows knit in concern. "Yeah?"

"Chad?" I swung my gaze wildly, people blurring in my vision.

"Um, so I forgot to tell you, but"—she dropped her voice conspiratorially—"we got back together."

"But—"

"Later, B! You're staying until the end of the night, right? We'll catch up then!" She blew an air kiss at Levi. "Enjoy the party. See you at the center on Monday!" she called over her shoulder as she swept away.

"Hey, can you just give me a minute?" My fingers tightened around the neck of the bottle. "I have to catch up with her really quick."

His lips parted like he was about to ask if everything was okay, but he swallowed hard and said, "Yeah, sure."

I dashed after Penny. She was disappearing into her bedroom at the back of the houseboat. I pushed my way past everyone, ignoring their greetings. I got to her bedroom door before she pushed it shut. "Penny," I said breathlessly.

She wasn't alone.

"Babe?" Chad stood in the center of the room, face mirroring my shock. Guilt fanned across his cheeks in a flaming streak of red as he looked between us, mouth agape.

I shut the door. "You guys really got back together." I swallowed. "When did you two—"

"Not long. I texted him before the party," Penny said quickly. She flicked her eyes to Chad. "We've been together so long. It was silly to end it over nothing."

I could have told her that.

Actually, I was pretty sure I *did* tell her that.

I fastened my eyes on Chad. "I didn't think you'd be here," I said.

Tension squirmed in my belly. He didn't owe me anything, but I couldn't believe he'd just gone back to Penny. Anger replaced the confusion. He'd kissed me on a whim. I'd been right after all. He was scared to be alone, scared to find out who Chad Ainswick was without Penny Wang in his life. And I'd been . . . convenient. I'd been there when she wasn't.

He'd jeopardized what should have been the best summer of our lives just because he was *scared*.

Chad looked cornered. He glanced between us, gnawing on his lip.

"You're both freaking me out." Penny put her hands on her hips. "Chad, what did you want to tell me?"

He shot me a look that was filled with a thousand things. I didn't have time to decipher them all before he said, "I tried to tell you earlier but you were too busy. It's okay, I can just tell you later."

The music faded. The world slowed. I knew what he was going to say next. Why he'd called her in here. It wasn't supposed to happen like this. *I* was supposed to tell her—it had to come from me. I kicked myself for waiting so long. I'd had days to tell Penny what had happened, but I'd been a coward and let it slide.

"Tell me what?" asked Penny. She flounced down on the bed and patted either side of her. "Sit down, guys."

Chad sat.

I couldn't. I felt like a prisoner at my own trial, hands and legs manacled to prevent movement, escape. My mouth tasted like ash.

I sent Chad an entreaty with my eyes. *Don't. Please don't.*

"I can't do this again with a secret between us," said Chad. He was still looking at me, but his words were for her. "We've always been honest with each other. All three of us."

Something in Penny's face shifted. It was like she knew what was coming.

Chad went for the death blow. "When you sent Babe to meet me that day . . . I was a mess. I was angry and sad and missing you, and—" It wasn't the end of the story. "We kissed."

"You what?" Penny's voice was inscrutable.

"It happened so fast, we didn't mean for it to," said Chad. He reached out for Penny's hand, and a second later, she gave it. "She didn't start it. It was my fault. It was nothing, it didn't mean anything."

The kiss was nothing. That foolishness was a wisp of nostalgia that I'd already brushed away. I didn't want to be with Chad. I just wanted this summer, and both my best friends. The kiss was nothing, but our friendship was everything. It was years of togetherness, of having each other's backs. We'd shared so much. We'd shared each other. Penny would understand, wouldn't she? This was *Penny*. My best friend.

But when she looked at me, there was no sign of the girl who I had spent my life with. The girl whose Easy-Bake Oven I'd learned my love of baking from, the girl who let me cry until snot bubbles burst when Elodie left, the girl who used to leave Post-it doodles in my school textbooks to encourage me before a test.

"You kissed my boyfriend." Penny's voice wobbled. She pressed a fist to her mouth, then pulled it away. "My boyfriend and my *best* friend."

"That's what I wanted to talk to you about," I whispered. "I wanted to—"

"This is unbelievable." Penny's voice was undone, shrill and hysterical. "Seriously? You . . . do you have any idea . . ." She pulled her hands from Chad before rearing back. Her palm arced through the air, making contact with his cheek.

His face swung to the side, redder than before.

She looked as shocked as I felt. I didn't think she meant to do it.

"There's nothing between us," I said. The sound of her flesh meeting his echoed in the room, the slap sounding about ten times louder. "I swear to you, Pen."

"And that's supposed to make me feel better?" Penny shot to her feet. "This is my fault. I . . . I invited you to everything. I wanted to make sure that you never felt left out, especially after Elodie left. But you . . . you just took advantage of that, didn't you? You took advantage of me."

My chest felt stretched tighter than a rubber band. Any second, I expected myself to snap and fly off. "I didn't." I gestured toward Chad. My breathing was shallow and my breath caught. "*We* didn't."

"Vince said it was weird, the three of us always being together. That sooner or later, you and he . . ." She pointed to Chad. "That you couldn't just be *friends*," she said with a sneer.

"Why the hell are you listening to what Vince says?" I asked, remembering the goon who had stuffed my cookies into his face.

Penny, voice growing louder, kept talking like I hadn't said anything. "He wasn't the only one who thought I was making a mistake. But I said you weren't like that. I stood up for you."

Was that what she thought? That I'd been eyeing Chad ever since the start? I thought of all those people outside, most of whom I knew and some of whom I didn't. People who showed up at Penny's parties every week. Her friends. Who didn't like me. Who mistrusted me.

And I had proved them right, hadn't I?

Hopelessness reached a crescendo inside me, and I wanted to throw myself at her, beg and cry for her forgiveness, if that was what it took. Anything to make her stop looking at me like that.

"You don't know me at all if you think I'd do anything to hurt you," I said.

"You just did!" Penny almost screamed.

"Hey," Chad started to say, but she quelled him with a slicing look over her shoulder.

When she turned back to me, her voice was quieter than I'd ever heard it before. "Get out." All trace of her tears was gone. The shattered porcelain had sharpened into steel.

"Penny—"

"You are uninvited. I don't want to see you here anymore. I don't want to see you at all." She laughed, all kinds of brittle. The sound shredded my heart. "In fact," Penny whispered, "the next time you see me? We don't know each other."

My ears were hot. Everything pounded. My vision blurred. The memory of Elodie crossing the street to avoid me flashed into my mind. Only now her face was replaced with Penny's. "Let's talk about this," I said. "Please, let's—"

Penny opened the door. "What are you waiting for?" Her voice cut straight through me.

I fled, not caring who I jostled on my way through her tiny living room, past the kitchen, and finally onto the deck. There was nowhere here where I could breathe. I put the bottle I was somehow still holding to my lips. The now-warm beer tasted disgusting, but I swallowed it down.

"Hey, you okay?" Levi was at my side.

I could only imagine how I looked. Pale. Shaken. Unhinged.

"I'm fine," I said, my voice louder than I'd intended. It seemed magnified to my own ears. "I just . . . can we get out of here? Go to the beach. Anywhere else."

I could see his concern from the way his eyes crinkled. But, to my relief, he didn't press me on it. "Yeah, of course," he said.

The journey there seemed to take an eternity, or maybe it only felt like it because I was reliving the memory of Penny's cold words and colder eyes. Over and over I heard her clear voice say, *Get out get out get out.* I'd barely had any beer, but the world still looked dizzying. I sank my bare feet into the sand, trying to hold back the tidal wave of emotion that threatened to take me under. "Here's good," I said.

We sat next to each other on the beach, backs resting against a log. When I looked at Levi, I didn't know what he saw in my face.

He gave me a crooked smile. "Shall we?" he asked, nodding toward our beers.

Wordlessly, I nodded.

"To summer," he said, tipping his bottle toward me. "And new friends."

And to losing old ones.

Our bottles made a satisfying *clink* when they met.

I could sense him looking at me, so I wasn't surprised when he asked, ever so carefully, "What happened back there?"

Oh, you know, just an implosion of a decade-long friendship.

I shook my head. "It's just better out here."

Levi didn't break the silence with another question. Silently, we sipped our beers—well, he sipped, I just tightly clung to the neck—and watched the waves foam and recede. We sat like that for minutes, until I heard him inhale. He put the bottle on the sand between his legs, then met my eyes. "Can I say something?"

Warily, I asked, "Is it about the party?"

"No."

"Okay." I nodded for him to continue.

He put his palms together, tentlike. Now that he had the floor, he seemed a little shy. I held his gaze, waiting. He drew closer. "I hope this isn't bad timing, but . . . I like you."

111

I glanced away, running my thumb across the lip of the bottle. It was almost like I'd been waiting for one of us to say it, and now it was finally out there. "It's not bad timing. There's nothing bad about it."

His eyes softened and he leaned back, looking relieved. "Good," he said, voice a little rougher than before. "I'm glad."

So was I. But I wasn't ready to say anything more about it. Because now I knew what good my attraction was—it was everything. It was a safe harbor before I was brave enough to head back into the storm.

seven

I tried to go back to Penny's twice in the next week. She wouldn't talk to me either time. I called her name, pounded on her door, even begged a little. But from her side, there was only silence. My very foundation seemed to wobble. The bricks of my life had been built with my friends, and without them, I'd never felt more unsteady.

Even Chad, shamefaced, had ducked into Busy's only long enough to say he was so sorry and would definitely speak to Penny, but thought that to keep the peace it would be better if we didn't hang out for a while. I doubted he would have much better luck wearing her down than I did.

Levi had continued to visit Busy's, sometimes with his sketch-book, always with a smile. The breakup might have been unbearable if it wasn't for him. The week after we'd toasted to new beginnings, he surprised me with an invitation to go out for dinner. A thank-you for the warm welcome to Oar's Rest, he'd said, his treat. At first, seeing his number flash on my phone screen had set off alarm bells—had he run into a problem with the house? Washing machine conked out? Electricity on the fritz? Weird leaks?

Instead, I was joining him for a meal.

"It's still a date; it totally counts," Lucy insisted.

"It's really not," I said. "It's a return invitation. He's being polite."

"He wouldn't do that for third-wheeling on a party he wasn't even invited to." Lucy waved at the book club ladies who had just come in. "I'm telling you, it's a date. Maybe it's a date masquerading as a thank-you, but it's still a date!" And with that, she swished off to take orders.

I dwelled on Lucy's words, replaying Levi's invitation in my head until I'd talked myself into it. She was right, he'd never ask me to dinner just as a thank-you—it was Our First Date. Maybe. Probably.

"Hey, Babe!"

I froze. Ariel, who was supposed to have been here hours ago, had just entered.

"Ugh." She stalked behind the counter and grabbed her apron. A few drops of water landed on the floor. Everything about her was disheveled, from her wet hair to her rumpled clothing.

"You're late," I pointed out. "Why didn't you call in to say you wouldn't be here?"

"Sorry, I slept in. I'm here now." Ariel cast me an irritated look. "Why didn't *you* call me?"

I blinked. "Ariel, this is . . . I mean, wow, okay. Do you even want this job? Because it seems like you're doing everything to prove you don't."

"I need the money," said Ariel. "Of course I want to work here." She had the temerity to scowl like I'd insulted her by asking.

I hesitated. "Is everything okay?"

"Stupid boyfriend drama. Sometimes I think you have the right idea about being anti-men. I'm swearing off guys, too." Ariel reached out to grab one of the lemon bars I'd brought in this morning. "Hey, do you mind? I haven't had breakfast." She took a bite before I could answer. "This is *amazing*. You should bring these to the fish fry next month."

"I'm not anti-men," I said stiffly.

"I've never seen you with a guy." She paused. "I mean, other than Chad."

Even her appreciation for my pastry didn't shake my annoyance with her behavior. She'd been here a couple of months and she'd never put in an honest week's work. She had a few good days, a few no-shows, but mostly she just drifted in and out like her job was an afterthought. I was tired of carrying her weight.

"You haven't dated anyone since I've been working here, right?" she asked, oblivious to my mounting anger.

"That's super none of your business," I said.

Lucy, returning with the book club orders, eyed Ariel. "Eight iced caramel frappes, one iced green tea, and one pot of lemon and hibiscus."

Ariel popped the rest of the lemon bar in her mouth and chewed. "Sorry, Babe. I just assumed. But it's fine. Dating isn't for everyone." It wasn't much of an apology.

For a girl in desperate need of allies, she has an awful lot of sass. I gritted my teeth.

But then the door opened again and in our distraction, Ariel pulled a Houdini.

I sighed. "What do you wanna bet we don't see her again until after the lunch rush?"

"Try closing time," said Lucy, filling up the orders with the practiced ease of a barista. "Hand me the caramel sauce, would you?"

♥ ♥ ♥

As expected, Ariel didn't reappear until the end of the day, just in time to show her face. Tom, who had come in for his usual game of chess with Ralph, asked once again if the deliveries had been checked against the invoice so he could pay the bill. Ariel swore up and down that she had done it, even though I was pretty sure she hadn't.

When Levi came to pick me up, I'd never been so eager to leave.

"Hey, Levi," chirped Lucy when he came through the door, looking like the quintessential summer boy in his blue plaid American Eagle button-down.

"Hey," he greeted us as he approached. "Ready to go?" He gave Lucy a wave, and as I turned to do the same, she gave me a quick thumbs-up.

Butterflies were raging in my stomach like they were on freaking Molly. "I'd love to introduce you to Tom and Ralph," I said. "Ralph was on the art center's selection committee."

Levi nodded eagerly. "I'd love that."

Ariel hung around for a few minutes, clearly angling for an introduction, but Tom and Ralph monopolized the conversation with questions about the art residency. Levi had his sketchbook in a beat-up messenger bag and flipped it open to familiar scenes of Oar's Rest: the post office's window boxes, overflowing with flowers; vibrant shutters on whitewashed cottages; a huge wedge of pie from Kimble's Diner, blueberry filling oozing onto the plate.

Appropriately impressed, Tom had sent us on our way, giving me his blessing with a hearty wink that I hoped Levi didn't catch.

"They were nice," Levi said once we were out the door.

"They are," I said, smiling.

We were moving in the direction of the sun now. The warm rays were making me feel sticky with perspiration and I swiped at my forehead when I felt drops of sweat cling to my hairline.

"I can see your mom's house from here," said Levi. He raised his arm, pointing to the colorful row of houses lining the commercial pier.

Shading my eyes with the palm of my hand, I squinted into the sunburst glow of the horizon. The houses there were built by the first fishermen who inhabited Oar's Rest and had been carefully renovated over the years by their descendants. In more recent years, the families had moved out, choosing to take their fishing fortunes and buy newer homes in the town itself. Most of the fishermen's cottages were now rented out to tourists, many of them city slickers who wanted a taste of the humble, quiet life.

"I see it," I said. The house was a mossy green, like the color of the algae infesting the submerged wooden beams in the pier. Mom's favorite color.

We lapsed into silence. I kept waiting for him to duck into the shade of one of the restaurant awnings, but he continued walking at a leisurely pace. The sun glinted in his hair, each strand lit with a multidimensional golden shine.

"What?" He'd caught me staring.

"Uh, just . . ." I gestured to his hair. "You have Disney princess hair." I could tell I'd surprised him from the slow smile that spread over his face. "Ugh, pretend I didn't say that?"

"Why would I do a dumb thing like that? That's pretty much the best compliment anyone's ever given me." A beat. "Plus, it means you were checking me out. Again."

"That wasn't—okay, it was." I laughed. "You busted me. I have zero game. I'm an open book."

We stopped walking. "Suits me," he said. "When I told you I liked you, it was because I don't want to spend the summer going back and forth on whether or not I should tell you. I don't play games, and guessing games are the worst."

I felt my rib cage shift in a fluttery plummet, all the way down to my stomach. "Then you're the opposite of every guy I went to high school with." A good thing, definitely.

"Good. I don't do games. I do grown-up." He flashed me the kind of smile that he probably threw around all the time like confetti. One part earnest, one part sweet. So deliciously genuine that my fingers itched to reach out and touch his face, make sure he was real. Because no one had smiled at me like that in a long time. Any wisecracks or flirtations withered in my throat. It felt wrong to tease after what he'd said.

"I like you, too," I said. Honesty sort of demanded it. And I *had* left him hanging last week when he'd told me how he felt.

His smile turned shy. "I sort of figured. You wouldn't be here otherwise."

We kept walking, our arms grazing every time one of us veered a little too close. My body hummed in response, tingling with awareness. The first time it happened, I glanced at him, but he wasn't looking at me. The second time, I wanted to let my fingers casually-on-purpose slide against his, but Levi simply murmured a "Sorry" to me and course-corrected himself.

I waved at some younger kids from high school who were lounging outside the Dairy Bar. Recognition lit up their faces and they eagerly returned my wave between licks of their ice cream cones. Their blueberry streusel ice cream was the best I'd ever tasted, and I made a mental note to bring Levi here.

The Dairy Bar was one of the many establishments along the wide expanse of beach. Mom's house, Busy's, and the ice cream shop were close to the wharf. The semicircle of sand allowed someone to stand at one end and see across the water to the other end, with the pier, wharf, rowboats, and fishing trawlers in between.

As we came to a halt in front of a cheerful yellow flower shop, he pointed ahead to a peeling-paint little eatery a few stores ahead of us. A whitewashed piece of driftwood was nailed above the door, with thin hangul brushstrokes spelling out the name of the restaurant.

Levi squinted up at it. "You up for some Korean food?"

The tacos they served would remind me too much of Penny and the last time we'd been there. I could still taste the kimchi on my tongue. Swallowing, I gestured to the beach. "I thought we could try something a little more local."

"Seafood?"

I nodded, hopping off the cobbled path and onto soft sand. My feet were swallowed by the hungry cling of the beach, warm sand slipping into my flip-flops. Levi fared better in his sturdy sandals. I made a face and pulled off my flip-flops, letting them swing between my fingers.

He let silence descend before breaking it. "Have you lived here your whole life?"

I made my way through a cluster of sandcastles. "Yeah. Born and raised."

"Must be nice. This place is like paradise."

I glanced at him, watching his eyes flutter closed. "Close enough. It's home."

"Never wanted to leave?"

"Would you?"

"Fair enough," Levi said, laughing.

I gave him a good-natured shoulder bump. "Come on, let's get some grub." I pointed to a little shanty about a hundred feet ahead of us. "I hope you're hungry, because this place definitely does not skimp."

Ahead of us, a small crowd had already gathered. There was a buzz of excited energy as everyone waited for their order to be ready. The smell of grilled fish and the smokiness of the firepit made both my eyes and mouth water.

I could sense Levi's skepticism as we approached the little sea shack. "Lamer?" he said, looking up at the hanging wooden sign above the counter. A second later, I saw the realization dawn on his face.

"La Mer." Lorcan, the owner, a curly-haired Poseidon with rippling arm and chest muscles, straightened himself behind the counter. "It means 'the sea.'"

"The letters are a little close together," Levi mumbled, still looking at the sign.

I tried not to giggle. "Levi, this is Lorcan. He's Lucy's boyfriend."

Levi nodded. "Hey."

Lorcan grinned at me. "Hey, man. Good to meet you. What can I get you two?" he asked, waving his hand at the gathering of people in front of us. Everyone made room for Levi and me to step through the gap.

"You can't go wrong with anything at Lorcan's place." I grinned at the owner. "What do you recommend for a city boy who's about to get his first real taste of Maine seafood?"

"Literally anything on my menu." Lorcan folded his arms across his chest and smiled at me.

"The Fisherman's Sampler," Levi read out loud from the chalkboard sign behind Lorcan's head. "Fish, shrimp, scallops, clam strips, calamari, crab cakes, and two sides."

"Sides are corn on the cob, roasted on the pit or boiled and buttered, and French fries." Lorcan sized us up. "That's more than enough for two people on a date."

Levi shot me a quick glance. He took a breath. "What do you think, Babe? Do you want the sampler?"

The total cost of the meal would be forty dollars, more if we added drinks. That was a bit more than I wanted Levi to spend on our date tonight. "Could we just go with a basket of shrimp?" I looked at Levi for approval before saying, "And nix the appendages, please, Lorcan."

Lorcan gave me an openly amused smile. "Anything for you, Babe." He winked. "Go take a seat. I'll give you a shout when your order's ready."

"What do you want to drink? Soda, water?" Levi asked, skimming the menu.

"Make that two Moxies," I said, figuring he'd never had one before. "It's sort of like root beer."

At his quizzical smile, I knew I was right.

"Nah," said Lorcan. "I'd say it tastes way more like a Dr Pepper."

"Yeah, you're right." I grinned at Levi. "You'll love it."

As Levi paid, I scanned the beach for a good spot to sit and eat. Some of the other diners had brought their own picnic blankets and were sprawled out nearby. The soft drone of their chatter was accompanied by the lulling sounds of foamy swash rolling onto the sand.

Those people were definitely on a date, I thought, stomach tightening. Unbidden, a memory started to take shape. Chad, Penny, and me eating on the smooth, flat rocks by the wharf, watching the fishermen bring in the evening's catch.

"Babe?" Levi appeared at my side, stuffing his wallet into his back pocket, two bottles of Moxie nestled in the crook of his arm. "Where should we sit?"

"There are some picnic tables over there," I said, pointing to a grassy knoll straight ahead of Lorcan's crab shack. Separating the beach and the rest of the town was a wide stretch of grass where a few picnic tables were scattered in between children's playground equipment and an ice cream vendor. "When I was a little kid, my mom and grandma used to bring me here. There was this crabber's shanty near where Lorcan's place is now." I smiled at the memory. "This old gruff guy with a beard and eyebrows so thick you could barely see his eyes. He sold the best steamed crabs I've ever eaten. Gran showed me how to crack open the crabs. She gave me a little wooden hammer and I just whaled away on the little suckers."

Levi glanced down the beach like he could actually picture the shanty still standing there. "I don't remember doing anything like that with my parents. Dad mostly just stuck me in front of the TV or sent me out to play with the neighborhood kids. We didn't do things together like that."

"What about art? Didn't your mom color with you or anything like that?"

He shook his head. "Not since I was really little. Like elementary school."

We stood in silence, until Levi shifted his stance. "Until I got good at something—drawing—they didn't have a lot of interest in what I was interested in. Dad loved travel shows and those luxury vacation magazines. We didn't have the money, but it was pretty much the main thing we ever talked about." He shrugged. "He didn't care about sports or movies or cars, nothing like that. But if I needed help on a world history paper or something . . ."

"What about your mom?"

"She works for a museum, but she's not really artistic." A faint smile flickered over his face. "She was excited when my art teacher told her I had talent. She'd just read all these articles about teen entrepreneurs, and she wanted me to have my shot. So I started posting online. Doodles at first, then more serious stuff. Anywhere that would get me exposure. And then I got on Instagram, just posting my art up there and racking up a following. Then commissions came along. Some people reached out to me, but it wasn't until some huge influencers started talking about me and tagging me that things really kicked off."

"And then your parents got you an agent," I said.

"It was pretty surreal. I have no idea if this is what I want to do for the rest of my life. I just graduated from high school; I don't have to have it all figured out." He exhaled through his nose. "They keep telling me I have potential, but they act like it's something that goes bad or spoils if you leave it alone too long. Like one day I'll wake up and have to pour it down the drain like sour milk."

I lightly touched his shoulder. "Hey. If it helps, I don't think your talent is something that'll fade or go away if you don't squeeze every drop out right now. You're right. It's hard to figure out if you want something to be a career. Like when people find out I'm not going to college, they get all awkward. They think staying at Busy's and being a barista is . . . a stepping-stone job. And for most people, it is." I shrugged. "But I've never wanted to do anything else in my entire life. Making people happy with food is something special. So is your art."

The wind teased his hair, lifting it up with an adorable little flip. "Yeah?" Levi smiled, then ran a hand through his hair, ruffling it all up. "I hope you're right. I talked to my high school art teacher in the winter about how my parents were trying to strong-arm me. She knows someone at the RISD admissions office who can help, even though I missed the application deadline by a few days. No promises or anything, but I'm on the priority waitlist." He shrugged helplessly. "I don't even know how I'll tell my parents if it works out."

Almost everyone pronounced the Rhode Island School of Design as *ris-dee*, but I remembered the first time Elodie told me about her dream school, she'd mispronounced it as *rised* the first time. Thinking about my girlfriend—ex-girlfriend—cast a shadow over me, so I swept the memory aside, focusing on the here and now instead.

"Wow. That's a good school," I said.

He shrugged, grinning. "I probably won't even get in. But whatever. It's taking the chance that counts, right? Anyway, it'd be nice to get out of the city, go someplace smaller." He glanced around us, eyes soft. "Like this."

I smiled. "You know, it used to be that everyone in my senior year wanted to get out of a place this small." I stretched both my arms behind my back, lacing my fingers together until the ache in my lower back went away. "Not me. I think it's nice to be in a place where everybody knows your name."

"Like *Cheers*?"

"What?"

"It's an old television show. It's about this bar where all the main characters hang out. They're like a family." He gave me a crooked grin. "Look it up on Netflix sometime."

"Okay." I rubbed an itch on my nose. "I'm surprised. Most New Yorkers who come here say that they could never imagine leaving the city."

His brow furrowed, like he was really thinking about it. "People always talk about getting out of New York, but . . ." He glanced at me. "I think my dad would love it here. So would Mom. They just never get around to leaving. Sometimes I think they're so scared of change that it paralyzes them into doing nothing, because *nothing* is better than making the wrong decision."

"How do you mean?" I found myself stepping closer to him, drawn like a honeybee to the secret parts of him.

"It's one of those vague 'in the future' things they think they want to do—or they *want* to want to do. But when it comes down to it, they can't imagine living anywhere else." Levi rolled his eyes. "And as much as they complain about it, it's home."

"I don't know if I'd ever find home somewhere other than here.

There's memories in every inch of Oar's Rest. The beach, the light-house. Busy's. Everywhere." Dangling my legs off the pier, watching hermit crabs hunt for shells during molting season, burying my fingers in the hot white-gold sand . . . a lifetime of memories coursed through my mind. I clung to them like old friends, taking solace in how solid they felt.

"You'd make new memories," he said.

I would. But the same memories that made Oar's Rest painful at times were also the ones that contained worlds. First kisses and dripping ice cream cones. Fumbled sex and really good weed. Sleepovers at Penny's and racing hermit crabs with Chad. Learning how to make soup dumplings and sandcastles. The awning Elodie had been standing under when I'd first realized I had feelings for her.

Summer boys were made for outgrowing places like this, but I wasn't. Every time I was with him, it was so easy to think of him as just a boy, but he wasn't, was he? He was just another memory waiting to happen.

I switched the subject. "What do you miss about New York?" I wanted to gauge his reaction, see how homesick he was. Or . . . if he wasn't.

He shot me a half smile. "There's always a twenty-four-hour place open if you're hungry. And when you look out your window at night, it's like you have the whole galaxy of stars looking back at you. Grabbing the subway with your friends, getting really good food whenever you want it . . . yeah, I guess I miss that." He looked at me almost shyly. "But I'd take a few *real* stars over thousands of sparkling lights any day."

My heart expanded. The way he was looking at me was all too

real, all too tender. No one had ever looked at me like that before. Not Elodie, not any of the guys who tried to hit on me when I was behind the counter.

"And of course, the coffee here is better than anything back home," Levi added.

"There's no way that's true."

"I'm telling you that it is," he said softly. This time, it didn't take an accidental graze for us to touch. His hand hesitantly reached out, his eyes on mine the whole time.

I curled my fingers around his, tiny thrills springing up my wrist. "Careful," I murmured, before I could think better of it. "Any more flattery and I might just hold on to you for good."

"Maybe I'd let you."

We stood in silence, savoring the rare breeze that blew our way. It was balmy and warm and did nothing to alleviate the wetness on my brow. Using the back of my free hand, I smoothed it backward into my hair.

From here, the town of Oar's Rest resembled a labyrinth of houses and a warren of winding streets. Colorful paint peeked out, everything bright and happy like in a storybook.

"It's beautiful here," he said.

I hid my ridiculously happy grin. "Yeah, it is."

Birds arced above us. The salt breeze drifted toward us, and the sand, smoothed by the lacy waves of the tide, shimmered with flecks of mica.

I chanced a peek at Levi. His face was serene, tipped upward. Maybe without my friends, I should have felt bereft, but I didn't—not with him here. The thought brought an unbidden smile to my lips.

Embarrassed, I tamped it down. It felt wrong somehow to be happy in this moment when things seemed so irreparable with Penny. I pulled my hand away from him under the pretense of messing with my ponytail.

"Don't take this the wrong way," said Levi, breaking the unhurried silence, "but you don't feel like a stranger to me. Even though, you know, you sort of are." He threw me a quick glance. "I've never—I mean, this hasn't ever happened to me."

I thought about Chad and Penny and wondered if we really knew each other as well as we thought, or if we'd just gotten content with being friends out of habit. I shifted on my feet. "Maybe we knew each other in another life."

"Nah," said Levi. "Trust me, I'd remember." He playfully nudged my shoulder.

My bare skin tingled at the unexpected, pleasurable contact. I wanted him to do it again. And again. And again. It startled me how *young* I felt right then. Not the kind of young that made someone go head over heels, wanting to tattoo someone's name on their shoulder or anything like that. But for the first time in years, I wondered what it would be like to kiss someone other than Elodie. The taper of his neck made me uncomfortably, wonderfully aware of how much I wanted to press my lips to the warm hollow under his jawline.

"You wouldn't," I said. I meant it to sound like a joke, but it came out like a challenge. My body prickled. What was I *doing*? I couldn't flirt with a summer boy!

He caught my eye, the breeze ruffling his hair just right so he looked like he was in the frame of a movie. "Yeah," he confirmed, voice grave and studious. "I would."

My reservations whooshed out of me.

We shared the moment, smiles lingering on both our faces, until it was broken by Lorcan's shout of "Hey, Babe!"

I headed back to the shack, squeezing my way through the throng of people, to accept the newspaper-clad bundle Lorcan handed me. "Bon appétit," he said, handing me a bunch of napkins.

"Thanks."

"Who's he?" Lorcan asked with frank interest. He wiggled his eyebrows in Levi's direction. "Doesn't look like one of Penny's friends."

"He's here for the residency at the art center. He's, uh, Penny's mentor." I immediately wanted to kick myself. He was more mine than he was Penny's. Then I wanted to kick myself again. Levi wasn't a rope in a game of tug-of-war; he belonged to himself first and only.

Lorcan's eyebrows shot up. "And you're dating him?" Even he knew how well that would go over with my possessive ex–best friend.

"It's *a* date. One. Dating would imply plural dates." I cleared my throat. "And we're just hanging out, it's really casual."

"Then why are you so pink?"

"It's hot over here! Your firepit is making it about a hundred degrees!"

"Sure, sure. Blame it on the heat," he said with a grin.

"And this is why we're sitting all the way over there, so I don't have to worry about you embarrassing me."

"*Moi?* Never."

I rolled my eyes good-naturedly. "Bye, Lorc."

"See ya, Babe."

I left Lorcan to his customers and maneuvered my way back to Levi, the makeshift basket of shrimp extended in front of me like a sacrificial offering. "Dinner," I said. "The best meal you'll ever eat."

"As long as it doesn't have legs, I'm in," Levi said, and I laughed.

We hustled to the picnic tables, narrowly dodging a Frisbee, a dog, and a scampering child in the process. "Watch out!" I called.

With Levi on one bench and me on the other, I put the still-scalding basket of shrimp between us in no-man's-land. "Dig in."

He slid one of the bottles to me. "Cheers. To new friends." He held his bottle by the neck and tilted the wide bottom toward me in a toast.

"To new friends," I repeated, tapping my bottle against his in a gentle clink. I felt a lot more confident making this toast the second time around.

eight

Fingers sticky, we found clean corners of the newspaper to wipe our fingers on when we ran out of napkins. Any second now, the night would come to an end—and I didn't want it to.

"I can't believe I was nervous about La Mer." Levi blew out a breath, his cheeks puffed. "I'd seen the lines here before, but you know how I feel about seafood." His eyes crinkled in a smile. "But this . . . it's amazing."

He glanced toward the boats moored at the dock, eyes flitting around until he found what he was looking for. I followed his gaze to Penny's houseboat, stiffening.

"So, tell me if I'm wrong, but did something happen between you and Penny at the party last week? I hope it wasn't because I showed up with you." Catching the panic on my face, he shook his head. "No, sorry. It's not my business."

"No, it's okay. It's just stupid friend stuff."

He nodded slowly. "*Stupid friend* stuff or stupid *friend* stuff?"

Penny didn't really feel like a friend right now. She just happened to be in the same town as I was. One sliver of hope—there was only so long you could go, brushing against the same people, before you finally had to admit you were more than just strangers.

"Long story," I said. "Some friendships just . . . start to fall apart after high school."

"It's not weird that I'm mentoring her at the art center, is it?" he asked, taking a swig of his soda.

I shook my head. "Not for me." My stomach twisted as I thought about a possible reason for his question. "Why, did she . . . did she say anything to you?"

"No. I just saw her and that guy who ate your cookies head to her houseboat with some other people a while ago. She saw us, but she didn't come over. Or wave. She just . . . kept going." He shrugged. "Thought it was worth asking about."

Penny was with Vince. No wonder Chad was worried she was moving on with other people. "It's not about you," I said. "I don't think it's really about me or Penny, either." I tried to hold the question back, but not hard enough. "So . . . what do you talk about?"

It was weird not talking to Penny. Not knowing the ins and outs of her day, the things that made her smile and the things that made her mad. Despite the fact that I'd dropped by her houseboat a couple of times hoping for reconciliation, she'd turned from fire to ice. I knew she was inside, I'd seen her, but she refused to open the door. Even though I pounded against the door, even if I begged. She wasn't ready to thaw yet. Our Cold War wasn't over.

He shrugged. "Anything, really. Art, movies, cat videos." He paused. "She's invited me down to her houseboat a couple of times to hang out. I kind of thought you would be there."

It sounded like they were friends. A little curl of jealousy tugged at me, but I didn't know whether it was toward Levi or Penny.

"Maybe I'll see you there another time," I said lightly. He didn't have to know I wasn't welcome there anymore.

"I can let you know if I'm going," said Levi. "That way we can meet up."

The back of my neck burned. I couldn't even imagine the humiliation of showing up with him and being turned away. Or worse, if she made a scene in front of Levi and the whole awful story came tumbling out into the open.

"Mmm." I made a vague sound of agreement, hoping he wouldn't push further.

He didn't.

I wanted to ask him if he'd seen Elodie at the center, but I couldn't. I may not have wanted to think about the future, but I definitely wanted to keep my past and present as separate as possible. And if tonight had told me anything, it was that, summer boy or not, I definitely wanted Levi in my present.

"I don't want this night to end," I said.

"I don't, either." Levi smiled as he wiped the corner of his mouth. "I'm glad you said yes to going out with me. Eating out is always more fun with a friend." He glanced back in the direction of Lorcan's crab shack, where business was finally winding down. "Do you and your mom still come here a lot?"

"We used to, but now not so much," I said. "She's home a lot more in winter, but summer and fall she belongs to the cruise line."

"Does it get lonely?" He lifted his hand to gesture to the lighthouse.

"No, I have Pen—"

Silence hung between us.

"I have Lucy, Tom, Busy's. And you," I said. "New friends, remember?"

Levi chuckled. "I'm yours."

Playing along, I asked, "And what if I decide to keep you?"

"I *might* let you," he said gravely.

It was just banter-y banter. He didn't mean it. He was a freshly minted eighteen-year-old; he couldn't make a decision just like that. Not when he had family and friends back home, college to decide about. Glum at the realization, I balled up the rest of our trash. "How's the house and everything? All of it okay?"

"Yeah, perfect." His throat bobbed as he took a long sip. "Except for one thing."

"What?" I ran through the entire checklist of things I'd made sure were in order before he arrived. I couldn't think of a single problem.

He mock-shivered. "The sounds here are different. *Creepier.* Like at night, when the rumble of someone's air-conditioning kicks in, or the shadows that jump around on the walls when noisy drunks stumble by the house on their way home. The house groans and creaks sometimes. It's a little disconcerting. Those are the things you never notice in the city."

"Seriously? Old houses groan a little bit, you know." I smiled around the mouth of the Moxie bottle.

"Seriously. That'll teach me to read Stephen King late at night."

"You know he lives nearby, right?" I asked. "And some of the movies were filmed in Maine, too."

"What? Really?" He blinked.

"Yeah. I don't think his house was marked on your map, but I could take you." I peeked at him from under lowered lashes. "If you wanted."

"I want," said Levi, each word emphatic and eager.

"I don't read a lot of horror myself, but I've never been weirded out by scary stuff," I said. "Even though I'm on my own, I like living up there at the lighthouse. Because it's like I'm alone, but also not alone. I can see *everyone* right below me. I can even see my mom's house—your place." I blushed a little, admitting that. "Though I'm technically watching over them, it feels more like they're watching over me. Does that make sense?"

"It does, actually."

I tapped a fingernail against my bottle of Moxie. "How are you liking the residency so far?"

"It's pretty great." Levi's eyes lit up. "I know I'm here as a mentor, but I think I'm learning as much as the mentees. Back home, it was me painting by myself. Here, I'm part of a community. There's always someone I can talk to, bounce ideas off of. Learn something from." He cleared his throat. "That stuff makes a difference."

I thought about the watercolor he'd been working on at the lighthouse. "What I saw of your work was pretty great. And I know Tom and Ralph were super impressed with your sketches."

His smile was adorably shy. "Thanks."

"Can I ask you something about RISD?"

"Shoot."

"Did you apply anywhere else?"

He shook his head. I could tell that he didn't see what I was getting at.

"Um, it's just . . . you said you wanted to see if there was anything else you were passionate about, too. Can you do that at an art school? It doesn't seem like you're actually getting away from anything."

"I . . ."

I wasn't prepared for the look of panic on his face. "Ignore me," I said quickly. "I shouldn't have said anything."

"I didn't even—" He broke off, swallowing hard. "I'm an idiot. You're right, I'm—I'm not—I didn't think this through. I just drove up here a day early, running away, and it turns out what I'm running *to* is the same thing that I thought I would be getting away *from*."

"You're not an idiot. You're eighteen. Give yourself a break."

"But you're right, Babe. I didn't think any of this through. I was rebelling against a decision that I somehow wound right back up at. I chose RISD. Not my parents, not my agent. Me."

"That still doesn't make you an idiot. You can apply somewhere else, if you want."

He still looked a little shell-shocked. "Or I could just do what everyone wants me to do."

"Everyone but you."

"If I do what I want, I'll spend years running around for a degree, and maybe I'll never be as good at anything as I am at art right now."

"Potential doesn't go bad, remember?" But he didn't seem to believe in those words anymore. I could see it in his face. "So what if you waste a year? Two years? Four? You have everything you need to succeed. You're smart, talented, tenacious. Way more driven than I was when I was your age."

"Which, for the record," said Levi, "was just a year ago, Grandma."

"Sorry." I blushed. "I wasn't pulling the I'm-older-than-you card, I swear. I'm just saying that you . . . you have *it*. Whatever the it-factor is, you do. You do, Levi."

"What if I don't want to waste any time? What if it's easier to just walk the path that's charted for me?"

In that moment, it wasn't Levi with me, but Penny. Penny with her dark glittering eyes and her fear of never being anything more than the slurred-together *PennynChad* package deal. If she'd told me she planned to break up with Chad, I hoped I would have had the courage and selflessness to say the same thing to her.

"It would probably be easier in the short run," I agreed. "But if it's already charted, you're not really going to discover anything new, are you? Success, or anything, really, doesn't come with a pushpin. You can't just stick a destination into a map and think there's just the one route that gets you there. And if you wind up right back where you started . . . well, that's okay, too. We get to come back from our mistakes. We have to believe that's possible. We're too young not to."

This time, I took his hand. And there was no hesitation. Not in the way I squeezed or in the way he held on tight.

It took several moments for him to speak. "So you're my Yoda now, basically. All wise and shit." He rubbed distracting circles over my hand in a way that made me feel totally boneless.

Mouth dry, I said, "Your Yoda, I am."

Then, in a swift change of subject, he asked, "Are you seeing anybody?"

"Whoa! Smooth."

He broke into a chuckle. Eyes lingering on my face, he said, "Just making sure there wasn't some boyfriend in the wings who was going to kiss my ass for taking his girl on a date."

I tried not to smile and failed spectacularly. "Kiss? I think you mean *kick*."

He blinked slowly. "That's what I said."

I wasn't buying his wide-eyed, innocent act, no matter how cute he made it look. There were two things I was suddenly very sure of: This was definitely a date. And judging by Levi's Freudian slip, he was as into me as Lucy had thought.

"Riiiiight," I said. "I must have misheard."

His grin spread slowly over his face until there was no mistaking the chemistry between us. "Must have."

He was still looking at me with expectation, so I swallowed past the swimming serpents in my throat. I wanted to kiss him, I wanted to taste him. A shiver danced down my back. And judging from his slip, he wanted to kiss me, too.

This was getting dangerous. Changes had never been for the better, not in my experience. Breaking my own rule and kissing Levi right now would be a big change. And in the end, no matter what the rest of this summer brought us, I would lose him like I'd lost everyone else.

I gently extricated my hand and cleared my throat. "There is no jealous boyfriend waiting in the wings to beat you up. I haven't been serious about a guy for a while. My ex and I . . . She was a year ahead of me in school. But she didn't really believe in long-distance relationships—so she went to college, I stayed here." I waited to see if he would show any reaction. He didn't.

"Sorry." He made eye contact with me. "That sucks. I know what it's like to have someone move on without you."

"What happened? If you want to tell me, I mean."

"A girl I liked in high school made me think that she liked me, too." He locked his fingers together like a cradle. "I thought she was my girlfriend, but she actually wanted to be some other guy's girlfriend. I was just some dude she kissed a few times to make him jealous."

"Shit."

"Yeah, sounds about right." He shot me a half smile. "I was just there. You know?"

I did know. More than he knew.

"I thought she liked me," said Levi, "but all the time she was waiting for him to get jealous and do something about it. One day he did, and then she stopped being my girlfriend after that. They moved on and got their happy ending."

"Happy endings aren't all they're cracked up to be," I said. I was thinking of how abruptly Penny and Chad's golden relationship had tarnished.

"I'm definitely not into her anymore. I've moved on. I'm not still . . . pining. Or whatever." Levi's cheeks were pink.

I got the idea that he was trying to convince me. My stomach quivered. "Are they still together?"

"Plot twist. He lost his field hockey scholarship because he got caught with drugs, and she has a baby with someone else."

"Well, there you go. He may have got the girl, but he didn't get a happy ending with her."

"True." He unhooked his fingers and let one hand drum lightly against the table. "And it made me realize I don't like games. I don't want to be a stop along the way. I never want someone to drop my heart like that again."

The serious tone in his voice sent my pulse racing. The words untangled themselves, hovering for a second before I said, "It hurts to be the one left behind, but I'm not the kind of person whose world falls apart because of someone else." It felt important that I told him that, but as soon as the words were out of my mouth, I knew I wasn't just talking about El.

He seemed to know it, too. "You mean Penny."

I toyed with the corner of a newspaper, struggling to find the words. "Did you ever have friends where . . . sometimes you think you're only friends because you don't know how to be anything else?"

Levi shook his head.

"We just sort of fell into each other. Grew up together, grew into each other. Me, Chad, Penny. We've always been there."

He lightly bumped his fist against mine. "And maybe you still will be. And if not, there's a lot of fish in the sea. We'll both find our forever fish one day."

I smiled at the cheese. "I like the sound of that."

The minutes dragged on, neither of us in a rush to say anything to fill the silence. It was enough to just sit there together, enjoying each other's company instead of being freaked out by the lapse in conversation.

"Can I sketch you?"

Jolted, I stared at him a moment before nodding slowly, tentatively. "Okaaay."

He already had a small sketchbook out. I watched in amusement as he scrounged in his pocket for a stubby four-inch pencil.

"Are you always this prepared?"

"Yup." He said it in a matter-of-fact way, which I couldn't help but smile about.

"This is my first time being anyone's muse, so feel free to tell me I'm doing it wrong, Boy Scout."

His hand stilled over the paper he was smoothing out in copious motions with the flat of his palm. "Just relax."

He held the pencil between his thumb and forefinger, his grasp light. In elegant strokes, he began to skim the paper with the blunt graphite. Scratches filled the air as the pencil nub worked its way across the paper.

I kept still, leaning slightly forward, my arms folded across the picnic table. *Just relax?* That was the advice the dentist gave you before doing something heinous, like pulling a tooth or poking you in the gums with the anesthetic needle.

A stray gust of wind blew my hair into my face and I sputtered, frowning into the windswept mess. As I sat there deliberating on whether it would break my pose if I straightened my hair, Levi broke his meticulous concentration. "Um, thanks," I murmured as I felt his hand smooth out the hair on my temple. It was just a brush of his warm fingers against my forehead, nothing more, but I still felt self-conscious at the gesture.

We resumed our silence until the last of the kids were called away by their parents. The sky had deepened to the color of a grapefruit. Pink and orange battled for dominance as the sun began to set, streaking the sky like a watercolor painting. The faint yips of a dog faded away until all I could hear was the soft rasp of Levi's quick pencil strokes.

I envied his concentration. My own mind was a whorl of uncertainty, dragging me under like a mighty wave. I wanted Levi—*wanted* him, wanted him.

But I didn't know if I wanted him for him . . . or because he was here and Penny and Chad weren't. Even if I did, he was a summer boy. When the last warmth of summer fled, so would he. But it was getting harder and harder to remember that. I'd held his hand, I'd listened to his fears and his dreams. It was more intimate than a kiss. It was more real than anything I'd done with another person, ever.

"Penny for your thoughts?" he murmured. "You look a little sad."

"Um, just wondering how much longer I have to hold this pose."

He hummed under his breath. "Not much longer. Almost done."

While he worked, I found myself entranced with the intensity of his eyes, the squareness of his jaw. His hands slender and tapered, from the narrow width of his wrist to his long fingers. Light golden hair dusted his knuckles. Every so often, he'd bring his hand to his mouth and press his lips against the knobs of his knuckles, or tap the end of the pencil against the side of his nose.

He tilted his svelte neck to either side, stretching out the kinks. His lips pursed and began to move, but it took me a second to realize he was directing a question to me.

"—fun?"

"Uh, what?" One corner of my mouth lifted.

He laughed, arching forward to lightly tap the end of the pencil against my temple. "I said," Levi murmured, "are you having fun?"

Realizing I'd been caught staring at him, I flashed him a smile. "Of course."

"Good," he said. His pencil stub kept scratching away.

"Are you?" I asked to be polite, even though I could tell he was in his element.

"Yes. I used to do this with my mom." He didn't look up as he spoke, still fixated on his drawing. "When I was younger, I mean. She had more time then."

"What changed?"

He paused mid-stroke. "Well, when her company offered free tuition, she went back to school. Since she had to spend a lot of time studying, we'd sit together on the sofa just like this. Her on one end, me tucked into the other. Both doing our homework. She wasn't one of those moms who insisted I do it as soon as I came home from school. She let me do it before bed, along with her, so it was like we were doing it together, helping each other. I always saved my art projects until she came home so she could see them, too." He smiled, and it was so beautifully wistful that I wished I could capture the moment in my memory's camera roll. "She knew me better then."

On impulse, I reached out. He startled, but let me clasp his hand. "I think your parents would still be really proud to see what you're accomplishing here."

I didn't know if he believed me, but at his tiny nod, I pulled away and resumed my pose. As his pencil returned to scratching out my likeness, a rush of affection went through me, pooling into liquid heat. I could get my summer back and still explore whatever this thing was with him, couldn't I? It didn't have to be one or the other. I could want it all. I could *have* it all.

One way or the other, I promised myself, I'd go for it before the night was through. I would kiss Levi Keller.

♥ ♥ ♥

It couldn't have been more than fifteen minutes since my vow, but it felt like in that moment, a lifetime had passed. Meteors crashed into

Earth, species went extinct, creatures emerged from the water and crawled onto land on hands and knees—and we were still there.

"Done." Levi eyed the sketch critically for a moment, his eyebrows scrunched together. He held it up at face level and gave a satisfied nod. "Not a perfect likeness, but—"

The rest of his sentence got cut off as an enormous drop of rain plopped onto the sketchbook. Within seconds, another followed, each of them staining the paper.

"Shit!" I snatched up our trash at the same moment he tucked the book under his arm. "We'll have to make a run for it."

"Where?" he asked, the words almost lost as a clap of thunder rolled overhead. The once-vibrant sky was now a haunted, dull gray, the vicious smears of cloud stamping out the other colors. His face tilted skyward. "Lightning."

I hustled to throw the trash away, my hair sticking to the back of my neck and plastered down the side of my face. "I know a place; come on!"

Without hesitation, he took off after me.

It felt glorious, the world bracing and fresh. Even though water was pelting me at every angle and sharp cracks of yellow-white lightning peppered the sky, I felt free and wild. A whoop burst out of me as I raced madcap down the beach, sand unceremoniously infiltrating my flip-flops.

It was like an out-of-body experience. I wasn't myself, I wasn't a girl who missed her mom and her friends and the way things used to be. I was part of the storm. I was in the eye of it.

"This doesn't bother you?" Levi shouted.

"Why would it? It's nature!"

Our destination was a network of sea caves on the north end of the beach. The pristine golden sand, now mottled with rain, grew more rocky and craggy here, with broken bits of glass and fragments of seashells littering the area near the mouth of the cave.

We dashed inside to escape the pelting rain. My exhilarated laughter echoed, bouncing off the walls and coming back to us with eerie, hollow volume. Once the adrenaline faded a little, I peered out into the gray haze. "It'll pass soon. We can ride it out in here."

Levi folded his arms across his chest. "It's cold."

"Drama queen," I accused him without heat. "It's just a little rain."

My back to the cave wall, I slid down until my butt hit the sand. From here, I was shielded from the elements while still having a window to the outside world. Clouds, dark and ominous, rolled overhead. Every time I blinked there was a resounding clap of thunder, and a second later, the crackle of lightning.

"May as well sit down, Levi. Looks like it could be a while."

He muttered something under his breath before slinking down across from me. A sheet of rain lashed against the sand, sending a light spray toward him. With a soft curse, Levi inched away from the entrance.

"It was a perfect evening until we got pelted," I said, watching as he drew his legs up and balanced his wrists on his knees.

"I think it's still going pretty good. Things don't have to be perfect to still be pretty great." His eyes crinkled when he smiled. "I'm alone with a pretty girl in a cave. In fact, if this was a movie, this is the time one of us would suggest snuggling up for warmth."

Oh my God, this was the perfect moment to get a little closer . . .

Energy thrummed through my body, adrenaline dulled by a sudden hesitancy. I wasn't used to second-guessing myself or feeling shy around someone. This would be the first kiss I wanted to share with someone who I hadn't known my whole life.

Warring emotions battled in my chest. One part of me wanted to take a breath and step away from this huge change, this beautiful boy. The other wanted to plunge right in. We only had summer. I didn't have the luxury of taking things slow.

Caution won out. A beat passed before I asked, "Can I see the drawing of me?"

For a moment, I thought he would refuse. A stunned expression played over his face, as if the idea embarrassed him. "I mean," I added, "unless you don't want to show me?"

"No, it's fine." He leaned forward, meeting me halfway.

He was entrusting me with the most intimate part of himself. Reverence draped around us, suspending the moment until the book was in my hand. Turning each page slowly, carefully, was a torment. I ached to pry open its precious secrets with eager, greedy fingers.

"No, here, let me," Levi said quickly, turning the pages with urgency. He handed the sketchbook back with pink-tinged cheeks.

I saw the eyes first—my eyes—and then the lips. My smile died.

Levi had not captured a happy girl. My lips didn't curve in a welcoming smile and my eyes didn't radiate happiness. Something *else* lurked in my face, something undefinable and unreachable, but no less beautiful.

I looked like art. I wasn't sure I liked it.

"It's . . ." I couldn't finish the sentence. I didn't know *what* to say. Whether I even should.

"You don't like it," Levi said, his voice disappointed.

"No, it's not—" I sucked in a breath, trying to find the words. "You know that Vermeer painting? Of the girl with the pearl earring?"

Okay, I'd never seen the *actual* painting, but I used to have the biggest crush on Scarlett Johansson and would watch any movie she starred in. It started with her badassery as Black Widow, but it hadn't taken me long to dig up *The Other Boleyn Girl* and *Girl with a Pearl Earring*.

He nodded.

"I look like that."

"Glad to see that being my muse has made you retain your modesty," he said with the most heart-stopping smile I'd seen in . . . ever. "I mean, comparing yourself to priceless art."

Heat stole across my cheeks. Even Elodie at her most romantic had never looked at me like that. His eyes were languid and warm, and I wanted to get closer, wanted to see the night off with my lips on his.

"Oh, shut up." I turned the sketch to face him. "There's something in her eyes that makes you think she wants to say something but her lips can't."

His face went slack. He inhaled, sharp and quick. "That's . . . that's how I feel about art. The best art. There's always something under the surface."

"Is this how you see me?"

"No. Not now. But for a moment, before the wind blew your hair into your eyes, you looked like that. People who fake smile all the time, people who are too aware of their looks, they don't fascinate me."

"But I do?" I raised an eyebrow, not totally sure how to take that.

Levi's eyes smoldered with intensity. "Yeah."

I leaned forward, returning the sketchbook to him.

Outside, the storm was abating, the tumult of cloud and rain petering down to a light shower. The pitter-patter against the ceiling slowed and my heartbeat with it.

Levi still looked at me. He made no move to leave.

"We can head out now." I stood; he did, too.

"Wait." Levi reached out and lightly touched my shoulder.

His face was *so* close to mine. As much as I tried not to be aware of it, the difficulty grew. Everything felt like it was moving in slow motion.

"I think it's only fair to warn you that I *really* want to kiss you right now," said Levi.

And then the slow gave way to the fast, and before I knew what I was doing, I'd taken a step closer. His hands cupped my face, and instinctively, I looped my arms around his neck. "Okay," I whispered.

And with that, he leaned in and kissed me. It felt like it took forever in coming, but when it did, I wished we'd been doing it all along. It wasn't just the desire I felt, or the adrenaline, or the connection to another person. It was how right it was. Maybe this wasn't the right move, but this felt right in the right now. His lips moved. Not in a kiss, but in a smile.

Forging ahead, I deepened the kiss, tracing the seam of his mouth with a light graze of my tongue. His lips parted and his hands landed on my lower back, hugging me even closer. I felt the heat of his stomach against mine, and the hard knobs of his knees against my legs.

"You're a good kisser," I murmured, rewarded by his dimpled grin.

His laugh ended on an exhale. His forehead met mine, our noses touching. "So are you."

I peeked at him, but his eyes were closed. I kissed the corner of his mouth, lightly and daintily, in a way I knew would tickle.

He opened his eyes, right cheek dimpling at me in a way that made me want to kiss him all over again. Luckily, we were on the same page, because he leaned in again. My fingers curled in the fabric of his shirt. Our kiss was short, sweet, and over all too soon. In other words, everything I wanted our first kiss to be.

Thunder clapped, reverberating down the cave walls. And my rib cage. It felt like everything was collapsing in on itself, just a matchstick house and other fragile things. My legs jellified as I tasted the mint of his breath on my mouth. Lightning clashed in the sky, sending a brilliant crackle of white light through the mouth of the cave. The wall glowed for an instant, but that was enough. I had just enough time to see someone's childish scrawl of MISCHA + KATE BFFS FOREVER etched into the stone. Just enough time to be reminded of Penny and all the reasons why kissing Levi was a bad idea.

He leaned in again, but this time, it wasn't okay. I pulled back, and his lips closed around air. Levi froze, lips still pursed. "Is this . . . is this not okay?"

This cave felt like a liminal space, a world where it was just us and the other things didn't matter. A before and an after. The end of my friendship with Penny and the beginning of something that could potentially be amazing with Levi. If I chose him, I would be giving up everything that this summer was supposed to have been. Was a boy, any boy, even one as great as Levi, worth a best friend?

My heart stuttered. "Levi, I don't know if we should do this," I said quietly, the words tugged from my mouth almost unwillingly. He was a summer boy. They always went home. But Penny wasn't going anywhere. I couldn't think just of my present anymore. I had to think of the future. And that was a future Levi probably wouldn't be part of—Penny would.

It wasn't just about Penny, though. It was because when he left, I wouldn't be able to come to this cave without remembering our kiss. I wouldn't be able to look at his regular table at Busy's without imagining him sitting there. I wouldn't be able to be eat shrimp without remembering the cautious way he'd peeled back the shells and licked his fingers. His departure would turn me into a ghost town of *us*.

He bit his lip. "Did I do something wrong?"

"No! It's just . . ."

He nodded as if he understood. "This is too fast."

"No, it's not that. I . . ." It felt like I was choking on the words. "I don't get involved with summer boys."

"Summer boys?"

I heard it the way he must have heard it. Like a slur. I hadn't meant for it to sound that way—when locals used it, we knew it was derogatory, but it was also accepted. But hearing it now made me feel sick.

"Um, it's just what we call the guys who wind up in Oar's Rest during the summer. The tourists. Because they go home at the end of the season."

Hurt flashed in Levi's eyes. He turned away. "Oh. Um, yeah, that, uh . . . that makes sense." He stretched his arm behind his head to scratch his neck. "Sorry. I shouldn't have—"

"No, it's not you. I wanted to. It's just that I got caught up in the moment and . . ." I sucked in my cheeks and turned away, facing the mouth of the cave. The faintest spray of water wetted my cheeks. "We've had a lot of fun tonight. And we're friends, right? You and me, we're good?"

Even though I still felt the delicious tingle of his mouth against mine, *friends* I could handle. Just about.

"Definitely," he said at once, like he'd just been waiting for me to offer. The palpable relief in his voice was impossible to miss. He opened his mouth, but I held up my hand.

"Please don't apologize again," I said. "Let's just say we got caught up in the heat of the moment. It happens in summer. When everything feels just right and everyone is their Summer Self. The self that doesn't fit into who they think they are the rest of the year. No one is their Usual Self in summer, not here. So, um, yeah. Heat of the moment."

He let me ramble on while he stayed quiet. Listening, actually listening. Even if none of it made sense to him, he didn't push. A hint of Levi's playful side came to the front as he tilted his head toward the rain. "Heat?"

"Okay, we got caught up in the rain of the moment." I poked my elbow into his side—not hard enough to hurt, just enough so he knew we were good.

He nudged me back.

Shoulder to shoulder, we stood together, watching as the rain faded to a drizzle. And just like that, we were back to normal. Just a girl and a boy in a cave, letting the world come rushing back.

nine

The hum of energy was palpable from the moment I biked down to town the next morning. Main Street was lined with cars, most of them with out-of-state license plates, windshields dusty and bug-spattered from travel. A little girl and her labradoodle waved energetically at me from the back-seat window while the parents lugged coolers and beach umbrellas from the trunk.

I trekked across the beach and down the pier. Here, at least, there was no activity. No prying eyes to hide myself from, no cheerful tourists who wanted to smile at me, no old friends who would make an inconvenient appearance. There was just me and Penny, and the front door that stood between us. The houseboat was her kingdom. I just needed her to let down the drawbridge and let me back in. I sucked in a breath, rallied all my courage, and knocked.

Nothing. Well, that was okay. I wasn't expecting her to answer it right away.

"Penny, it's me." Then, uselessly, I added, "Babe." I waited. "Please, can I come in?" I pressed my lips to the door, close enough to touch. "Can we talk?"

There was no way our friendship was this impermanent. I silently willed her to open the door, to give me even a sliver of hope that things could go back to normal. The morning breeze brushed my neck, but it felt like it went all the way through me. My bare legs trembled with the cold. I was paper-thin, seconds from crumpling into a ball.

"Penny, I am so sorry. The kiss meant nothing to either of us. He's your boyfriend. I don't want Chad, you know that. It was just— he was being stupid. But it's not me he wants." I hesitated. "It's always been you. You know that."

She had to remember that. She had to remember *all* our good times. Baking with her Easy-Bake Oven as children, my head lolling against hers as we smoked our first joint, passing notes in the back row at school. I still had a box of falling-apart notes, all of them written in the violet ballpoint we thought was *so* cool. Making daisy chains and napping under the huge tree in front of the library, lurid, dog-eared romance novels tucked in our backpacks.

"Penny!" I raised my fist and pounded on the door. "C'mon. Don't do this."

I waited for a scathing *Go away!* or even a text message asking to be left alone. But there was nothing. Cold crept into my chest. She didn't even care enough to text me.

"Remember all those plans we had about this summer?" I said. "We were going to spend all summer together. You, me, Chad. We were going to eat fish tacos and ice cream every day. You said you wanted to go to Bar Harbor for shopping. You even got me to agree to that yoga class!"

My pleas fell on deaf ears.

It didn't matter if she forgot all those promises, because she was already breaking the most important one of all. It was silent, something we never had to talk about, because we knew it, felt it, deep in our bones. When you were best friends with someone, it just went without saying that you would always stand with them. You'd fight side by side, against any obstacle, to get past anything.

"Penny," I whispered. This was me, showing up, fighting. My best friend was nowhere in sight.

Just as I turned to leave, the door swung open. Penny was wearing a tank top and sleep shorts, a pink eye mask pushed into her hair. She was clutching a steaming mug of coffee in her hands, and her eyes weren't bleary from sleep. Somewhere inside, a fan was whirring.

Relief flooded through me. I started to take a step forward, but she didn't let me in. Body still blocking the doorway, she looked back at me coolly.

I came to a stop. "I'm sorry, Penny. I know you're feeling—"

"No, you don't," she flared. "Did I kiss your boyfriend? No? So then you don't know what I'm feeling."

My throat was scratchy. "Fair enough."

She sighed. For the briefest of moments, I thought she was relenting. "Babe, I get to be mad."

"I know you do."

"All those things about summer . . . those are things you decided. I don't want to do the same things we've spent our whole lives doing. There's other stuff, you know? I don't want be . . ." She gestured with her hands. "I don't want to be small-town Penny. There's more to me than—than Chad, than this, than you—"

My heart was in my throat.

She stopped, her eyes darting away. "This summer wasn't the end of anything. It was just another beginning. And those can be wonderful and scary, but mostly wonderful, and I know you think endings are really sad, but . . . but the world isn't split into beginnings and endings. There's all that stuff in the middle. The *getting there*. That's what I want. The not knowing. Adapting to the change." Penny took a deep breath. "I want to change. I want to muddle through shit and make mistakes, and I want to come back from those mistakes, if I want to. But I can't stay the same. Not for me. And not for you."

"Penny—"

She wasn't done. "I thought I was safe with you."

My heart clenched. "You are."

"I thought my *relationship* was safe with you," she clarified. When she looked at me, her eyes were glassy. "I didn't want to be one of those girls who ditched their friends the second they got a boyfriend. I promised myself that no matter what, you'd be as important in my life as Chad. And we'd all been best friends for so long, I didn't want to exclude you. It wouldn't have been the same without you there, not really." Penny wet her lips before taking a deep breath. "There were times . . . when I thought maybe you two were getting close—too close. Closer than me and Chad." She hesitated. "Closer than me and you, too."

That took the wind right out of my sails. The gasp tore itself from my mouth before I could take it back. It wasn't as simple as I'd thought. Penny wasn't just jealous because of the kiss . . . it was because she was afraid *she* was the odd woman out.

Tears welled in my eyes and my chest tightened, as if every bad decision was inflating inside me like a blow-up pool toy. I was barely able to keep my head above water, treading between the person I was now and who I used to be.

I couldn't keep doing this. I couldn't keep feeling this way. I knew she was entitled to her anger and pain—even if most of it seemed to be directed at me. I didn't begrudge her wanting space. Though I wasn't thrilled about being cut out, I'd suck it up if that was what she needed. But I had to know if there was a chance, like Chad said, of forgiveness. I needed her to throw me a life raft.

My hands balled into fists at my side. I blinked back the tears.

Penny spoke first. "I . . . I didn't want to lose either of you. I thought if I tried harder, if I included you, we wouldn't drift apart. I didn't want you to be jealous I was spending more time with Chad, or think I was leaving you behind." She inhaled sharply, like maybe she was on the verge of tears, too. "I guess I had this idea that it all rested on me. I wanted us to keep going on like we always had. The three of us."

The boat was too small, this conversation too hard. It wasn't going the way I had hoped for. My nails were digging into my palms, and my throat felt sandpapered rough. When I loosened my fists, relief surged up through my arms. *The three of us.*

I barely recognized the gravelly voice as my own when I asked, "So what does this mean for you and me?"

"I just think we need to be our own people for a while. We've been together so long that our roots are tangled. Thorny." She cleared her throat. "We can't grow if we're still holding on to each other so tight." She recited it like it was something she'd memorized already.

My dry lips parted. "Are you saying you don't want me to hang out with Chad?" I asked, incredulous.

She hesitated, patchy color taking over her cheeks. "And about the sandcastle . . ."

She was skirting around the rest of the sentence. But I sensed what was coming. Icy heat shot down my arms. "You don't want me and Chad to partner up," I said, hearing the dull, finite tone in my voice. I should have seen it coming. "You don't even *like* making sandcastles."

"But we're back together now."

I understood. Translation: *I'm his girlfriend and you're not.*

"What about Chad?" I asked, my voice raw. "You trust him but not me." It wasn't a question.

Penny closed her eyes. "I'm in *love* with Chad."

"You love someone who you could just throw overboard like"— I snapped my fingers—"that?"

"I think you should go."

"Wait!" I stuck my foot in the door before she could close it. "Where does this leave us?"

"Nothing's changed, Babe. I still don't want to—" She sucked in a sharp breath. "I love you, but you kissed my boyfriend."

"What if that was me changing?" I asked desperately.

"Into what, though?" A flicker of a frown crossed her face.

I didn't have an answer for her. It had been a dumb thing to say. I didn't want to change into someone who kissed the wrong people.

She exhaled. "Yeah, I thought so. Change isn't your get-out-of-jail-free card. It's real. People aren't meant to stay the same forever. You shouldn't even want them to."

"So what is it?" My eyes burned, my nostrils tingled hot and cold. "You're mad because Chad kissed me or you're mad because you only want the changes that *you* decide?"

"You haven't changed," Penny said emphatically. She used her flip-flopped foot to wedge mine out of the doorway. I let her. "You're just trying to give me an answer you think I'll fall for."

"That's not what I'm—"

Her voice turned sharp. "Yeah. It is."

"I don't know how to get you back," I said, voice small.

"Then don't."

My insides ached. Everything felt cold and hollow and carved-out.

"That's for me to figure out," said Penny. "Not for you. *I get to be mad*, Babe." And then she closed the door.

Was I guilty of more than just kissing Chad? Was I guilty of everything else she'd accused me of? The anger felt different this time, muddied with confusion and hurt and the kind of loneliness that came from breaking up with your best friend. It felt like she had outgrown me in some way, as though I had clung too hard and held her back. Like she was static because of me.

"You sure everything in the delivery was in order?" Tom was asking Lucy as I entered Busy's. He bent over the counter to peer at the huge pile of mail. Envelopes of all colors and sizes were dumped in front of him.

Dazed, I glanced at the ripped-open envelopes on the counter. "What's up?"

"One of our suppliers has sent a bill for the coffee beans," said Tom. "And I checked the back. Looks like we're a little short. Has everything been unboxed and checked against the invoice?"

"Are you sure you looked everywhere? Maybe it's still buried in the back somewhere?" suggested Lucy. "Ariel said she had done some, and then we finished the rest."

"You girls are supposed to sort the mail, too," said Tom. He swatted an envelope down on the counter. "Get rid of all the junk and hand the important stuff to me. Why is there such a pile here?"

Another one of Ariel's jobs she'd failed to do.

While Tom ducked his head to sort through the envelopes, Lucy caught my eye. *Ariel*, she mouthed.

"Is Ariel coming in today?" Tom asked gruffly as I reached for my apron.

"No." I tied the strings behind my back. "We, um, actually haven't seen her too much lately."

Tom's face was resigned. "Had a feeling this would be coming," he said with a sound that was halfway between a grunt and a scoff. "Babe. What are we doing about her?"

"She . . . she has to go," I said. I shifted under Tom's gaze. "I'm the manager. I'll do it the next time she comes in and give her whatever she's owed for the hours she's actually worked."

My earlier empathy for her had fizzled out as quickly as it'd started. Ariel's situation wasn't like mine. She'd used up her second chance. And her third. And her fourth. I still had my second chance.

Tom nodded slowly. "Sounds good. I'll put up a sign in the window once that's done."

"For a waitress?" asked Lucy.

"And the fish fry is coming up, too," said Tom. "We could use the extra hands."

"We don't even need to hire anyone new," said Lucy. She placed a hand on my shoulder. "We've got this, don't we, Babe?"

"Do you, now?" Tom smiled at me. "Like mother, like daughter."

A rush of pride swelled through me. *Like mother, like daughter.*

160

The words rang in my ears long after Tom retired to a table in the back and Lucy began humming Taylor Swift's latest single.

My mother, Jenna, had worked at Busy's, too. The best waitress and manager he'd ever had, Tom once proclaimed, though her coffee-making skills didn't have a lick on mine. The affection Tom had for Mom was like that of a father.

"Does he look more tired lately to you?" Lucy whispered once Tom left.

Alarm flared through me. I hoped it wasn't Ariel that was stressing him out. I glanced at our boss. He was over sixty, but he looked younger. His skin didn't sag, and the lines on his face were all from laughter.

"I don't know," I said. "A little, maybe. But it's probably only because it looks like it's going to be a busy summer. It's the fiftieth anniversary of the sandcastle competition. I heard someone say that a lot more people are coming because of the press coverage."

"Maybe." Lucy gnawed on a nail. "How are things with Penny?"

"Nonexistent." Since our fight, she'd already avoided me in town twice, and after the talk we'd just had, I didn't see that changing. It wasn't like she'd crossed the street like El had, but the cool way her eyes looked right through me was worse somehow.

"And Chad?"

I shrugged. "He doesn't want to rock the boat right now with Penny. She's . . . she's sort of icing me out. Um, she kicked me out of an iMessage group chat last night. Surprised it took this long, honestly."

"Mmm. Well, you still have to let me know what you think about us doing the pageant together," said Lucy. "It's okay if you don't want to come dress shopping, but maybe we could just get ready together or something."

After our conversation on the houseboat, I knew there wasn't any chance I'd be doing the pageant with Penny. And it was really more her thing than mine.

Looking into Lucy's face, I was suddenly overcome with affection. I pulled her into a hug. "Thanks for being good to me," I said, the words muffled into her hair.

"Don't get all sappy on me! It's just makeup!" She hugged me back.

It was more than that, and we both knew it.

We broke apart when the door swung open and the bell chimed. The first day of tourist season was well and truly underway.

♥ ♥ ♥

It was almost closing time and only a few customers still lingered at Busy's when the door opened and Elodie walked in. "Hey, Babe," she said, smiling prettily. "Got any of that German chocolate cake left? I promised my mom I'd get her a slice."

So was this the way it was now? Two strangers pretending like they hadn't once kissed and touched and loved? My eyes smarted. I didn't want her back, but I didn't want her pretense, either. I was tired of things being secret and messy. Nothing good had ever come of it.

I was incredibly conscious of Levi sitting at his usual table. Any second now, Elodie would see him, too. I didn't want to see them talking, getting along. I'd deliberately avoided talking to Levi too much about the art center for this specific reason. I didn't want El to come up, and I especially didn't want to feel compelled to explain to him that she was the ex I'd told him about.

Her eyes were on me.

I swallowed. "Yeah. I'll just wrap the cake up for you." I grabbed a to-go box and slid the cake in, careful with the caramel coconut frosting. While my eyes were focused on the packaging, she stepped away from the counter.

"Hey," said Elodie.

I jerked my head up.

She'd headed to Levi's table. With a hand perched on her hip, she smiled at him. "I've seen you at the art center. You're Penny's mentor, right?"

Levi closed his sketchbook. "Hey," he said, voice cautious with surprise. His eyes slid to me for a brief second before flickering back to Elodie. "Yeah, I'm with the art center's summer residency program. You are, too?"

She nodded.

He held out a hand. "I'm Levi Keller."

I could see the recognition flutter over her face. My insides squirmed.

"Wait." El drew the word out like taffy. "Not . . . *the* Levi Keller? From Instagram?"

"Um, yeah. How do you—"

"I love your Instagram! I've been a fan of yours since forever. Even before you got big," Elodie enthused at once, voice going high and squeaky with excitement.

I knew how much being one of the early fans mattered to her. She always looked down her nose a bit at people who became fans only after someone got popular.

She swung her face back to me. I could see her accusation plainly—*why didn't you tell me my idol was living in Oar's Rest?*

Yeah, well. There were a lot of things she didn't exactly keep me informed about, too. I pushed her cake to the customer's side of the counter and bit the inside of my cheek. She had her cake, now she could leave. "Cake's ready!" I called out.

Elodie waved her hand in a *yeah, yeah* motion. "So what are you working on right now?" she asked, nodding toward Levi's sketchbook.

"Nothing ready to share," he said with an awkward smile, getting up. "I'm kind of looking at this residency as a way of resetting my creativity. Getting back to why I started doing this in the first place."

"Oh."

I smiled to myself, pleased to see her excitement deflate. If I was being totally honest, I was glad he hadn't shown her.

Not skipping a beat, Elodie followed him up to the counter. "I think that's a really good idea. Refilling your creative well." She smiled and pushed her hair over her shoulder. "I'm renting studio time this week at the center. I'd love to maybe collab on something with you," she said. She pulled her wallet from the back pocket of her shorts and peeled a bill out.

While I gave her the change, Levi caught my eye and gave me a crooked smile.

"I'm Elodie, by the way," she continued, undeterred. "I'm back from CalArts for the summer." She moved out of the way so he could pay his bill.

"CalArts, huh?" Levi glanced at her sideways. "I've heard that's a good school."

Elodie's smile turned even brighter. "It is! What about you—are you in art school? Or, like, what else are you up to?"

"I'm still figuring it out," said Levi, taking his change.

I was hyperaware of Levi's warmth and the way the tips of our fingers grazed as I pulled my hand away.

"You could take your pick of any school you wanted," said Elodie.

"Yeah, maybe." He fidgeted with the coins in his hand. He caught my eye and I knew he was remembering the same night on the beach that I was.

Elodie didn't take the hint. "Any thoughts yet about where you might want to apply?"

"It might be nice to do something other than art," he said.

I sent him an encouraging smile.

"Oh," said Elodie, tilting her head to the side. I could read the doubt on her face. "But why would you want to? You've already made it on the art scene. Why would you major in anything else?"

"You sound like my parents," said Levi. His smile dimmed. "They're not crazy about me pursuing other options."

El laughed, a soft, uncomfortable thing. I knew her enough to tell she was embarrassed. "Opposite of my parents, then. They like my art, but only as a hobby. They don't think I'll be able to support myself or do anything in the real world with it."

There was an awkward pause.

"I should, uh . . ." Elodie tilted her head toward the door.

"See ya," I said.

Levi hung back, and just as I was about to ask him if he wanted to grab dinner, Elodie whirled around. All her embarrassment was gone. "Hey, I was just heading to the Dairy Bar," she said. "Have you been there yet? They have amazing ice cream. Wanna come? My treat."

Before he could say anything, she took hold of his arm. "Seriously, it's the best." With a tug, she'd already started shepherding him toward the door.

Look back, look back, I chanted in my mind. I didn't know what I thought it would prove, but I wanted to count on Levi. My perfect summer wasn't exclusive to my friends. It could still be a perfect summer with Levi in the picture.

She kept up a stream of conversation, but he twisted around and shot me an apologetic smile.

It was cold comfort.

At the end of the day, after the last customers had shuffled out, we got to work tidying up. Soon, Busy's was spotless, everything ready for the next morning.

"Wanna grab some dinner from Lorcan's?" I wrung out the last wet rag in the sink before slapping it into the washing basket. "Elodie dragged Levi off, and kinda took my dinner plans with her."

Lucy gave me a sympathetic look. "Mom is expecting me for dinner. Meatloaf night." Her lips turned glum, curved to the floor.

I laughed. I knew what that meant. Lots and lots of ketchup. Lucy's aversion to ketchup-smothered meatloaf was legendary, and everyone except her mother knew about it. "Sorry. I didn't mean to laugh. It's just so weird she keeps forgetting you hate it."

Lucy made an unhappy face. "She claims it's out of habit.

Apparently three generations of Bishop women have been ketchup lovers. It's in our blood, she says, which is a whole new level of gross I don't want to think about."

We said our goodbyes, exchanged hugs, and went our separate ways. Lucy, owning a car, lugged the leftover confectionary delights in her trunk. On her way home, she'd drop them off at the soup kitchen or the food pantry, whoever's turn it was this week.

My bike ride took me up the bluffs. My thighs burned pleasantly from the strain of my rapid pumping and the wind blew through my hair, cooling my sweaty scalp. The waves surged below me and the entire town was suffused in an amber glow. In the flattering evening light, even my own skin looked bathed in bronze.

The lighthouse was getting closer and closer. From a distant, toy-size structure, it now stood tall and proud, reaching toward the heavens. I breathed it all in, feeling sea air enter my lungs and puff me with renewed life. It almost put Elodie and Levi out of my mind.

"Babe!"

Shit.

My joy at coming home dissipated like a wisp of candle smoke after the flame had been blown out. I braked, twisting my hips to stare. "Chad?" I hadn't expected to see him anytime soon.

Chad approached, his stocky frame somehow appearing even more larger-than-life. His bike lay discarded at his feet, tossed down instead of leaning against the kickstand.

"Hi," he said, voice breathless. Before I could formulate a thought and get my mouth to follow through, Chad was embracing me. His bear hugs used to feel safe, like they were holding me close, but now they felt claustrophobic. It felt like his arms were a vise around me, much like the way a snake strangled its prey before swallowing it whole.

"How the hell are you?" he asked, releasing me at last. "I'm so sorry. After what happened . . . I didn't think you'd want to see me. I had no idea what to say."

"Why are you here now?" I folded my arms over my chest and stared at him.

I should have been overjoyed to see him, but all I could think about was Penny's soft, dreamy eyes and Chad's tanned, freckled face. Back together again. The fact that the two of them fit together so much better when I wasn't there.

I closed my eyes against the image—and accompanying nausea—and took a step backward.

Chad's face twisted into something wounded and grotesque. "Babe . . ."

I had the sudden, wild thought of getting back on my bike—of never having stopped for Chad in the first place—and spinning away too fast to care about anyone.

"Uh, earlier." He rubbed his nose, not looking at me. "Don't think I haven't been trying to talk Penny 'round. Because I have. She's just . . . being stubborn. I know she misses you." Then, in those familiar, fateful words that shattered me, "I miss the three of us, too."

Me, Penny, Chad. The three of us.

My heart squeezed, sharp and tart and bitter.

He waved a hand at the lighthouse. "Can we go inside?" he asked. His eyes roved with a beady scan I could only describe as rodent fear.

A vise clamped around my chest. Understanding flushed through me, hot and sharp. He was afraid of being seen with me.

"Seriously, Chad?" I scoffed.

I didn't buy the guile in his voice as he said, "What?"

"You . . . Did you come up here only because you won't run into anyone from town?" I dropped my voice to a scathing note. "Like *Penny*?"

Chad's cheeks reddened into splotchy patches. "Wha—no, what?"

"Oh my God."

"What? Are you . . . are you being serious right now? Of course that's not why—*Jesus*, Babe!" he said.

"Well, what am I supposed to think? You've been avoiding me! The last thing I have from you is that stupid text!" I scowled. "You said it'd be better to lie low until she cools down. That it'd be better if I didn't show my face, if we weren't seen together. Do you have *any* idea how that made me feel?"

"I . . . I thought it was the right thing to do."

"No. Hiding wasn't the right choice. It was the easy choice."

"You think anything about this has been easy?"

"Yeah, because you've been the one iced out, right? Wait, that was me." I shook my head. "Nice try."

"You are so mistaken if you think you're the only one who has to earn her forgiveness," he said in a low voice.

"Yeah?" I rolled my eyes. "What was your crime? Because clearly I'm the shitty best friend who kissed her boyfriend. You? She took you back. She could have ended things—again—but she didn't."

The silence felt loud as my words bobbed to the surface like jagged bits of driftwood. Oh, but there was so much more below. There was a whole shipwreck of our friendship.

"Babe . . ."

I hated the plea in his voice. I couldn't deal with it.

"I'm sorry. I know it was my fault. Maybe I shouldn't have told her that we kissed, but I didn't feel right in hiding it." His cheeks flamed again, even more vivid and angry than they were before.

"*That* wasn't your mistake." My chest heaved. "Why did you do it, Chad?"

"I don't understand," Chad said, the words as careful as if they were walking over broken glass.

I stared at him, committing his face to memory. There was something comforting in his face, something that still made me feel safe despite it all. Despite everything. "Why did you kiss me?" I whispered. "Did you kiss me for me, or because I reminded you of her?"

The silence lingered too long for it to mean anything other than agreement. I didn't know to which part of my question, but it didn't matter anymore. Maybe he didn't know the answer any more than I did. I felt like the mythical Odysseus, so far from home and his loved ones, about a million obstacles in front of him.

The memories of our good times came in an onslaught, too fast and too bittersweet to fight them off. I felt like someone was taking my ribs and tying them into sailing knots. And then, just as quickly, I saw the twinkling stars and whispered conversations and booze-free recklessness drift away, a curl of smoke on the stub of a burned-out candle.

That was the thing about the good old days, I thought. No one told you at the time that they *were* the good old days.

"I don't want to fight," said Chad. "If you don't want me to come in . . ."

"Then you'll do what you do best and take off?" I asked.

Chad still looked like he didn't understand what was happening. "That's not what I'm going to do," he said finally. "I hate that everything is so messy, Babe. I swear, if I could go back and—but I can't. I wish I could, but it's just easier to do things Penny's way for now. She won't stay mad forever."

"Won't she?" She still hated the boys who had made fun of her for being different when we were kids.

Chad must have been remembering her tendency to hold on to grudges between tight fists, too. He sighed and scratched the back of his neck. The silence was deafening. He shifted on his feet, raised one shoulder in a hopeful shrug. "Can I get another hug?" he asked, not even realizing that my feet were dragging and my heart was sinking.

I wanted the hug more than I wanted to deny him. "Sure." I put my arms around him and wondered how *he* became *hers* and I was the one in the middle of the ocean, alone against the waves. I was a ship in distress, desperate for a guiding light, but all I had was the soft pressure of Chad's arms around my back.

"I'm really sorry," he whispered into my ear.

Distracted by a lone figure coming up the hill, I didn't answer Chad. The figure came closer and closer, golden with the sun, and as every second in Chad's embrace seemed to drag on, Levi sharpened in visibility.

He froze, expression still too far away for me to see, and I wanted to shout out to him, *Come up! Come up!*

His easel was still here, so I knew he'd come to continue painting. I kept waiting for him to approach, but he didn't make a move. I raised the arm that was around Chad and waved.

Levi waved back.

I wiggled in Chad's arms until he let me go. "I guess I'll see you around, then," I said, dragging my eyes away from Levi. I had to get rid of Chad—quickly.

While Chad gripped the handlebars to pull the bike up, I scanned the hill for Levi.

What? My lips parted in surprise. He was *leaving*. He'd turned around and was heading back to town, now too far away for me to call back unless I screeched. And God, did I feel like screeching just then.

"See ya, B." Chad waved over his shoulder.

I watched him go, wheeling his bike away, with tears of frustration pricking my eyes. Once again, it looked like we were both trying to score an A on Penny's test. I waited until he was safely out of sight before retreating inside, blinking back my tears.

When I heard the knock on the door a few minutes later, my heart sped up. I doubted it would be Chad again . . . but what if it was Levi? Maybe Chad biked past him on the way down, and Levi doubled back. Prickles ran into my hairline, over my arms, down my legs. I knew, without even opening the door, that it would be Levi on the other side.

ten

It wasn't.

My face must have given me away.

"Expecting someone else?" asked Elodie.

I couldn't tell if she'd seen Levi. I settled for a nonchalant shrug, leaning against the doorframe. I couldn't trust my voice to speak. With how screwy my life was at the moment, maybe I should have anticipated yet another curveball. Murphy's Law. But with everything else going on, Elodie's reappearance had taken a back seat. She was the last person I would have expected to be here, but actually, now that I thought about it, it was weird that she hadn't come earlier.

The lighthouse had always been our place. The place where she could be herself, and we could be together, and no one had to know. It hadn't been enough, even when I tried to tell myself that it was. Seeing her back here was disconcerting, especially when I wished there was someone else in her place.

The silence lingered until it became almost oppressive. Elodie's eyes flicked beyond me, into the lighthouse, and I knew she was wondering why I wasn't inviting her in. Part of me wanted to pretend that nothing had happened, that she was just here for a visit. But I could tell from the determined set of her mouth that this wasn't going to be a casual meeting between two people who had once known each other.

"I was thinking about you today," said Elodie. She dug the scuffed toes of her sneakers into the grass. "A lot of days, actually. Most of them."

I waited for her to continue.

She exhaled. "Can I come in?"

"I don't—"

"Please."

The honesty in her voice whittled away at my reservations. I took a step back, away from the doorway, letting Elodie know it was okay to come in.

After only a brief hesitation on the threshold, she did. She smelled like cotton candy body spray and fresh-cut grass.

The rooms inside the lighthouse were circular, small. The ground floor kitchen was narrow and the stovetop sticky with the remnants of week-old oil spatter. Above the sink I had a plate rack stacked with colorful dishes. The rest of the wall had open cabinets with bowls, glasses, coffee mugs, and a gargantuan spice rack. It was a present from Penny that she'd picked up at an artisan gift shop two years ago because the crushed oregano, basil, and sage leaves reminded her of weed.

Elodie moved toward the kitchen table and sat down, hands clasped primly in front of her. The table was just big enough for two, and even though I had the space for something a little bigger, the table served as the perfect nail-polish station, laptop dock, and grub hub. Each fleck of paint told a story. Some splotches were canary yellow: the day I'd gotten my first paycheck, Penny and I drunkenly painted our nails in celebration. A swipe of peach was where Chad had insisted on painting my nails when we were both high out of our minds and it took three swipes before he realized he was painting the table instead.

The last splotch was my favorite, and even reliving the memory now brought a smile to my face. A flamingo pink, one of El's polish colors. It had been an accident—she was distracted by me singing along, badly, to her then-favorite boy band. That was when she'd first started to fall for me, she told me later. When I was comfortable enough to be a complete idiot around her.

The memory brought a smile to my face. As I sat down opposite her, I traced my fingertips over the paint streaks, remembering laughter and sweet kisses and badly painted nails—all courtesy of the three most important people in my life.

Elodie was looking at the paint streaks as well. A half smile had tweaked her lips upward, but the moment she saw me looking, she let it drop. "We haven't missed our summer, have we?"

There was no right answer. Knowing exactly what to say when someone threw you for a loop was a myth. It didn't exist. The right words were never there when you wanted them, only hours later when you had time to drive yourself crazy going over and over what you *should* have said. Words eluded me now as I stared back at her, at the face I knew so well. The pert, slightly upturned nose. The slant of her cheekbones, the stretch of collarbone I'd once peppered kisses across. The thickness of her lashes, the fullness of her lower lip.

She stretched her hand across the table as if she expected me to reach for it. I was too knotted up, too held in place. What was she doing? I wanted to recoil. Looking at her too long was like staring into the sun.

"You look good," said Elodie after a long pause. She drew her hand back.

So do you. But then, she always did. My lips tightened. I didn't say a word.

"I thought you wanted me to say hi." Her voice turned light, coy.

"Saying hi is different from ambushing me like this."

Her eyes widened. "Ambushing? That's not what this is."

My mouth wouldn't unstick for the longest moment. Finally, I managed to get out, "Why are you here?"

Her finger traced the pink splotch. I wondered if she even knew that she was doing it. "For you," said Elodie, just like that, like the last year hadn't happened. Like my heart hadn't been ripped out of my chest and thrown into the sea.

I clenched my mouth—hard. My jaw began to ache from the pressure of my teeth. I hated the lilt of her voice, the earnestness in her face. I hated everything about this. "No, this is for you."

"What do you—"

"This," I said loudly. I gestured around my kitchen. "Coming here. Here, El. You're still"—my breath caught—"hiding."

"No, that's not—"

"Like everything is the same," I finished.

"You're the same," she said. "I'm glad. I didn't want you to be anything other than how I remembered you."

I stiffened. She didn't seem to realize how entitled and unreasonable she sounded. I knew that I wasn't the same. Not anymore. Not like she thought I was. Not like she wanted me to be. Because if I was the same Babe who was willing to hide her relationship, that would make it easy for her. And because I'd once loved her—loved her so much—I wanted to make it easy for her. But if I dug deeper, I knew that making it easy for her would only make it harder on me. And I was tired of things being hard for me.

"I don't think I am the same," I said after a long pause. "I think you want me to be, because if I was, it'd mean you know how the rest of this goes."

"How would it go?" she asked quietly.

"Like this." I stretched my hand out to touch hers. Just for a second. "It would start with this."

"I sense a but." She tried to twist her hand to capture my fingers, but I pulled back just in time.

"I moved on, El. I moved on without you. You should, too."

"But . . . but I'm back now."

"You've been back for a while. It took you until now to come up here."

"It wasn't so easy! You were so . . ." She paused. "Mean."

"Mean? That wasn't mean."

"Pissed off, then."

I stared at her. She was deflecting, trying to unload the responsibility of her decisions on me. The moment was maple-candy brittle. "I don't want to be anything, El. I'm just done. *We're* done."

Elodie inhaled, but it sounded like a horrible, shaky gulp. "But I want to be with *you*."

"You say that, but for how long?" I challenged her. "I want more than a summer, El. I want more than keeping secrets and sneaking up here because you're too scared to go anywhere else. I don't judge you or hate you for not being ready, but I've been out for years. I'm not ready to go back in just so I don't draw attention to you. I'm sorry."

"Do you want me to—"

"No," I blurted out, reading the question in her eyes. "I don't want you to do anything you're not ready for. Especially if you'd only be doing it for me. If you come out . . . it should be for you. But I don't think I can do this again."

She shoved her chair back, hard enough to scrape, and stood, shoulders quaking. I was a bystander to her pain, too shattered myself to do anything to help. Tears streaming down her face, dripping from her chin, she streaked past me.

I followed after her. She'd left the front door open on her way out. I wrapped my arms around myself as I stood in the doorway, eyes focused on the road Elodie had taken to return to town. My shoulders ached with renewed discomfort. The weight of a first love was no small burden. It was a heavy anchor. Looking out the window, at the beach tinged with the dusky pinks and purples of sunset, I knew my best thinking wouldn't be done at home.

I could see the moon. The sky was a purple gray, and the houses of Oar's Rest twinkled with light. Lorcan's crab shack still boasted an impressive mini-army of couples and families within a twenty-foot radius.

A book lay in my lap, a page fluttering in the breeze. Walt Whitman's words swayed, an unintelligible rippling of letters. I dropped my finger from where it was keeping my place. Though I had been out here for a while, I was no closer to figuring out what to do.

Penny's words from this morning ran through my mind. Seconds later, they overlapped with Elodie's until I couldn't even hear the words anymore, just the barrage of noise. Penny wanted me to be different, but when Elodie came to the lighthouse, she was clearly counting on me to be the same. What was the balance? Did anyone know, or was this a struggle that only my own fucked-up life dished out? Everything I thought I knew about my friends, about myself, now it was just replaced by giant question marks. My world was shaken, unsteady. I still couldn't believe Elodie's gall in coming to the lighthouse, in thinking our relationship was suspended in the same place after all this time.

Feet padded through the sand. Stopped right in front of me. "Hey."

"Hey." The words came automatically. I looked up, squinted.

Levi loomed above me, a large waffle cone in each hand. One was starting to drip. He folded his knees and sank into the warm sand beside me. He licked the white river of ice cream and held out the other one to me.

I took it, held it uncertainly for a moment, then scooped the tip of the ice cream off. "Thanks. What're you doing here?"

"I was out for a walk. I saw you sitting here, so I went back to the ice cream shop to grab us a couple cones."

The vanilla was cold and sweet on my tongue, coating my throat. "What if I'd left?" I asked, unable to hold back my curiosity.

He chuckled, the noise reverberating in his chest like the soft purr of an engine. "Then I guess I'd have eaten them both." He saw my book and his smile deepened, his top lip thinning even further as his mouth stretched to accommodate his amusement.

"This?" I lifted the book, closing the front and back. "I found it on the beach. Half buried in the sand, like maybe someone left it here, went for a swim, and forgot about it."

"You're smiling." He bumped his shoulder against mine. His eyelashes looked particularly golden in the twilight hour, the color of his eyes a haunted gray instead of a keen, piercing blue.

I took a swipe of ice cream. "I am. I came here to think, be alone—"

"Oh, sorry, I can just go—"

"No!" I blurted out. "I didn't mean for you to leave. I can be alone with you here."

We fell into silence, broken only by the low calls of gulls and strains of chatter from Lorcan's. I looked at Levi from the corner of my eye, enchanted with the way the dying light played on his face, casting him in an ethereal glow. At the same time, I kept spying his glances at me. Furtive little things, not long enough to linger, but enough for me to catch the turn of his head and the angle of his nose.

Now would be the time to tell him about Elodie and what had just happened. I ached to, but when I parted my lips, the words didn't come. I didn't want them to. And even if I did, how could I tell him without also outing her secret? She wasn't ready for people to know—not then, not now. Even her family was in the dark. If I told Levi, I'd be shining a light on the very thing she wanted kept private. I had no right to do that to her. It wouldn't matter that I trusted Levi to keep it to himself—even if it was my past, it was someone else's secret.

"Must be something big," said Levi.

Arrested, I swung to look at him. "What?"

"Whatever you're thinking about." He lightly tapped my forehead. "You're looking like it's something big."

Under his gaze, any thought I had about anything else seemed insignificant and small. "Have you ever had a hard decision to make, but you don't know how to make it?" I asked, licking a rivulet of ice cream that had snaked its way down my thumb.

He thought for a moment, head endearingly cocked. "Yeah, but you know it already."

I turned his words over in my mind. "I do?"

His eyes shone like sea glass. He didn't look away when he answered. "Coming here. I knew I'd have to leave home one day, but it was still one of the toughest decisions I've ever made. The last year has been full of them. Side effect of growing up, I guess. But if I'd stayed in New York, my whole career would have been mapped out for me. The time in my life when most other teenagers are finding themselves . . . I'd never be able to figure out what I wanted, or who I am, unless something changed. Unless I made it change."

"You don't think people can grow at the place they're already at?"

He paused for a moment before answering. "Maybe they can. I don't think *everyone* has to actually leave their life in the rearview mirror like I did," he said with a crooked smile. "What gets left behind doesn't even have to be a place. It could be anything. A mind-set, a bad decision, a person—anything at all. I think the point is that I had to get out of my comfort zone."

Levi's words tugged at me. What he was saying could have described me over the past few weeks. The push and pull between everything I thought I wanted and everything I wanted now. The before and the after. No matter what happened this summer, I knew that I would never be the same. He was right. Sometimes you just had to leave behind what didn't fit.

The corners of his eyes crinkled as he smiled, leaning a little closer toward me. "Like coming here. It was a good decision."

He didn't have to say it, but I heard what was left unsaid: If he'd never come here, we would never have met.

Levi used his pointer finger to trace doodles in the sand. "I wanted to get away, become someone new." He tilted his head, looking sweet and boyish and a million other things I couldn't put into words.

I slipped my fingers through his. It seemed like the right thing to do. "I think you've done a pretty good job of finding yourself," I murmured. "It's like you told Elodie. You're pushing the reset button. You're losing yourself in order to find yourself."

He looked startled for an instant, lips parting like he was going to say something. I'd never seen him look taken aback before, even though I knew other things about him: His eyelashes went still when he was being serious, and his blinks would grow slow and measured with every answer. The side of his palm was almost always silvery with graphite. The higher up his wrist the smudge traveled, the more lost in his sketching he had been.

How had I noticed all the little things about him and ignored the big one? He was a summer boy, which meant that no matter how eloquent and handsome he was, there was one thing he would do at the end of his residency . . . and that was leave.

"What are you doing?" he asked as I began to dig in the sand with one hand.

"Putting the book back."

He laughed. "You should keep it. No one is going to come back for it. It'll just get waterlogged and someone will throw it away."

"This is where I found it," I explained. "I kinda like the idea of giving it back to the beach. And we're far enough away from the water that it won't get ruined. Probably someone just forgot to take it away with them. I want them to find it if they come back, but if it's still here tomorrow, I'll take it to the lost and found." Sand was getting under my nails, but I kept digging until the hole was large enough. I put the book in and then pushed sand in to fill the depression, supporting the book so it wouldn't topple the moment I took my hands away.

Levi hummed in response. When I turned to look at him, he'd almost finished his ice cream and had started taking small nibbles of the rim of the waffle cone.

We ate our ice cream in silence, watching as the sun went down and the tide started coming in. The tang of salt water was sharp and just a little bit acrid. I took a deep breath of it, savoring it like my mom relished her Chanel No. 5.

It struck me then that no matter what choice I made, he would always be one step away from leaving. This wasn't his life. He'd said it himself—this was paradise. And one day, Levi would leave paradise behind and go back to the real world, to his Usual Self. His time here was fleeting, temporary. He wasn't for keeps.

"I love it here," he said, breaking the silence with the timbre of his voice. He drew his knees up and hunched forward, wrapping his arms loosely around his legs.

I chomped on the soggy bottom of the cone. "What's the most beautiful place you've ever seen?"

"Mavora Lakes," said Levi. "Definitely."

"Where's that?"

He grinned. "Remember Fangorn Forest, where Merry and Pippin escaped from the Orcs?" At my nod, he said, "This was the filming location."

"No way. You were in New Zealand?"

"Yeah, a couple of years ago during Christmas break with my friend's family. Dad was, like, a step away from asking if he could come with," he said with a faint laugh. "He was more excited than I was. There's a few pushpins in New Zealand on his map."

Not sure what to say, I settled for a nod.

"What about you?" Levi asked. "What's the most beautiful place you've been?"

"Honestly? I haven't been to a lot of places outside of Maine. Once to Disneyland, and once to DC on a school trip."

He shrugged. "If you could, though. Go anywhere. Where would it be?"

"I have *no* idea."

"Indecisive or evasive?" he asked with a grin.

I gave him a look. "Indecisive. There's not much that I try to hide, you know. I'm the definition of an open book." Even as I said it, I knew it wasn't the truth.

"I don't know if I would agree with that," Levi said easily.

I arched an eyebrow. "No?"

Levi's eyes smiled down at me. *Really* smiled. The kind of smile that was absolutely genuine because it wasn't just muscles moving lips, but reached his eyes, too. "No," he said simply.

"How do you figure?" I tipped my head back, smiling.

"Do you remember in English class we learned about the story pyramid thing?"

I nodded.

"Well, here's my thinking." Levi leaned forward. "We're eighteen—"

"I'm nineteen," I said.

"We're still teenagers," he said. "So if life was a plot structure, we'd still be in the rising action stage. Our lives are just beginning. Your big *aha!* moments are waiting for you. Mine, too. Somewhere out there." He grinned. "In baking terms, I guess you could think about it like a cookie that isn't done baking."

I liked the way he put it, like I was the hero in this story and not just someone else's sidekick. Like somewhere beyond imagining, plot devices were murmuring among themselves, wondering when to kick in and to set me off on my hero quest. I'd given up on thinking I'd have one ever since I turned eighteen and no one showed up to tell me I was the Chosen One.

Part of me wanted to laugh it off, minimize how much I liked his fanciful analogy. Because suddenly, it all felt too real. The more I let him in, the more I let him mean to me . . . the harder it would be to let him go. *Let him go*. My stomach twisted. I would be doing to Levi what Tom did when he went fishing—catch and release.

Could I do that to him? To myself?

"You never know," he continued. "Maybe we were meant to meet. I mean, what were the chances that the waitress at Busy's also happened to be my landlady?"

"I love that you think it's fate," I said. "Not everyone believes in it."

"Well, I do," he declared. His eyes darted over my shoulder, forehead scrunched like he was trying to focus.

I twisted around. "What is it?"

"I think I see something over there," he said, pulling his hand loose. His pinkie hooked around mine for just a second. "Hold on, I'll get it."

I swallowed my surprise as I watched him get to his feet and amble toward an abandoned plastic pail and a miniature spade with a broken handle. It had been there for weeks, too old and broken for any of the children to touch. Levi crouched down, brushed the crusted sand off them, and then returned to me, loot in tow.

"You want to make a sandcastle?" I asked, amused.

He grinned at me. "Up for it?" The pail dangled from his pointer.

"Always."

We got to work, and in silence, we created a messy imitation castle. It leaned a little to the right, like the Leaning Tower of Pisa, but remained standing.

"It's going to fall over," said Levi.

"Don't be a Debbie Downer! We built it with a good foundation. For anything to work, it needs that."

"Aye, aye." He grinned.

"It looks like Hogwarts." I smoothed my finger over a tower. The sand was still wet, and I tried to shave the sides of it with the edges of my palms, slicing upward so the tip of the spire narrowed like the point of a number-two pencil. "Here's Gryffindor Tower."

Levi chuckled as he crouched forward to watch what I was doing. "Potterhead?"

I flicked some sand at his leg. "I solemnly swear that I am up to no good."

"So what else do you like?" He rocked back on his heels, smiling.

"I like all *kinds* of stuff." I returned his smile, dreamy and soft and warm and so, so, so in like that I let myself ramble. "I like Star Wars and rereading things I've already read a dozen times and too many marshmallows in my hot chocolate." I raised my finger, pointed at the moon. "I like looking at the stars and the clouds and seeing the shapes the ancients used to see."

And I like you.

"Kind of like now," he said, glancing up.

I followed his gaze. Face upturned, I almost missed him pulling his phone out of his pocket and turning on the flashlight app. Light flooded above in a line. "May the Force be with you," he said solemnly, earning a laugh from me.

"Nerd," I teased, sprawling out in the sand next to him. It had taken me a second to remember he wasn't one of my best friends whose lap I could settle my head in.

He lay down on the sand, one arm crooked under his ear to support his head. He shot me a lazy smile. "If Oar's Rest is paradise, then you're Eve."

I grimaced. "As in biblical, gets-blamed-for-everything Eve?"

"Nah." Levi didn't seem to mind the sand getting on his clothing. "More like beautiful Eve in her paradise."

I barely heard the incessant, buzzing cricket chirps or the gentle splash of tide as it rolled up on the sand. Sound faded, receding from my ears like the roll of water as it headed back to the sea.

I had been grappling with my feelings toward him, but now it all seemed so clear. The moment had shifted from two friends sitting together to a girl who might, just might, be falling for a boy.

Everything felt still. My stomach clenched and loosened, clenched and loosened. My heart jackrabbited and my breath came out in soft, shallow breaths. He seemed unaware of my internal turmoil—or that he was the cause of it.

Levi was right. Beginnings could be scary, and there was always a chance that the ending wouldn't be pretty, but the middle was what made it all worth it. Penny was right, too. People weren't meant to be preserved in amber. Maybe there were no happily ever afters. But there could be happiness, if I was brave enough to go for it. Though I knew Levi would leave, I wasn't ready to give up the possibility of us.

I'd been so confused for so long, I just wanted one thing, just *one* thing that made sense. And the only thing that that made sense to me in that moment was him. So I didn't stop myself when I tilted forward.

"Babe?"

I closed the distance between us. Before my eyes shut, his face broke into a smile and he leaned toward me. One hand cupped my cheek while the other lightly clutched my shoulder, pulling me closer. Our kiss was sweet and gentle, and when we both pulled away, gasping, he didn't let me go.

eleven

lmost a week later, my feelings hadn't abated one tiny bit. The shiny newness of being in *like* with someone made everything speed up. Minutes didn't drag, conversations didn't bore. I was on point, springily refilling coffee and getting orders out at record speed. It had been so long since my last crush that this one hit me with all the weight of a freighter. Even a coffee shop full of hungry customers all vying for my attention didn't put me off my stride. I was aware of him with every step I took. Aware of this spine-tingling relationship between us that made my eyes trail him without even noticing. What he was doing, what he was reading, whether he had finished his coffee yet . . . It was a little bit disconcerting, but mostly exhilarating.

At his usual table, Levi sketched. Every few seconds I heard the sharp scratch of the pen against the paper. His breathing had slowed as he devoted himself with singular focus to the task at hand. I envied him his concentration. When he was around, I found myself distracted. It was a smile when no one was watching, it was graphite-stained fingers combing through hair. The cord in his neck that tightened when he couldn't get something the exact way he wanted it. The hunch of his shoulders and furrow in his brow when he was utterly and completely absorbed by his work.

I pulled my hair out of its bun, letting the sea-salt-crunchy waves from my early-morning swim tangle in my fingers before spilling over my shoulders. Lucy, who was mediating Tom and Ralph's latest Battleship blowup, caught my eye over the heads of our customers. *Excited for tonight?* she mouthed, nodding subtly to Levi.

Levi and I had plans to hang out this evening, and I hadn't been able to stop thinking about it all day.

I let my smile answer for me. Lucy flashed me a sly grin and a thumbs-up.

♥ ♥ ♥

The beach was serene. I couldn't even hear the usual sound of seagulls calling to each other over the water. Noises of children playing had receded to a soft hum as they headed home, and the shops lining the boardwalk had all turned off their lights, casting the beach in a romantic, dusky glow.

Lorcan's crab shack was lit up in fairy lights strung from post to post, creating a canopy of twinkles above his customers' heads. Hushed voices spoke over the gentle roar from the firepit.

I leaned back on my elbows, watching as one of his waiters, a tanned blond with a conch-shell necklace, lit the tea-light candles on the empty tables. In the evenings, when there were a lot of tourist couples in Oar's Rest, Lorcan liked to go the extra mile. Gauzy canopies if it was drizzling, candles on the tables, and clusters of shells around the candles to add to the vibe. He would always scatter the smaller shells on the beach for hermit crabs to adopt as their home when it was time to molt.

A shadow fell over me. "Babe?"

I looked up, heart sinking into my growling stomach. "Hi," I said, pushing myself into a cross-legged position.

Chad and Penny stood above me, their faces searching mine. For what, I didn't know. "What are you doing here by yourself?" Chad asked. His voice wavered as he said, "You should join us."

Penny's eyes darted away. She seemed engrossed in watching Lorcan brush stray embers from his leg. She held a tub of potato salad in her hands. Peeking out from the pocket of her sundress were plastic-wrapped forks. Chad had a brown paper bag dangling near his knee. The grease stains saturated the bottom in the way that the waffle and chicken place in town always served it.

Chad was waiting for an answer. It was on the tip of my tongue to tell them I wasn't by myself, but with Penny right there, and her words still echoing in my ears, I couldn't. Instinctively, I prayed that Levi wouldn't show up while they were still here. A second later, I shook it off. I wasn't doing anything wrong.

"I'm waiting for someone," I said coolly.

Penny jerked her head back to me. Her eyes narrowed but she said nothing.

"Lucy?" Chad was still making an effort to be pleasant, like this wasn't the first time the three of us were back together since Penny had told me we weren't friends anymore. He shifted the paper bag in his hands.

Penny tugged at Chad's arm. "Let's eat," she said, cradling the tub in her arms.

I wove my fingers through my hair, thankful I didn't have to answer him.

"Yeah." He lightly clasped Penny's wrist when she began to walk away. She stopped. "It'd be cool for the three of us to hang out again. Wouldn't it, Pen?"

The ball was in her court now. Penny didn't say anything.

Even as I waited . . . and waited . . . and waited. When the silence became uncomfortably thick, almost suffocating in expectation, Chad's smile slipped. It was just like when we were kids and someone pissed her off. She was punishing me, withholding the thing I needed most of all. Her friendship.

Before she passed, Gran had been fond of saying that your family gave you roots, your past made you who you were. Both gave you a home, a place to go back to. I'd always liked that idea. When I was little, I thought of it as a save-game point in a video game, a way to reset your bad decisions and go back to a time when it all worked.

I hadn't realized that roots could also be a noose around your neck, anchoring you to a point in your life that felt as ill-fitting and oppressive as a scratchy, too-small sweater. It strangled you into compliance and habit. It made you love being held in place.

My blood blazed hot. Any trace of my guilt at being here with Levi burned away, leaving her in my path of fire. I wanted to scorch away the thorns and bramble tangled with my roots. I wanted to be who *I* was. Me. Just Babe, not Babe *and* Penny *and* Chad.

Penny's eyes, dark and starry as the night, crackled with the reflection of the fairy lights. I remembered my crush on her in middle school, something that had faded and flared intermittently until she began dating Chad. As I looked upon the two faces that I knew so well, it was painfully obvious that the three of us didn't know what to say to each other anymore. Their loss was painful, but it was a phantom ache. Like with Elodie, maybe we made better strangers than friends. I had to move on. It was scary, but not any scarier than standing still in a dynamic that didn't fit me anymore.

Grief welled in my throat, diffusing the fire. Voice thick, I said, "It was nice seeing you guys."

Chad's lips parted. In his face, I thought I saw some of the torture I was feeling. For a horrible moment I didn't think they were going to leave. I sensed he wanted to say more, but he didn't.

Please just go.

Penny swallowed. Hard. "See ya around, Babe," she said. Her fingers curled around Chad's bicep.

Chad's eyes turned downcast. He ground the toe of his shoe into the sand, eyelashes golden. His eyes were hidden from me. "Bye." He let himself be led away, loping after Penny.

Neither one of them looked back.

I exhaled and closed my eyes. My stomach churned and suddenly I wasn't sure I was hungry at all.

A pretty blonde stepped out of the crowd of Lorcan's regulars. She wiggled her fingers, smiling invitingly.

Dani. The first person I'd gone out with after Elodie dumped me. She still wore the same round glasses and magenta lipstick. Her other hand was draped around a girl I didn't know, a girlfriend maybe. I shyly waved back, mouthing *Hi*. I pulled my cell phone from the wristlet looped around my wrist, digging past the makeup and crumpled bills. Checking the time, I saw that it wasn't yet eight.

While I was stuffing my phone inside my wristlet, something landed on the sand next to me. Not Chad and Penny *again*. I looked up.

"Levi!" I stamped down the unease my friends had caused. Then I looked at the basket lying in the sand. "Picnic?" I reached out to open it, but he made a soft tsking noise.

"Let me spread out the blanket first," he said, unfolding one from under his arm.

Obligingly, I sat up, shook sand off my clothing, and helped him flap the checkered sheet over the spot I was sitting on.

"Did you cook?" I asked with interest, watching as he pulled out two bottles of lemonade and several containers of food.

He chuckled and ran a hand through his loose waves. "Only some of it. The rest is from the deli."

I hummed in appreciation as I recognized some of the goodies he spread out on the sheet. A cold chicken-and-rice pilaf, lobster rolls drizzled with curry mayonnaise and crunchy kaffir leaves, black bean and cherry tomato quinoa salad, and two bulging pulled-chicken sandwiches.

"Oh my God. We're going to eat all this?"

"I didn't know what you'd be in the mood for," he said with a laugh. "I wound up getting a few different things." He handed me a paper plate. "Eat up. I don't want to take any of this back."

"Good thing I came hungry," I said, reaching for the fork he offered me. "So what did *you* make?"

Levi grinned. "The drink." He pulled a clear bottle from the basket. Blood-colored liquid sloshed inside, along with a few lumpy pieces of fruit. "I found some booze in your mom's kitchen. Hope you don't mind," he said. Flashing a smile, he passed me a red Dixie cup.

I laughed. "Not at all." I knew Mom wouldn't notice.

After he poured us both a generous serving, he raised his glass toward me in a toast. "To new friends."

I touched my glass against his, reminded of the first time we'd done this. "To new friends." My first sip had me sputtering. Something went down spicy—not enough to overpower the sweetness of the fruit and rosé, but enough to make me cough.

"I should have mentioned." Levi's eyes glowed amber in the flickering firelight. "There's a bit of a kick."

I gasped. "I'll say!"

"Crushed red pepper." With an abashed smile, he spooned food onto my plate. "Eat, it'll help."

I gulped down a bite of quinoa salad. The juice from the tomato soothed my irritated throat and the gentle, almost bland, flavor of the quinoa calmed down my protesting taste buds. "You put red pepper in the sangria?" I asked with a wince.

He tugged at his left earlobe. "Uh, yeah. Too much?"

"Well, after the initial burn, it's actually pretty sweet. Like a Red Hot."

He grinned. "I had this in Spain. The Spanish Club went on a two-week trip between my junior and senior year. A bunch of us snuck out one night and went down to a beach in Costa Brava and had this. I'm trying to perfect the recipe by autumn. It's perfect for drinking in front of a roaring fireplace with a good book in hand. This heat makes me nostalgic for sweater weather."

"You've been everywhere and you still love it here," I said, smiling.

"I haven't really been everywhere," said Levi. His ears turned pink and he ducked his head. "Just lucky enough to go to a couple of places. I had some money saved up from selling some of my work and taking a couple commissions. But going to Spain meant asking for all my birthday money in advance and working for my dad at his office supply store to make up the rest."

I took another sip. This time I was prepared for the burn, so I didn't even notice it. The fruit exploded with flavor, secreting wine-flavored juices. "Cinnamon?" I ran my tongue over my lower lip. "And . . . there's a hint of something else."

He nodded encouragingly. "Syrup mixed with port, Cointreau, cranberry juice, and rosé. I fiddled with the recipe a bit."

"It's good," I said. And it was.

"Good," he echoed, the word seeping with relief. It was good to know that I wasn't the only one who was a little nervous.

"I saw you come up to the lighthouse the other day," I said, the words offhand even though the air was charged with an electric energy.

His fork jerked. "Oh yeah?" He stabbed at a black bean.

"Yup." I fiddled with the lobster roll on my plate before taking a bite. The bread hugged the chopped lobster, the whiteness of the inside stained yellow and softened from absorbing the curry mayo. "Why did you"—I chewed—"leave without saying hello?" When he was silent, I added, "That guy, he was just a friend."

Levi nodded slowly. "I guess I just didn't want to interrupt anything. It looked pretty serious."

"It wasn't," I said quickly. "It was just my friend. Best friend, actually. He wanted to say hi. That's it." I pointed Chad and Penny out. "And he's dating Penny."

"Your best friends are dating each other?" He paused. "That sounds . . . messy."

"We've been best friends since we were kids." I didn't know why I felt the need to justify that our friendship worked—especially since right now, it didn't. Maybe it never would again.

"So is that part of the weirdness I sensed between you and her that night at her party?"

Yikes. I wasn't expecting him to bring that up again. There was no way to tell the story from the middle—but how could I even begin to explain a lifetime of friendship? If I told him about the kiss and the fight, all he would hear was the worst part of it all. But he'd already picked up on the weirdness, so not telling him would just make it weirder.

I'd taken too long to answer. Levi clasped his hands together. "Hey, you don't have to answer that."

"No, I can. I . . . I want to." I swallowed hard. "So, um, this was before I met you. Penny broke up with him. She had this idea that she . . . wanted a fresh start? Didn't want a high school sweetheart anymore."

He blinked at me. "That's sort of shitty."

I hoped it was dark enough that he couldn't see my face. "She asked me to keep him away from her one night, because she told me she didn't want to have a face-to-face. I didn't want to do it, and Chad didn't take it that great. We—the three of us—aren't used to change. It wrecked everything." I took a deep, bracing breath. "He kissed me."

I cleared my throat, glad to have that particular hurdle over with. "It didn't mean anything. Chad was just confused. He's in love with Penny. But Penny . . . she found out about it the night of the party. That's why I wanted to leave early. She's been keeping her distance since then, and Chad's going along with it. That's what he came by my house to say that he's going to be playing by her rules."

I waited for him to ask me something, but I was met with silence.

His head was bowed, eyes shielded from view. I watched his golden eyelashes flutter against his cheek as he fiddled with the picnic basket.

"Thanks for sharing that with me," he said at last. "I wish I hadn't turned around that day."

I wished he hadn't, too.

"So you and Chad . . ." His eyes met mine in question, lips stilling on their journey to a smile.

"There's nothing going on," I said quickly. "Chad wasn't thinking straight when he kissed me. He just . . . lost his way for a second there."

Levi frowned. "They're back together now, though. It's super not fair to you."

He'd voiced what I'd been thinking. Gratitude rushed through me. I was both embarrassed and touched that he was on my side. Tears pricked at my eyes, so I quickly waved my hand at the picnic in front of us. "Thank you. I know I was the one who brought it up, but do you mind if we don't talk about them?"

"Oh, yeah. Of course." Levi reached for the picnic basket and pulled out a bouquet of bruised wildflowers. His smile was a little lopsided. Petals hung limply from stems like dangling threads from a shirt.

I took the bouquet, fighting back a grin as I recognized some of the flowers from my mom's yard. "Thanks?"

"They weren't supposed to look like that."

Putting a daisy out of its misery, I snapped off the flower and tucked it behind my ear.

"The bottles dented them." Levi's lips twisted in a bit of a pout. He took a deep breath, as if realizing the agony of the dearly departed.

I liked that he cared enough to be upset about it. I reached out to touch his hand. My fingers slid down his, and as I passed the knuckles, I felt the friction of our touch. No sparks, just the soft understanding of two people who really got each other.

"I stole them," he whispered, his voice breaking the stillness.

"You what?" My laugh came out in a whoosh.

"Nabbed them," he confirmed, grinning. "From your mom's front lawn. They were just *there*, a ton of them, under the mailbox with all the weeds. Actually, I think most of them might be weeds themselves."

I laughed and took a sip of the chilled lemonade. "Yeah, some of them are."

"I'll get you proper flowers for the next date," Levi announced.

Next date? I went tingly all over. He was already thinking about the next date. I flushed warm, mind whirring at his words. "Not necessary," I said.

"The date or the flowers?" he countered.

I laughed. "The flowers." The date I would take with open arms.

"Not a flower kind of girl?"

"It's not that." I ran my pinkie over a soft petal. "It's just that . . . you don't have to do all that. For me, flowers mean . . ." I trailed off. We attached so much ridiculous weight to romantic gestures, and flowers were a big one. I didn't love change, but I'd already dipped my toe in the water with spending so much time with Levi. If I actually dated him—*really* dated him, flowers and all—then it would be like doing a cannonball into the sea. And the ripple effect was something I couldn't foresee.

His voice was soft. "Flowers mean what?"

I wasn't thinking. I just spoke, giving the words free rein to tumble out. "Something that means . . . I want to get to know you. I want you."

Levi stared at me so long that I didn't realize how much I'd admitted, how willingly I'd dipped into my thoughts.

"Or something like that," I said lamely, trying to steer our conversation to safer waters.

Oh my God, why did I say all that?

I hadn't been thinking about protecting my heart. In fact, in those few short words, I'd handed it over to him on a platter. Exhilaration sent moonbeams through my bones, carving through the fear in swaths. Instead of treading water, I'd tucked my knees and cannonballed in, consequences be damned.

"What makes you think I don't want all that with you?"

I looked up. His voice, louder and deeper. His eyes, brighter and fiercer. The scrunch of his eyebrows. The tenseness of his mouth. My fierce, wonderful summer boy.

My heart thrilled. Unlike some of our banter before, this didn't seem like an idle comment, did it? The way he said it . . . it was like he actually meant every word. I wanted to kiss him senseless under the starry skies and feel him shiver when I touched his spine. I wanted him to cup my chin, gently, and then lean in, slowly, and show me how much he wanted me, too.

Every bit of me was alive, thrumming for his touch. My heart yearned to kiss him, but my head reminded me to be careful. Levi

Keller was a flower that I could pick and keep as my own, but the roots wouldn't be mine. I'd only be uprooting something beautiful from its own habitat. At the end of summer, he'd go home, and I'd stay here. I was a perennial, an eternal summer girl year-round. Levi was as annual as they came.

So I didn't kiss him then, even though I wanted to.

♥ ♥ ♥

"Let me walk you home," he said a little while later as I helped him pack away empty containers.

"You don't have a bike and you'd have to walk all the way uphill in the dark," I pointed out. My fingers tightened on the handlebars of my bike as I pulled it upright. "Don't worry about it."

Levi handed me my bouquet of squashed flowers. "Are you sure?"

I tucked the bouquet into the crook of my arm. Maybe it was a little old-fashioned, but I could picture a young Levi being coached by his father about being a gentleman. Never kissing a girl on the first date, pulling her chair out for her even if she didn't expect him to, walking her to the door and waiting until she got inside before leaving. His Levi-ness was ingrained in him so true and so solid that I knew I would miss it once it wasn't mine anymore.

"That's really sweet of you, but I'm fine getting home alone," I said. "Honestly, it's out of your way and I've walked home by myself a million times."

The sun tended to set a little after eight p.m., and that hour had come and gone. Now it was after ten. Only Lorcan was still around, serving late-night drinks to stragglers who loitered on the beach. He sent us a wave as he stamped out the fire and pulled his grate off for cleaning.

"Okay," said Levi. "Sorry, I know it's dumb. I just wanted to, I don't know, end the night right?"

"It's not dumb." I smiled at him. "And we did end the night right."

He slung an arm around my shoulder and pressed a kiss to my temple. "Yeah, I guess we did."

"Hey," I said as we turned to make the trek back into town, "we forgot to look for our sandcastle."

Levi turned around, scanning the beach. With disappointment, he said, "Kids probably smashed it by now. Or the tide took it away."

I shook my head. "Sandcastles are sacred in Oar's Rest, Levi. It's sacrilegious to destroy one."

"Hey, I've been meaning to ask you," said Levi.

We picked our way across the sand, arms bumping as I walked my bike next to me. "Yeah?" I asked.

"I saw something about the fiftieth anniversary of a sandcastle competition." He ran his free hand through his hair. The picnic basket jogged against the back of my knee. "Would you want to . . . with me?"

"Do I want to build castles with you?" The butterfly flaps in my stomach beat faster. "I'd love to."

His eyes pierced into mine, more golden now than they were before. He leaned in. For a moment, it looked like he was going to capture my lips, but then he kissed my cheek. "Good night, Babe. Thanks for a wonderful date."

"Thank *you*," I said in return, blushing. "Tonight was . . ." There was only one word for it. "Magical."

We parted ways. In the lamplight, I watched him walk away. I felt so full—more full than I had felt in my entire life. Full of experiences and happiness and hope. I clung to it greedily. I wanted so much life, wanted to swell up and just fly away, a balloon adrift in the sky. Away and away and away.

Even though we'd left each other a few minutes ago, I wanted to see him again. I didn't want to go to sleep, because part of me felt the memory of today would slip out of my tight hold. That was what had happened with Chad and Penny, after all. The two people who I thought would always be mine, without a shadow of a doubt. But now they were just ghosts of good times creaking around in my memory.

Levi wasn't a ghost. I didn't want him to be.

I wanted this summer to last forever.

twelve

The weekend passed in the numbing monotony of lighthouse tours, shifts at Busy's, and the never-ending cycle of baking, cleaning, eating. Rinse and repeat. I perfected Nutella cookies, thin and brittle like gingersnaps, and buttery Earl Grey shortbread cookies.

I sank my teeth into a shortbread cookie that wasn't perfectly round. The sweet, smoky notes of tea blended with the crushed vanilla beans I'd sprinkled into the cookie batter. The flavor was incredible—like sweet, crumbly autumn goodness. Like fragrant, floral tea and crisp breaths in brisk air. Like fingertips warmed by hot cocoa and enormous woolly sweaters wrapped around me.

My famous cinnamon waffle cookies completed the trio, brushed on top with a maple glaze and a dusting of brown sugar. On several trays, I arranged dozens of each cookie, layering them to maximize space. I stretched plastic wrap over the top and bunched it up at the bottom, pressing it flat.

I stacked the trays in the basket of my bicycle and pedaled to Busy's to get ready for the fish fry.

Inside, Lucy was slicing vegetables, a table fan aimed straight at her. "Hey," she said, covering her mouth with the back of her hand, yawning. "That for the fish fry?"

"Yup. I'm just gonna put this away." In a mock-whisper, I added, "Before people start gobbling them up."

"Good idea," Lucy deadpanned. "But leave a few out for us; getting ready for the fish fry is hungry work."

Every year, after the Fourth of July, Oar's Rest threw a huge feast for everyone in the town, locals and tourists alike. For the local businesses, it was something of a tradition to drag their seating outdoors, share grills, and dish up plate after plate of mouthwatering food.

Tom was on coffee duty, refilling French press after French press to make our signature iced coffee, while Lucy and I tackled the panini press. We sliced loaves, caramelized onions, and prepared the meat, cheese, and vegetables.

"Here, slide in a few extra of these," I said, handing sizzling bacon to Lucy. It wouldn't be an onion-bacon-Gouda without the perfect ratio of bacon to cheese.

While she finished up the BLTs with avocado and fried egg, I whipped up a plate of caprese paninis.

"I'll start cutting those up for samples," said Tom, peering over our shoulders. "After I get started on the whoopie pies and poutine."

"You outdid yourself this year, Babe." Lucy grinned. "Salted buttercream, Nutella, and vanilla cream cheese fillings? How did you find the time to make three kinds of pies?"

"*Everyone* makes whoopies. Figured we should do something to stand out a little," I said.

The three of us pitched in without mentioning Ariel. She hadn't come to work in so long that I figured she'd realized it wasn't working out. Rather than let it drag out, I sent her a text to come and collect her wages.

Later, laughing at one of Lucy's jokes, I felt rather than heard the door open. A gust of hot air hit the backs of my legs. "Levi," I said, surprised to see him so early. "What are you doing here? The fish fry won't start for another hour."

Levi grinned, the indent of a dimple faint in his left cheek. "And the valiant prince showed up to save the princess, and she looked him up and down with disdain, and could only utter: 'What are you doing here?'"

"Damn straight." I smirked at him. "The princess saved herself by the time the prince finally showed up."

"Oh, did she?" One eyebrow rose. "I guess you won't be needing me, then." He turned as if to leave, cheeky grin still tugging at the corners of his mouth.

His playfulness was too cute to ignore, so I gave in. I grabbed his sleeve. "So, brave knight, are you really here to save me?"

"Depends." His eyes twinkled. "Can I have a cookie?"

At my nod, he moved forward, hand snaking behind me to take a waffle cookie. His sharp jaw came close to my neck as he bent his head; his angles and lines invaded my personal space until all I could smell was him.

I ached to kiss him. I inhaled as he drew away, popping the cookie in his mouth.

"This is really good," he said. "Now, how can I help?"

"Let me give you a hand," said Levi, already moving to help Tom with the crate of water and iced tea. Lucy held the door open for Tom and Ralph, who filed out with platters of steaming food.

The three men put the cookie and sandwich platters on the tables that stretched through Main Street. Each platter looked even more delectable than the last.

Lorcan's tables were next to ours. He'd placed grilled tilapia and catfish on an enormous bed of parsley rice. The smokiness of the fish made my mouth water. The next platter held snow crabs dripping in a garlic butter sauce, ears of grilled corn lightly coated with a lime salt and paprika seasoning, and yellow baby potatoes. The last platter held a variety of skewers: grilled pineapple and honey-ginger scallops, tricolored bell peppers, and charred red onion and shrimp.

The food was the piper's song, luring townspeople and tourists alike to the party. Within minutes, people crowded around our tables, jostling elbows as they placed orders and handed over cash.

Local businesses had taken over the entire length of Main Street, the seating spilling into side streets. Gingham tablecloths fluttered in the summer breeze, homemade signs and streamers billowing overhead in a riot of colors.

The park, usually full of squalling children and dogs, had now been transformed into an adults-only beer garden. Tables were loaded down with burgers, lagers, and wines. People milled around, waiting for spare seats, but the shared picnic tables weren't having a quick turnover. Nearby, the historical society volunteers were setting up the gazebo for live music, and some local bluegrass legends were plucking away at their mandolins and banjos. Bunting was strung up on streetlights and storefronts, coastal blue and white flapping in the breeze.

A huddle of children was grouped in front of the toy store, where the owner and his wife were giving away free balloon animals. Next door, the bookstore had placed huge signs in the window advertising a fifty-percent-off sale on the books of local authors.

"Can't believe we're still not old enough for the beer garden," said Lucy. She eyed the park enviously. It had been roped off with plenty of signs that said 21+ ONLY. "Another two years until we won't get carded."

"It's two for Babe, *three* for you," said Tom, wincing as he straightened his back. "Ladies, I need to sit myself down. Might head on over to the park for a bit." He clapped Ralph on the shoulder.

"Beer sounds good," said Ralph, and the two of them moved off.

While Lucy took over the flurry of customers, Levi and I headed inside to pull the French presses out of the fridge. "These are pretty heavy," he said, hefting two in his arms as I began mixing drinks at the counter.

We were able to thin the crowd in the street by rerouting them indoors to pick up their coffees before sending them on their way. By lunchtime, all the coffee ran out, and Tom and Ralph were back to take over our stall.

Lucy's mom accompanied them, and even though she wasn't dressed for handling food, she rolled up her sleeves, donned a spare apron, and got to work taking orders inside Busy's. "Hi, Babe," she said cheerfully. "Ran into these two codgers at the garden and thought I'd give you a hand."

"We definitely won't turn down the help," I said with a smile, turning away to help another customer. "Thanks, Mrs. Bishop."

As I packed cookies into a to-go box, the woman I was serving asked, "Do you have a website?"

"For Busy's? No, sorry, not yet. We're working on it, though! Hope to have it up soon."

She tucked her black hair behind her ear. "My husband and I were here last year and we just loved your food. In winter, we thought about your shortbread tea cookies quite a bit. I tried re-creating them, but I never get the perfect balance of tea." She laughed. "Have you ever thought about taking online orders?"

I knew Busy's had great reviews on TripAdvisor, in no small part because of my baking, but I knew I wanted to talk to Tom before making a business decision like that. Right now, it felt a little wrong to commercialize my baked goods; Tom's cozy, homey coffee shop was where they—we—belonged. "I have," I said, lips quirking up in a smile. "I'd love to do something like that one day, but my grandma once told me not to dance faster than the music."

The woman smiled and accepted the bag I slid across the counter. "Sounds like a smart woman," she said, setting down a crisp bill. "Keep the change. Hope to see you again next year!"

Business kept rolling steadily for two hours, and by the time it slowed enough that we could take a break, we were bone-tired. With hugs all around, Lucy's mom left Busy's to join her husband at the gazebo. I glanced over what remained of the food—we were almost sold out of everything.

"I've never been so tired in my whole life," Lucy moaned as she stood up from her chair. She'd said that last year, too.

Even from here we could hear the twangs of the banjo and the boisterous cheers of the crowd as the town outside geared up for the fireworks display.

"You kids get a move on," said Tom. "We've worked hard today, and you should enjoy the rest of the fish fry. Ralph and I can handle things here. Just put the money in the cash register, would you?"

"Sure thing, boss." I took the bills from the cash box and headed into the cool, air-conditioned coffee shop to tuck them into the register.

When I came out, Levi and Lucy were helping Lorcan with his stall. My gaze traveled down the street for a minute, enjoying the hustle of activity. I froze when I saw Elodie in my line of sight. She was watching me. Her hand half rose, then fluttered down to her side. For a moment, I almost wanted to wave back, just to show there were no hard feelings. But then a flash of irritation went through me. Why? Why should I be the one to ease the way? It was always me. Same old Elodie. She couldn't talk to me in public, now she couldn't even wave? I was tired of being the understanding one. So I breezed past the crowd and headed to our stall instead.

"I'm almost out of food, so I asked my dad to send one of my brothers over to take over my table while I cook, but—" Lorcan's lips flattened into a thin line. "Yeah, didn't happen."

"Are they seriously still pissed you didn't want to work at the pub anymore?" I asked.

"I told them I'd help out in the winter, but you know Dad. He saw me doing my own thing as disloyalty," Lorcan scoffed, and wiped his sweaty brow with a napkin. "Well, that's the last of the shrimp and catfish."

"What if I helped you?" Lucy suggested. She seemed to have forgotten how tired she was.

"I can't ask you to do that," said Lorcan. He ducked his head. "Enjoy the fish fry."

Lucy fell silent while Lorcan helped a middle-aged couple. She made change while he handed them their shopping bag.

"Thanks, have a great time," said Lorcan.

"Lorc, you're running low on a lot of things," said Lucy, eyeing the table. "The corn and potatoes are over, and you only have a couple of crab legs left. They were really popular. If you have time to make more, you should. Plus they'll be fresh and hot, so the smell should get you more customers. I can man your stall while you head back to cook."

Lorcan bit his lip.

"We can help," said Levi, glancing at me. "Right?"

"Definitely," I said, heart happily constricting at his offer.

"No need for that, Levi. We'll help Lucy look after Lorcan's table while he skedaddles on back to his crab shack," Tom said firmly. "Three of us between two tables will be no trouble."

"There, it's settled," said Lucy, squeezing Lorcan's arm.

Lorcan thanked everyone before dashing away to cook. "We can stay if you want," I whispered to Lucy as we watched him weave through the crowd.

"No, you two go ahead and enjoy the rest of the fish fry." Lucy smiled. "I think we've got things handled here."

"Let me get some more water from inside," I said. The sun was beating down relentlessly and the top of Ralph's bald head was already sunburned. "And maybe a couple umbrella stands, too. They still in the storeroom?"

"Yup," said Tom.

"I'll go with you," said Levi. He paused when he passed Ralph, touching his shoulder. "I'll catch up with you later."

Curious, I caught Levi's eye, but he smiled brightly and didn't give anything else away.

We headed into the dark chill of the storeroom. I flicked on the switch, and unflattering fluorescent lighting flooded the room with an unforgiving luminosity. I reached up and pulled my hair from its messy bun, letting the damp strands fall around my ears. Sweeping my hair over one shoulder to let my neck cool, I scanned the room for the white umbrellas.

Levi moved behind me. A moment later, his hands settled on my waist.

"Trying to get me alone?" I teased.

"Look," he said, resting his chin on my shoulder.

I couldn't see anything out of the ordinary, just boxes, boxes, and more boxes. "I'm not following, Levi."

"Next to the shelves. Wrapped in brown paper." Levi dipped his head in a *go on* gesture.

I looked. A two-foot-tall, narrow object was wedged between the wall and the shelf. After a questioning look over my shoulder at Levi, I moved forward and pulled the object free. At once, I could feel it was a frame. "A painting?" My eyes widened. At his nod, I asked, "When did you put it here?"

He grinned. "I snuck it in when I was helping out earlier."

"I didn't even notice," I said. I split the brown paper with the sharp edge of my nail, revealing my secret superpower of being an excellent paper ripper.

It wasn't the same painting he'd been working on at the lighthouse. This one was smaller and the colors were a little brighter, and instead of the entire town of Oar's Rest, Busy's took front and center. The frame was simple wood, the corners edged in shiny metal. I held it at arm's length to take it all in. While most of the other businesses and homes were too small to be recognizable, I made out Dan's Bike Shop, the book I'd buried in the sand, the B&Bs and crab shacks and even the hint of a little red dot in the top corner that looked like my lighthouse.

Levi hadn't just painted a picture. He'd painted home. *My* home. Tears grew in my eyes and I laughed, mostly because if I didn't, then I was bound to cry. "This is perfect," I said.

"I was hoping you'd love it. It's a gift for you."

"This is . . . I don't even have the words, Levi. Thank you."

"Don't go selling it or anything."

I gawked at him. "I wouldn't!"

He chuckled and wrapped his arms around me, grunting when the simple act became infinitely more cumbersome thanks to the painting in my arms. "I was teasing. But you never know, I could be worth a fortune one day."

"You're worth a fortune to me *now*." I hugged the painting to my chest. "I think I'd like to hang it up here for a while. So everyone can enjoy it. Can we go hang it?"

He agreed readily, and we found a spot on the wall where I could always see it when I was at the counter.

"It's perfect," I said, stepping away, satisfied with the tilt of the frame. "I love it."

Turning to Levi, I looped my arms around his neck and met his lips. We held them together for a few seconds before I took the lead. Our kiss was fast and slow, chaste and passionate. Every kiss with him felt like the first time.

Our tongues hungrily said hello, exploring each other with languid, unhurried curiosity. I felt each of his inhales and exhales against my skin, and I matched mine to his until even our breath thrust in and out in synchrony. His hand cupped my cheek and I melted against him. I pressed my lips to his wrist, satisfied on a primal level to hear his sharp, undone inhale.

His thumb gently rubbed against my lower lip. I knew it was swollen and red from his kiss, and I knew he knew it, too, judging by the way his eyes clouded with desire, growing a darker, indigo blue.

"We should join them," said Levi, his breath a little ragged. He brought my hand to his lips and kissed my palm.

"You go ahead," I said. "I just need to go to the restroom first."

When I came out a few minutes later, my eyes landed on his painting of Busy's. Warmth bloomed in my chest. Even when Levi left, a piece of him would still be here. A pleasant shiver went down my spine. A second later, the warm, cocooned feeling of being in *like* was blotted out with a splash of ice water.

Because Penny was standing in the doorway, mouth pulled into a sullen frown, while Mrs. Wang waved from behind her.

"Babe!" Mrs. Wang bustled into the coffee shop, quickly enveloping me in a hug that smelled like honeysuckle and sunshine. "You look like a tomato, sweetie," she said with a cluck of her tongue, studying my face. "Are you drinking enough water? It's so hot out there." She fanned my face with the flyer she was holding.

If I was flushed, it was entirely because of Levi, and nothing at all to do with the temperature. I felt my face warm even more when Mrs. Wang vigorously began to swish the flyer through the air. "I'm fine, really. Thank you."

"Mom," said Penny. She still hadn't come in. "Let's get something to drink."

"We can get something here," said Mrs. Wang. She pursed her rosebud mouth. "Penny tells me you didn't want to do the Clamshell Queen pageant this year?"

"Uh, I—" Stricken, I tore my eyes away from Mrs. Wang's concerned face to look at Penny. She'd told her mom that it was my decision?

"You girls have done it together every year, so I was surprised," her mom continued. "Are you sure? I still have lots of fabric, so you could just drop by whenever you—"

"*Mom*," said Penny. "She doesn't want to." Her eyes cut to me. "And Babe's working. We're holding her up. Let's go to the Dairy Bar for a milkshake."

"Why don't you join us afterward?" suggested Mrs. Wang.

I wanted to say yes. I wanted, in that minute, to take Mrs. Wang up on her offer and ask her to help me sew a dress for the pageant. If I did, Penny would be forced to keep her mouth shut. She wouldn't contradict me in front of her mom. This could be my in, my way back to everything I'd lost when I'd kissed Chad.

But I couldn't do it. I didn't know this side of Penny, which meant I didn't know what she would do next. What if she didn't like me pulling a fast one on her and turned the tables? What if she called me on it, outed me to her mom right here and now? She could reveal the story, tell her mom what Chad and I had done. It wouldn't matter that they'd been broken up, not to a mother. She'd take her daughter's side, obviously. I didn't want Mrs. Wang to look at me with disappointment. So I held my tongue.

"Penny's right," I said. "It's pretty busy and, um, Tom's counting on me out there, so . . ."

"Of course." Mrs. Wang smiled. "The offer's still open, though. Just drop in if you change your mind about the pageant." She squeezed my shoulder before heading for the door.

Penny shot me one last look before spinning on her heel and following her mom. She had lied. She'd pretended it was my idea not to join them this year. I felt numb all over, then icy hot, then nothing. Then I felt the grief rise through my belly and into my throat. It crested into a brilliant, agonizing sob of hurt and pain and every emotion in between. I didn't feel nothing anymore. I felt everything.

thirteen

A few evenings later, Levi and I padded our way across the beach to the wreckage of our castle. Even from a distance, I could see that the towers and once-packed sand had crumbled in little chunks at the base. His face fell as we got closer.

"We can't even be sure that's ours," said Levi, sounding hopeful.

"Oh, it's ours all right," I said dryly. "I remember because it still looks lopsided."

We stared at it, both a bit dejected, before I slapped my palms against the tops of my thighs. "Okay. Time to practice."

He wore a look of determination as he sank into the sand.

I slid my sunglasses from my hair to my nose. "I know we built a sandcastle just for fun a few days ago, but I'm about to take you into the big leagues. You ready, Keller?"

"It can't be too different than sculpting, right?" There was a hopeful lilt at the end of his sentence.

I grinned. "So . . . you haven't made a *real* sandcastle before, I'm guessing."

He winced. "Nope. Sorry."

"Okay, no worries." I pursed my lips. "I can walk you through the basics."

I'd selected a spot close enough to the water so we didn't have to keep refilling our five-gallon bucket. Tools lay scattered in front of me, and I lifted each one up to explain its purpose. The spade was for scooping and packing, and the smaller buckets and yogurt containers were for towers. An old funnel made for a pretty good roof, a trick I'd picked up from Chad, and a few other kitchen and home improvement tools would finesse our creation into a professional sandcastle.

We used the spades to scoop a big mound of sand in front of us, building it higher and higher into a bowl shape. The sand was already a little wet, but I tilted the big bucket and poured more water on it. "Now we tamp it down with our feet so we get an even foundation to build on," I said. While I bounded over our workspace, Levi was more self-conscious, patting the sand gingerly with his bare feet.

"Not like that," I said, fighting back a grin. Taking his hands in mine, I drummed my feet into the sand, flattening it even further. "Come on, put your heart into it." It took a few tries, but he finally got it, stomping with abandon. Once that was done, we had a four-by-four plot of sand that was ready to build on.

"Here, take this." I pressed a bucket into his hands. "Fill it almost to the top with sand, pour water in, and pack it down." I watched as he followed my directions, packing the sand as tight as he could.

"Now what?"

"Flip it."

Immediately, Levi began to pull the bucket off.

"Wait!" I exclaimed.

His forehead scrunched. "Why?" he asked, sounding adorably puzzled. A lock of hair fell into his eyes.

"Use your hands to tap the sides and remove any excess air. It'll come out smoother."

With his open palm, he slapped the bucket on all sides until he determined it was ready to lift. "I'm nervous about getting this right," he said with a laugh.

I reached for his hand. "Don't be."

He gave me a squeeze. "Building a sandcastle for the first time makes me feel like a kid again." His eyes skimmed the beach.

I followed his gaze. The other teams that had claimed their spots were already working on elaborate towers and turrets, their castles twice the size of ours. "Don't worry about it. I'll get you caught up in no time." With an encouraging smile, I nodded to his bucket. "Go ahead and lift it up."

Grasping the sides, Levi began to slowly pull it upward.

"Gently," I coaxed.

The bucket came off, but an area where the sand hadn't totally been tamped down crumbled immediately.

"Try it again," I said. "Try adding a little more water this time."

Once he mastered that, I showed him how to repeat the process with the funnel roof. The good thing about building sandcastles was that once you knew the basics, there were so many different ways you could apply the same knowledge to get different results. Once we had a few different towers going, I showed him how to roughly shape a wall with our hands, using a spackle knife to get the edges sharp and neat. Once the wall was level, we used the knife to create little cuts at the top to resemble battlements.

"It's always way easier to cut away than to add more sand, so I like to kind of keep it a little messy when I'm building," I explained. "It can always be tidied up at the end."

The peal of his cell phone made us both jump. With an apologetic smile, he reached into his pocket. "Just a second," he said. "It's my mom."

"No problem." I waited for him to move away, but he didn't. Weirdly, it felt good that he didn't want privacy.

"Hey, Mom." He paused. "Yeah, I'm doing fine. Just out on the beach." He shot me a helpless glance and mouthed *Sorry*. "Yeah, it's going really well. You saw my photos, right?" Another pause. "Yeah, Dad would like it here. Did he see them, too?"

He tilted his head to the side, balancing the phone between his ear and shoulder. "I'm still sharing my art on Instagram, yeah. I don't know if you noticed, but I've gotten a lot more engagement since— no, I'm not accusing you of stalking my account. I'm not trying to hide anything, Mom. Go! Look all you want. Everyone loves the new stuff I'm putting up."

I flashed him a thumbs-up.

He made a sound of frustration. "I'm just saying that it's not the career killer you and that hack agent thought it was." He made a face at me. "Yeah, I have gotten a lot of interest. Some new commissions, too. Someone asked me if I could do her wedding invitations for her. She wants to get married right here in Oar's Rest. She fell in love with the lighthouse." He caught my eye and shot me a small smile.

He spoke to his mom for another couple of minutes, assuring her he was eating well and that he was super happy here. By the time he hung up, his cheeks were a little pink. "Sorry," he apologized again. "She hates that I'm so far away. She's been calling me a lot since we made up. I think I'm wearing her down about everything, though. Maybe by the end of summer, she'll actually let me do things my way."

"She gets why you had to leave?"

Levi nodded. "Yeah. Dad does, too. He's still pissed about the hole my pushpin left in his map, though." A half smile curled his lips. "But that's just how he is."

"You're getting more commissions," I said. "That's really good."

"It's different from what I've painted before. They were pretty, but a little generic. Since coming here, I feel like my style has evolved into something with more character."

I nodded. I could see the new nuance in his work, too. "Maine left its mark on you."

"Or you did," he said lightly.

My face warmed. I hoped that was true.

"What now?" he asked, leaning forward to survey the rest of the tools. "Measuring spoons?" He lifted them out with a wry grin.

"For decorations." I pulled out some starfish and clamshell cookie cutters. "The sandcastles look really pretty when you decorate them with seaweed and shells."

"Could we try making something bigger?" he suggested, pointing to the nearest sandcastle.

I grinned. "Let's go for it."

This time, we piled up a ton of sand and then got to work shaving away the walls so we were left with a huge foundation about three feet tall. We added a keep in each of the four corners, slicing the rounded bucket walls so they became squares. Walls connected each keep, creating a perimeter for our project. Levi was exacting enough to cut out the battlements just right, while I focused my attention on creating ledges. Holding the knife at a downward angle, I cut into the keep, then dragged straight down. The sand neatly fell away.

Levi paused in his work when I grabbed the melon baller. "What are you doing with that?" he asked curiously.

"Watch." I hovered the melon baller under the ledge until I had the angle just right, then scooped.

"Whoa." A grin spread over his face. "Lookout windows."

"Exactly."

He crouched forward to study the battlements. "That gives me a great idea. You think I could make arrow slits on these battlements?"

"I don't know if you could carve out something so skinny," I admitted. "But you could try drawing them on with the knife and see if that works."

It did, although the detail was too fine to be easily noticeable. Still, Levi seemed proud to have attempted it.

"We forgot the door," he said, frowning. "I could try my hand at a really shitty drawbridge?"

"This is easier." I held the knife in front of the center of the wall and carved out an arch. "Here's the doorway. Now I'll just do a second one inside it." Once they were both carved out, I smoothed down the door to make it flat.

"Here, I collected these." Levi dropped small shell fragments in front of me. "Maybe you could stick these in the arch so it stands out?"

"Perfect." I grinned at him. "See? You've totally got the hang of this!"

"I'm getting there," he said. "Super slowly."

"Seriously, don't sweat it too much. It's just for fun."

"Don't you want to beat Lucy?" he asked with a grin.

I laughed. "Okay, so maybe I am in it to win it. But you're

already leagues ahead of the partner I had last year, so I'm not too worried."

"Who did you partner with before?"

"Just whoever else needs a partner. There's no shortage of sand-castle enthusiasts in town. Note that I said *enthusiasts*, though."

He blinked. "No one at your level?"

"Nope."

"That actually makes me feel a little better about our chances of winning this," he said. "If I get another practice in, maybe I'll go pro."

"And discover your lifelong dream of building sandcastles for a living?"

"Hey, don't knock it. Everyone needs a passion." He waggled his eyebrows.

"Don't get too cocky, buddy," I teased. "Next, I'm going to show you how to do a staircase."

He burst into nervous laughter. "You're kidding, right?" Catching the look on my face, he said in a low, serious voice, "Okay, you're not kidding."

"The night's not over yet, Levi Keller," I said.

By the time we mastered the art of winding a staircase around the outside of a tower, we were working in unison. Words had given way to perfect bodily synchrony. He knew what tool I wanted without my having to ask for it, and I evened out his trouble spots before he could get frustrated.

By the end of the lesson we had lapsed into complete silence. Exhausted, we lay back on the sand and watched the coral-strewn sun deepen into tangerine. I turned to glance at Levi. His eyelashes were tipped in gold, face sun-speckled and bronzed. He sensed my eyes on him and tilted his head, lips curving into a sensual, lazy smile.

I gave in to temptation and leaned forward, pressing a soft kiss to the corner of his mouth. Feeling a little playful, I nipped at the fullness of his lower lip. He leaned into the kiss, hands tangling in my hair, and pulled me onto his chest. He deepened the kiss, sliding his hands to my hips.

Warmth settled in my soul and I wanted it to stay there forever. By the time the stars came, I had realized one very crucial thing: Levi was my shooting star. Blistering and bright and riveting, he split the sky into two things. A before and an after.

In the course of our silent camaraderie, I'd wound up with my legs splayed at a right angle to his body, my head resting on his chest. One of his hands played with my hair. I reveled in the gentle massage.

"The residency will be over soon," he said, and I could hear the truth of the statement coming deep from his chest, right where the heart lived.

"I wish you didn't have to go so soon." My admission was quiet and I was glad he couldn't see me. I felt his fingers still in my hair. He didn't say anything, and I wasn't sure if I was grateful for that or not.

"Maybe I don't have to," he said, eyes closed, but the ghost of a smile on his lips. "I'm glad we became friends."

"Me too." I curled up at his side.

"What about you?" he asked. "What are your plans after this summer?"

"I hadn't really thought about it, honestly. I'm happy with what I'm doing. In the way, way future, I'd like to buy Busy's. But for right now, maybe just get the shop's website up and running. Someone asked about online orders. I think maybe that's something I'd like to talk to Tom about. I love making people happy with food. The sweetness of a slice of cake has the ability to turn a bad day around. There's a lot of memories in food, you know."

"That would be really cool," Levi said. "You'd be a small business owner."

I smiled faintly. "Yeah." I pulled away from him and drew my knees to my chin, staring out at the serene water.

"What just happened?"

I half turned, resting my chin on my shoulder. "What do you mean?"

"You went away from me for a second there." He followed my lead and propped himself up on his elbows.

"I guess it's just weird to think about you leaving. About doing all these things without you here. It feels like you've always been in Oar's Rest. Almost since we first met, you've never felt like a stranger. There's already been so many changes this summer that I hate to think of another one." I shook my head. "Please don't be creeped out."

"I'm not," said Levi. He wrapped an arm around me and kissed my temple. He held his nose there a moment longer before drawing back. "The truth is, I don't want to leave here. My gut's saying—" He broke off. "I feel like this place—you—is the right place for me. Does that sound crazy?" His voice was so soft I had to strain my ears to hear him.

"Not at all," I murmured, reaching to run my thumb across his exposed wrist. I pressed a kiss to his palm and sighed. I understood more than he knew. Since the beginning of the summer, I'd felt like I was walking on shifting sand. First with graduation, then Penny, then Elodie.

With Levi, there were no games. No second-guessing. No strings. It was easy in a way none of my relationships had ever been. Elodie had always been afraid to embrace the idea of us, always looking over her shoulder. Chad had always been more Penny's than mine, even if it sometimes felt the opposite. And Penny, well, I didn't want to think about Penny.

All I wanted right then was to be just Levi and me. No one else.

Levi flicked some sand from between his fingers. "What will happen to us?"

I startled. The terms of my relationship always seemed to be decided for me. For the first time, someone was looking to *me* to set the pace. "Um, what would you want to happen? Would you want more than a summer romance?"

"Yes," he said, without the slightest hesitation.

I warmed all over. "How would that work? With you, wherever you end up, and me here?"

"Maine isn't that far from New York. Or Rhode Island, depending on if I get into RISD or not. Being on the waitlist was making me nervous, so I called to follow up. I actually have a good chance of getting in."

I squeezed his hand. "Oh my gosh, that's amazing." I could be happy for him and bummed for me at the same time. "So a long-distance relationship?"

"Would you be into that?" he asked.

I didn't even have to think about it. I didn't want a part-time relationship after being able to see Levi every day, holding his hand whenever I wanted to. I didn't want a relationship with a screen. Suddenly, I could see why a clean break seemed like the right choice for Elodie.

"We should have talked about this before," I said softly. "Whether this was just a—"

"Please don't say a fling." He made a face. "That sounds so immature. Kleenex-y. Like use it once and toss it."

I hesitated. I wanted to say yes because it would be easy. I wanted my time with him to stretch for as long as it could. But it would only be easy for right now. Long-distance wasn't right for me, even if it worked for other people. I wanted someone here, someone who would be mine. Someone who I could belong to and wake up next to.

"Remember what you said about different paths leading to the same place? Don't tell me that only applied to me," he said.

"I can take my own advice." I couldn't. Every word felt like sticky taffy in my mouth. But I had to see this through, didn't I? I had to try. I couldn't be like Elodie, like Penny. Snipping people out. I *wouldn't* be like them.

"So is that a . . ."

"Yes. It's a yes," I said. "I don't know where this thing between us will go, but I want to find out."

"Me too." He leaned down to graze his lips across the knob of my shoulder.

I shivered at the cool sensation that tickled its way up my neck and down my arm. "That tickles." When he started to move away, I quickly added, "But don't stop."

"Your wish is my command."

"Anything?" I asked mischievously.

Levi moved to my neck, planting soft, open-mouthed kisses behind my ear. "Hmm?"

I cupped his jaw, stopping him. "Have you been in the ocean yet?"

"Babe?" Levi's eyes were wide, luminous. "What are you—"

I threw my hair over one shoulder and reached back to pull the strings of my sundress, sending the yellow paisley print to the sand, revealing the bikini underneath. "Come on," I said, already moving. My feet kicked up sand, generating a blizzard. The sand changed as I got closer to the shore. Dry to wet. Loose to dense. "Follow me!"

I ran into the water, letting the sea tug me out into its cold embrace. Salt water invaded my senses, crashing against my body. I turned, kicking my feet in the water. Levi stood as if rooted to the spot. I kept my eyes steady, silently willing him to join me.

Behind him, the sand looked taupe. The town, plunged into blue-black, windows and doors glowing with streetlight. The sea itself appeared like black glass and my arms skimmed the surface as I turned left, then right, creating small waves. The only sound was the soft whispering of the sea and the sand. If I tried to focus on the whispers, tried to make sense of them, I could have sworn I heard *our* names. Oar's Rest could be seductive like that, stealing away slivers of us and occasionally returning the favor with tricks of the wind.

My lips parted. I waited for him to make his move.

He was already wearing swim trunks for his sandcastle crash course. All he had to do was yank the shirt over his head and walk to the water. He did so, keeping his eyes steadily on me.

My uncertainty drifted away, replaced by want and need. The moment felt charged with a sensual undercurrent. Feet treaded water, hands extended in front of me, reaching for the boy I liked, for the town I loved, for the moon I would never reach.

His fingertips touched mine. "Hi," he said, and I was lost.

I kissed him and the whole world fell away. It felt like the sea was just for us, lapping at our backs, sending cool shivers down our spines when the night breeze touched us.

His mouth was hot, and he kissed me back with the kind of desperation that mirrored my own. Levi's lips clung to mine, kissing the seam of my mouth, coaxing entry with his tongue. He tasted rich and velvety, like the black coffee he drank, and his skin was salt-stroked.

"Levi," I whispered against his lips. His name was a benediction. A curse.

"Babe." His voice had lowered several octaves, guttural to my ear.

I felt his hands on my waist and tingles went through me, the happy, inexplicable kind that I hadn't felt since Elodie. I laid my forehead against the curve of his shoulder. "I wasn't sure you'd join me," I said, my lips grazing his warm skin. I pressed a kiss against the freckle on his collarbone, and I felt his body shiver.

"I wasn't sure I would, either," he admitted.

"What changed your mind?"

"You did."

My legs relaxed, sliding down his hips, caressing his legs, and finally began to tread water again. Beyond us, the town crowned against the beach.

"We should head back," I said.

Levi took a shaky breath. "Yes."

We dripped our way back to the town, to the place where sand turned to concrete. Under the yellow glow of the streetlights, we couldn't look at each other. I was a little taken aback by the ferocity of our ocean kiss, the hot and cold of our mouths melding together. I could still feel his mouth against mine, the seamless rhythm we'd both locked into like we'd been kissing for years. A shiver went through me. I was eager to resume where we'd left off, my body throbbing for him in every muscle, in every heartbeat—I hoped he felt the same way.

"You're soaked," said Levi, running a hand over my hair. "Do you want to come over and dry off?" His words were spoken quickly, in a low whisper, as if there was anyone outside to hear us.

Everyone was tucked away in their cozy houses. I could see the shifting colors of the television glinting against open windows, could hear the hushed rumble of dissonant voices and music.

"Nah, I'm fine. It'll dry on the bike ride up." I reached back to gather my hair in a low ponytail and squeezed my hair at the base of my neck, feeling the cool water drench the back of my dress.

"Well, at least let me cook us some dinner. We haven't eaten."

His eyes glowed soft and fey in the lamplight. I looked at him from under lowered lashes, the clumpy, wet spikes obscuring most of my vision. "Okay," I agreed. I resisted the shiver that went over my shoulders. I wondered—hoped—that he wanted to pick up where we left off.

My hair was already starting to dry. I scrunched it in my palm, feeling the saltwater stiffness. But I trailed after him all the same, the only noise in the thick blanket of night coming from the steady glide of my bike wheels.

His porch light was our beacon, one of the few on the street.

"It's always so dark here," Levi muttered. I heard the click of his

230

key in the lock and the sharp finality of the lock giving way. He pushed the door open.

I stepped through the doorway, the hairs on my arms prickling. It was cooler inside.

Absently, I said, "During the Revolutionary War, the people of Oar's Rest had a strict curfew in place. These were the days when they were afraid of marauders and soldiers coming across the sea. When the sun set, they would turn off all their lights—the lighthouse hadn't been built then—and the whole town would be plunged into darkness."

"And it's still so dark after all this time," he said. "Maybe the town never forgot the memory."

I smiled, sweeping my eyes over the house. "Memories do tend to linger here."

The lights flicked on and a second later, the door closed behind us. "Make yourself at home," he said. "I'll grab some towels."

Before I could assure him that I was already well on my way to dry, he disappeared up the stairs. I was too wired to sit, so I walked around the living room instead.

The coffee table books I'd laid out for his arrival had been stacked to one side, replaced with pencils, sheets of paper, and a thin layer of dust. I ran my finger over his coffee table, creating a large heart. It was more of an absent doodle than a confession, but the thought struck me that he might not see it that way. Quickly, I used my forearm to wipe the heart away, leaving a clean, rectangular splotch in its place.

My hand brushed a familiar notebook. Tan, nondescript cover, smudged with charcoal pencil. The moment hung suspended in front of me. I was still, eyeing it like a predator. Levi's sketchbook. Right in front of me.

There was no sound of footsteps, no voice to alert me of his impending arrival. I sucked in a breath and sat down. I knew it was wrong, knew it was a betrayal to violate his privacy, but it was too late—I was already reaching for it. Curiosity had me in its thrall as I remembered the secrecy with which he'd sidestepped Elodie's nosiness a few weeks ago. She'd wanted to poke into his sketches, but he'd said whatever he'd been working on wasn't ready to share. Maybe now it was.

The first few pages were of buildings and churches, probably places he'd been inspired by during his travels. A ton of faces, some landscapes, even the odd floral arrangement or two. Then the sketches began to change. The pencil more ferocious, the color rich and dark and smudged with fingerprints. The gray stains had transferred to the back of the preceding page.

One face became more common, standing out from the sea of eyes and noses and lips. A girl with long hair down to mid-back, diamond-bright eyes standing out like moons, and rounded, impish eyebrows. She wasn't smiling but she still looked back *smilingly* at me, a secret in her eyes and on her lips. I traced my finger over her cheekbones, recognizing myself.

My mouth turned dry; I couldn't look away.

Levi still wasn't back. I continued flipping pages. My face made an appearance every so often, in different poses, but with the same look on her beautiful face. Like she and the artist shared a secret.

My stomach squirmed. I closed the book.

"I've got the towels!" he called out.

I jerked back to reality. It felt like so much longer, but it couldn't have been more than a minute. Guiltily, I shot to my feet.

Whatever might have happened between us in the future now seemed out of the question. Everything was ripped and shredded. How would I be okay with a long-distance relationship? It wouldn't be any better than the secrecy of my relationship with Elodie. It would still be sporadic, relying on stolen moments and long treks. I couldn't put myself through that again. I hadn't been thinking; I'd just gotten caught up in the moment. If I felt more for him than I did for El, then I didn't even want to imagine the carnage left behind when my heart broke all over again. Did I want to risk hooking up with Levi when our future was still uncharted? I was out of my depth—I couldn't navigate my love life by myself. If Penny were here, she would know what the right call was. She'd put those Slytherin smarts to use and come up with a plan that didn't Avada everything.

Levi entered the living room—and bless his soul, there was no indication that he suspected me of invading his privacy, which only made me feel worse—and handed me a towel.

In silence, I dabbed my arms, neck, and legs. "Thanks." I handed it back to him.

"So can I offer you anything before I start dinner? I can brew some cof—"

"No," I said quickly.

"Oh. Right." His lips tugged upward. "Stupid. I should have known after working in a coffee shop, coffee would be the last thing you'd want to drink."

"I love coffee." I shot him a nervous smile. "But it is pretty late."

Levi stared. Under his scrutiny, guilty heat crept over me.

233

"You just got here," he said. "I thought you were staying for dinner."

I could see him trying to work out what had changed since he'd gone upstairs. His lips parted, but before he could say anything, before I could be convinced to stay, I blurted out, "*Okaybettergobye!*"

"What?"

I took a deep breath. "I have to go. I'll take a rain check on dinner. Thanks." I wasn't proud of fleeing but I couldn't stay, either.

"Babe, wait."

He caught up to me outside his front door. Levi stood in the doorway, leaning against the doorjamb with a crinkled expression of worry on his forehead. "Is it something I—" He paused, coughed delicately. "Is everything okay?"

I stared at his face, twinges of electricity still pulsing through me. The long lines of his jaw led to a squared chin and a tapered neck. The muscles in his neck were taut.

"Will you text me when you get home?" Levi asked, still not looking happy at the idea of my leaving.

Touched at his concern, I nodded. "Yeah. I'll let you know I got there okay." I swung one leg over the bicycle and adjusted myself on the seat, wincing at the hot leather.

"Good night, Levi!" I called over my shoulder as I pedaled away. More than anything, I wanted to turn around and go back to him, dive into his arms, and kiss him again. I wanted to assure him he hadn't done anything wrong, that everything was still okay. I wanted to lead him upstairs and close the bedroom door. But I didn't do any of those things. It was usually me getting left behind, but this time, I was the one doing the leaving.

fourteen

Sleep didn't come easy after I left Levi's place. Too on edge to stay still, I'd paced in my kitchen until realizing how unproductive that was. Then I'd swapped walking for baking, and my stomach had thanked me for it. But even that didn't help me go to bed. All I could see stretching in front of me were the next four years he'd be at college. The times he'd be too busy studying, or hanging out with his dorm friends, or the moment he realized long-distance just wasn't cutting it. Being without him.

I'd done this song and dance with Elodie already. I didn't want a repeat. I didn't want to pull a Band-Aid off slow. I'd rather let the hurt in all at once instead of little by little, torturing myself over the months, the years.

I knew what Lucy would tell me. I'd say *What if we break up? What if it ends in heartbreak?* And she'd say *What if it doesn't?* She'd tell me to go after what I wanted, even if it meant letting someone in. Letting them have the power to hurt me just by being them. Like Mom. Like El.

Which was why, the next day, when I woke up after a restless night's sleep, I decided not to tell her. She was coming over to get ready for the Clamshell Queen pageant. I wouldn't be entering this year—I didn't have a chance without Mrs. Wang and her sewing machine to help me with a dress. My heart wasn't in it, anyway. The years I'd competed had been because Penny signed us up. It wasn't really my thing.

I didn't mind not being part of it, though. It was one thing to compete *with* Penny, and another to compete against her. So I'd taken Lucy up on her offer to get ready, much to her delight. She and her mom were coming up to my lighthouse for a photo shoot, too, while her dad was painting her clamshell backdrop in their garage. I told them to come for lunch, so at noon, I started getting everything together. My bamboo cutting board was the bed for thin slices of a ripe Roma tomato, wedges of avocado, onion, different kinds of cheese, and crusty bread.

I hummed while I pulled three glasses from a shelf. I examined the rims to make sure there were no finger smudges; satisfied that the glasses were clean, I turned my attention to my hair. I was expecting the Bishops for lunch in a few minutes, and the day was so warm that my hair already felt a little damp. I pulled the claw clip free, wincing when the prongs snagged on my hair. I flipped my head so my blonde hair pointed at the floor, then began ruffling it at the scalp to fluff up the volume.

"Babe?" a male voice called out.

Levi? A grin spread over my face as I whipped my head back up. "It's open!" I shouted in the direction of the door, knowing it would carry. On the exposed beam next to the counter I'd nailed a thrift-store mirror. The filigree oval mirror had reminded me of the wicked queen's magic mirror from *Snow White*, and at just under five dollars, I would have been *dopey* not to buy it.

Some of the freckles on my face were more prominent from the sun, and the blonde streaks looked extra bleached. My cheeks were pink from my blush stick, but my upper lip looked a little sweaty. Frowning at my reflection, I used a clean kitchen towel to dab above my mouth.

"Hey."

I turned, smile at the ready. My stomach sank like a stone. "Chad?" I asked in disbelief. "What are you doing here?"

Chad's eyes volleyed around my kitchen as he shoved his hands into the pockets of his baggy shorts. He glanced at the six slices of rustic country bread. "Expecting company?"

"Yeah." I rocked on my heels, playing with my fingers. "I'm expecting Lucy and her mom for lunch. She's getting ready for the Clamshell Queen pageant here."

He laughed, but it sounded nervous. "Penny wants me to escort her there later. So, um, I guess I'll see you there."

"Guess you will."

He didn't take the hint. "Things seemed weird the other night. Between you and me," he said.

The beach.

"When you were on a date with Penny?" My lips pursed.

Before I knew what was happening, he had crossed the kitchen and was in front of me. I wasn't expecting the hug or the muffled "God, wasn't that awkward" in the crook of my neck.

It was easy to hold still in his embrace, but then I stiffened and placed my hands on his waist, pushing him back. "I can't do this right now, Chad. Why are you *here?*"

"I told you." There was an undercurrent of frustration in his voice. "When I saw you on the beach, you were waiting for—" He broke off, frowning like he couldn't remember the name. That was because I hadn't given it to him.

"Levi," I supplied.

"Levi?" Chad stared at me. "Penny's mentor?" His eyes searched my face.

I frowned. Technically, I'd known him before she had. "Yeah," I said, "*my* friend Levi. I wasn't trying to hide it."

Okay, so I sort of had been. But at the same time, I wasn't trying to keep my relationship with him a secret. Everything we did, we did in public, not squirreled away in stolen moments. Unlike Chad and Elodie, I would *never* hide what I felt for Levi. I'd never sneak around with him, using my lighthouse as cover. A touch of anger ignited in my chest as I remembered the shifty way Chad had snuck up here last time.

"Does Penny know you're here?" I asked, knowing I'd hit home when he flinched.

"I care about her." He paused, then, hesitantly: "I care about y—"

"Don't," I said savagely, interrupting his sentence. "*Don't*. If you cared about me, you wouldn't have gone along with her icing me out. When I run into her on the street, she stares past me like I'm not even there. Things I used to be invited to?" I laughed bitterly. "I'm persona non grata around here these days because of her."

Best friends weren't supposed to be like paper kites in the wind. They were supposed to be people who wouldn't float away, who would always be there.

His sigh was loud, heavy. It took up too much space in my small kitchen. "I thought I was making headway with her . . . and then when I saw you by yourself at the beach, I thought I'd try my luck. It just made things worse. I didn't know she'd already told you about needing to take a break from each other." Chad's smile was sad. "Weird how I'm her boyfriend but you're always the first one to know everything."

"Weird how you think that's some kind of honor," I said with a snort. "So you snuck up here again to do what, exactly? Tell me to be patient? Tell me you're"—I air-quoted—"'*working on it?*'"

"I love you." Chad shuffled his feet. "I don't want to lose you." Clarifying, he added, "Or her."

I flattened my hands against my stomach and looked away. "Please don't say that."

His breath was loud in my small kitchen. "Why not?"

My stomach clenched. "Because I think Penny had the right idea when she broke up with me."

He looked stunned. It must have been the last thing he'd expected me to say, after everything we'd been through together. "W-what does that mean?"

"We've done everything together all our lives, and the one thing that should have been just you two . . . You never had a chance to figure out what you were like as a couple, or as people, because in a way, we never really grew up. We stayed the same. And it can't be like that anymore—it shouldn't be."

And then, because I was afraid my voice had sounded hesitant and unsure, I repeated, more firmly, "She may have said it for the wrong reasons, Chad, but Penny was right. About all of it. Whatever was good about us, we're choking it to death. Our roots are too tangled. We need to have space to breathe." Relief came over me as I realized I had finally said what I had struggled with articulating for so long.

His forehead scrunched as he took it all in. "You actually agree with Penny? But she just did that to hurt you."

I shook my head. "I don't think she did. She can be mean, but she's not cruel."

"So what changed? Why do you agree with her now?"

"Just . . . space. Distance from the whole situation."

Chad's expression cleared. "You love him, don't you?"

He meant Levi. I didn't pretend to misunderstand. "I barely *know* him!" I exclaimed.

"You want to, though. On the beach, when you were on a picnic with him . . ." Chad swallowed. "You looked at him the way you used to look at Elodie when you didn't think anyone was watching."

The kitchen felt too small to keep looking at him, so I turned around. I knew it was childish but I didn't care. My world felt small and suffocating and for the first time, I wondered what it would be like to just leave. Not tell anyone where I was going and vanish. Do what Levi did—pick a place with a pretty name and reinvent myself, become someone new, someone without a past.

"Hey." Chad moved behind me, hugging my waist for a brief moment before pulling away. "Don't cry."

"I'm not." I turned around and laughed, partly from embarrassment, and partly because my eyes *were* wet.

"Listen," said Chad, rubbing the side of his nose in an awkward gesture that I'd learned to associate with his discomfort. "If you like this guy . . ."

I swiped at my eyes. "Not sure I'm in the place to start swapping relationship advice with my best friend's boyfriend," I said, trying to make a joke.

He ducked his head, running his hand through his hair. "I was always your friend before I was anything else," he said. "I'd . . . I'd like to be that again. If you'd let me."

My breath was deep, steadying. "I'd like that."

He looked up at me, the barest glimmer of a smile on his face. "All right." He glanced away and then back at me. "I should go. You have people coming." He retraced his steps to the front door.

He was halfway out when I blurted out, "Wait. Chad."

He stopped.

"You never told me why you came here in the first place."

"I wanted to tell you I was sorry," he said.

"You've already apologized."

"For fucking everything up, sure. But not to *you*, for what I did. I shouldn't have kissed you, Babe. Maybe there's always been a little of what-could-have-been between you and me." He paused. "I love you, but I'm *in* love with Penny."

I nodded. I knew that. No matter how close Penny drew me into their relationship, I'd always known I didn't want to get between them. "Chad . . . I know I said we weren't really at the swapping advice phase, but can I give you some anyway?"

"Sure."

"I know you love Penny, but if you're just with her because, I don't know, you're scared to be alone? You shouldn't be."

His grin turned crooked. "You can't just tell someone how to feel."

241

"Right. Sorry. I didn't mean to do that." I shook my head. "You can totally be scared. But you shouldn't let it hold you back from doing what's right for you. She broke up with you and didn't even tell you why."

"What are you getting at?"

"Think about it. What's changed? What's less same-y now?"

He didn't have an answer.

"She's scared to be the same, and you're scared to be different," I said. "Shouldn't that be sort of a concern?"

"I don't know, a little?" He shuffled his feet. "But it's about to be the end of everything, Babe. It's fucking terrifying. We're legally adults, but I don't feel like one. Not in any of the ways that matter."

I wrapped my arms around myself. We should have talked about this weeks ago. I should have told him I was scared, too.

"I'm turning nineteen in fall and I still have Spider-Man bedsheets," he burst out. "I wake up some mornings so stunned that I'm supposed to be an adult, and I don't even feel like it. I feel so ripped off that high school is over, that Real Life is so long and everything else is so short," he said, and every part of me ached at the helplessness in his voice. "I don't want to be at the end of high school without my girlfriend. I know how this goes. Couples who go to college together usually break up. If she changed her mind, then . . . then maybe we're not one of those couples. Maybe we're the exception."

Or maybe they weren't. I'd tried to get him to think about things, but this was as far as I went. I was sad for him, but I drew the line at telling him he needed to talk with Penny about their future. I knew better now. No more getting involved in their relationship.

"You think it'll happen again," Chad said. "That she'll realize nothing's different and she'll make the same decision again."

"I'm just looking out for you. You can be an idiot sometimes, like when you go around kissing people who aren't her, but you deserved better than—than what she did."

"You're the only person who's said that." He glanced down, then back up at me with an unreadable expression on his face. "John, Cary, the other guys . . . they just think I'm lucky to get her back."

"What are you listening to them for? They cheated all the way through high school and still got Cs."

"Ha. Yeah." He ran a hand through his hair. "Seriously, though. I should go. She'll get pissed if she has to wait for me."

He wasn't wrong, but it still rankled. Penny always expected more from other people. She never stopped to think about what would happen if they had enough. Maybe because it had never happened before.

"Sure. Guess I'll see you down on the beach for the pageant." Whether or not he'd acknowledge me with Penny right there watching him was a different story. "Good luck with . . ." Would it be rude to say Penny? "Everything," I finally settled on.

"You too. I'm rooting for you and Summer Boy." Chad's smile was stronger than before. "See ya, B." With one last wave, he left.

Mrs. Bishop drove us down to the beach after we finished lunch and put all the finishing touches on Lucy's hair and makeup. Vendors had set up colorful booths along the beach, and a row of striped umbrellas provided shade for children and the elderly. The sizzle of hamburgers and hot dogs carried into the car, and the Dairy Bar's ice cream truck was doing brisk business in the parking lot.

The moment Lucy saw the crowd already gathered, she buried her face in her hands.

"Hey!" I yelped. "Your makeup!"

Lucy stopped herself just in time. "There's so many people," she whispered.

"You'll be just fine, honey," said Mrs. Bishop. She met her daughter's eyes in the rearview mirror. "You look beautiful."

Lucy hunched her shoulders and didn't reply.

I squeezed her knee. "You've got this."

Parking was impossible to find, so Mrs. Bishop dropped us off near the raised stage where the clamshells were being arranged in a row. Some of the pageant contestants were already up on the stage, posing for the cameras. As we got out of the car, Lucy froze.

"Honey?" Mrs. Bishop called from the front seat. "You okay? You can just get back in the car if you've changed your mind."

"No, I'm going to do it." Lucy pressed her lips together.

We waved as the car drove off, but once the car was out of sight, Lucy fidgeted with her curls. "Penny looks gorgeous," she said. "And Dad put my clamshell right next to hers. Ugh."

Penny was playing up her pale skin and black hair with a striking red silk *qipao*. There was a slit in the side of the Chinese-inspired dress that went all the way up to her hip, golden chains underneath for a hint of modesty. Gold fish scales were painted on the fabric from the waist down, reaching her pointy golden heels. Mrs. Wang had outdone herself this year.

But so had Mrs. Bishop. She'd designed Lucy's dress with chiffon, dying it in a gradient of black to turquoise to white. The bottom was flounced with fabric, made to resemble frothy waves. The pretty ombré dress flowed like water itself, and was offset with tiny white pearl beads stitched over the bodice. Lucy had even made herself a wire crown, stringing the same pearls onto them and forming a coral-like creation.

"Babe!"

Lucy and I both swung around in surprise to see Lorcan jogging over.

He shot me a wink. "Sorry, not you," he said, wrapping an arm around Lucy. "You look incredible," he said, kissing her temple. "What are you still doing down here?"

"I feel a little sick," said Lucy, pressing a hand to her stomach.

"Want me to get you some water?" I suggested, pointing to a cold-drink vendor who'd set up his cart nearby. I could see Chad farther away with Penny's parents, buying hot dogs. Mrs. Wang caught me looking and waved. After a slightly guilty glance at Penny, I waved back.

Lucy shook her head and nestled into Lorcan's chest. "No, thanks. I'm trying to remember I have more confidence than this," she said with a laugh. "I don't know how you did it last year, Babe."

"I thought Penny won last year." Lorcan glanced at me.

"Um, she won the previous year. Last year I won," I explained. "But she just looked so crushed that I told the judges I was going to share it with my best friend."

I hadn't minded sharing my win—hadn't she shared everything else in her life with me? Her mom, her boyfriend? She was generous. Maybe she'd been too generous for too long, though. That was when it had all turned sour.

"Oh, that was a nice thing to do," said Lorcan. But the way he said it made me think he didn't quite believe it. "Is Levi coming?"

Levi would be at the art center today. He'd offered to join me to cheer Lucy on, but I knew how motivated he was to work on his latest painting. "Nah, he had some work to do. He said he'd meet us later, though."

Lorcan nodded. "Cool."

Truthfully, I could do with the space. It hadn't come up again, but the long-distance thing . . . I wasn't sure it was going to work. Seeing Lucy and Lorcan together just cemented it further in my mind. They did everything together, whether it was sandcastle building or working at the fish fry. Those were things you couldn't do through a computer screen. Skype was no substitute for the things I wanted— for the things I'd never had.

As much as I'd loved Elodie, it had burned when I'd seen other couples holding hands at the beach, kissing in the park, slinging their arms around each other as they made their way home at night, slightly tipsy. I'd wanted all those dumb little inside jokes and embarrassing pet names that everyone would make fun of us for, and I had wanted those things with her. And all she wanted was for us to be kept a secret. We wanted different things, and I was always the one folding. I couldn't compromise again—my heart couldn't take it. Not with him.

I glanced up at the stage. Penny was looking right at me. There was a hint of something on her face, something that gave me pause. It looked so much like sorrow that my knees threatened to buckle.

She slowly descended the stage. The crowd parted for her, all eyes focused on the spectacle in red she made as she strode in a

246

straight line to where I stood. I didn't dare move. Our eyes were still locked together.

"Hey, I'm going to head up there," said Lucy, eyeing Penny's progression with apprehension. "C'mon, Lorc. Four's a crowd."

They exchanged nods with Penny as they left. I almost wanted to tell them not to go, because I had no idea what she wanted to say to me. Part of me didn't want to know.

"Did you tell Chad to break up with me?" was the first thing out of her mouth.

"What? No!"

Even though her nails had been painted a scarlet red, she gnawed on her thumbnail. "He sneaks off to see you, and comes back all . . . different. Then he says we need to talk about what's next for us, and I just *know* that you said something to him."

Oh my God, Chad. He always had the shittiest timing.

I swallowed. "He did come see me, but—"

"I knew it." She screwed up her face. "God, you can't stop, can you?" I hated that even her scowl was pretty.

"Penny, come on. That's not fair and you know it," I said. "You're painting me as the villain, and I *get it*, okay? You want to punish me. But enough is enough. I apologized to you so many times, I asked you what you needed from me to make this right, but it feels like you just want to blame me for *everything*."

Her face turned ashen. "Do you actually think you can turn Chad against me? Do you seriously think you're the victim?" Her eyes snapped fire. "Are you forgetting that you kissed my boyfriend?"

"You were already broken up! And I wasn't the one who initiated it!"

"Technicalities," she shot back. "Do you want to know the truth? It wasn't even the kiss that pissed me off, it was that *you* didn't tell me. What kind of best friend does that?" She kept going. "If you think that makes me such a terrible person, then maybe you should think about how you would feel if it was me and Levi. Seriously. Think about me for once."

I reeled back, tears stinging. Hurt surged through me. I couldn't believe she'd gone there. I'd always done what she asked me, even if I didn't want to. Her accusation was unfair, and she knew it. She damn well knew it. The way Penny was looking at me, not an ounce of remorse on her face, I wondered if she hated me that much. If there was no hope left for us.

The fanfare began, and the pageant contestants all began to take their places in front of their decked-out clamshells. For the longest moment, Penny didn't move. It was as if she was waiting for me to say something. Maybe it would have fueled her wrath if I tried to defend myself, if I unsheathed my own claws in return.

"Hey, Babe. You okay?" Lorcan appeared beside me. He eyed Penny, then said quietly, "I think they want you onstage."

Her eyes flicked between me and him, amusement registering on her face. "Unbelievable. You've already lined up a replacement for us," she said. There was an edge to her voice that hadn't been there before. "I guess that makes you Chad 2.0."

"I think you should go," Lorcan said firmly.

Penny sucked in her cheeks, then turned and stalked toward the stage. She looked less regal now, but her eyes still singed with fire. Even all the way up there, I could feel her contempt.

When she'd said we weren't friends anymore, I didn't think that meant we were enemies. I could only give half my attention to the pageant. I clapped and smiled at the right moments, but I couldn't unsee the look of sorrow on Penny's face. If I focused too hard on it, it morphed into her rage. Neither was an image I wanted to remember.

"Babe!" Lorcan clapped me on the shoulder. "She won!"

Dazed, I blearily tried to focus on Lucy. She'd stepped forward to accept her crown and was giggling and waving shyly at the crowd. I waited until she saw me before I flashed her a thumbs-up. I knew she could do it.

Unable to stop myself, I slid my gaze to Penny. She wasn't looking at Lucy with jealousy, as I'd thought. She was looking at me with the same look of sorrow she'd worn before. She didn't mask her expression before I saw it, though. Her eyes widened when she realized I'd spotted her. The veneer slipped over her face again, sneering and hard. She was back to being all sharp angles and cutting eyes. But it didn't matter, though, because I had seen. She still cared about me, whether she wanted to admit it or not.

I tore my eyes away as another cheer for Lucy went up. Tom and Ralph were front and center, encouraging the crowd to get louder. I joined in, clapping and whistling. By the time all the fanfare died down and Lucy posed for the newspaper photographer, confident and radiant, I scanned the beach for Penny. Whatever had happened with Chad, I needed her to know I would never willingly hurt her—not like she'd accused me of.

But none of the faces in the crowd were hers.

fifteen

For the next few days, Lucy wore her crown to work every day. The tips in our tip jar doubled.

"Hey, Babe. Busy day?"

I recognized that voice. Turning, smile in place, I prepared to answer, but then I caught sight of Elodie behind Levi. Looking at her instead of him, I nodded. "Lucy's becoming a bit of a celebrity. Ha. What's up?"

My eyes tried to read the expression on Elodie's face. She seemed uncomfortable in my presence but had mustered a smile that looked forced. A twang of guilt went through me.

He didn't know so many people in Oar's Rest, and he seemed to have hit it off with her since their first meeting at Busy's. And I knew that she was a huge fan of his. There was no reason they shouldn't be friends. Another reason I couldn't tell him about her. And after my friendship with Penny turned so rocky, I didn't really want to risk telling him there was yet another girl we both knew who I had history with.

Elodie renewed her smile my way, but I couldn't return it. My brain was in overdrive, drawing a conclusion about the fact they'd walked in together. A few days ago she'd been at the lighthouse saying she wanted me back, and now she was hanging all over Levi? Okay, so she wasn't exactly all over him, but they *were* standing awfully close. They made a beautiful couple. They looked like they belonged together, and I had the sudden, paranoid thought that she could be attracted to Levi.

My mouth went dry. *My* Levi. I tamped down the budding jealousy. Just because he and Elodie were friends didn't mean anything was taken away from me. I mean, it was totally possible they'd met along the way and just happened to both be coming to the same destination, but . . .

Elodie adjusted her hat. It was one of those ridiculous felt hats with a wide brim and a thick band of ribbon, the kind that people wore in high fashion magazines and not in real life. Her brown hair looked full and light, pointing to a professional blowout and not a wash-and-go like mine.

"Coffee," Levi said. "My usual, please."

"A caramel macchiato for me," Elodie put in, giving me the full force of her megawatt smile.

"I'll get that for you," I said, wiping my hands on my apron. "Here or to go?"

"Here," said Levi.

As Levi and Elodie made their way to his usual corner, I stifled the twist in my gut by using a clean, damp rag to give the table a vicious once-over. The heat evaporated the light sheen of water within seconds. I joined Lucy behind the counter.

"Please don't look at me like that," I said, pouring milk into a small pitcher before placing it under the machine's nozzle.

With grim determination, I jabbed another button on the machine to get a double shot streaming into the white cup. With my free hand, I started the steaming process. The nozzle that descended into the

251

pitcher began to whir, steaming the contents to a fluffy froth. Timing was everything in making a macchiato the right way.

"When did those two become friends?" asked Lucy.

I glanced up. Elodie said something to Levi that made him laugh. She never even had to try, never even had to demand attention. It just gravitated toward her like it was her birthright. In her bohemian top and high-waisted denim shorts, she looked like the picture of summer itself.

"They're both mentoring at the art center." I gave Lucy a wry smile before tipping the milk froth onto the top of the coffee. The trick was to steam the milk enough so that what I poured was all froth and not hot milk, which would dilute the espresso and move us into cappuccino territory.

"I'll take it over," she said.

"Thanks." I was grateful.

The door swung open again, bringing with it John Martin and some of his friends. "Hey, Elodie!" a few of them called out, surrounding the table.

As Elodie began the introductions, John stepped up to the counter. He swung his eyes over me with appreciation. "Looking good, Babe."

I rolled my eyes. He hadn't outgrown his high-school-dude broness. "Thanks. What can I get you?"

John passed along his friends' drink orders, and Lucy and I got to work.

While I popped on the covers, I caught snatches of their table's conversation. Two of the guys had bent over Levi's shoulders, pointing out something on an iPad. "And if we take this road, we can shave off ten minutes," Cary said.

"Where are you headed?" I asked, working free a take-out cup carrier from the stack with the tips of my nails.

"You know the Stephen King house in Bangor?" John fished out his wallet and handed me a twenty-dollar bill. "We're driving up to see it. My cousin from out of town is a big fan, so we're doing the nerdy tourist stuff."

"I figured you weren't the fanboy in the bunch," Lucy teased, handing John a small clump of napkins. "And here's your straws."

While I counted out John's change, I couldn't help looking back at the occupied table where Levi was laughing and joking with Elodie and her friends. "Will you all fit in the car?" I asked lightly, trying to affect an uninterested tone. But inside, I was trying not to seethe. Hadn't I offered to take Levi there when he told me he loved Stephen King?

"We're taking two cars. There's room if you two wanna come," said John.

"We're working until closing time," Lucy said regretfully, sighing. "I wish, though. Sounds like fun. Ordering any food for the road?"

"Nah, we'll grab some lunch in Bangor. It'll be cool." John shrugged. "Maybe another time, yeah?" He tilted his head toward the door. "Let's head out," he said to his friends.

As everyone ambled toward the exit, John smiled. "Thanks, Babe."

"No problem," I said, speaking to John even though my eyes were zeroed in on Levi. He'd gotten up with the others and was approaching the counter.

Elodie came up behind him, reaching for her purse, but Levi

waved her off. "Nah, I've got it," he said, shooting me a crooked smile as he put a five-dollar bill on the counter.

He was paying for her now?

Seething inside, I returned his change in unsmiling, stoic silence.

"Babe, please tell Levi he has to come with us," said Elodie in a wheedling tone. "Cary and John are making a whole day of it, and *this* guy refuses to come."

Words stuttered on my tongue. I couldn't move my suddenly dry lips. My eyes flicked to Levi. If he said yes, if he left with Elodie . . . I would crumple. Swift, merciless realization made me open my eyes to what was happening right in front of me. Something I couldn't do and that Levi *could*. Was this what a long-distance relationship would be like? One of us always being left out of things the other person enjoyed, and trying to fake being happy for them anyway?

I couldn't do this, I knew it in my bones. I wanted what Lucy and Lorcan had. I wanted a hand to hold, a face to cup, an ear to whisper into. I didn't want a relationship with someone who wasn't there in the way I needed him to be there. I didn't want to be jealous of all the people who could see and do things with him every day. Couples did it successfully every day, but it wasn't for me. If I didn't want Levi to leave with them now, how okay would I be with something like this happening all the time?

"They're getting in the car," said Elodie. She touched Levi's wrist. "We better hustle."

Levi shook his head, alternating his weight from foot to foot. "Thank Cary for inviting me, but honestly, I'm just swamped today."

Elodie pouted.

"Seriously!" Levi said with a laugh. "And, um, I have a friend who promised she'd take me."

Elodie put a hand on her hip. "Who else do you know here? Not Penny—she'd never be into something like this."

"Oh, um, it's Babe, actually," said Levi, glancing at me.

"Babe?" Elodie stared at me, saucerlike eyes stunned. "I didn't know you two were . . ."

Levi reached across the counter to take my hand. "Yeah, you know that girl I told you I was sort of seeing?" He shot me a shy look.

"Babe," said Elodie. Her exhale seemed to rattle her whole body. "Right. Yeah. I should have guessed." Her mouth worked itself into a wooden smile.

We all turned toward the door when the car ignitions started in the parking lot.

"I think they're leaving," said Lucy, pointing at the window.

Elodie swallowed. "Thanks for the coffee, Levi. I'll see you at the center." With one last, inscrutable look my way, she flew out the door toward her waiting friends.

Lucy, Levi, and I watched as two sedans made their way to the main road.

"You didn't have to do that," I said, even though I was secretly thrilled he did. "You would have had fun with them."

"I'd rather have fun with you," Levi said with a shrug. "And we can make plans to go to Bangor whenever." He surprised me by cupping my cheek in front of Lucy. "Honestly, it wouldn't matter that much to me even if we didn't go." His thumb idly caressed the bottom of my jaw. "I'm fine right here."

From the corner of my eye, I noticed Lucy quietly slipping away. I leaned forward so we could meet halfway across the counter, and pecked Levi's lips. "You're sweet," I murmured, gently butting his nose with mine.

"Sweet on you," he said, and it was so corny that I dissolved into giggles. But not before I kissed him soundly.

sixteen

The next morning, I woke up to an iMessage from Chad saying he'd broken up with Penny overnight. My fingers flew over the keyboard: *Why?????*

The response came immediately. *You were right.*

I didn't want to crow. I didn't feel victorious. Nothing about it felt good.

The sun scorched my back as I made the short jog to the pier, where the last stragglers of Penny's never-ending party were leaving. Their red, bleary eyes avoided meeting my face, although I got a couple of "Hey, Babe" mumbles and tired nods. Like a line of ants, they all trailed from Penny's houseboat.

I cringed at the heavy, musty smell of weed. "Penny?" I picked my way over a pile of clothes and flattened cans of beer. "You decent?"

I couldn't give up on my friendship with Penny, despite her anger and accusations at the pageant a few days ago. I would give it another try. It wasn't hard to guess why she'd erupted that day. Seeing me there with Lucy and Lorcan must have made her realize that I wasn't as alone as she thought I would be without her. This time, she was the one who didn't have me or Chad. I hoped that revelation would make her more open to talking things out with me.

The galley kitchen was speckled with red sauce, and the empty jar of Ragu and random pieces of spaghetti on the floor made me think someone had had a late-night craving for pasta.

"Penny?" I called out again, rapping on her bedroom door. No answer. I pressed my ear against the wood and listened, but there were no signs of life. I put my hand on the doorknob and gave it a firm turn. The door squeaked open, and I poked my head in, scanning the bed and the beanbags.

Vince lay naked on the bed with a fishing magazine open on his soft stomach. Next to him was Penny, shrugging her shoulders into a bloodred dressing gown.

"Morning," she whispered, keeping her voice low. She darted a glance at Vince and scuttled out of the bedroom, brushing me to the side and closing the door.

"You hooked up with him?" I said, my voice tight. What had she been thinking? Was she trying to lash out at Chad?

Penny's gaze was unfocused. "Why is that any of your business?"

"Just because you decided you're not my friend anymore doesn't mean I'm not yours."

She rubbed her forehead and looked at me. Not one of her hostile, dark stares, or one of her seeing-through-me looks. But like she was finally, really seeing me. "Do you want coffee?"

"No, thanks."

I watched in concern as she stumbled to kitchen cupboards, pulling them open at random until she found a cup. "I don't have anything clean," she muttered, more to herself than to me, and then, without warning, she reached up, the cup still clasped in her hand.

I didn't realize what she was planning to do until the ceramic met the wood floor and the fractured pieces skidded all around us. I saw the look of rapture on Penny's face, and the vague, incoherent thought flitted through my brain that she'd never looked quite as beautiful in her destruction.

Neither of us moved.

She made to bend, hand outstretched toward each itty-bitty piece.

"Don't, you'll cut yourself," I said.

She didn't listen.

I moved forward, delicately weaving around the broken cup. "Come on, get up." When she didn't move, I reached down, hooked my fingers under her armpit, and began to pull. It was easier than I thought it would be. Penny had always been slender, but this was different—her skin felt papery and she looked frail and tired in a way she hadn't looked when I'd first brought Levi here.

"Is everything okay?" I dropped my voice. "With Vince?"

"Of course," she said, slumping back down.

"Get up." When she made no move to comply, I dug my fingers even harder into her skin. "Get up," I insisted. "I'm getting you out of here."

"I need to sweep," she tried to say, but I'd already started leading her away.

"Forget about that." I helped her stumble onto the pier and when both her feet were on solid ground, they finally gave out.

I couldn't support her weight any longer and had no choice but to break her fall as gently as I could. "Penny? Penny? What are you on?" I peered into her eyes, but they didn't appear dilated. "Are you high right now?"

Her stare was blank.

I hauled her up again, almost falling over when her dead weight fell against me. "Come on, Penny. You're going to start walking. One foot in front of the other. There, that's it."

With my coaching, she managed to steady her legs and walk down the pier, her arms hugging her body. My arm was wrapped around her waist, making sure she stayed upright. Between the two of us, we managed to get her off the pier and into the soft, golden sands of the beach.

"Good. Feet hurt," she mumbled.

I spotted a mother with two little girls looking our way. Under the brim of her straw hat, the mother shot me a frown and held her hand out to the girls, saying something I couldn't hear at such a distance.

I realized that not only had Penny's robe flapped open again, giving everyone a free show, but in my haste to get out of there, I'd forgotten to put shoes on her feet. "Damn it," I swore, closing my eyes in frustration. Easing us both down to the sand, I pulled the robe closed.

When I opened them again, she still hadn't closed her robe. Hickeys blotched her torso, bruised and already purpling. Vince. Ugh.

"Babe?"

I turned around, using my hand to shield my eyes from the glare of the sun. "Lorcan?"

He jogged over to us, his golden retriever puppy, Merlin, and his cavoodle, Lulu, dashing ahead of him. They were so well trained he never had them on a leash, and they skidded up to me, yipping in recognition.

"What's wrong with her?" Lorcan said in a whisper, noticing Penny's drowsy expression and bare feet. To his credit, he didn't gape at the scene we made.

I told him, as quickly and discreetly as I could manage.

"She hooked up with Vince?" Lorcan widened his eyes. "I never got good vibes from that guy."

"I think it's because Chad broke up with her," I said in a small voice.

At the sound of his name, Penny murmured something under her breath and moved closer to me. I pulled her onto my lap, letting her head drape on my left thigh. Missing my usual scratches and pets, Merlin gently butted Penny's leg in affront before burrowing his way underneath her to head for Lorcan.

Lorcan's face darkened. "I know Vince. What did he give her?" He bent forward and snapped his fingers under Penny's nose. "Come on, wake up. Yes, that's it." The moment her eyes fluttered open, he used his finger to peel back her eyelashes so her eyelid stayed open. I vaguely remembered he'd taken junior EMT classes in high school.

"Lor—" Penny scrunched her eyes, forcing him to let go long enough for her to blink. "What are you doing?"

"I don't think she's that high. Just drunk. She just looks exhausted. When's the last time she slept?" he asked, directing the question at me.

Flummoxed, I shook my head. "I don't know."

"The party don't start till I walk in," Penny mumbled.

I gave her shoulder a little shake. "Penny? Did you sleep at all last night?"

She didn't reply.

"Were you up all night? Partying?"

She nodded.

"How long did the party last?" Lorcan looked grim. "Did you take anything else?"

"Um, just since last night, I think? It's just booze and *this* much weed, I swear. I'm fine." Penny tried to roll off my leg.

I let her, but made sure she didn't face-plant into the sand. With effort, I helped her sit upright. Her expression still looked glazed, but her voice seemed steadier, and she didn't wobble when my arms fell away from her.

Sitting there in the sand, she reminded me of a child.

"It's exhaustion," Lorcan determined. "She's dehydrated, sleep-deprived, and is probably going to regret this tomorrow."

"Are you sure she's okay?" I whispered, terrified she could have alcohol poisoning.

"She'll be fine," said Lorcan. "But let's take her home?" At my start, he clarified, "Her parents' house, I mean."

"No shoes!" Penny whined.

"I'll carry her." Without waiting for an answer, Lorcan leaned forward, clinically grabbing whatever parts of her were still covered by the flapping kimono and pulling her into his arms.

"Lulu, Merlin, time to go!" I called out, clapping my hands. With Lorcan in the lead, a limp Penny cradled against his chest, the three of us followed behind him.

I knew the Wangs hid their spare key in the vase next to the front door. When I overturned it, the key fell into my palm. Her parents were still asleep, so I woke up her mom while Lorcan carried Penny into her old bedroom. He moved a wastepaper basket by her bedside along with a glass of water. Mrs. Wang hurried in, her face ashen.

Allowing myself a gesture of affection before we left, I brushed my palm over Penny's forehead. I could have sworn she leaned into my touch for a moment.

"We should get him out of her houseboat," said Lorcan as we slipped out the front door again.

I dropped the key back into the vase.

In the pocket of my black romper dress, I found a couple of sticky, warm peppermint candies. I offered Lorcan one, which he took. I unwrapped the other and popped it in my mouth, sucking hard. My tongue was dry and sour, and my heart was still beating fast. I glanced up at Penny's bedroom window as I crinkled the wrapper in my fist and shoved it back into my pocket.

Outside, the dogs were waiting for us. Lulu's face was cocked to the side as she waited for us to join them on the sidewalk. Her tail slapped against the ground. Merlin brushed against me, his nose butting against the back of my calves.

"Thanks for being here, Lorcan," I said, falling into step beside him. "I wouldn't have been able to get her here without you."

He cast me a sidelong glance. "Don't be mad at her, but Lucy told me a little bit of what's going on with you three."

"She did?" There was no judgment in his voice, but I still felt the finger of blame.

He nodded. "I better go finish my run. These guys will go stir-crazy if I don't tire them out a little bit." He whistled to Merlin and Lulu before breaking into a jog, the two dogs yipping in unison before chasing after him.

I watched him go, a faint smile ghosting across my lips. Growing up, it had always been Chad and Penny who had my back. I thought now of Lucy's resilient optimism and Tom's grumpy affection, of Lorcan's true-blue steadiness and Levi's heart-stopping smile.

With that thought, I turned and headed back to Busy's.

Lucy was pissed when she heard me relate what had just happened. "I wish you guys had roughed him up a little bit," she said, surprising me with the anger in her voice. "I never liked Vince. He's mega skeevy. Plus it was super irresponsible of him to get her drunk and not even make sure she was okay. That's the least you do for someone you hook up with." She cleared her throat. "Hey, can you pass me the cake? The window table wants a couple slices."

Lorcan had already rounded up a few local fishermen to haul Vince out of Penny's houseboat. Their gnarled hands wore battle scars with pride; gashes and ancient scars where flesh had once been gouged by fishhooks; their arms muscled, faces unforgiving. They were the true Old Men of the Sea, strong as krakens, legendary as Cthulhu. Lorcan had called us and said that although Vince had created a scene and refused to go quietly, they'd dealt with him easily enough.

I handed Lucy the cake platter. "Being thrown naked onto the pier was punishment enough. Lorcan said if Vince didn't want to be arrested for public indecency, he'd better run as fast as he could to whatever gutter he crawled out of."

"He's pretty good at playing the knight in shining armor." Lucy laid the last piece of cake onto its side, easing it on the plate carefully so the mocha icing didn't smear and the layers of raspberry and chocolate chip could be seen.

I would have loved to use blueberries, but I hadn't had a chance to go berry picking at one of the local farms with everything else that had been vying for my attention lately.

"Is she still asleep?" Lucy asked. "Will she be okay?"

"She was knocked out when we left," I said. "And . . . I think she will be."

I had a feeling we all would be.

seventeen

I once saw a snake slithering up the road just outside of Busy's. It didn't move in a straight line, even though it would have been much faster. It wove left and right in a slow, hypnotizing dance, each zig followed by a zag. Predictable. It took its sweet time going where it wanted to go.

The weeks after the fish fry felt like that—languid and neverending. Tourists came, tourists left. Tom and Ralph continued to be fixtures, alternating between playing chess and arguing about how far they got with the girls in their youth.

Every time the stories were told, they grew in the telling. The girls had grown up and grown away and were now relegated to challenges for my friends to win. If Tom had kissed Elaine under the stars, then Ralph took her out in his granddad's boat. If Ralph got Annie's number, then Tom had been the one to kiss her in the back of the old movie theater. Their competition over days long past had been amusing at first, but quickly paled. They knocked it off after we pointed out that their nostalgia was just on the side of skeevy.

The boat on the beach grew more and more each day. With so many people from Oar's Rest pitching in, the bones of the boat were filled in with old planks from the pier and leftover wood from forgotten DIY projects. People contributed what they had—the boat was a patchwork of projects and lives. Then, using remnant silk from the craft store, someone made bloodred sails. Every day we saw the ripple of the sails from Busy's, heard the hammers and the jovial, muffled voices of the boat builders.

"There's got to be a story behind that," Levi said one day as we sprawled on the beach after a long sandcastle practice.

The blanket beneath us was hot from the sand and my legs stretched in front of me, looking impossibly lean and long. My stomach peeked out from my crop top, a glorious, creamy golden-tan.

"The boat?" I opened one bleary eye to look at it. Everyone had long since gone home, and it stood there, tall and proud, just a few yards away. I closed my eye again. "Mmm, yeah."

I rolled onto my side. "We do it every year. After the tourists leave, we have a huge bonfire on the beach, light it on fire, and drink the night away. It's sort of the town's giant *fuck you* to the people from the city who come down here and wear out their welcome."

"Definitely feeling the love," he said dryly.

"You don't count," I explained, smiling.

"What's a guy gotta do to count?"

"Buying a bike would be a good first step, I guess."

He didn't say anything, so I opened my eyes. He was staring blankly, apparently lost in thought, at the strip of my stomach exposed to the last lingering rays of the sun. An inch of tanned flesh, the hint of a hip bone.

"I wish . . ." He let his words trail off, sighing. He pulled his legs up and folded his arms across his knees.

My heart clenched. *I wish you didn't have to leave.*

Soon, I wouldn't see his face every day at Busy's. We wouldn't joke over the fact that he never varied his coffee order, we wouldn't exchange smiles over the heads of other customers. If I couldn't have my first wish, then I wished I could go back, tell him I didn't want a long-distance relationship. That the risk outweighed the reward. That I was no brave Gryffindor to barrel headfirst into things, nor an optimistic Hufflepuff who would try, try, try. I swallowed, waiting for him to speak.

He never finished his sentence, but I knew how it would go as well as if I'd said it myself: *I wish this summer could last forever.*

Finally, he wetted his lips, which were chapped from the wind and from too much kissing. "I wasn't supposed to fall in love with—with this place."

I was willing to bet that he wasn't the first summer boy to feel that way. My chest felt hollow. A thought pierced me, sharp and true: Had other people in Oar's Rest felt this way? And then a deep and profound sadness for all the other summer boys and summer girls who had left Oar's Rest and the people who loved them behind. I thought about all the people who came into Busy's, locals and tourists alike. Who knew what drew them here, and what would draw them away? Because, as I'd told Lucy at the start of summer, tourists always left.

The sun drooped, coating the sky with amber glow, tingeing the water gold and fiery. Levi's hair looked dipped in stardust. Impossible things suddenly seemed possible.

"What if you didn't have to leave?" I murmured. "What if you weren't a tourist anymore?"

"I kind of like the idea of being a townie." His lips quirked into a smile. "Rest my oars here for good."

"It sounds nice put like that."

He caught my eye. "Yeah, it does, doesn't it? I could paint, maybe go to college here, learn how to sail . . ."

My stomach happily squirmed. I wanted *everything* about the picture he was painting. If he could see a real future here, then we could just ax the whole long-distance plan. We could keep going just as we were. "Learn how to eat things with arms and legs."

"Hard pass."

I laughed at the horrified look on his face. "Oh, come on! You know things taste better when you cook them in the shell, right?"

"Fake news."

"Baby," I teased, throwing an arm around his shoulder. "But seriously, though. There's cool classes at Oar's Rest Tech, and if you wanted to paint, the art center usually has some highbrow artist in residence during the year to teach. Ralph could get you more info about it."

"Great minds," said Levi, pressing a kiss to my temple. "I've already spoken to him about it and he's getting back to me."

My insides thrilled. He'd done it on his own, without us even needing to talk about it. No one I knew had ever taken this kind of initiative in order to *stay*. Mouth dry, I managed to ask, "So . . . you're thinking about staying?"

"I think I'd have to be an idiot not to at least consider it. I'm more creative than I've been in a long time, everything about Oar's Rest is inspiring, and then there's . . ." He broke off, lowering his eyes to the curve of my neck. "And then there's you."

I could feel my cheeks heating up. "What about RISD?"

"Still trying to figure it all out. School starts in September. It's way too late to apply for any scholarships. I mean, if the money doesn't come together, RISD could still be a big nope."

It could also be a yes. If Levi was making plans for the future—our future—based on whether or not he got into his dream school, then he could just as easily unmake them. My hope faltered, squeezing my insides hard. Everything rested on the thin, flimsy edge of an envelope—acceptance or rejection. I squeezed my eyes shut.

"Hey, it's okay." He drew me into his arms, breathing into my hairline. "It's not the end of the world if it's a no. You have a college here, right?"

He knew we did. His tone was light, cheery. Meant to make me feel better, I knew. But even the safety of his arms didn't quell the unease that gripped my mind. His words should have been everything I wanted to hear, but they were wrong somehow, too. He shouldn't go to a local school that couldn't offer him the kind of program he deserved. He should have the best education available, and Oar's Rest Tech wasn't it.

I rested my cheek in the crook of his neck. He was sensitive there and went tense when I brushed my lips against his clavicle. "Your art is amazing," I whispered. "If you get in, you should go to RISD."

I felt rather than heard him exhale. "You're still up for a long-distance relationship, right?" he asked.

This was it, my chance to come clean. But taking it back was cruel, even if it was true, and I didn't want to let him go. Maybe throwing everything into the ring and doing something scary and potentially heartbreaking was the right call. Maybe everything was aligning this way to make me see that a long-distance relationship wasn't the end of a relationship, but just another path to get where I needed to go.

He was waiting for an answer. I swallowed. "I—I said I was, remember?"

"No, I remember. I just wanted to double-check."

"I'm not a multiple-choice quiz," I said with a smile that felt just a little bit wooden. Pulling away to look at the boat, I let my smile drop the moment he couldn't see me anymore. The truth was that he was right to second-guess me. I wished I had a life eraser that could sweep away the wrong answer and give him the right one this time.

He opened his mouth—maybe to talk about RISD, maybe to press me further—but I knew I couldn't let the conversation keep going. I didn't want to talk about plans that might or might not happen. I'd done that often enough with Elodie; I wasn't up for a round two.

Choosing to focus on a different plan instead, I asked, "Hey, do you still want to visit Stephen King's house? I have the day off tomorrow."

Levi shrugged, looking embarrassed. "You know, the main reason I said yes was so I could spend more time with you. I love his books but don't really want to gawk outside his house. I'm up for doing anything that you want to do."

I thought for a moment, then asked, "Would you like to go blueberry picking? They're in season right now and I'd love to use some in my baking." Judging from the grin that slipped over his face, he was into the idea.

"How far is it? I can drive us," he offered. "I've already exhausted all the places you circled for me."

I felt bad that I didn't feel guilty about distracting him. Maybe I had some of Penny's Slytherin wiles after all. "Not too far. We could stop at some pretty spots and you could sketch, if you wanted. I know a couple that weren't on your map."

"I'm in," he said, a smile spreading from cheek to cheek. "Can you meet me at the house at nine in the morning?"

"Absolutely," I said.

♥ ♥ ♥

I could have chosen one of the many blueberry stands that dotted Maine's highways, but I had a special destination in mind.

"Hey!" I called out, approaching Levi's house. He was waiting for me on the porch and raised a hand in greeting.

"What's that?" he asked as I got closer, eyes trained on the bright blue cooler I had in my hand. "Did you walk all the way down with that? You could have called me."

He'd noticed my lack of bike. "Got a ride from someone," I said. "Mind if I put this in the back?"

When he unlocked the car door for me, I leaned in and slid the cooler onto the floor. His sketchbook lay on the seat, a freshly sharpened charcoal pencil point sticking out to mark his place.

"Just some lunch," I explained, closing the door behind me.

His face lit up. "Yum. I thought we could just grab sandwiches somewhere, but your cooking sounds way better. What do you have for us?"

"Cobb salad, sans blue cheese because I didn't know how you felt about it, Mexican Coke, and pecan pie brownies."

He made a noise of appreciation and I grinned, thinking of the age-old adage that the way to a man's heart was through his stomach. Food was something my mom's boyfriends had always appreciated, because she'd taken it to heart, if her amazing Sunday dinners were anything to go by.

More interested in hanging out with my friends than playing happy families, I usually spent Friday night and all of Saturday with Penny. Mom probably intended for me to stay at one of my preppy friends' houses, where the mother and the father wore Ralph Lauren polos and kissed their kids good night, but instead, I spent those lost weekends at Penny's. Her parents were happy to let us use the kitchen under supervision, which was great for when the novelty of Penny's Easy-Bake Oven paled.

The drive to Nectar Creek Farm took about an hour, but we took a few stops along the way. This part of Maine wasn't lush and green, but I loved letting my head rest against the window and watching the stark, craggy coastline whiz by. The highway we took was rock-bound, water on one side of us, soaring granite cliff on the other. Every so often there'd be a pullout, and whenever we found one with available parking, Levi would scoot in.

Forty miles away from home, we took our third stop and Levi reached for the back seat, snagging his sketchbook. "Last one, I promise," he said as we got out of the car.

"I don't mind," I told him, watching as the awe on his face morphed into studious concentration as he flicked his dulling pencil point in long, sharp strokes across the paper.

I wasn't immune to Maine's beauty. Happy to let him have all the time he wanted, I wandered away, leaving him to lean against the wooden railing, sketching furiously. My feet tumbled over pebbles and sandy beach and grassy dunes until I came to the water. It was calm, unbroken by seagulls or children splashing. It pulled me in, seducing me with its endlessness. I stood there for what could have only been a few minutes, but it felt like much longer.

A young couple with a toddler stood at the water's edge, both parents pointing to the waves. In the distance, a foghorn bellowed.

"I get it now."

I started, my shoulders jerking forward when I heard Levi's unexpected voice next to me. "Get what?"

"Why you don't want Oar's Rest to become commercialized. No chain hotels or five-star restaurants. No real estate tycoons buying up land and spitting out parking garages and shopping centers." Levi stared across the water.

I shoved my hands into the pockets of my shorts. "Yeah." Eyeing him sideways, I asked, "Did you get your sketch?"

He exhaled roughly. "Yes. But I can't replicate the water and the sand." He stared at the sea and its vastness. "When I look out there . . . it's so haunting. I don't know how to explain it."

He didn't have to. I understood.

Levi looked up at the sky, his unneeded sunglasses tucked into the V of his neckline. "Even though the world is so gray right now, which you'd think would make sketching easy . . ." He laughed. "It somehow seems harder."

"You'll get it."

Levi's grin was blinding. "Thank you. It's sweet you're trying to make me feel better," he said, voice light and teasing. "But the way our eyes perceive color and depth and just . . . everything? It sometimes feels impossible to re-create, and maybe we're not supposed to. Maybe we're just supposed to enjoy it the way it is." He stared directly at me as he said the last sentence, and I felt heat creep down my neck.

"Do you want to stay?" I asked, breaking the intensity of the moment.

"It's beautiful here. We could stay a bit longer, if you don't mind?" His eyes searched mine. "Unless we're in a rush to get to the blueberry farm."

The low growl of my stomach decided for me. "Nah, we can stay. I'm hungry. I'll grab the food," I said, already breaking into a jog as I beelined back to the car. The door was unlocked, and after I grabbed the cooler I joined Levi on the beach.

It wasn't clean like Oar's Rest's beach, pristine with looked-after sand, free of trash and debris. The place we'd stopped looked like a party spot, with broken bottles near the shore, amber shards embedded in the damp, packed sand.

Sprinkled among them were flat, smooth stones in varying shades of green. Some were deep green, like moss or the underbelly of a frog. Others were almost white, resembling the surface of a honeydew melon. And falling in the middle were green stones that were the color of a dying fern, the shade dull and uninspiring.

"These are pretty." With careful fingers I pried tiny pieces of stone from the sand, sifting through muddy grain. Using some water, I washed the grit off the rocks. "Probably just pieces of a bottle, though."

Levi got up from the grassy patch we were sitting on, leaving the cooler lid open. He crouched at my side and took my hand in his. He lowered his eyes, gazing at the rocks. "The edges don't look sharp."

"I think it's just because they've been polished smooth from the water." I closed my fingers over them, made to throw them back into the sea, but Levi's gentle touch on my wrist stopped me.

"Wait. They're pretty," he said. He uncurled my fingers and with an indulgent smile, I scattered the pieces into his waiting palm.

"They're junk," I said mildly. "Smashed glass that's been in the water too long."

"Beauty is in the eye of the beholder!"

"And this is beauty to you?" Amused, I smiled at him. "Treasure, even?" I nudged him in the side.

Levi grinned. "Something like that. Everyone's a bit of a diamond in the rough, aren't they?"

I thought of myself, all my uneven edges and chipped shoulders, and gave him a rueful shrug.

He pocketed his treasure trove, and together, we made our way back to the cooler, me thinking of the many faces of jewels and how, in the right circumstances, all of us could be those rubbed-smooth bits of glass, just waiting for someone like Levi to think they were worth hanging on to.

We returned from Nectar Creek Farm with purple stains on our fingers and tongues. With Levi's help, I carried wooden crates of blueberries inside Busy's, much to Lucy's amazement. Using her back, she held the door open and gaped after us. Her face was shiny, tendrils of hair stuck against her forehead in damp curls. "You guys picked a *shit-ton*," she said.

Inside, the place was stuffed to the gills. Every single table was full. The book club ladies were back, making no secret that they were more interested in the crumb cake than in conversing—they were eating more than they were talking.

Lucy returned to the clamor, shuffling between tables, her hair escaping her messy bun. Her pencil worked feverishly over a note-pad as she took orders.

Ralph was engaged in a heated game of chess with one of the fishermen from the docks, and their match had garnered a small but vocal audience of other old-timers. From the way he was rubbing his hand over the shiny baldness of his head in swift, agitated motions, I could tell that Ralph was trying to worm his way out of a corner.

Middle schoolers were curled up in the corner booths. A few of the girls were resting their heads on their friends' shoulders as they slurped frothy beverages and scrolled through their phones. The guys were at the table next to them, an impressive number of empty milkshake glasses pushed to the center as they gestured animatedly through some story, voices overlapping and fighting for dominance. There was also a steady, impatient line at the counter. Tom was working the register, apologizing profusely, and his elbow knocked over a to-go cup.

"Oh shit," said Lucy, rewinding her thick brown hair into a messy bun.

Tom would never ask me to pitch in on my day off, but I didn't hesitate to grab my apron. "Lucy, can you get those berries in the fridge? I'll take over here." I shot a welcoming smile at a customer.

"I'll help, too," Levi said, slinging his arm around my shoulder just long enough to give me a kiss on the cheek. "Hand me an apron, ladies."

My heart went all soft and squishy. "You've got it," I said, pulling a fresh one out of a drawer.

Lucy shot him a smile of thanks and joined me on the other side of the counter. "Levi, do you think you could slice and plate four pieces of chocolate cake? And take this tray of coffees to"—she pointed—"that table?"

"Sure thing." Levi reached behind the counter to grab a knife.

I started the blender, churning cold-pressed coffee and ice together until clear fragments bobbed to the surface of the pale, caramel-colored liquid. A generous dollop of whipped cream and butterscotch drizzle later, I had three tall glasses of sugary goodness.

I threw Levi an appreciative glance as he mopped up a spill. "Thanks."

He grinned. "No problem."

The activity didn't let up for the next thirty minutes as customers poured in and out of Busy's. By the time the line dissipated, I was exhausted. I had no idea how Lucy had kept up with the pace all day.

"Thanks, Babe." Tom included Levi in his appreciation, giving us both a huge, tired smile. "It's been a crazy day."

The next hour passed quickly between dishwashing, tidying, and swabbing down tables. Lucy gave Levi a crash course in cappuccino foam art—after swearing him to keep all our secrets, of course—while Tom poured fresh beans into the coffee grinder and set it whirring. While Lucy and Levi perfected their foam hearts, I began to count up how many of my pastries were missing from the display case in order to calculate the day's takings.

Freshly ground beans always made the coffee taste a little nuttier, a little richer, and no one said no to my complimentary top-up. By the time I returned to the counter, coffeepot empty, it was time to start winding down.

"We've got things covered here. You should take off early," I said, squeezing Lucy's shoulder.

"I think I saw Lorcan out there with his dogs earlier," said Levi, forehead scrunching as he tried to replicate the heart Lucy had shown him.

Lucy's eyes sought out mine. "Are you sure? It's your day off."

"Positive. I'm the manager, so it's my call," I said.

"Authoritative." Lucy's nose crinkled as she laughed. She removed her apron. "So this is me falling in line, I guess."

Levi glanced up at us. "Did I steam the milk enough? It looks frothy to me, but I'm no expert."

Lucy waved a hand at the still-hot stove. "Yes, that needs to be steamed more." She headed to the door. "Hey, did you guys see what's going on out there?"

"What?" I asked.

"A ton of people are showing up with their sandcastle equipment." She twisted around. "You two have been practicing, right? We could really do with some solid competition this year."

"Fighting words, Lucy Bishop," I said, laughing. I met Levi's eyes. "Trust me, we'll be ready for you."

eighteen

"So when am I going to get to taste some of your blueberry concoctions?" Levi asked me the next day at Busy's.

I laughed. "Tomorrow morning I'll be here early. You, Tom, Ralph, and Lucy will get first crack at the blueberry streusel when it comes out of the oven. I'm stopping at the Dairy Bar for some of their blueberry ice cream, too. It's the best combination."

"I'll be here," said Levi. "And don't forget about the exhibition this weekend. I can't wait for you to see what I've spent the summer on."

It was like a sucker punch. His words were a reminder that summer was nearly over. He hadn't mentioned staying here to continue art classes again, and I didn't know how to ask, even though I desperately wanted to know. If that didn't pan out, it was long-distance or bust. I forced a smile. "I can't wait to see," I said, remembering the watercolors of Busy's and Oar's Rest. "Are they all the landscapes you showed me?"

"Not all of them," Levi said, mouth quirking into a slow smile. His blue eyes smoldered in a way that made me wonder what he meant.

"Indecisive or evasive?" I quipped.

He shrugged in an *I'm-so-innocent* way that I didn't buy.

"I knew I called you Mystery Boy for a reason," I said.

He burst into laughter. "When did you do that?"

"The first day we met! I didn't know your name, remember?"

"And you couldn't come up with anything sexier than Mystery Boy?" he asked with a good-natured grumble.

"You're the exact opposite of mysterious. You always tell me what you're thinking. That's a pretty sexy quality in a boyfriend," I said. A second later, I realized that the title of *boyfriend* wasn't likely to last for long. The countdown to the exhibition had started.

If it surprised him, he didn't let on. "I'm gonna get going. I have some very mysterious boyfriend stuff to work on at the art center," he said with an exaggerated wink. "I'll see you at the lighthouse for dinner, though?" He glanced down at his berry-stained hands, which, even after thorough washing, hadn't quite scrubbed the bruised, purple tint.

Before I could say "Okay," he leaned forward, pressed a soft kiss to my cheek, just enough that I felt the tip of his nose graze my skin, and then drew away.

"Thanks again for yesterday," I said, a little breathless from the rush of butterfly flaps in my rib cage.

"No problem. I had fun."

I smiled. "Me too." I looked behind Levi, where the gaggle of teens in the corner booth had just started getting up, everyone making a reach for purses and phones. They'd left a mess on the table: crumbs, napkins, and messily stacked cups and plates. "I'd better get that," I said, already reaching under the counter for a wet rag.

He followed my gaze and nodded. "See you soon."

I felt my eyes crinkle when my smile widened. I couldn't keep the silly grin off my face. Convinced I was sporting a pretty Joker-esque expression, I tried to downplay it. Was this how everyone felt when they were with someone who made their heart beat faster? When they didn't have to hold back and keep each other a secret? When they could be unashamedly, unreservedly happy? I couldn't believe I'd gone without it for years.

"You look happy," Lucy said, reaching for the tip jar. "It's a good look on you," she said with a soft smile.

I ducked my head, blushing. "Yeah? I feel like the whole town has seen our PDA, but I don't even care. This feels—I've never—" I couldn't even articulate it. "God, I've lost the ability to word."

"A known side effect," she said with a wicked smirk. "In the book of *Babe and Levi: A Love Story*, make sure I get all the credit!"

"Oh, I don't know if it's lo—" I stopped. She'd already dumped the tip jar upside down and was busy counting out the coins.

Before she noticed the pause, I started the dishwasher, unplugged all our appliances, and turned the air-conditioning down. By the time the dishwasher was halfway through the rinse cycle, Busy's was empty.

"Divided up the tips," said Lucy, pointing to two small piles on the counter. "I know you have a date tonight, so I can close up here, if you want."

I shot her a grateful smile. "I owe you one."

My bike made it up to the lighthouse in ten minutes. When I turned around, right at the crest of the hill, I could see Busy's below, warm and lit from within with a rosy glow. A second later, the lights flickered off, and I knew that Lucy would be heading home.

Hunching my shoulders against the cool night air, I headed inside.

The faintest whisper of vanilla lingered in the air, a remnant of last night's candle, along with the morning's slow-cooker seafood chowder. I had half a loaf of rustic bread on the counter, and in the fridge, a wedge of cheese, a plump handful of grapes, and some crisp romaine lettuce leaves.

I lifted the lid of the slow cooker and inhaled. The savory scent of potato, carrot, and onion cooked in broth wafted upward, along with the coastal freshness of clam and shrimp. I sprinkled in a touch of pepper, putting the pepper grinder down just as the door shut.

"Hey."

I glanced up to see a pink-cheeked Levi in front of me, tugging off his shoes. "The door was open," he said.

I turned around to grab bowls and spoons. "Can you give me a hand with the salad?"

"Of course." He began mixing in shredded cheese and baby tomatoes.

I started sawing through the crusty bread. "I'm kind of nervous about the exhibition," I admitted, unable to look at him directly while I said it.

It would mean coming face-to-face with Elodie again. I'd been able to justify keeping my past with her private before, but if there was a possibility he'd stay in town . . .

"Why?" His nose scrunched adorably when the dressing bottle farted out a huge dollop of ranch. "Penny?"

No, but close enough. "No," I admitted. "My ex will probably be there. I don't really want to see her."

I almost wanted him to ask me who it was. I wanted to be put on the spot, so I would have to answer. I stared into his face with anticipation, waiting for him to ask. It would make things so much easier if he asked me straight up.

"I'll run interference if you want me to," he said, a glint in his eye.

Disappointment sagged against me. Still, I appreciated the offer and was reminded once again how different he was from some of the guys I'd grown up with here. On my few post-Elodie dates, Neanderthal boys had seemed intensely threatened by my bisexuality, finding reasons to be jealous even when there was zero cause for it. Or, worse, thought it meant I'd put out just because they'd paid for dinner. My skin burned at the memories. I could still remember the crude jokes and wet kissing noises some of the middle school boys made when Penny and I walked down the hallway arm in arm.

Levi stopped tossing the salad. I could sense him looking at me, and with a hint of self-consciousness, I said, "I might just take you up on that."

He smiled faintly as he put the bowl of salad on the kitchen table.

I pulled the grapes and cheese from the fridge. "It feels like the summer just got started, doesn't it?" I said. "Seems like just yesterday I was handing you the keys and telling you how to work the wonky dials on the washing machine."

It had been a strange kind of summer, fast and slow all at once. Beautiful and sorrowful. A summer of possibilities and adventure and growing up. Now, so close to the brittle fall, I felt older all too quickly. It had been the other way around before I'd graduated. Then, summer break had made me feel young, innocent, wild. Not having bedtimes or homework made summer all the more delicious. This summer hadn't been delicious, but bittersweet. With a start, I realized that in the future, if I ever had to reach back and point to the summer when it all changed . . . this would be it.

I wanted to ask him if he'd heard back from RISD yet, but

I wasn't sure I wanted to hear the answer. I figured if there was something to tell, he would have. A queasy thought occurred to me: What if he *had* heard back, but just didn't want to say anything before he absolutely had to? What if, like me, he was holding back? I hated keeping up the pretense of being okay with it, but I also didn't want him to think I was trying to manipulate him into staying.

Still lost in thought, I ladled soup into the bowls. A layer of orange oil skimmed the surface, sloshing gently against the sides of the white ceramic. Levi accepted the steaming bowls from me while I carried the rest of the food over to my paint-splotched table.

"It's been a good summer for falling in love," he said.

I tensed. There it was again, that word. *Love.* Whether he meant with me or this town was unclear.

We sat down and as I reached for a thick hunk of bread, I said, "Yeah, Oar's Rest tends to do that to people. The love creeps up on you." I kept my eyes on him, waiting for a reaction.

Levi brought the spoon to his lips and blew on it. "Yes, yes, it does. It was the last thing I expected when I came here," he said. "What about you?"

He was looking at me with expectation, but my heart was hammering wildly, echoing in my ears like a wooden spoon banging on the bottom of a steel pot.

"I definitely wasn't expecting to break up with my friends," I said, swishing my spoon across the surface of the soup.

"I get it," said Levi, nodding. He ripped off a small piece of bread, then swirled the soft insides in the soup and took a bite. "Anyway, I'm jealous."

"Of what?"

"Of the fact that everyone here knows each other, is here for each other," he said, looking a little bashful. "It's nice. Like everyone's family. The way everyone pitched in after the fish fry? That was kind of incredible."

"Why?"

"Well, most people wouldn't be so eager to help clean up a dirty street after a festival, you know? No one *wants* to chase after loose streamers or sweep up trash and food that's fallen on the ground. But here everyone just rolled up their sleeves and got to work." He shrugged. "I don't know where else you'd find that."

I skimmed the spoon through the half-eaten soup and licked the back. I gave him a soft smile. "Probably nowhere."

I didn't need Levi to tell me that this town was special. There were many things you couldn't find elsewhere. Trees that seemed to whisper lost lovers' names when the wind blew just right, a beach that swallowed flip-flops and gave back books. Memories containing whole worlds.

That was what Levi forgot. Oar's Rest held on to memories. Every first kiss, every last kiss. Every tragedy, every miracle. It was greedy for them. We'd talked about it before, but I didn't think he realized that Oar's Rest would hold on to *him*, too. The memories he left behind would be there in every grain of sand, in every wobbly plank on the pier, in every corner of my world. Places like Oar's Rest were like that—they held on tight, tugged memories close, and gave life to the people who weren't there anymore.

nineteen

The original *Girl with Summertime in Her Eyes* hung in the art center. The water-spattered sketch from almost three months ago now seemed like a distant memory. It was wild to think of how many people would view my likeness, brought to life by slashes of watercolor on sturdy white paper, framed in thin black plastic. Once Levi put it up on Instagram, that number would explode exponentially. He'd immortalized me. Not even Elodie had thought to do that before.

From across the room, Penny stood in front of her mosaic paintings, looking frustrated and embarrassed. Her parents were both animatedly snapping photos at dozens of angles. She said something to them that made them stop for a moment, but then Mrs. Wang went right back to taking pictures, and Penny threw her hands up and spun around.

Our eyes locked. An eternity seemed to hover. Just as I thought she was going to look through me, her face eased into a slow, hesitant smile. Warmth stole across my chest.

It was all the ice-breaking I needed. I pointed to her art, then gave her a thumbs-up. Each canvas depicted an animal from the Chinese zodiac. The dragon was her masterstroke, the ferocity in his face almost popping off the canvas. It must have taken her hours to get the azure-to-jade gradient just right, but she'd pulled it off.

Thank you, she mouthed back.

The moment lingered. Neither of us looked away. Maybe we were both scared that if we did, we'd never be this okay again. But one of us had to make the first move. We couldn't hold still because we were scared of what might happen. Even if it had been for only a few seconds, the gap between us seemed a little less wide. It would be that way again. I had to trust that it would.

I was the first to look away. And, curiously, the warm feeling didn't go away.

A second later, Levi's arms wrapped around my waist. His breath was warm against my neck as he whispered, "You look beautiful." His hands settled on the white lace of my dress.

Turning around, I pretended to fuss with his black tie. "I was wondering where you'd gotten to."

"How long are you going to stand here?"

"Until someone asks me if I'm the model. A few minutes ago a woman behind me kept talking about the sketch, and I was silently willing something about the back of my head to nudge her in the right direction."

Levi's lips stretched in a laugh, and he gently bumped his nose against mine. "Do you remember the cave?"

The memory of our first kiss brought a warm smile to my face. "Like it was yesterday."

"Me too," he said, touching the back of his neck in a bashful way that I found absolutely, indescribably hot.

The exhibition was a huge success, admiring out-of-towners and locals alike packed into the art center gallery. Statues were scattered around the room: men and women sculpted to scale, and abstract and geometric metal floor pieces and wall art. Some artists had opted to display their work on easels, while Levi had arranged all his watercolors together on the wood-paneled wall.

My own face smiled at me from the canvas, radiant in its happiness. Blonde hair spilling over sun-kissed shoulders, eyes alight with the kind of pervasive happiness that only an artist could capture. My face looked almost three-dimensional, the fine, precise brushstrokes both curving and harshly defined. The colors were subdued, except for the eyes. The eyes—my eyes—looked like a novel condensed into one page, like they'd leeched and muted the pigment from the rest of the canvas. They'd swallowed it all up.

"I love it," I told him. I would have said more, but his mouth cut me off as it landed over mine. It was a slow, sweet, languid kiss. I breathed in the scent of his skin, the pine and toothpaste smell that made my nose tingle like I was about to sneeze.

By the time we pulled away, a little out of breath, and a lot smiling, I had the ridiculous urge to say *Thank you*.

"Sorry." Levi rested his forehead against mine. "I just really wanted to do that."

I tilted my lips up for a soft kiss, nibbling at the V of his upper lip. Every time he leaned forward and tried to capture my kiss, I moved, inching butterfly kisses over his lips.

"Don't apologize," I said. "I love kissing you." I wrapped my arms around his middle and pressed myself close. I hugged his warmth to me, his soft shirt rubbing against my cheek. A whiff of light, woodsy cologne brushed my nostrils.

His breath hitched. My heart began a frantic thumping, fast as children's exuberant feet as they ran themselves to exhaustion.

Levi's laugh ghosted warm breath across my face. "Okay."

We held the position for several seconds before he pulled away with reluctance.

"Want some canapés?" he asked.

"I'm dying for another one of those stuffed mushrooms," I admitted, but tugged him back when he started to move away. "Wait!"

Levi lifted an eyebrow.

"Don't you want a photo?" I pointed to one of his seascapes.

I purposely didn't say *to send your parents* because I knew it was a sore spot. They'd wanted to come, but it hadn't panned out. I knew, even though Levi didn't talk about it, that he was disappointed.

He pressed his lips together and glanced around the gallery. Many of the other artists had brought their families for the exhibition. Achievements always seemed more exciting when you shared them with people you loved.

"Yeah, let's do it," he finally decided. "Where should I stand? Is here okay?"

I took my phone out of my clutch. "No, a little to the left—wait!—no, that's it—perfect." I snapped the picture.

"Oh my God, delete that one," he said, covering his laugh with his hand. "I wasn't ready."

"It's cute," I protested, but I took another shot.

Levi groaned over my giggle. "Okay, let's go eat."

I was introduced to some of the program mentors over refreshments, which somewhat prevented me from scarfing as many mushrooms as I'd have liked. There was no polite way Levi could get out of receiving compliments, even though it was hard to keep a conversation going when I could see how quickly the mushrooms were being depleted.

Levi's look of misery was almost comical by the time we finally got around to the salmon toast. "Why are there two platters of deviled eggs? Who decided that we really needed two dozen eggs?"

"Okay, I'm seriously going to make you some sriracha deviled eggs one day. You'll convert."

He made a face. "Doubt it."

As I popped an hors d'oeuvre into my mouth, Levi put a hand at the small of my back. "Your friends are coming over," he said.

Lorcan and Lucy, both dressed in black, had glided across the room to join us. Lucy's smile sparkled brighter than the glittery pins in her upswept brown hair. "I saw your paintings," she said. "They look so good."

"Thanks," said Levi. "I'm glad you like them." He bumped fists with Lorcan.

The four of us moved through the room, recognizing some familiar scenery and faces along the way. A goateed guy in his late thirties—"That's Aaron, the pretentious one of the group. He's always name-dropping all the artists he knows," Levi whispered—was monopolizing Ralph in a steady stream of chatter. The black-and-white photographs Aaron had taken of Oar's Rest were stark in their simplicity, black waves crashing against rock. With some masterful photo editing, he'd created an underwater kingdom below. Tentacled creatures and hideous mermaids swam between the bones of sailors who couldn't let go of their treasure hoard.

"Beautiful," I whispered to Levi. "But eerie." I wouldn't want to look at them for too long.

Next to the photographs was an array of canvases propped up on easels. At first glance, they looked like feverish charcoal scribbles. Almost none of the white canvas was visible. Elodie stood behind them. Her eyes were on me, hard. I didn't want to stop in front of her work; I didn't even want to look at it. Her work was always evocative, if disquieting. It was like staring into the sun. Blinding and uncomfortable.

"The metalwork looks really nice," I tried to say, pulling Levi away, but Elodie called out crisply, "Levi!"

Fear pushed against me. *Please, please, if she hasn't told him about me yet, don't let her do it now.*

"Hey, Elodie." Levi changed course, and we came face-to-face with her paintings.

Or rather, we came face-to-face with me. Lucy couldn't hold back her shock, hand flying to her mouth. Of the eight canvases in front of us, four were of me. The charcoal looked frenzied, angry. My face was brought to life in an abstract of angry geometry, tumbling strokes of unrestrained, uncontrolled passion streaking across a white canvas. Was that how she felt?

My breath became stilted the longer I looked at myself. If the drawings had been of anyone else, I might have said they were incredible. The first charcoal sketch was of me at Busy's, hand wrapped around a cup. The smile was in my eyes, and the care in each tendril of hair, each freckle on my nose . . . it wasn't just art. It was deeply personal. The second and the third were of me in the sand. One was an aerial shot where I appeared to be asleep, the other was a day I remembered I'd been building a sandcastle with Levi. She hadn't included him in the scene.

But the fourth charcoal, that was the one that made my stomach tighten and cramp. It was the day we'd broken up. Behind me was the lighthouse, just barely visible, houses dotted below in minute detail. My face looked stricken, pale, even though there was no other way I could look on canvas. Despite the lack of color, the look in my eyes was vivid, inviting me into the pain on my face. The pull I had to the sketch was undeniable.

This sketch was softer, almost reverent and tender. Where Levi's painting of me played it safe, Elodie's looked like it was designed in emotional free-fall. My stomach tightened, twisted, plummeted. There was nothing to hold on to, nothing to soften the fall.

I remembered the sting of my tears, the way the chill kissed my cheeks raw and pink. The circling gulls over the lighthouse, the fishing fleet in the distance. I remembered the muted gray of the day, El's hair whipping into a bird's nest, her crying as she told me I deserved better. I'd felt like when she ripped away from me, she'd taken all the color with her. The gulls' cries had taunted me as my legs buckled and gave out. As I sank to the ground, grief tumbling over and over in resounding crashes.

I felt exposed, laid bare. Everything I'd felt that day was mirrored in her canvas, as though she was trying to tell me that she understood. That she wasn't as impervious or unaffected as I'd thought. Next to me, Levi stiffened. Vaguely, I realized Lucy and Lorcan had edged away.

The sights and sounds around me faded, drained of color, of life, of everything. How could she do this to me? Betrayal twisted in my gut. My pain was not hers to use, hers to display. How many people had seen this? Wasn't she scared by what her sketches would reveal about her? About us? About everything she said she wasn't ready to share? The music, playing from chameleon-like hidden speakers, was drowned out by the erratic, sharp thumps of my heart.

Elodie's eyes swallowed the room. I could only see her face, my face, her face, my face. The look of control she always wore like battle armor had slipped, leaving behind an unnerving storm in her eyes. Tension crackled between us. It was only my opinion of the drawing that she cared about, I realized. It was for me. It was all for me.

"This is . . ." Levi sounded unmoored. There was wonder and confusion in his voice, tinged with something else that I couldn't place. He couldn't look away from Elodie's work, his face calm, but his jaw was clenched tight. Like me, he wasn't immune to the chaos of the strokes, the palpable energy of the piece.

He swung his eyes to me, as if hoping I'd finish the rest of his sentence.

I didn't have the words.

Desperate, I stared at Levi, willing him to say something. The muscles in his face were taut. This was the moment that he knew, I realized. Who my ex was. Maybe it hadn't mattered to him before, maybe he wanted to let the past stay where it was . . . but this. This was an ambush. Not just for me, but for him, too.

Anger lanced through me. How dare Elodie pull this? This was hugely inappropriate. Tonight was about the artists, not us. She had no right to put me on the spot, to confront me with these memories. She'd had her chance. If she'd wanted to, she could have let us be in a real relationship two years ago. She could have thought about how devastated I would be when she said she didn't even want to keep in touch. She could have *not* crossed the street to avoid me that first day I saw her after she came back.

I was with Levi now, didn't she get that? He'd told her as much on the day she and her friends went to Bangor. I wasn't hers anymore. Not hers to draw or hers to reclaim. It was too late for that.

In a cacophony of sound, the world came rushing back. My head pounded and my ears were hot. I didn't want to stay in front of Elodie's work for another minute.

I tucked my hand into the crook of Levi's elbow. "Let's go."

Elodie's eyes were bright. She made to reach out, but I flung myself away, taking Levi with me.

As we walked, my heartbeat calmed. Next to me, Levi was still. He gave me a long look when we came to a stop in a private alcove, away from the crowd. I waited for him to speak first. For a long, terrible moment, I thought he would say nothing. Then he sucked in his cheeks. "Are you all right?" he asked.

There was nothing strange in his voice, no undercurrent of anger or jealousy. I paused, weighing my answer. "I'm okay. I didn't know she was going to do that." I peered up, unable to read him.

"So." He gestured behind him. "You and Elodie. She's your ex."

"Y-yes."

"Why didn't you tell me?" His voice resonated with confusion and the first brim of anger. There was a hard edge I'd never heard before—not from him. "I knew you were bi. You were up front about that. You were up front about everything except her."

"I did tell you about Elodie," I said. "I just didn't tell you her name."

"The most important part! Do you still have feelings for her?"

"No!" I took a deep breath. "When we were together, she wasn't ready to come out," I said. "I didn't like having to hide our relationship, but I understood. She hasn't even come out to her family yet. Jesus, Levi!"

I willed him to say something, but he seemed more at a loss than I was. I knew he was stalling and I knew why—he didn't know how to approach this any more than I did, but it was hell waiting for his response. I knew it was entirely unfair to expect him to take the lead on what was absolutely my fault, but everything felt so adrift that it was all I could do to stay upright.

"Levi," I whispered.

This seemed to snap him out of it. He swallowed once, hard, then ran a hand through his hair, savagely enough to look disheveled. "I get it," he said. "I just . . . I wish you'd said something before we saw—"

"I know." I took his hands between mine. "I don't even have the words. I was horrified when I saw—"

"No, they were beautiful." Levi shook his head. "I recognized you immediately. Only someone who knew you really well could have—" He broke off. "I had no idea she was this talented. I've seen her sketches before, but they were nothing like this."

Those sketches weren't just talent. They were anger, too. I'd seen it in Elodie's face when she looked at me. I'd seen it in the harsh strokes of charcoal across the canvas. She'd done them in a furor, and they were masterpieces. Her art wasn't just beautiful— it was *her*. In painting the sorrow on my face, she'd exposed something else, too. Herself. Anyone who saw her work would wonder at the artist's relationship to the subject. It wasn't a huge leap to make.

Whether she knew it or not, this had been her coming out.

"I think I need some water," Levi said.

"Do you want me to come wi—"

"No."

I nodded, throat choked up. "Okay." When he left, I closed my eyes. Shame prickled down my neck. I hadn't intended to hide things from Levi, truly I hadn't. But as long as Elodie didn't say anything, things went on as they had been. I'd thought after she'd come to the lighthouse, she understood that there wasn't any hope for us. I'd been wrong. If her art was anything to go by, she'd taken my turning her away as a challenge. As something she had to prove.

"Babe?"

My eyes flew open. *Elodie.*

"Did he ditch you?" she asked, a mini-scowl on her lips. She glanced around.

I stiffened. "He just stepped away for a minute. He'll be back." I didn't know if that was the truth. "What are you doing here?" On the tip of my tongue were the words *Haven't you done enough?*

Elodie's brow creased. "I had to come after you. I saw the way you looked at my work." Before I could stop her, she'd taken my hand. She held it between her own, and I tried not to think that just a few minutes ago, I'd been holding Levi's hand instead.

"El, don't." I pulled free, holding my hand against my chest like an injured bird. "What do you want?"

I knew what she wanted, but I needed to hear her say it.

"I told my mom about us," said Elodie.

My eyes widened.

"She . . . she didn't really understand. But she was supportive. Mostly she just cried. She didn't understand why I didn't tell her. She thinks she's been a bad mom for not suspecting sooner." The words were flooding out of Elodie, a dam bursting free. She hung her head, then abruptly jerked her neck back up to look at me. "I told her for *you*," she said, almost pleading.

"No, that isn't fair."

"Babe—"

"I'm with Levi now!" I said sharply.

I might as well have slapped her. Her head swung to the side and she clenched her eyes shut. I was saying words she didn't want to hear. But she had to hear them.

"El, I'm glad you told your mom, but whatever you think is going to happen between us . . . it's not. Okay? It's just not. We had fun. We were each other's firsts. But our summer is over now."

"But I still love you," she said in a small voice. Then, before I could stop her, she was leaning in. There was a recklessness in her eyes, and her impassioned charcoal sketches flashed into my mind. Even though I didn't think she'd done this for the right reasons, for a tiny, microscopic moment, I wanted to let her kiss me.

But I'd been here before with Chad. Sometimes the past had to stay in the past. When you brought it into the present? Calamity.

"No," I said. One word. Soft, gentle.

Her lips stopped, hovering an inch from mine. "But I did it all for you," she said quietly. "If you don't want me, it was for nothing."

It wasn't for nothing. But it was more for her than for me.

I kissed her on the cheek, and tried to ignore the taste of salt. I tried to pour everything I had into that tiny peck, every last bit of love that her leaving had wrung out of me. "You will always be my first love," I whispered. "But we both need to move on."

The muscles in her cheek twitched. She pressed her lips together until the rasping gasps subsided. I could tell she was trying to stop crying.

I blinked back my own tears. As the blurriness went away, I saw Levi standing in front of us. Before the relief at his return could sink in, I saw his face change. He took in the scene, me and Elodie standing too close, our mouths too near. His cheeks bloomed red, and his mouth pinched into a hard, straight line. His fingers tightened around the bottle of water. Then he turned away and began walking toward the exit on his long legs. He didn't look back once. Each stride took him farther, and further, away from me.

The room spun. My legs were shackled in place. I felt my chest tighten and snap, like a used rubber band. Scraped thin, yanked around and around. I pressed my fingers to my temple and took several ragged breaths. Around me, the animated chatter faded to the buzzing drone of an insect. Too close to be avoided, but flying past my ears at breakneck speed.

"Babe?" Elodie's face swam into my vision. Smile composed, cheeks dry. She held my face, but her touch was all wrong.

The world came rushing back, every sound and sight and smell overwhelming and obnoxious in its vibrancy. Shame stabbed at me. I'd ruined Levi's exhibition. He'd stalked out of here and was probably halfway to the parking lot by now. I gasped, tearing myself away from Elodie.

I couldn't let him leave like this.

I ran after him, determined to catch him before he got into his car. I rounded the corner of the hallway, shoes slapping against the wooden floor. When I burst through the door, I swung my gaze, trying to find him. He was almost halfway to his car.

"Levi!" I shouted. His feet faltered in a fumbling half step, but he didn't stop.

I caught up to him easily, catching his swinging arm and stopping him in his tracks. "It wasn't what it looked like," I said, and I knew at once it was the wrong thing to say, before his pained expression turned angry in a heartbeat.

"Seriously?" He wrenched himself free. "That's all you have to say?"

"I'm sorry! I didn't mean it that way. *Nothing* happened, I swear."

"You know, I really want to believe you, but . . ." He took a step away.

"How could you"—I stabbed my finger in his direction—"think that I would kiss her when I'm here with you?"

"Because I saw the two of you!" Levi's eyes glowed, hurt, furious. "God!"

He was overreacting, he had to see that, I had to *make* him see that. "Levi, no—"

He threw his hands up. "Are you trying to make me jealous? Or this whole summer, you and me, was this you trying to make her jealous?" he asked, voice sad and angry and broken all at the same time. He went for the killing blow. His words were coming out faster and faster. "You must have thought I was such an idiot. Falling for it again." His laugh was full of biting cold. "All those kisses on the beach."

My stomach bottomed out. He thought I was just like his ex. Someone who just wanted to use him to make another person jealous.

I wasn't like her; I would never do that to anybody. But I could see from the inflexible set of his face that I wouldn't be able to convince him of that.

In the thorny seconds that passed, I was drowning. Every breath was a battle, gasped and rasping. My fingernails were embedded in my palms so hard that I knew there would be eight perfect half-moon indents.

My mouth tasted sour like vinegar. Blood rushed to my ears. He was so wrong, and yet, how could I blame him for coming to that conclusion? He'd told me weeks ago what his last girlfriend had done. In his eyes, this looked like a repeat of the same situation.

Realization crashed in his eyes. "So that's a yes, then. To me being an idiot."

"No, I wasn't pretending, I wasn't faking, it wasn't like that," I tried to say, but he wasn't having it.

"Then what was it like?"

"*It wasn't my secret to tell!* I'm out; she's not! I have *no right* to tell anyone her business. How are you not getting this?!" My voice cracked, but I kept going. "I don't want to be with her, I want to be with you! Yes, okay, yes, she wanted to kiss me! But I wasn't going to let her. I stopped her; I told her I was with you. The only person I want is you, Levi Keller, even if you're being a huge fucking jerk right now!"

The secret hadn't been that I'd withheld my ex-girlfriend's identity. The real secret was that we'd both forgotten how much we could hurt each other. Though I'd been a hair's breadth away from major drama all summer, it hadn't touched us much. Even if I'd gotten nothing else right, *we* had been right. Even though Mom never came to visit me like she promised, even though I never got my perfect summer with my friends. Even if nothing else worked out the way I wanted it to, I'd had Levi, and that had been an awful lot like having a home.

"What else don't I know?" Levi asked, chest heaving like he was struggling for breath.

Him being in pain was worse than me being in pain. I didn't mean to say it, but something inside me unleashed, came sprawling out in a torrent before I could think. "Idon'tthinkIwanttohavealong-distancerelationship."

"What?"

I said it again, this time slower. "I don't think I want to have a long-distance relationship."

There were no secrets left. They were all out in the open.

He blanched. "I think—I'm just gonna—" Levi edged away, hand raking through his hair. His face was bleached of all color, except for the two bright patches of pink in his cheeks. He made it to his car without looking at me.

I wanted to follow, but my legs had jellied. I swallowed. "You don't have to—" I tried, but it was no good.

"Can you get a ride back home with someone?"

I nodded. "Lucy'll drive me."

His key fumbled in the lock, but then he got it to slide in evenly, and with a quick twist, he was inside. The door slammed. He was my ride, but now he was leaving alone.

He stared at me through the glass for a long moment, then started the ignition. I wanted to tell him not to go, that I was sorry, but what came out was: "What about the exhibition?"

"The only person I really cared about showing my art to was you," he said, and then he was reversing out of the parking space.

An infinity passed between our eyes. My chest felt raw, shaky. Everything hung in the balance. Would he still think about staying? The things I had counted on an hour ago now seemed elusive, out of reach.

He waited until I took a step back before peeling out of the parking lot. I watched the taillights until they faded, and only then did I remember to blink.

♥ ♥ ♥

I didn't know how long I was out there, leaning against Lucy's car, struggling to process. Going back inside wasn't an option. I didn't want to be stared at, didn't want to see Elodie again. Didn't want her to try to win me back. Didn't want her or anyone else to wonder where Levi had gone. I'd just wait for Lucy out here.

So this was it. Whatever remained of summer, here it was. This was how it all ended, in a dimly lit parking lot with my makeup running down my face. My eyes burned, and when I swiped at them, a black mascara smear rubbed off.

"You look like shit."

I didn't even have to look up. "Thanks, Penny. Really what I needed to hear right now." I wiped at my nose.

I felt the tiny shift of the car as she joined me in leaning against it. Instead of crying harder or feeling upset that she was witnessing my epic breakdown, all I could think about was how long her legs looked in her black velvet skirt and Doc Martens. The thought was so unexpected that I laughed, a horrible, snot-nosed, bubbly laugh that made Penny flinch.

Half waiting for her to make some kind of remark, I was surprised when she just put her arm around me. Naturally. Not like she had to think about it first. Just as easily, I found myself leaning into her.

"Saw the two of you coming out here," she said. "Figured you might need a friend."

"Is that what we are?"

"I was actually going to say that you needed *me* and the solace only I can provide, but that seemed egotistical," she said, deadpan.

"It's all about you," I said through a watery laugh, not really meaning it. She'd made me smile, and that was what she'd intended all along, I realized.

A shadow fell in front of us. "Room for one more?" Chad's unsure voice asked.

I couldn't hold back my gape. "W-what are you doing here? You didn't say you were coming tonight."

Silence.

Chad joined us, flanking my other side. He breathed noisily. "I came with my parents," he said. "I saw him stalk out. Then you chasing him."

"I guess everybody did," I said, a little sourly.

"If you mean Elodie, I doubt it," said Penny. "She's parading around on John's arm."

Somehow that didn't surprise me. Elodie was always good at rallying. "Oh," I whispered. "Were you watching me?"

"Not the whole time." Penny let her head rest against mine. "Just when you stopped in front of her work. I kept an eye, you know, just in case you needed backup." A beat passed. Then: "I'm sorry," she whispered. "I know I was being a colossal bitch. I just . . . I just couldn't stop. I hated myself."

Next to me, Chad stiffened. I knew he was listening.

"I know the kiss didn't mean anything," Penny continued. "It was just the thing that set me off. It's so much easier to be angry than it is to face up to things."

The three of us stood there in silence until I regained control of myself. My soft, shuddering breaths gave way to the chirps of crickets. It wasn't just my strength that pulled me through; it was knowing that my friends were with me, too.

"Should I get you something?" asked Chad. "Anything. Just name it. Tea?"

"Beer," said Penny. "God, Chad. She doesn't drink *tea*. What is she, ninety?"

"I drink tea," he said.

"Since when?!"

"And it's good for shock."

"Says who?!"

Neither of them realized they'd fallen back into an old pattern until they both caught sight of me smiling. Penny burst into helpless laughter and sagged against the car.

"I don't need anything," I said. I held a hand out to each of my friends. "Just stay with me?"

They didn't hesitate. Their hands found mine, and for a moment, I wasn't thinking about everything else that had just slipped away.

twenty

Every day of summer, Levi Keller had been a clockwork boy—black coffee, baby blues, lopsided smile. But the last couple of days, he hadn't come to Busy's at all. If he even left the house, that was news to me. I didn't see him anywhere. Not his house, not the beach, not in any of the shops along Main Street. It was a little humiliating that he was still the first person I looked for in a crowd, especially since he was probably ignoring me.

I threw myself into baking. Like a madwoman, I worked every minute I wasn't at Busy's. It wasn't exactly soothing, but it gave me something to do that didn't involve moping. I knew if I started, I wouldn't stop. In one summer, three of my relationships had fallen apart. Chad, Penny, and now Levi. So no, I couldn't slow down and give myself time to feel sad. As long as I kept baking, my mind was consumed with measurements and instructions, things that wouldn't let me down. When it came to food, at least, I didn't make mistakes.

The morning of the sandcastle competition, I woke before dawn. As I headed out of my lighthouse, I paused, arrested by the sight of the sun peeping over the horizon. Molten and rippling on the water, the sun rose like a California poppy unfurling its petals. Blush pink and peach and tangerine watercolors streaked and muddled across the sky. Morning dew squelched under my flip-flops as I pulled a patio chair out to watch the sunrise.

Unlike the sea of nighttime, inked black and midnight blue, the sea now shone glasslike and cerulean. The morning was illuminated by scattered pockets of silver light reflecting on the surface of the water. The lobster boats heading out of harbor were tipped in gold, like they were wearing crowns.

The breath paused in my lungs—it was like time had stopped and I was here, witnessing the beginning of everything. I could hear the faraway barks of seals and the mournful, haunting wails of a loon's cries. Turning my face up to the sun, I basked in the persimmon, pearly light. It now hung fully suspended in the sky, sending the water to liquid gold. The early morning's lavender and gray had scrolled back to reveal the bejeweled, sequin-silver sky and the egg-yolk sun. It was a day for magic, miracles, and new beginnings.

As I finally got up, dragging my unwilling feet, the chorus of birds chirping their dawn song followed me into town. A cool breeze brushed my forearms as I biked down the narrow, winding streets to the beach.

Tom was just opening Busy's. "Morning!" he called out, turning the key in the lock.

I slowed down, coming to a stop. The bucket of tools hanging on my handlebars rattled. "Hey, Tom. Thought you were closing this morning for the sandcastle competition."

"Just getting my coffee!" he said cheerfully. "Ready for the big showdown?" He grinned. "I've seen you and Levi practicing the last couple weeks. My money's on you to take home the gold."

"You're betting on us?" I asked with a laugh.

Then I remembered there wasn't really an *us* anymore.

It was just me.

"Friendly betting," said Tom. I didn't buy his innocent face for a minute.

Once he went inside, I clenched my handlebars and kicked off, heading for Levi's house. It wasn't about the competition; I just wanted to talk to him. To work things out. To tell him that whether he was here or there, I still wanted him.

His car wasn't parked out front, but I hopped off my bike and made my way to the door anyway. I knocked twice. When he didn't appear even after I counted to twenty, I tried again, this time with solid, loud knocks. Still nothing.

I stepped off the porch and called up to the bedroom window, "Levi?"

I waited to see if the curtain would flutter or if I could see his figure move. I didn't even make it to twenty before I tried again. "Levi, can we talk? Please?"

At this point, I just had to face it. He either wasn't there or he wasn't answering the door. Of the two, I hoped it was the former. Dejected, I got back on my bike. There wasn't much point in going to the sandcastle competition, but it beat skulking around his house like a gremlin.

I was the last participant to make it out to the beach. The parking lot was already packed with locals and tourists alike. Mr. and Mrs. Bishop waved to me from their car, where they were eating breakfast, and a few other regulars called out their support as I jogged across the sand. Penny and Chad were among them, too far away for me to talk to. Stunned, I watched as Chad laid out all his equipment and pointed to each piece in turn, presumably explaining their purpose. They said they weren't back together, but maybe, just maybe, this was a step in that direction. I scanned the beach for Levi, dejected when I couldn't find him.

There was only one other place he could be.

The lighthouse.

I grabbed my bike from where I'd left it in front of Busy's, fingers shaking too much to deal with the lock. Winning the competition didn't matter anymore. Whether he stayed or left didn't, either. The destination mattered way less than the journey. And I would never know if there was a future for us unless I was willing to take it. Whether that meant Skype calls and flying back and forth from Rhode Island or staying in Oar's Rest, I wanted him in whatever way I could get him. Part of me had always known that, but it had taken our time apart for it to cement in my head.

Tom came out with his coffee as I swung onto my bike. "Where are you going?" he called as I pedaled away. "It's about to start!"

I waved at him over my shoulder and kept going. The streets were empty because everyone was gathering at the beach. I traced the route up to the lighthouse with my eyes, hoping to see a flash of his car.

Nada.

I biked as fast as I could, panting for breath by the time the lighthouse came into view. What if we'd missed each other? I hovered on the hill for a long moment. From here, I could see that no one was waiting at my home. What could I do now?

There was no point going back to town—without Levi, I couldn't take part in the competition. I wasn't even sure I wanted to anymore. Without him, winning didn't mean a thing. But if I stayed here, I'd just replay everything and drive myself crazy. So I twisted the handlebars and biked down to cheer for my friends.

Busy's was locked up by the time I got back. While I bent down to secure my bike, I heard footsteps approaching. I expected them to keep going, but they stopped.

"Where have you been?" an exasperated voice asked from behind me.

I whirled. Hard to do while still crouched. "Levi! I–I've been here. I was waiting for you and I didn't think you'd show up and I went to your house and then went back to—" I stopped talking as he helped me get up. I didn't want to let go of his hand, so I held on.

"Later," he said, that one word soft and silky and oh so safe.

"But—"

He cocked his head. "Don't you want to win this thing?"

"I do," I said. "But I want you more. I told you, Levi. There's nothing else—no one else."

"I'm yours." His blue eyes settled on me. "If you still want me, that is," he said, the words sounding too careful, too deliberate to not take at face value. He didn't mean just for the sandcastle competition, I realized.

"We'll have to run," I said.

"I'm okay with that. We have the rest of our lives to take it slow."

"I meant to the beach."

"I didn't. But it works for that, too."

So that was exactly what we did. We skidded into our place just as the judge began counting down *ten, nine, eight* . . .

I ached to talk to Levi about everything that had gone wrong, but now we were at *five, four, three* . . . There was no time for me to do anything else but plunge my spade into the sand and start digging.

It was as if no time had passed. In perfect harmony, Levi and I began to move, arms furiously tamping down wet sand, forming the early shape of the castle we'd been practicing. The lumps of sand slowly began to come together in towers and walls, larger and grander than we'd made them before.

I drowned out everything else, focusing only on the sand sifting through my fingers and the rasp of the knife as it cut through walls. The sun, low in the sky when we started, rose higher and higher until it hit its noonday peak. We were approaching the end of our four-hour limit, and as the judge gave us a thirty-minute warning, I cast a wild-eyed look at Levi. While I was etching in doors and windows, and studding seashells into turrets, he was painstakingly working on a staircase for each of the four keeps.

He was being too ambitious. We'd only ever done one staircase before, and that had been during practice. Though we'd kept up a feverish pace since the start of the competition, even I doubted he'd be able to get them done in time. Without asking, I grabbed another knife and got to work. I was faster at it, I reasoned, so with any luck, we'd be able to get done.

The last half hour passed in a frenzy. It blurred past me, and by the time the judge called time, I'd only just finished crowning each tower with a tiny starfish. Levi stepped away from the castle and dropped his knife, blinking in weary exhaustion at our creation. I shaded my eyes against the sun to look at it. It was a masterpiece, way better than anything we'd done before.

"Oh my God, yours looks so good," squealed Lucy.

A relieved laugh burst out of me. "So does yours," I said, raking my eyes over the tall tower they'd built. It had been hand-molded to look like coral, twining and twisting to almost five feet. They'd dug a moat around it and filled it with water, lining the perimeter with beautiful shells Lorcan had bought for the hermit crabs.

"Wow, this is fantastic," said Chad appreciatively as he ambled over. Penny trailed behind him, looking a little skittish all of a sudden, like maybe she wasn't sure whether Lorcan and Lucy would want to hang with her after what happened at the pageant.

"Your castle looks pretty good," said Lucy. She leveled a solid look at Penny. "Ours is better, though."

Penny peeped at her from under her eyelashes. "Yeah. I'd be really surprised if yours or Babe's didn't win."

While everyone else chatted and waited for the results of the competition, I turned to Levi. "You came."

There wasn't a trace of the betrayal I'd seen at the exhibition. Just the same soft promise I'd seen before. "Hi, Babe," he said quietly, shuffling toward with me with his hands buried deep in his pockets, bunched up into balls like he was nervous.

"How are you?" I asked at the same time he opened his mouth.

A rueful smile tugged at his lips. "I was about to ask you the same thing." He pulled one hand out of his pocket and unfurled his fist, revealing a shiny silver bracelet set with the sea glass he'd picked up that day we'd gone blueberry picking.

"Is this the sea glass?" I asked, picking it up. "You polished it. It's beautiful."

The cuff bracelet was thin and delicate, spidery in the silver wire filigree work. In the center, several glossy, imperfect pieces of sea glass were lined neatly in a row.

"Someone at the art center showed me how to do the metalwork," said Levi. "I was going to give it to you the night of the exhibition. I know my timing sucks, but I made it for you and I think it should be with you. May I?" At my nod, he slipped it over my wrist.

My skin tingled where his fingertips touched me.

"I'm sorry," he said, breaking the pregnant pause.

"Don't be," I said. "You came in the end. I didn't think you would."

His eyes flew to mine. "I wasn't talking about this." He gestured to the beach, where the judges were still walking around with their clipboards, taking notes on the sandcastles.

"I'm sorry. Not for keeping Elodie's name secret, because that was her call, but for you finding out the way you did," I said. I took a deep breath. "I never meant for you to think I was using you to make her jealous. It was never like that. She's my past, you're my—" I had to stop myself. I had no idea if he was my future anymore, let alone my present.

"I realized when I got home that night that I hadn't really given you a chance to explain. I wanted to go to you, talk things through, but after those things I'd said . . ." Levi exhaled. "The way I acted." He shook his head. "I was sure you were going to tell me to go to hell."

"You had every right to be pissed at me. I know how it looked. She—she came to find me, Levi. Those paintings, they were some kind of tribute to me, a way for her to declare what she felt, but—but—the thing is, I'm not in love with her, Levi. I'm in love with you. I'll still be in love with you, no matter where you go or how hard it is to make it work."

He stared at me for so long that I grew self-conscious, tucking hair behind my ear and darting my eyes away from him. "Babe," he began to say, but then the megaphone boomed, and we both turned.

The judges were standing in front of our sandcastle. "We have a winner!" the head judge said with a broad grin. "Will the architects of this castle come forward, please?"

It took a minute for it to sink in.

"Babe, it's you!" Lucy shouted, setting off a round of cheers and hoots.

Levi stepped next to me, hand on my back. He met my eyes, and wordlessly, we both stepped forward at the same time, heading toward our creation. The judges pinned blue first-place ribbons on us. Lorcan and Lucy were awarded red ribbons for second place, and another team won third.

"I suck!" Penny shouted dramatically over the commotion. "Chad was robbed!" Even Lucy cracked a smile.

John and Cary kicked their sandcastle back into the beach, which wasn't hard, considering it was falling apart anyway.

Camera flashes went off, the crowd surged forward. Everyone was in my face, buzzing in my ear, asking me how it felt to break Lorcan and Lucy's winning streak.

"Everything okay?" Levi whispered in my ear, though it was really more of a shout to make himself heard over all the festivity.

"It will be!" I shouted back.

Over the next week, the coffee shop was jam-packed with people eager to congratulate me and Levi. Lucy and Lorcan, the former reigning champs, swore that next year they'd steal first back from us. It titillated the crowd to think we had a friendly rivalry going on, and someone shouted, "Drinks on me!" which got all the tourists excited until they realized we didn't serve alcohol.

As a result of all my baking, Busy's smelled like sugary pecans. The aromatic, spicy scent of cinnamon and nuts brought back fond memories of winters I'd spent with Penny and Chad, all of us tucked away in her parents' kitchen, eating fruitcake and spilling sugar on the floor, then arguing about who would wipe it up. It was usually Chad, since it was Penny's house and her parents' stolen mulled wine, and in solidarity, she'd point out that it couldn't be me since I'd made the fruitcake.

Still reliving old memories before closing time, I arranged some spice cake and hot black tea for Ralph to carry out, while Lucy made a gift arrangement of mango-macadamia cake and oatmeal-walnut cookies to deliver tomorrow.

The last of our customers skedaddled out the door into the navy-blue, ink-splotched sky. The days were getting darker earlier, and the air cooler, to match. From here, I could see autumn poking its head around the corner. The dog days of summer were behind us, replaced by shivery night chill and a vibrant carnival of colors. Pastel-colored houses, shrouded in leafy canopies of green and gold and merlot, glowed with a marzipan ethereality. Lampposts and restaurant windows slanted just enough shadows and illumination to look eerie, the boat on the beach the unsuspecting backdrop for accidental shadow puppetry.

Tonight was the Burning Boat Festival. Summer already seemed like a faded memory.

"Hurry! It's about to start," said Lucy.

"I heard you the first time," I said with a laugh.

Within ten minutes, we'd locked up and run to the beach, our feet kicking up sand, our laughs caught and swallowed by the wind.

Down on the beach, a crowd had already gathered, stacking logs inside the boat so the fire would burn long and hard through the night, burning down to crackling embers by morning. This was Tom's year to light the fire; he crouched down and started the blaze. White smoke would soon curl upward, swelling the air with the sweet spice of autumn, making everyone yearn for sweet apples, just off the branch, and pecan pies, warm out of the oven.

Our friends were already there, part of the circle that surrounded the bonfire. Penny stood next to Chad, her hair disheveled from the wind. With the light casting shadows on her face, her cheekbones and jawline looked sharp enough to cut a man. She wore a shapeless black dress that billowed around her thin frame. Penny fiddled with the sleeve of the cardigan tied around her waist before catching my eye. Her smile was a thousand things all at once: *I'm sorry, I miss you, I love you, I'm sorry I'm sorry I'm sorry.*

The air burned with the smell of autumn, the spicy tang of cinnamon and cloves swirling around us like my favorite Yankee Candle. Flames leapt feverishly like flamenco skirts, whipping and snapping around us in dizzying billows. Levi and I both watched, enraptured, as flames lapped over the wooden boat, devouring planks and nails. Within moments, they had spread to the bow, tendrils twirling in a fiery, dancing blaze.

If August had a color, it would be gold. Brighter than a lion. Twenty-four-karat beauty. Levi's presence in Oar's Rest had stretched from summer into the beginnings of brittle fall. Spiderwebbed leaves turned from green to gold, the edges a rich burnt amber and persimmon orange.

"I'm glad you got to see this," I whispered to Levi. Witnesses to the much-beloved boat festival were few and far between. Secrets didn't stay secrets for long in a small town, but this was one we all universally kept from strangers, hidden up our sleeves and close to our chests. The last thing any of us wanted was for Oar's Rest to become another Bar Harbor.

"Me too." Levi's smile was luminous. A light show of primal, twisting orange flames flickered across his pupils.

The Burning Boat Festival was basically destruction dressed up as a party, and as the flames rose higher and higher, the party well and truly got underway. Someone was blasting a mix of folk tunes from their iPod, and bodies swayed around the engulfed boat, tan legs kicking up golden sand, and bronzed arms wrapping around friends and lovers.

A few feet away, Lorcan and Penny tipped back bottles of beer before Lucy pulled Lorcan into the firelight to join in the jigs of the revelers. "Come on, Babe!" she screamed, hair bouncing up and down as she bounded around the bonfire with the rest of the young people. Laughing, Lorcan let himself get pulled along, stumbling a little as he tried to keep up with Lucy's jittery dance steps.

"There's the guys," said Chad, stubbing his toes into the sand. "I'm gonna catch up with them for a minute." He turned to leave, then paused. "Um, do you wanna come, Penny?"

Her eyes widened. "Sure." She turned to me. "I'll see you two later?" At my nod, they both drifted away like shadow, the black plumes of Penny's dress fading, fading, fading. Just the two of them this time. As it should be.

"She looks a lot happier," said Levi. "Do you think they'll get back together?"

I agreed with him in wholehearted relief. It had hurt to see her painfully thin body, the skin bruised like day-old supermarket fruit, the hazy uncertainty in her eyes the day after her last party. "I don't know. Maybe. But maybe not."

We stood there for several minutes, both of us content with the silence. It was broken only when Levi reached into his back pocket. Something crinkled. I watched with interest as he pulled out an envelope. He let me read the return address for only a second before he flung it into the bonfire. In seconds, the corners of the envelope curled up and blackened.

I gasped. "Levi, that was from RISD!"

"I know."

"Why did you—" I shook my head. "Did you even open it?"

He grinned at me, utterly unrepentant. "What, do you think I'm crazy? Of course I did. That was just a grand gesture, since I didn't have anything else I wanted to throw into the fire."

I was in no mood for his cuteness. Especially when it wasn't giving me the answer I wanted to know. "But . . ." I bit my lip, watching as the envelope disintegrated, becoming one with the flame. "What did it say?"

"I got in," he confided. "I had the online acceptance a while back."

"You got—!" I stared him down. "Levi! Oh my God! Congratulations."

"I was going to tell you after the exhibition." *Oh.* "I asked for my acceptance to be deferred until the spring semester," he said. "It'll give me time to apply for as many scholarships as I can before I officially start school." His voice held more hope than I'd ever heard before when he added, "Dad said he'd help as much as he could."

I knew what that meant to him. His eyes were so intense that I never wanted to look away. If I did, it wouldn't come true. If I even blinked, it wouldn't—

"Babe, say something."

Words weren't enough. I wrapped my arms around his middle and pressed myself close. I hugged his warmth to me, his soft shirt rubbing against my cheek. A whiff of familiar woodsy cologne brushed my nostrils. "You're staying for a semester," I said, mostly for myself but also for confirmation. This didn't make any sense. What about RISD? What about figuring out if he had other passions besides art?

Levi cuddled me close. "I'm staying. I've been talking to Ralph about it. He got me a place here for a semester. I spoke to the art program coordinator and she said if I come up with a rigorous program, she'll consider giving me course credit. And I don't have to worry about, well, money. As long as I keep painting, I'll keep getting commissions. And maybe after this, I won't want to pick up a paintbrush again. Maybe I'll do something totally different. I'm not in a rush to figure it out."

He brushed his knuckles over my cheek. "And you have time to figure it out, too. Whether you can do something long-distance or not. We haven't been together long enough for that kind of commitment, maybe." He paused. "I feel like I'm not supposed to say that."

But I was glad he did. "I don't think we have, either," I said. "Summers anywhere, but especially here . . . it makes everything fast-forward. I guess that's why we have Real Life, to keep us from burning ourselves out. Summer's good for a lot of things, but the real test is what comes next."

"What comes next for this summer boy is this," he said, and then he kissed me. It was just as short and sweet as the first time, and it ended the same way, him smiling against my mouth.

"That was a good decision," I whispered.

"I think so, too." He opened his eyes to look at me. Our noses brushed. "It's just a semester. But maybe one day I'll stay for us. Or you'll leave for us. Whichever. Maybe neither. You were right before. RISD is a great school, but it will still be there a few months from now. Maybe staying here for a semester isn't the right choice, or maybe it is, but we won't know until we try, you know?"

"I don't know what to say," I said, heart thudding. "I feel like the right thing for me to do is tell you not to wait for me."

"I'm not waiting for you."

"You're *deferring*, Levi."

His voice was coaxing. "Nothing's going to expire if we take a few extra months together. Remember?"

"But it's selfish of me to let you."

He frowned. "Let me?"

"Bad word choice. I know you can make your own decisions, I do, but if I'm a factor in it, then—"

"Of course you're a factor. But you're not the *only* factor. I told you, I'm doing good here. I'm inspired, I'm creating, I've made friends. I have a life here that goes beyond you, Babe. I love you, and you're part of that life, but you're not my *whole* life."

"That's super unromantic and yet incredibly reassuring. You're not just saying that, are you?"

"No more secrets," he said. "Let's say what we mean from now on."

That I could agree with. I'd had enough of all the secrets this summer. "Then I want you to kiss me again," I said boldly.

"Trust me, I plan on it." He smiled. "But first . . . just look." This time, what he pulled from his pocket wasn't an envelope but a postcard. The corner was bent just slightly.

My breath caught. This was Oar's Rest. Even in miniature, I could see the bright colors of the beach houses dotting the coast, the familiar slant of the Busy Bean's roof, and the slick red of my lighthouse.

On the path uphill, the same one I took every day, were two figures on bicycles. One was a boy with short hair, the other a girl with wavy blonde hair trailing behind her. I blinked, lips parted. *This was us.*

In the top corner, nestled in the clouds, were the words *Oar's Rest* in graceful illustration, each word resembling rope. Levi's name was written in black ink on the bottom, small, so as to fit inside the sandcastle that peeped from the edge.

I flipped the postcard over. On the back were the familiar three lines for an address, but on the opposite end something was written: The words *A place to rest your oars* between two crossed wooden oars.

A place to rest your oars.

"Oh," I whispered. I looked up at the sky before the tears could plop onto the postcard. Instead, I blinked, and I felt hot wetness cling to my lower lashes.

"Those are happy tears, right?" he asked.

"Very happy tears," I said, laughing. "When did you have time to do this?"

"Last week. I went to the tourist office and suggested I could do a postcard series for the whole of Maine. They loved the idea. They wanted a mock-up done first, but if they like it, they're going to order a whole print run."

"You'll have to buy a bike if you decide to stick around," I said, only half-kidding.

"I know. Maybe tomorrow after work you can help me pick one out?"

I wound my arms around his neck. "It's a date."

Levi bent his head; his lips trailed kisses from my shoulder to my ear.

I shivered with pleasure when I felt blunt teeth against my pulse, felt his breath on my earlobe a second before his lips followed.

His warm fingers painted pictures over my wrist, shooting tingles up my arm. "You're ticklish," he murmured.

We stood there for what felt like an eternity, holding each other tight.

"I love you, Babe Vogel," he whispered against my hair.

I glanced back at my friends, at the flames, at the town I knew and loved. This was the summer that everything had come undone, unspooling our lives like the wickedest of storms. Now there was only the calm, the after. It would start in picking up the pieces, making sure everyone was okay. But where it ended? That was anyone's guess. Like Levi once told me, we were beginnings and middles, but we weren't endings. They were still up there in the clouds somewhere, waiting for us to catch up.

I looked up at the lighthouse, then back at Levi. "Let's go home."

"You don't want to stay for the rest of the bonfire? I thought this was supposed to be a sacred Oar's Rest tradition."

"It is, but now that my Jedi's returned . . ." I trailed off suggestively.

He grinned. "Wanna see my lightsaber?"

"Want to see lightsaber, I do," I said in a Yoda voice.

"Okay, the mood's shot." But he grinned and kissed me quick, and I could tell that the Force was with him.

"We'll be back fast enough to catch the end of it," I promised. Right then, I wasn't interested in taking it slow.

"Ha." Levi's mouth curved into a slow, lush smile, full of promise and a thousand everythings. "Maybe not that fast."

And then I was reaching out. Reaching for the boy I loved, for the town I belonged to, for the moon I could almost reach. For all those things that seemed near and far away. For summer and everything that came after.

acknowledgments

I t would be impossible to begin without first acknowledging my parents for their support, guidance, and unflinching ability to read all my manuscripts. Mom, you gave me the love of stories and a library card without parental restrictions—any coarse language is therefore not my fault. Dad, I can't thank you enough for being my biggest cheerleader and helping me find the first spark of "fire in the belly." Without you both, I wouldn't be able to follow my dream.

Thank you to Jean Feiwel, Lauren Scobell, my editor Kat Brzozowski, and the entire Macmillan/Swoon Reads team for helping this book come together. Kat, I hope *Small Town Hearts* makes you *really* hungry. Thank you for always asking the right questions to make me dig deeper and, on occasion, reminding my characters to be a bit less murder-y (this will always be my favorite comment). Big thanks to André-Naquian Wheeler, Hayley Jozwiak, and Jessica White for their sharp eyes and insightful copyediting. Swoon Squad, you've been the best crew I could hope to sail with. Especially when the seas get rough. I'm also grateful to have the Novel19s community and my Twitter writing pals just a click away.

Thanks to Jen Dibble, the first person outside of family to believe in me. When you reached out that day in 2015, you helped set my life on a new course. And the journey wouldn't have been half as fun without my pals Sam Pennington and Alessandra Ferreri, who are the best people to fangirl with. You three are truly the best. My sanity and I also thank my best friend Kate Holiday, who was always a willing ear, shoulder, and everything in between. You're my fairy-tale sister. Here's to slaying more dragons together.

And, of course, this would be incomplete without mentioning Charlotte and Wolf for being the start. You guys know what you did. Bev and Sean, I owe you for the laughs and for telling it like it is. Embarking on this publishing journey would have been unimaginable without the people who had been there from the start: Pragati, Vicky, Mandee, and the many others who read, loved, and championed . . . you have my heart. The last thank-you is reserved for my readers, old and new, and to all the ones I've yet to meet. I wouldn't be here without you.

DID YOU KNOW...

READER
Swoon
READS
APPROVED

readers like you
helped to get this
book published?

Join our book-obsessed community and help us
discover awesome new writing talent.

1

Write it.
Share your original YA manuscript.

2

Read it.
Discover bright new bookish talent.

3

Share it.
Discuss, rate, and share your faves.

4

Love it.
Help us publish the books you love.

Share your own manuscript or dive between the pages
at **swoonreads.com** or by downloading the **Swoon Reads app.**